About the Authors

Addicted to daydreaming and romance from a young age, **Angela Bissell** suspects she was destined to become a writer, although she did travel a convoluted career path on her way to authordom. Like many an intrepid Kiwi she also travelled the world, backpacking through Europe, Egypt, Israel, Turkey and the Greek Islands before settling for a time in London. Now she lives back home in New Zealand, never taking a day in her beautiful country for granted and loving the challenge of pursuing her writerly dreams.

Maisey Yates is a *New York Times* bestselling author of over one hundred romance novels. Whether she's writing strong, hardworking cowboys, dissolute princes or multigenerational family stories, she loves getting lost in fictional worlds. An avid knitter with a dangerous yarn addiction and an aversion to housework, Maisey lives with her husband and three kids in rural Oregon. Check out her website, maiseyyates.com or find her on Facebook.

USA Today bestselling, *RITA*®-nominated, and critically acclaimed author **Caitlin Crews** has written more than 130 books and counting. She has a Master's and Ph.D. in English Literature, thinks everyone should read more category romance, and is always available to discuss her beloved alpha heroes. Just ask. She lives in the Pacific Northwest with her comic book artist husband, is always planning her next trip, and will never, ever, read all the books in her to-be-read pile. Thank goodness.

European Escapes

July 2023
Madrid

August 2023
Sicily

September 2023
Sweden

January 2024
Paris

February 2024
Prague

March 2024
Athens

April 2024
London

May 2024
Berlin

European Escapes:
Paris

ANGELA BISSELL

MAISEY YATES

CAITLIN CREWS

MILLS & BOON

First Published in Great Britain 2024
by Mills & Boon, an imprint of HarperCollins*Publishers* Ltd,
1 London Bridge Street, London, SE1 9GF

www.harpercollins.co.uk

HarperCollins*Publishers*
Macken House, 39/40 Mayor Street Upper,
Dublin 1, D01 C9W8, Ireland

European Escapes: Paris © 2024 Harlequin Enterprises ULC.

A Night, A Consequence, A Vow © 2017 Angela Bissell
Heir to a Dark Inheritance © 2013 Maisey Yates
Tempt Me © 2020 Caitlin Crews

ISBN: 978-0-263-32265-1

This book is produced from independently certified FSC™ paper
to ensure responsible forest management.

For more information visit: www.harpercollins.co.uk/green

Printed and Bound in the UK using 100% Renewable Electricity
at CPI Group (UK) Ltd, Croydon, CR0 4YY

A NIGHT,
A CONSEQUENCE,
A VOW

ANGELA BISSELL

For Bron – author, mentor and friend.

Your support and encouragement have meant the world.

CHAPTER ONE

'You owe me for this, Xav.'

Ramon de la Vega dropped into a chair in front of his brother's desk and stretched out his legs.

Eight hours on a transatlantic commercial flight, another hour in the back of a company limo inching through endless queues of bumper-to-bumper traffic, and he felt as if he'd been straitjacketed for a week.

His mood carefully harnessed, he lounged back and perched his feet on the corner of his brother's desk. 'I had planned to spend the weekend in Vegas,' he added.

His brother, Xavier, sat in a high-backed chair on the other side of the massive oak desk—an antique heirloom their father had handed down along with the company reins to his eldest son. Behind him a thick pane of wall-to-wall glass framed a sweeping view of Barcelona that drew no more than a brief, disinterested glance from Ramon. Instead, he focused on his brother, who looked impossibly cool and immaculate in a dark tailored suit in spite of the mid-August heat. As always, Xav's features were stern, his posture stiff. Only his right hand moved, his fingertips drumming an incessant beat on the desktop's fine leather inlay.

The sound, amplified by the dearth of any other in the vast corner office, penetrated Ramon's eardrums like a blunt needle and reminded him that flying and alcohol made for an unwise mix.

'Doing what?' Xav's voice carried the hint of a sneer. 'Gambling or womanising?'

Ramon ignored the disdain in his brother's voice and unleashed his grin—the one he knew could fell a woman at fifty paces. Or tease the tension out of an uptight client in a matter of seconds. Against his only sibling, however, the impact was negligible. 'It is called recreation, brother.' He kept his tone light. 'You should try it some time.'

The deep plunge of Xav's eyebrows suggested he'd sooner lose an arm than indulge in such hedonistic pursuits. His fingers stopped drumming—*mercifully*—and curled into a loose fist. 'Get your feet off my desk.' His gaze raked over Ramon's jeans and shirt before snapping back to his feet. 'And where the hell are your shoes?'

Ramon dropped his feet to the floor. His loafers were… He squinted, trying to remember where he'd left them. *Ah, yes.* In the outer office. Under the desk of the pretty brunette whose name had already escaped him. He considered the rest of his appearance: stonewashed designer jeans; a loose open-necked white shirt, creased from travel; and a jaw darkened by eighteen-plus hours' worth of stubble. A far cry from his brother's impeccable attire and his own usual standard, but a man had to travel in comfort. Especially when his brother had had the nerve to issue an urgent summons and then deny him use of the company jet.

Ramon made a mental note.

Buy my own plane.

At least the curvy redheaded flight attendant in First Class who'd served him meals and refreshments during the flight from New York hadn't minded his attire. But, yes, for the Vega Corporation's head office in the heart of Barcelona's thriving business district, he was most definitely under-dressed.

Still, Xav needed to chill. Cut him some slack. He had ditched everything, including a weekend in Las Vegas with his old Harvard pals, and flown nearly four thousand miles across the North Atlantic—all because his brother had called out of the blue and told him he needed him.

Needed him, no less.

Words Ramon had once imagined would never tumble from his proud brother's mouth.

Yet, incredibly, they had.

Beyond that surprising entreaty, Xav had offered no more by way of explanation and Ramon had not demanded one. As CEO, Xav technically outranked him but it wasn't his seniority that commanded Ramon's loyalty. Xav was family. And when it came to family there was one truth Ramon could never escape.

He owed them.

Still, he allowed his grin to linger. Not because his mood leaned towards humour—nothing about being back in Spain tickled his funny bone—but rather because he knew it would irritate his brother. 'Flying makes my feet swell,' he said, 'and your secretary offered to massage them while you were wrapping up your meeting.'

A look of revulsion slid over Xav's face. 'Please tell me you are joking.'

'*Sí*, brother.' Ramon broadened his grin. 'I am.'

Though he *had* got the impression as he'd kicked off his shoes and settled in for a friendly chat with… Lola?… Lorda?…that she'd happily massage a lot more than his feet if he gave her half a chance. And maybe he would if she was willing. Because God knew he'd need a distraction while he was here. Some way to escape the toxic memories that sooner or later would defy his conscious mind and claw their way to the surface.

Xav pinched the bridge of his nose, a *Lord give me patience* gesture that reminded Ramon of their father, Vittorio. Not that any likeness could be attributed to genetics: Xav had been adopted at birth by their parents after two failed pregnancies. Four years later Ramon had come along—the miracle child the doctors had told his mother she'd never conceive let alone carry to term.

Miracle Child.

The moniker made Ramon's gut burn. He hated it. He was no heaven-sent miracle. Just ask the Castano family, or the Mendosas. No doubt they would all vehemently agree and then, for good measure, throw in a few fitting alternatives.

Ramon could think of one or two himself.

Like Angel of Death.

Or maybe Devil Incarnate.

He snapped his thoughts out of the dark mire of his past. This was why he gave Spain a wide berth whenever possible. Too many ghosts lurked here. Too many reminders. 'Tell me why I'm here,' he demanded, his patience dwindling.

'There's a board meeting tomorrow.'

He frowned. 'I thought the next quarterly meeting was six weeks from now.' He made a point of knowing when the board meetings were scheduled for so he could arrange to be elsewhere. In his experience, day-long gatherings with a bunch of pedantic, censorious old men were a special brand of torture to be studiously avoided. 'Since when does our board meet on a Saturday?'

'Since I decided to call an emergency meeting less than twenty-four hours ago.'

Ramon felt his mood start to unravel. 'Why the hell didn't you say over the phone it was a board meeting you were dragging me over here for?'

'Because you would have found an excuse not to come,' Xav snapped. 'You would rather waste your time at a poker table—or buried between the legs of some entirely unsuitable woman!'

Ramon's brows jerked down. 'That's out of order,' he growled.

Abruptly Xav stood up, stalked to the window behind him and stared out. Ramon glowered at his back. Xav *was* out of order. Yes, Ramon avoided the boardroom. Pandering to the board, keeping the old cronies happy, was his brother's responsibility. Not his. But no one could deny that he gave his pound of flesh to the Vega Corporation. He'd done so every year for the last five years, in fact. Ever since he'd accepted the vice-presidential role his father had offered him on his twenty-fifth birthday. He'd side-lined his architectural career. Gone from designing luxury hotels and upscale entertainment complexes to buying them and overseeing their management.

He'd excelled—and he'd realised in that first year of working hard to prove himself that this was how he could repay his family. How he could compensate in a tangible way for the pain he'd inflicted, the destruction his eighteen-year-old self had wrought and the shame he'd brought on his family. He could stamp his mark on the business. Contribute to its success.

It had been a tall order. The de la Vega empire was well-established. Successful. It spanned continents and industries, from construction and real estate to hospitality and entertainment. Any contribution Ramon made had to be significant.

He had risen to the challenge.

First with his acquisition of the Chastain Group—a collection of luxury resorts and boutique hotels which had doubled Vega Corporation's market share on the European continent, and then with the expansion of their portfolio of private members' clubs into a lucrative network of sophisticated high-end establishments.

Yes, he had made his mark.

And yet to his brother—and most of the board—the spectacular results he'd achieved year upon year seemed to matter far less than how he chose to conduct his personal life.

It rankled.

He didn't deliberately court the press but neither did he

waste his time trying to dodge the attention. Evade one paparazzo and ten more would materialise from the shadows. It was easier to give them what they wanted. Flash his trademark grin at the cameras, drape his arm around the waist of a beautiful woman and the tabloids and their gossip-hungry readers would be satisfied.

But dare to deny them and they'd stalk you like prey. Look for scandal where none existed. Or, worse, where it *did* exist. And the last thing he needed was someone digging into his past and shining a spotlight on his teenage transgressions. Nurturing his playboy reputation served a purpose. The tabloids saw what he wanted them to see. A successful, wealthy, aristocratic bachelor who pursued pleasure as doggedly as he pursued his next acquisition.

He reined in his anger. 'Why an emergency meeting?'

Xav turned, his expression grim. 'Hector is making a play for the chairman's role.'

Ramon narrowed his eyes. 'I thought you and Papá had earmarked Sanchez for the role,' he said, referring to their newest and most dynamic board member—an accomplished former leader of industry who Xav had persuaded the board to accept in an attempt to inject some fresh blood into the company's governance. Aside from Xav and their father, who was about to retire as Chairman, Sanchez was the only board member for whom Ramon had any genuine respect.

Hector, on the other hand, was a nightmare. Their father's second cousin, he craved power and status and resented anyone who possessed more than he did. The man was self-centred. Narrow-minded. Not figurehead material.

Ramon shook his head in disbelief. 'He'll never get the support he needs.'

'He already has it.' Xav dropped into his chair, nostrils flaring. 'He's been working behind my back, garnering support for a coup. Persuading the others that voting in Sanchez is a bad move.'

'Surely Papá can pull him into line?'

His brother threw him a look.

'Papá has already taken a step back. He's too unwell for such drama—something you would know if you made an effort to visit more often,' Xav said, the glint in his eyes hard. Accusatory.

A sharp jolt went through Ramon. He knew their father had high blood pressure, and had suffered from mild attacks of angina over the past two years, but he hadn't been aware of Vittorio's more recent decline. He tightened his jaw against the surge of guilt. He kept his distance from family gatherings for a reason. There was too much awkwardness there. Too many things left unsaid. No. Ramon would not let his brother guilt trip him. He did everyone a favour, himself included, by staying away.

'The board members respect you,' he pointed out, marshalling his thoughts back to the business at hand. 'Win them back.'

Xav's jaw clenched. He shook his head. 'Whatever diamond-studded carrot Hector is dangling to coerce their support, it's working. Lopez, Ruben, Anders and Ramirez have all avoided my calls this week.'

Ramon dragged a thumb over his bristled chin. 'So what's the purpose of the meeting?'

'To confront Hector out in the open. Force him to reveal his hand and compel the others to choose a side—show where their loyalties lie so we know what we're up against.'

'"We"?'

'I need your support. As does Sanchez, if we've any chance of seeing him voted in as Chairman. We need to provide a united front. A *strong* front. One that'll challenge Hector and test his alliances.'

A single bark of laughter escaped Ramon. 'I cannot see

how my presence will help your cause,' he said, and yet even as he spoke he could feel the sharp, addictive surge of adrenalin he always experienced in the face of a challenge.

Something else rose in him, too. A sense of familial duty he couldn't deny. A compulsion to help his brother.

He studied Xav's face for a moment. It wasn't only anger carving deep grooves around his brother's mouth.

'You're worried,' he observed. 'Why?'

'The Klein deal went belly up.'

Without thinking, Ramon pursed his lips and let out a low whistle. Xav's expression darkened.

'I'm sorry,' Ramon said, his sympathy genuine. He too had suffered the occasional business failure. Had experienced the disappointment and utter frustration that came after investing countless hours of manpower and resources into a potential deal only to see it fall over at the eleventh hour. 'You're concerned that your credibility with the board is damaged,' he surmised.

'Hector's already laid the failure squarely on my doorstep. Called my judgement into question.' Xav's voice grated with disgust. 'He'll use it to undermine the board's confidence in me. We need a win to regain the board's trust. Something that will make them forget about the Klein debacle and give us some leverage.' He sat forward, his grey eyes intense. 'Have you managed to secure a meeting with Royce yet?'

Ramon felt his spine tighten.

Speaking of failures.

'Not yet,' he said carefully.

Xav leaned back, the intensity in his eyes dimming. He breathed out heavily. 'It was always going to be a long shot.'

His tone was dismissive enough to needle under Ramon's skin. Setting his sights on The Royce—one of London's oldest, most prestigious and highly exclusive private clubs—was ambitious, but his brother shouldn't be so quick to underestimate him.

'Have a little faith, brother,' he said. 'I've hit a minor roadblock, that's all. Nothing I can't handle.'

'A roadblock?'

'Royce has a gatekeeper.' He downplayed the matter with a one-shoulder shrug. 'Getting access to him is proving…a challenge.'

Xav's frown deepened. 'Do they not know who you are?' His voice rang with a note of hauteur. 'Surely the de la Vega name is sufficient to grant you an audience with Royce?'

Ramon nearly barked out another derisory laugh.

The importance of the family name had always carried more weight in Xav's eyes than his. Their mother and her siblings were distant cousins of the King of Spain and directly descended from a centuries-old line of dukes. Marry that blue-blood lineage to the vast wealth and success of their father's industrialist family and the de la Vega name, since the early eighties when their parents had wedded, had been inextricably linked with affluence and status.

'Are you forgetting the clientele The Royce serves?' He watched Xav silently bristle over the fact that their family's power and influence, while not insignificant, did not merit any special recognition in this instance. Not from an establishment that catered to some of the wealthiest, most powerful men in the world.

'And yet if there is truth to the rumours you've heard, Maxwell Royce is not selective about the company he keeps. Surely a meeting with you is not beneath him?'

Ramon sensed a subtle insult in that statement. He gritted his teeth for a second before speaking. 'It's not rumour. The information I received comes from a trusted source. It's reliable.'

As reliable as it had been surprising, for the discreet disclosure had come from his friend Christophe completely out of the blue. 'Royce has a gambling problem and mounting debts,' he said. 'It came from the mouth of his own accountant.' Who apparently, after indulging in one too many Manhattans in a London cocktail bar with a pretty long-legged accountant—who happened to be Christophe's sister—had spilled the dirt on his employer. Christophe's sister had relayed the tale to her brother and Christophe, never one to sit idly on useful information, had called Ramon.

'Where trouble resides, so does opportunity,' he said, voicing a belief that had served him well over the years when scouting out potential acquisitions. People resistant to selling could quickly change their tune when faced with a financial crisis. A buyout offer or business proposal that had previously been rejected could suddenly seem an attractive option.

The Royce had been owned by the same family for over a hundred years, but it wasn't uncommon for third or fourth generation owners to opt to sell the family business. For legacies to be sacrificed expediently in favour of hard cash. And if Maxwell Royce needed cash... It was an opportunity too tempting not to pursue, long shot or not. Ramon's clubs were exclusive, sophisticated and world-class but The Royce was in a whole different league—one that only a dozen or so clubs on the planet could lay claim to. An establishment so revered would elevate his portfolio to a whole new level.

Xav sat forward again. 'I don't need to tell you how much an acquisition of this nature would impress the board.'

Ramon understood. It would be the win his brother was so desperately seeking. A way to cut Hector's critical narrative off at the knees, wrestle back control of the board and regain the directors' confidence.

'Deal with Royce's gatekeeper, whoever he is, and get that meeting,' Xav urged. *'Soon.'*

Ramon didn't care for his brother's imperious tone, but

he bit his tongue. Xav was under pressure. He'd asked for Ramon's support. How often did that happen?

Not often.

Besides, Ramon had as much desire as Xav to see Hector at the company's helm.

He thought of the obstacle in his path.

Not a *he*, as Xav had assumed, but a *she*.

A slender, blonde, not unattractive *she* who had, in recent weeks, proved something of a conundrum for Ramon.

He'd readily admit it was a rare occasion he came across a woman he couldn't charm into giving him what he wanted.

This woman would not be charmed.

Three times in two weeks she'd rejected him by phone, informing him in her very chilly, very proper, British accent that Mr Royce was too busy to receive unsolicited visitors.

Ramon had been undeterred. Confident he could net a far more desirable result in person, he'd flown to London and turned up at the club's understated front door on a quiet, dignified street in the heart of fashionable Mayfair.

As expected, security had been discreet but efficient. As soon as he'd been identified as a visitor and not a member, a dark-suited man had ushered him around the outside of the stately brick building to a side entrance. Like the simple, black front door with its decorative brass knocker, the black and white marble vestibule in which he'd been left to wait was further evidence of The Royce's quiet, restrained brand of elegance.

Ramon had got quite familiar with that vestibule. He'd found himself with enough time on his hands to count the marble squares on the floor fifty times over, plus make a detailed study of the individual mouldings on the ornate Georgian ceiling.

Because she had made him wait. Not for ten minutes. Not for twenty, or even forty. But for an *hour*.

Only through sheer determination and the freedom to stand up, stretch his legs and pace back and forth across the polished floor now and again had he waited her out.

After a while it felt like a grim little game between them, a challenge to see who'd relent first—him or her.

Ramon won, but his victory was limited to the brief surge of satisfaction that came when she finally appeared.

'You do not have an appointment, Mr de la Vega.' Grey eyes, so pale they possessed an extraordinary luminescence, flashed at him from out of a heart-shaped face, while the rest of her expression appeared carefully schooled.

Pretty, he thought upon first impression, but not his type. Too reserved. Too buttoned-up and prim. He preferred his women relaxed. Uninhibited. 'Because you would not give me one,' he responded easily.

'And you think I will now, just because you're here in person?'

'I think Mr Royce would benefit from the opportunity to meet with me,' he said smoothly. 'An opportunity you seem intent on denying him.'

The smile she bestowed on him then was unlike the smiles he was accustomed to receiving from women. Those smiles ranged from shy to seductive, and everything in between, but always they telegraphed some level of awareness and heat and, in many cases, a brazen invitation. But the tilt of her lips was neither warm nor inviting. It suggested sufferance, along with a hint of condescension.

'Let me tell you what *I* think, Mr de la Vega,' she said, her voice somehow sweet and icy at the same time—like a frozen dessert that gave you a painful case of brain freeze when you bit into it. 'I think I know Mr Royce better than you do and am therefore infinitely more qualified to determine what he will—and won't—find of benefit. I also think you underestimate my intelligence. I know who you are and I know there's only one reason you could want to meet with Mr Royce. So let me make something clear to you right now and save you some time. The Royce is *not* for sale.'

Colour had bloomed on her pale cheekbones, the streaks of pink an arresting contrast to her glittering grey eyes.

Interesting, he thought. Perhaps there was a bit of fire beneath that cool facade. He held out his business card and took a step towards her but she reared back, alarm flaring in her eyes as if he had crossed some invisible, inviolable boundary. *Huh.* Even more interesting. 'Ten minutes of Mr Royce's time,' he said. 'That is all I am asking for.'

'You're wasting your time. Mr Royce is not here.'

'Then perhaps you would call me when he is. I'll be in London for another forty-eight hours.'

He continued to hold out his card and finally she took it, exercising great care to ensure her fingers didn't brush against his. Then she gave him that smile again and this time it had the strangest effect, igniting a spark of irritation, followed by a rush of heat in the pit of his stomach. He imagined kissing that haughty little smile right off her pretty face. Backing her up against one of the hard marble pillars, taking her head in his hands and devouring her mouth under his until her lips softened, opened and she granted him entry.

Carefully he neutralised his expression, shocked by the direction of his thoughts. He'd never taken a woman with force. He had no aversion to boisterous sex, and he'd indulged more than one bed partner who demanded it rough and fast, but on the whole Ramon liked his lovers soft. Compliant. Willing.

She took another step back from him, the flush of pink in her cheeks growing more hectic, her eyes widening slightly. As if somehow she'd read his thoughts. 'Mr Royce will not be available this week,' she said, her smile replaced now by a thin, narrow-eyed stare. 'So unless you have extraordinary lung capacity, Mr de la Vega, I suggest you don't hold your breath.'

And she turned and walked away from him, high heels clicking on the shiny chequered marble as she made for the door across the small foyer from which she'd emerged.

She had a spectacular backside. Somehow Ramon's brain had registered that fact, his gaze transfixed by the movement of firm, shapely muscle under her navy blue pencil skirt even as a wave of anger and frustration had crashed through him.

The sound of Xav's desk phone ringing jolted him back to the present. He shifted in his chair.

Xav placed his hand on the receiver and looked at him. 'Speak with Lucia on your way out,' he said. 'I told her to make a dinner reservation for us this evening. Get the details off her and I'll see you at the restaurant. We'll talk more then.'

Ah. Lucia. Yes, that was the name of his brother's secretary. Not Lola or Lorda. Ironic that he couldn't recall the name of the attractive brunette he'd just met, and had already considered sleeping with, yet he had no trouble summoning the name of the English woman he'd rather throttle than bed.

Her name, it seemed, was indelibly inked on his brain, along with the enticing image of her tight, rounded posterior.

Emily.

CHAPTER TWO

EMILY ROYCE SAT behind her desk and took a deep breath that somehow failed to fill her lungs. For a moment she thought she might be sick and the feeling sent a rising tide of disbelief through her.

This was not how she reacted to bad news. Emily had learnt how to handle disappointment a long time ago. She did not buckle under its weight. When bad news came, she received it with equanimity. Practicality. Calm.

And yet there was no denying the sudden stab of nausea in her belly. Or the cold, prickling sensation sweeping over her skin.

She dug her fingers into the arms of her chair, some dark corner of her mind imagining her father's neck beneath her clenched hands.

She was going to kill him.

At the very least she was going to hunt him down, drag him out of whichever opulent hotel suite or illicit den of pleasure he was currently holed up in and yell at him until she was hoarse.

Except she wouldn't.

Emily knew she wouldn't.

Because no matter how many times in her life she'd imagined venting her anger, letting loose even a bit of the hurt and disappointment she'd stored up and kept tightly lidded over the years, she never had.

And this time would be no different. She would do what she always did. What she had to do. She would shove her emotions aside and pour all her energy into limiting the damage. Into doing whatever was necessary to sweep Maxwell Royce's latest indiscretion under the rug and in so doing keep his reputation—and, by association, the reputation of The Royce—intact.

Only this time, if what she had just been told was true, Maxwell had outdone himself. He'd created a situation so dire she struggled to accept that even he could have done such a stupid, irresponsible, *selfish* thing.

And this would not be a mere matter of slipping a wad of cash to some unscrupulous opportunist to prevent embarrassing, compromising photos of her father from finding their way to the tabloids. Or of dipping into her personal savings and hastily rebalancing the club's books, with the help of their accountant, to cover up Maxwell's misappropriation of funds from one of their business accounts.

Not that any of her father's prior indiscretions could be labelled trivial, but this...*this*...

Her grandfather would turn in his grave. As would his father, and his father before him.

Edward Royce, Emily's great-great-grandfather and a wealthy, respected pillar of British high society at the turn of the twentieth century, had founded the club on which he'd bestowed his name in 1904. Since then ownership of the prestigious establishment had been proudly passed down through three generations of Royces, all male heirs—until Emily. More than a hundred years later, The Royce remained a traditional gentlemen's club and one of western Europe's last great bastions of male exclusivity and chauvinism. A society of powerful, influential men who between them controlled a good portion of the world's major industries, not forgetting those who presided over governments and ruled their own countries and principalities.

On occasion Emily amused herself with thoughts of how the majority of their members would react to learning that fifty per cent of their precious club was now owned by a woman.

She imagined there'd be deep rumblings of discontent

and much sputtering of cigar smoke and Scotch beneath the lighted chandeliers in the Great Salon. But she also knew her grandfather had acted with calculated intent when he'd bequeathed half of the club's ownership to his only grand-child. Gordon Royce had known his errant son could not be trusted with sole proprietorship. Rewriting his will to leave fifty per cent of the shares to Emily—the granddaughter he'd wished had been born a boy—had surely been an un-desirable but necessary course of action in Gordon's mind.

Not that her grandfather had been able to overcome his misogynistic tendencies altogether. He'd gone to significant lengths to ensure the Royce name would live on through a male heir.

It was terribly ironic—that her grandfather should ma-nipulate her life from beyond the grave when he'd shown scarcely a flicker of interest in her while he'd been alive.

Emily closed her eyes a moment. Her mind was wan-dering. She needed to harness her thoughts, to wrestle her brain around the problem and come up with a solution. She needed time to think. Alone. Without the sinister presence of the man who sat in the upholstered chair on the other side of her desk.

She stood slowly, her features composed, her legs steady only through sheer force of will.

'I think you should leave now, Mr Skinner.'

She spoke with all the authority she could muster but her cool directive failed to have any visible impact on her visitor.

His head tilted to the side, his thin lips stretching into a humourless smile that sent an icy ripple down Emily's spine. 'That's a pity,' he said. 'I was just starting to enjoy our conversation.'

Emily didn't like the way he looked at her. Carl Skin-ner—one of London's most notorious loan sharks—looked old enough to be her father, yet there was nothing paternal in the way his gaze crawled over her body. She fisted her hands by her sides. Her pinstriped skirt and white silk blouse were smart and conservative and not the least bit revealing. There was nothing for him to feast his filthy eyes on, she assured herself—except maybe for the angry colour rising in her cheeks.

'Our conversation is over.' She gestured towards the single sheet of paper he'd produced with a smug flourish when she'd questioned the veracity of his claim. It lay upon her desk now, the signature scrawled at the foot of the agreement unmistakably her father's. 'I'll be seeking a legal opinion on this.'

'You can have a hundred lawyers look over it, sweetheart.'

Emily tried not to flinch at the endearment.

'It was legally binding when Royce signed it seven days ago,' he continued. 'And it'll be legally binding in another seven days when I collect on the debt.' He leaned back, his gaze roving around the interior of her small but beautifully appointed office, with its view overlooking one of Mayfair's most elegant streets, before landing back on her. 'You know, I've always fancied myself as a member of one of these clubs.'

Emily almost snorted. The idea of this man rubbing shoulders with princes and presidents was ludicrous, but she endeavoured to keep the thought from showing on her face. Skinner's business suit and neatly cropped hair might afford him a civilised veneer but she sensed the danger emanating from him. Insulting this man would be far from wise.

'Mr Royce's debt will be settled in full by the end of the week.' She injected her voice with a confidence she prayed wasn't misplaced. If her father's gambling debt wasn't settled within the week, the alternative—Carl Skinner getting his hands on a fifty per cent shareholding of The Royce—

was an outcome far too horrendous to contemplate. *She would not let it happen.*

'You sound very certain about that, little lady.'

'I am.'

Skinner's lips pursed. 'You understand that assurance would carry more weight if I heard it straight from your boss?'

'My boss is not here,' she reminded him, instinct urging her now—as it had twenty minutes earlier when he'd turned up without an appointment demanding to see her father—not to reveal her surname. She'd introduced herself simply as Emily, Administration Manager and Mr Royce's assistant, and agreed to meet with Skinner in Maxwell's absence only because instinct urged her to hear what he had to say.

She coerced her cheek muscles to move, pulling the corners of her mouth into a rigid smile. 'I'm afraid you'll have to settle for *my* assurance, Mr Skinner,' she said, walking around her desk as she continued to speak. 'Thank you for your visit. I believe we have nothing more to discuss at this point. I do have another appointment,' she lied, 'so if you don't mind...'

Skinner rose and stepped in front of her and Emily's voice died, her vocal cords paralysed by the violent lunge of her heart into her throat. Her legs froze. He was standing in her space, two feet at most between them, and she wasn't used to such close physical proximity with another person. Especially someone she didn't know and had zero desire to. 'Mr Skinner—'

'Carl,' he said, and took a step towards her.

She stepped backwards, glancing to the right of his thick-set frame to her closed office door. Her palms grew clammy. *Why hadn't she thought to leave it open?*

His smile returned, the narrow slant of his lips ten times more unsettling than before. 'There's no need to stand on ceremony, Emily. This time next week I could be your boss...'

Her eyes widened.

'And I'm not big on formality. I prefer my working relationships to be a little more...relaxed.'

Nausea bloomed anew and she fought the instinct to recoil. She tried to tell herself his sleazy innuendo didn't intimidate her, but the truth was she felt horribly unnerved. She inhabited a world dominated by men but she wasn't familiar with this kind of unsolicited attention. For the most part she was used to being invisible. Unseen.

She straightened her shoulders. 'Let me offer you one more assurance, Mr Skinner,' she said, her heart hammering even as common sense told her he couldn't pose any physical threat to her person. Her admin assistant, Marsha, unless she'd gone for her morning tea break, would be sitting at her desk right outside Emily's door, and Security was no further away than one push of a pre-programmed button on her desk phone. 'Not only will you never be my boss,' she said, a sliver of disdain working its way into her voice now, 'But you will never, so long as I have any say in the matter, set foot on these premises again.'

No sooner had the final word leapt off Emily's tongue than she knew she had made a grave mistake.

Skinner's expression had turned thunderous.

Terrifyingly thunderous.

And he moved so fast—looming over her, his big hands clamping onto her waist like concrete mitts as he pinned her against her desk—that she had no time to react.

An onslaught of fragmented impressions assailed her: the sight of Skinner's lips peeling back from his teeth; the dampness of his breath on her skin as he thrust his face too close to hers; the overpowering reek of his aftershave which made the lining of her nose sting.

Panic flared, driving the beginnings of a scream up her

throat, but she gripped the edge of her desk behind her and smothered the sound before it could emerge. 'Take your hands off me,' she hissed. 'Or I will shout for Security and an entire team of men will be here in less than ten seconds.'

For a moment his grip tightened, his fingers biting painfully into her sides. Then, abruptly, he released her and stepped away, his sudden retreat setting off a wave of relief so powerful her legs threatened to buckle. He ran a hand over his hair and adjusted the knot of his tie—as if smoothing his appearance would somehow make him appear less brutish.

'Seven days, little lady.' His voice was gruff. Menacing. 'And then I collect.' He jutted his chin in the direction of the paper on her desk. 'That's a copy, of course. You can assure your lawyer that I have the original tucked away safe and sound.' He sent her a hard, chilling smile then showed himself out, leaving her office door standing open in the wake of his exit.

Emily sagged against her desk, just as Marsha rushed in.

'My God!' the younger woman exclaimed. 'What on earth happened in here? The look on that man's face—' She stopped, her eyes growing rounder as they took in Emily's slumped posture and the pallor she knew without the aid of a mirror had stripped the colour from her cheeks. 'Emily...?'

Rousing herself, she pointed a trembling finger over Marsha's shoulder. 'Call Security. Tell them to make absolutely certain that man leaves the building.'

Marsha hurried back out and Emily moved on shaky legs to the other side of her desk. She picked up her phone, pulled in a fortifying breath and dialled her father's mobile number.

The call went straight to voice mail.

Surprise...*not*.

She slammed the phone back down, frustration, fury

and a host of other feelings she didn't want to acknowledge building with hot, bitter force inside her.

Her eyes prickled and the threat of tears was as unfamiliar and unwelcome as the nausea had been.

What had Maxwell done?

Her lips trembled and she pressed them together, closed her eyes and pushed the heels of her hands against her lids.

She knew what he had done.

He'd borrowed a monstrous sum of money to enter a high-stakes poker game and put up his fifty per cent shareholding of The Royce as collateral.

And then he had lost. Spectacularly.

She wanted to scream.

How could he? How *could* he?

No wonder he'd been incommunicado this last week. He was hiding, the coward. Leaving Emily to clean up the mess, like he always did.

Bitterness welled up inside her.

Why shouldn't he? She was his fixer, after all. The person who made things go away. Who kept his image, and by extension the image of The Royce, as pristine and stain-free as possible. Oh, yes. Her father might be a selfish, irresponsible man but he wasn't stupid.

He'd finally discovered a use for the daughter he'd ignored for most of her life.

Emily dropped into her chair.

It wasn't unusual for Maxwell to disappear. As a child she'd grown to accept his fleeting, infrequent appearances in her life, sensing from a young age that she made him uncomfortable even though she hadn't understood why. As an adult she'd hoped maturity and a shared interest in The Royce's future would give them common ground—a foundation upon which to forge a relationship—but within the first year after her grandfather's death it'd become clear her hopes were misguided. The loss of his father had not changed Maxwell one bit. If anything he'd become more remote. More unpredictable. More absent.

It was Emily who had run the club during his absences, assuming more and more of the management responsibilities in recent years. Oh, Maxwell would breeze in when the mood took him, but he rarely stayed at his desk for more than a few token minutes. Why stare at spreadsheets and have tedious discussions about staffing issues and running costs when he could be circulating in the restaurant or the Great Salon, pressing the flesh of their members and employing his innate silver-tongued charm?

Emily didn't care that her job title didn't reflect the true extent of her responsibilities. Didn't care that for seven years her part-ownership of the club had remained, by mutual agreement with her father, a well-guarded secret. She knew The Royce's membership wasn't ready for such a revelation. The club was steeped in tradition and history, mired in values that were steadfastly old-fashioned. Its members didn't object to female employees, but the idea of accepting women as equals within their hallowed halls remained anathema to most.

Emily had a vision for the club's future, one that was far more evolved and liberal, but changes had to be implemented gradually. Anything fundamental, such as opening their doors to women… Well, those kinds of changes would happen only when the time was right.

Or they wouldn't happen at all.

Not if Carl Skinner got his grubby hands on her father's share of The Royce. There'd be no controlling Skinner, no keeping the outcome under wraps. It would be an unmitigated scandal, ruinous to the club's image. There'd be a mass exodus of members to rival establishments. In short, there would be no club. Not one she'd want to be associated with, at any rate. Skinner would turn it into a cheap, distasteful imitation.

Oh, Lord.

This was exactly why her grandfather had bequeathed half of the club to Emily. To keep his son from destroying the family legacy.

And now it was happening.

Under her watch.

She reached for the phone again, imagining Gordon Royce's coffin rocking violently in the ground now.

Her first call, to the bank, told her what she already knew—they were at the limit of their debt facility. Raising cash via a bank loan wasn't an option. Her second call, to The Royce's corporate lawyer, left her feeling even worse.

'I'm sorry, Emily. The contract with Mr Skinner is valid,' Ray Carter told her after she'd emailed a scanned copy to him. 'You could contest it, but unless we can prove that Maxwell was of unsound mind when he executed the agreement there's no legally justifiable reason to nullify the contract.'

'Is there nothing we can do?'

'Pay Mr Skinner what he's owed,' he said bluntly.

'We don't have the money.'

'Then find an investor.'

Emily's heart stopped. 'Dilute the club's equity?'

'Or convince your father to sell his shares and retain your fifty per cent. One or the other. But whatever you do, do it fast.'

Emily hung up the phone and sat for a long moment, too shell-shocked to move. Too speechless to utter more than a weak, distracted word of thanks when Marsha came in, placed a cup of tea in front of her and said she'd be right outside the office if Emily needed to talk.

Alone again, she absentmindedly fingered the smooth surface of the pearl that hung from a silver chain around her neck.

An investor.

Slowly the idea turned over in her mind. There had to be members of The Royce who would be interested in owning a piece of their beloved club. She could put some feelers out, make a few discreet enquiries... But the delicacy required for such approaches and any ensuing negotiations would take time—and time was something she didn't have.

Whatever you do, do it fast.

Ray's warning pounded through her head.

Abruptly, she swivelled her chair, dragged open the middle drawer of her desk and rummaged through an assortment of notepads and stationery until her fingers touched on the item she was seeking. She held her breath for a moment, then shoved the drawer closed and slapped the business card on her desk.

She glared at the name emblazoned in big, black letters across the card's white background, as bold as the man himself.

Ramon de la Vega.

A bloom of inexplicable heat crept beneath the collar of her blouse. She'd intended to throw the card away as soon as she returned to her office after her brief encounter with the man, but at the last second she'd changed her mind and tossed the card into a drawer.

He had unsettled her.

She didn't like to admit it, but he had.

Oh, she knew his type well enough. He was a charmer, endowed with good looks and a smooth tongue just like her father, except she had to concede that 'good looks' was a rather feeble description of Ramon de la Vega's God-given assets.

The man was gorgeous. Tall and dark. Golden-skinned. And he oozed confidence and vitality, the kind that shimmered around some people like a magnetic force field and pulled others in.

She had almost been sucked in herself. Had felt the irresistible pull of his bold, male charisma the instant he'd stepped into her zone—that minimum three feet of space she liked to maintain between others and herself. She'd taken a hasty step backwards, not because he had repelled her, but rather because she had, in spite of her anger, found herself disconcertingly drawn to him. Drawn by the palpable energy he gave off and, more shockingly, by the hint of recklessness she had sensed was lurking beneath.

They were qualities that didn't attract her, she'd reminded herself sharply. Not in the slightest. And not in a man whose audacity had already set her fuming.

She leaned back in her chair, her breathing shallow, her pulse feeling a little erratic. Was she mad even to consider this?

Or would she be mad *not* to consider it?

Forced to choose between Carl Skinner and Ramon de la Vega, she couldn't deny which man was the lesser of two evils. De la Vega had a pedigree, not to mention an impressive business acumen. She knew because she'd done an Internet search and, once she'd got past the dozens of tabloid articles and photos of him with beautiful women, the long list of accolades lauding his accomplishments as both an architect and a smart, driven businessman had made for interesting reading.

Before she could change her mind, she snatched up her phone and dialled the mobile number on his card.

Two seconds later, she almost hung up.

Maybe this needed more thought. Maybe she should rehearse what she was going to say…

'*Sí?*'

The breath she'd unconsciously bottled in her lungs escaped on a little *whoosh* of surprise. For a second time that day, her vocal cords felt paralysed.

'Yes?' he said into the silence, his tone sharper. 'Who is this?'

Emily shook herself. 'Mr de la Vega?'

'Yes.'

'Good morning—I mean…' She paused as it occurred to her that he could be anywhere in the world—in a different time zone where it wasn't morning at all. She could have interrupted his evening meal. Or maybe it was the middle of the night wherever he was and he was in bed and… She froze, an unsettling thought flaring. Oh, no. Surely he wouldn't have answered the phone if…?

Before she could kill the thought, an X-rated image of entwined limbs and naked body parts—mostly naked *male* body parts—slammed into her mind.

She felt her cheeks flame. 'I'm sorry,' she said, mortified, even though he couldn't possibly know her thoughts. Where was her bulletproof composure? Skinner's visit must have unbalanced her more than she'd realised. 'I hope I'm not disturbing you. I'm—'

'Emily.'

Her breath locked in her throat for a moment.

'That's very impressive, Mr de la Vega.'

'Ramon. And you have a very memorable voice.'

Emily rolled her eyes. There was nothing special about her voice. There was nothing special about *her*. Ramon de la Vega was a silver-tongued fox, just like her father.

She sat straighter in her chair. 'Mr Royce would like to discuss a business proposition with you. Are you still interested in meeting with him?

'Of course.'

No hesitation. That was a good sign. She gripped the phone a little tighter. 'Nine o'clock tomorrow morning. Can you be here?'

'Yes.'

'Good.' She kept her voice professional. Courteous. 'We look forward to seeing you, Mr de la Vega.'

'Ramon,' he insisted. 'And I look forward to seeing you too, Emily.'

A flurry of goosebumps feathered over her skin. Had she imagined the sensual, lazy intonation to his voice that made her name sound almost...erotic? She cleared her throat. 'Actually,' she said, cooling her voice by several degrees. 'You may call me Ms Royce.'

Silence came down the line. In different circumstances, she might have allowed herself a smile.

Instead she hung up, before he could ruin her moment of satisfaction with a smooth comeback, and looked at her watch.

She had twenty-two hours to find her father.

CHAPTER THREE

RAMON DIDN'T BELIEVE in divine intervention.

Only once in his life had he prayed for help—with all the desperation of a young man facing his first lesson in mortality—and the silence in the wake of his plea on that disastrous day had been utterly, horrifyingly deafening.

These days he relied on no one but himself, and yet yesterday... Yesterday he had found himself wondering if some unseen hand was not indeed stacking the chips in his favour.

And today—today he felt as if he'd hit the jackpot.

Because the thing he wanted, the thing he needed after Saturday's volatile board meeting, had just dropped into his lap.

Almost.

'Fifty-one per cent,' he said.

The indrawn breaths of three people—two men and one woman—were clearly audible across the boardroom table.

Ramon zeroed in on the woman.

Ms Emily Royce.

Now, that was a surprise he hadn't seen coming.

Though admittedly it wasn't a patch on this morning's bombshell: Emily was not only the daughter of Maxwell Royce, she was a fifty per cent owner of the club.

Soon to be a forty-nine per cent owner, Ramon amended silently.

'Absolutely not,' she said, the incendiary flash of her silver-grey eyes telling him she wasn't the least bit impressed by his proposal.

His London-based lawyer leaned forward in the chair

beside him. 'We appreciate you're in a difficult situation, Ms Royce—'

'I don't think you *appreciate* our situation at all,' she cut in. 'I think Mr de la Vega wants to take advantage of it.'

'Emily.' Ray Carter, the grey-haired lawyer sitting on her left, touched her briefly on the arm. 'Let's hear what they have to say.'

Ramon watched her right hand curl into a delicate fist on the table-top. Knowing what he did now, he wouldn't have been surprised if she felt inclined to punch the man seated on her right, nor could he have blamed her. No one privy to the conversation that had just taken place could deny that Emily Royce had a right to be furious with her father.

Ramon and his lawyer had listened, incredulous, as Carter had laid out the facts, stating his clients were making full disclosure of the circumstances in the interests of trust and transparency.

And then Maxwell Royce had offered to sell his fifty per cent shareholding in The Royce in exchange for a swift and fair settlement.

It had taken less than an hour for both parties to agree on what constituted 'fair'. Royce's need for an expedient, unconventional deal had given Ramon leverage that he and his lawyer hadn't hesitated to use.

But it wasn't enough. Ramon wanted a majority shareholding. Wanted the control that additional one per cent would afford him.

Ms Royce mightn't like it, but if she and her father wanted a quick bailout she *was* going to sell him one per cent of her shares.

And if she didn't quit glaring at him as if he were the Antichrist, instead of the man about to save her from a far less desirable outcome, he was going to crush any sympathy he felt for her and damn well enjoy watching her yield.

He looked into those luminous, pale grey eyes.

'I am not unsympathetic to your situation,' he said, ensuring his gaze didn't encompass her father. For Maxwell Royce he felt not an iota of sympathy. The man had been reckless, irresponsible. Ramon was a risk-taker himself, and no saint, but he'd learned a long time ago the only kind of risk worth taking was a calculated one. You did not gamble with something—or some*one*—you weren't prepared to lose. 'But I think we can agree that your options are limited and what you need is a fast and effective solution to your problem.'

He leant his elbows on the table, his shoulders relaxed under the charcoal-grey suit jacket he'd donned over the matching waistcoat, white shirt and maroon tie that morning. He spread his hands, palms up in a gesture of conciliation. 'I believe that is what I am offering.'

'Demanding a majority shareholding is not a solution,' she said. 'It's a takeover.'

Angry colour rose in her face, the pink contrasting with her pale eyes and accentuating the elegant slant of her cheekbones. With her blonde hair scraped into a tight twist behind her head she looked as prim and buttoned up as she had the first time he'd met her. But now he found himself conceding that Emily Royce wasn't pretty...she was beautiful—despite the *back off* vibe she radiated with her prickly demeanour.

He dropped his gaze to her mouth. Remembered the swift, unexpected urge she'd aroused during their first encounter—the powerful desire to kiss her, to soften that condescending smile into something warmer, more inviting.

No smile adorned her mouth this morning but the tight moue of her lips did not diminish his appreciation of the fact they were lush and shapely.

Rather like her body, the generous curves of which he couldn't fail to notice. Not when the soft, pale blue top she wore moulded her ample breasts and slender midriff to utter perfection. He wasn't blind. He was a thirty-year-old red-blooded man who liked the opposite sex. A lot. When a desirable woman drifted into his orbit, his body was programmed to notice.

He clenched his jaw.

Lust had no place in this meeting. He was on the cusp of achieving what his brother had believed he couldn't. He wasn't about to lose focus.

He'd satisfy his libido later. Celebrate with a night out in London and find himself a woman who was warm and willing, not stiff and spiky, like the one sitting opposite.

'Correct me if I am wrong, Ms Royce,' he said. 'But my understanding from Mr Carter's summary of the situation is that you and Mr Royce have less than six days to raise the money required to settle his debt.'

Emily glanced at her father. Royce looked impeccable in a pinstriped navy suit but his clean-shaven face was noticeably drawn, his blue eyes underscored by dark shadows. In the moment his daughter looked at him, something that could have been regret, or shame, passed over his features.

Her gaze came back to Ramon. 'That is correct.'

'Then I will present you with two options. You can refuse my offer and watch me walk out of here—' he paused for a beat to let that threat sink in '—or you can sell one per cent of your shares to me in addition to your father's fifty and I will execute the deal and wire the money within the next forty-eight hours.'

Her eyes narrowed. 'Just like that?'

'We have established there is no time for prolonged negotiations, have we not?'

'What about due diligence?'

He waved a hand. 'Give us access to your books today and we'll satisfy ourselves there are no major issues for concern.'

She eyed him across the wide mahogany table, her head tilting to one side. 'I'm curious about your interest in The Royce, Mr de la Vega. Your own clubs seem to be doing rather well but they're hardly in the same league. This establishment is built on a foundation of prestige and tradition and we cater to an elite and very discerning clientele. We are not a playpen for the *nouveau riche*.'

She was baiting him and Ramon counselled himself not to bite. His clubs were not *doing rather well*, they were reaping the rewards of extraordinary success. Yes, they were luxurious—decadent, even—but every aspect of their design embodied taste and sophistication. And they were wildly popular. His newest club, launched in Paris just four weeks ago, had reached its full membership quota six months before opening night and now had a waiting list of hundreds.

'The Royce is an icon in the industry,' he said. 'I assure you I have no intention of doing anything that would undermine its reputation.'

Her mouth opened but her lawyer sat forward and spoke first.

'Naturally Ms Royce is passionate about the club and preserving both its reputation and heritage. As a traditional gentlemen's club, it embraces values that are very conservative and, since female members are still prohibited, Ms Royce's part-ownership is not common knowledge.' He put down his pen and folded his hands on top of his legal pad. 'That said, she is an integral part of the business. If she were to agree to become a minority shareholder, we would seek a guarantee that her job remains secure. In addition, she would expect a reasonable level of autonomy in managing the day-to-day operations.'

Ramon inclined his head. 'Of course.' He turned his gaze on her. 'I have no wish, nor reason, to oust you from your business.' He wrote a number on his lawyer's note-pad, locked his gaze onto those pale grey eyes again and slid the pad across the table.

She leaned forward to look, as did Carter. The two exchanged a glance, then she picked up her pen, slashed a line through the number Ramon had written and wrote down another. She pushed the pad back to him.

He glanced down at the number.

'Done,' he said, and ignored the small, wheezy cough that came from his lawyer.

Emily stared at him, wordless.

'I suggest we make an immediate start on reviewing the financials,' he said smoothly. 'That is, if we're all agreed…?'

A hush fell as all eyes looked to Emily. Ramon waited. Her features were composed but he knew she waged an internal battle.

Finally, she looked at Carter, gave the briefest of nods then stood and walked around the table. She extended her hand. 'Congratulations, Mr de la Vega.'

He rose, wrapped his much larger hand around hers and registered at once the warmth of her skin. Surprise flickered. For some reason he'd imagined her touch would feel cold. Clinical. But the heat filling his palm was intense, almost electric.

Her eyes widened as though she too had felt something unexpected. Abruptly, she pulled her hand out of his. 'If you'll excuse me, I'll talk to our accountant and arrange for our financial records to be made available to you.'

'Thank you.'

She started to turn away.

'Emily,' he said.

She paused. 'Yes?'

He flashed his trademark smile. 'You can call me Ramon.'

* * *

Emily locked the door of the powder room, turned on the cold tap over the basin and shoved her wrists under the water.

She felt flustered, unbearably hot, and she couldn't understand why. Couldn't understand why Ramon de la Vega should have this crazy, unbalancing effect on her. Just being in the same room as him somehow had elevated her body temperature. Made her lungs work twice as hard to get enough air into them. And when she'd touched his hand… Her nerve endings had reacted as if she'd grabbed an electrified wire.

She dried her hands and sank onto a stool.

Had she done the right thing?

She closed her eyes and rubbed her forehead.

What choice had she had?

Ramon de la Vega or Carl Skinner.

In the end she'd had no choice at all. Her hand had been forced. First by her father's irresponsible actions and then by Ramon de la Vega's ruthless, self-serving agenda.

In less than two days from now, the Vega Corporation would own fifty-one per cent of The Royce.

I'm so sorry, Grandfather.

She exhaled a shaky breath.

At least Maxwell had finally turned up, although she couldn't have said whether it was an attack of conscience or the four messages she'd left on his phone, ranging in tone from pleading, to furious, to coldly threatening, that had prompted his appearance.

He'd looked terrible, as if he hadn't slept in days, and part of her had hoped he hadn't.

Why should he get the luxury of sleep when she'd lain awake all night worrying?

And then he had agreed to sell his shares.

It had taken Emily a full minute to realise the tightness in her chest had been not only shock, but sadness.

The Royce was the one remaining connection she had to her father. Now that connection would be irreparably severed.

She stood up suddenly and smoothed her hands down the sides of her trousers. She wasn't going to do this. She wasn't going to get emotional. It would only make her feel worse.

Drawing a deep breath, she headed down the plush carpeted corridor and looked into the accounting office.

It was empty.

Further along, she stopped at Marsha's desk. 'Do you know where Jeremy is?'

'He called in sick this morning.'

She sighed. The news wasn't welcome, and not only because she needed financial data from Jeremy. He was one of the few people at The Royce she felt able to confide in—and the only other person aside from Ray Carter who knew about her father's gambling problem. It would have been nice to talk with him.

Marsha looked at her. 'Can I help with something?'

'Do you have access to the finance drive?'

Marsha nodded and Emily grabbed a pen and a piece of notepaper and scribbled out a list. 'Download these files onto a flash drive and take them to our guests in the board-room.'

'Mr de la Vega?'

There was a gleam in Marsha's eyes that Emily tried not to notice. 'Yes. And please also arrange for refreshments and lunch for our visitors.' She moved towards her office. 'Thanks, Marsha. I'm going to keep my door closed for a while. If Mr de la Vega or his lawyer ask for anything more, let me know.'

So I can tell them to go jump.

Except she wouldn't, because she didn't have that luxury. But the thought was satisfying, if nothing else.

Sitting at her desk, she forced herself to focus. This morning's outcome was not what she'd anticipated but she still owned forty-nine per cent of The Royce. She still had a job to do. The staffing budgets had to be completed and she'd promised the executive chef she'd look at his proposed changes to the seasonal menu and give her stamp of approval.

Plus there was the small matter of drafting a discreet communication to the members. Maxwell had agreed to a carefully worded announcement in his name welcoming the Vega Corporation as a shareholder. The members already believed he was the sole owner. Armed with only selective facts, they'd assume her father had retained the balance of the shares, and he and Emily and the club's new shareholder would allow that assumption to go unchallenged.

It wasn't ideal, but discretion was necessary. The club's stability had to be her priority.

An hour later, despite her good intentions, Emily had abandoned her desk. She stood at her office window, her arms wrapped around her middle, her mind a tangle of thoughts as she stared sightlessly through the glass.

A knock at her office door jarred her out of her head. 'Come in,' she called over her shoulder, assuming it was Marsha.

It wasn't. It was her father.

She turned around and he closed the door, pushed his hands into his trouser pockets.

After an awkward silence, he said, 'The lawyers are fleshing out the terms. Ray will bring you a draft to review as soon as it's ready.'

'Fine,' she said, but it wasn't.

None of this was fine.

She wasn't fine.

Maxwell looked away first. He always did. 'If you don't need me—' he spoke to a point somewhere beyond her left shoulder '—I'll head off and come back when the agreement is ready for signing.'

If you don't need me.

Emily almost let out a bitter laugh.

Of course she didn't need him. She had needed him as a child, but he'd never been there, so she had taught herself to need no one.

'What will you do?' she asked, forcing the words past the sudden, silly lump in her throat.

He shrugged. 'I don't know,' he confessed, and Emily didn't think she'd ever seen Maxwell look quite so defeated.

'You still have the Knightsbridge apartment?'

Or had he gambled that away too? As he had everything else, including his father's stately mansion where Emily had lived at weekends and holidays when she wasn't at boarding school.

He nodded and, though she shouldn't care, she felt relieved that her father wouldn't be homeless.

He turned to go and all of a sudden Emily felt as if she were six years old and her daddy was abandoning her again. Walking out of the front door of the mansion and leaving her in that big, silent house with only her grandfather, his stern-faced housekeeper and her mother's ghost for company.

'Was it really so hard to love me?'

The words blurted from her mouth before the left side of her brain could censor them.

Maxwell paused, half turned. 'Excuse me?'

'Did you love *her*?'

She clasped the pearl at her throat and saw the tension grip her father's body. He had never talked about the woman who'd died giving birth to his only child.

'Your mother...' he began, and Emily's breath caught, her heart lurching against her ribs as she waited for him to go on.

But he simply shook his head.

'I'm sorry,' he muttered.

And then he left, closing the office door behind him. *Gone.*

Just like all the times before.

Tightness gripped her throat and she blinked rapidly. *No tears*, she told herself fiercely. She returned to her desk, opened a spreadsheet on her computer and forced herself to concentrate. She hadn't allowed herself to cry in a very long time. She wouldn't start now.

Ramon draped his suit jacket over the back of the Chesterfield sofa in Maxwell Royce's soon-to-be ex-office and sat down. His briefcase, a sheaf of papers and his open laptop lay on the dark wood coffee table in front of him. He could have worked at the big hand-carved desk at the far end of the enormous office, but staking his claim before the deal was officially done felt a touch too arrogant, even for him.

He looked at his platinum wristwatch.

The lawyers had been hashing out terms in the boardroom for nearly two hours.

Trusting his own lawyer to nail down the finer details, he'd left them to it over an hour ago.

Several times since then he'd thought about seeking out Emily, but each time he'd curbed the impulse. This morning's meeting had been civil but tense. Allowing her a cooling-off period seemed sensible.

His phone buzzed and he pulled it from his pocket and checked the screen. Xav had sent a text:

Good work. Talk later.

He dropped the phone onto the table, annoyance flaring. After having sent his brother an update an hour and a half ago, he'd expected a more enthusiastic response.

He should have remembered Xav was not a man ruled by emotion.

The door to the office banged open. Jarred from his thoughts, Ramon looked up to see who had so abruptly intruded.

Emily.

Her fine features pinched into a scowl, she stood in the doorway with a sheet of paper clutched in one hand. She breathed hard, as though she had sprinted the length of the carpeted hall from the boardroom to the office. Her gaze found him and he felt the heat of her anger wash over him. Felt it reach into places he probably shouldn't have.

'Who said you could use this office?'

He rose to his feet. 'Your father,' he said, sliding his hands into his trouser pockets. 'Is that a problem?'

Stalking into the room, she raised the paper clenched in her fist. '*This* is a problem.'

He remained calm. 'Is my guessing what's on that paper part of the game?'

'This isn't a game, Mr de la Vega.' She threw the sheet of paper onto the coffee table and pointed a manicured finger at it. 'Care to explain?'

He glanced down. It was a page from the latest marked-up version of the agreement. He didn't need a closer look to guess which amendment had raised her ire.

He walked to the door and closed it. At her questioning frown, he said, 'We don't want the children overhearing our first argument, do we?'

Her eyes flashed, and the glimpse of a temper intrigued him. She grabbed the piece of paper off the table.

'We're not going to argue,' she said. 'You're going to take this to your lawyer—' she slapped the page against his chest, anchoring it there under her flattened hand '—and you're going to tell him to reinstate the bylaws under the list of matters that require shareholder unanimity.'

Ramon looked down at the slender hand splayed across his chest then back at Emily's upturned face. This close he could see the velvety texture of her long brown eyelashes and the rings of darker grey around the circumference of her irises.

When he breathed in, he caught a subtle fragrance that was musky and feminine.

For seconds neither of them moved.

Then, with her luminous eyes widening, she snatched her hand away, took a hasty step backwards and lost her balance.

Before she could fall, Ramon's reflexes kicked in and he caught her by the waist, hauling her against him. The paper fluttered to the floor and it took all of three seconds for his body to register the feel of her soft breasts against his chest, the shape of her delicate hips fitting to his.

His gaze went to her mouth. Her lips were no longer pursed in anger but slightly parted. A hot spark of appreciation ignited. When not taut with disapproval, those lips were sultry. Kissable...

'Stop.'

Emily's low, urgent command sent a jolt through Ramon. He realised he'd lowered his head—was millimetres away from satisfying his desire to know if she tasted as ripe and sweet as he imagined. He raised his head, noted the streaks of crimson over her cheekbones, the laboured quality of her breathing, and knew a rush of satisfaction.

The attraction was mutual.

She stiffened, even as she trembled. 'Let me go.'

His aroused body protested but his mind urged him to comply. He wasn't averse to mixing business with pleasure on occasion, but indulging his lust with the prickly

Ms Royce would be more complicated than a few hours or days of pleasure were worth.

Restored to his senses, he dropped his hands from her waist and stepped back.

She retrieved the paper from the floor and moved away, placing a good six feet of space between them. 'Is that how you settle disputes with your business partners?' Her face was flushed, her tone scathing. 'By kissing them?'

'Only the pretty ones,' he drawled.

She gave him a withering look. 'You're not funny, Mr de la Vega.'

'I thought I told you to call me Ramon.'

She flapped the paper in the air. 'And I thought you were serious about this deal.'

Her comeback sobered him. 'I am.'

'Then explain why you're proposing to curtail my voting rights.'

He pushed his hands back into his pockets. 'You want autonomy in the day-to-day operations,' he said. 'And I'm willing to grant you that. By the same token, as the majority shareholder I don't expect to need your agreement on minor policy changes.'

She sent him an incredulous look. 'Minor? The bylaws are hardly *minor*. They're the very foundation of the club. The rules and regulations that govern everything that's important to the members. Etiquette, dress code, membership—' She halted and, slowly, realisation dawned on her face. 'That's it, isn't it?' Her tone turned accusing. 'You want to push through a reciprocal membership arrangement with your own clubs.'

'No. But I do want to amend the membership protocols.'

Her eyes narrowed. 'Why?'

Because his brother needed leverage. Because it was an opportunity to counter Hector's underhanded power plays. Hector thought he could buy the loyalty of his fellow cronies, but what he failed to realise was that his supporters were no less duplicitous than he was. Offered the right incentive, they'd desert him in a heartbeat and give their allegiance to Xav.

And what better incentive than entry into a club where they'd rub shoulders with some of the most powerful, influential men in the world?

But first Ramon had to ensure there were no obstacles in the road.

'The approval process is archaic.' He went to the coffee table and picked up a bound copy of the club's rules and regulations. 'This says the protocol for accepting new members hasn't changed in more than sixty years.' He raised an eyebrow. 'Surely a review is overdue?'

She shook her head. 'You can't go changing the rules willy-nilly. The membership needs to be consulted. And the member who chairs the Admissions Committee is a stickler for tradition.' Her expression turned faintly smug. 'He won't be easily swayed.'

'Lord Hanover, you mean?' He smiled as the smugness slid from her face. 'A pleasant chap. At least, he seemed so when we spoke.'

Her mouth went slack. 'You…you spoke with Lord Hanover?'

'Briefly. Forty minutes ago. I've arranged to have lunch with him on Thursday.'

'You're *lunching* with Lord Hanover?' Her eyes narrowed. 'I don't believe you.'

He dropped the document, picked up his phone and started thumbing through his contacts. 'Would you like to ask his secretary?'

Emily snapped her mouth shut. 'Fine. I believe you. But aren't you jumping the gun? Our agreement isn't executed yet.'

He stilled. 'Are you suggesting it won't be?'

'Not in its present form.'

Tension clamped the back of Ramon's neck. 'There was a reason you called me yesterday,' he warned softly. 'Don't forget that.'

Her chin took on a mulish tilt. 'Are you saying this is a deal breaker?'

'Yes.'

Her head jerked back a little. Then she sucked in a sharp breath, crossed to the window and presented him with a perfect view of her long legs, graceful back and slender neck. Her blonde hair was still confined in a tight twist, but a few silky strands had escaped, and he was surprised to see how curly they were. He let his gaze slide lower. She wore black trousers that accentuated the gentle flare of her hips and, yes, her backside was spectacular.

She spun to face him. 'If I waive the unanimity requirement, I want something in return.'

He shifted his weight. 'Go on.'

'Grant my father an honorary position as chairman.'

He stared at her, his appreciation of her curves swiftly forgotten.

'Plus a modest monthly allowance.'

His disbelief ballooned. Sharp on its heels came a surge of anger. 'Your father's actions have jeopardised the future of this club, and you want to reward him with an honorary role and an *allowance*?'

Was the woman a complete fool? Or simply too forgiving? The latter possibility incensed him. Forgiveness had to be earned, and some deeds didn't deserve forgiveness. Some people didn't deserve forgiveness. Ramon knew that better than most.

She crossed her arms. 'My father can't disappear from the club altogether. It will raise questions. At worst, suspicion. For appearance's sake, he needs to maintain a presence, show his face occasionally.'

He gave her an assessing look. 'So this is about the club. Not your father?'

'Of course. The Royce needs stability. That's all I care about right now.'

He nearly bought the act, but her tone was too lofty, her body language defensive. The idea of Emily caring about her father's welfare after he'd risked her livelihood only deepened Ramon's anger. Royce didn't deserve his daughter's lenience.

Yet she made a good point. The stability of the club and its membership was paramount.

Abruptly, he said, 'An honorary position. No allowance.'

She pressed her lips together.

When she didn't respond after a moment he warned quietly, 'You need this deal, Emily.'

As did he.

She blew out a breath and closed her eyes. Finally, she looked at him again. 'Fine. Unless you have any more surprises to spring?'

He thought about the accountant and decided the issue could wait. 'No.'

To which she nodded wordlessly and strode from the room, giving him a very wide berth, he noted.

CHAPTER FOUR

THE DOCUMENT FORMALISING the sale of Maxwell Royce's fifty per cent shareholding in The Royce and a further one per cent of Emily Royce's shares to the Vega Corporation was signed by all three parties at six twenty p.m. on Tuesday night.

It would have happened sooner, but Maxwell had taken almost two hours to reappear after Emily had called him on his mobile to summon him back.

He hadn't been inebriated when he'd showed but the whisky fumes on his breath had been unmistakable. Ramon had snagged her eye as they'd congregated in the boardroom and she'd known from his hard expression that he too had detected the whiff of alcohol.

Emily's heart had pounded as she'd signed her name to the agreement, and once the deed had been done she'd escaped as quickly as she could.

Except Maxwell had followed her out of the room, and when he'd called her name it'd felt wrong to ignore him.

'The honorary role...' he'd said, examining his shoes. 'I don't know what to say.'

'"Thank you" will suffice,' she'd told him, mentally shredding the little vignette she'd created in her head— the one in which Maxwell wrapped his arms around her and expressed his gratitude with a hug.

Stupid, stupid girl.

When had her father ever hugged her?

She had turned her back on him then and walked away and now, a day later, that small act of rejection felt petty and mean.

A knock at the office door drew her gaze away from the

window. She swivelled her chair around and glanced un-happily at the papers strewn across her desk. She'd arrived into the office at seven a.m. and in the two hours since then had achieved precisely nothing.

'Come in,' she called, then wished she hadn't, when the man responsible for her lack of productivity opened the door and strode in.

She wanted to hate Ramon de la Vega in that moment. As much as she wanted to hate the uncontrollable way her body reacted to him. Just his presence had the ability to make her feel hot and unsettled, restless, in a way she'd never experienced before.

He closed the door and she curled her hands over the arms of her chair.

She wished she didn't know how hard and lean he was underneath his swanky designer suit. But after yesterday, when she'd stumbled in her haste to back away from him and he'd caught her, she knew there wasn't an ounce of ex-cess fat on his powerful frame. Every impressive inch of him was hard, masculine muscle.

She pressed her thighs together, remembering the alarm-ing flare of heat she'd felt between her legs, the tiny thrill of illicit excitement when his mouth had descended towards hers. The avalanche of sensations had been so unexpected, so different from the revulsion Carl Skinner had evoked, she'd barely returned to her senses in time to command Ramon to stop.

She still reeled from the encounter. He'd almost kissed her and for one crazy, reckless moment she'd wanted him to. Had wanted to know how his mouth would feel against hers and if he tasted the same as he smelled…earthy, with a hint of spice and an undertone of sin…

Emily had tried hard to forget everything about that moment, but not even last night's frenzied baking session or the double helping of dark chocolate mousse cake she'd devoured had helped. Afterwards, feeling slightly ill, she'd glared at the partly eaten cake as if it had failed her somehow. Baking treats in her kitchen and indulging her sweet tooth were her favourite forms of stress release, but last night neither had brought her comfort beyond the temporary sugar hit.

'Good morning,' he said, his deep voice, with its interesting mix of Spanish and American accents, as rich and decadent as the cake she'd gorged on last night.

He smiled and she ignored the way it made her stomach flutter. Reminded herself he was the kind of man who used his looks to flatter and seduce. It wouldn't surprise her if he practised that smile in front of the mirror every morning.

She said a brisk, 'Good morning,' then glanced at her watch. 'You're half an hour early.'

Last night, before leaving, she'd suggested an introductory meeting with the department heads at nine-thirty, followed by a tour of the club and, if he was interested, some one-on-one time with each manager for an overview of their respective areas.

It had only just gone nine.

Without asking, he took a seat on the other side of her desk—the same chair Skinner had sat in two days earlier—and scanned the room. 'You have a nice office,' he said, ignoring her comment about the time.

'Thank you,' she said, because her office *was* nice, and she liked it. It'd been her father's until her grandfather had died and Maxwell had taken the larger office further up the hall. After moving in, Emily had hung a piece of colourful artwork and applied a few feminine touches to the decor. The result was a professional but comfortable space that at times felt like a second home. 'I hope it remains that way.'

He raised an eyebrow. 'Nice?'

'Mine,' she said, and his dark brows angled into a frown.

'Your job is secure, Emily.'

Emily wanted to believe him, but having faith in people had never been her strong suit, and the last few days had tested her capacity for trust. She straightened a sheaf of papers on her desk. 'I've confirmed the meeting with the department heads for nine-thirty,' she told him, moving the conversation along so she could hasten his departure from her office. 'Is there something you need before then?'

He paused for a beat, his toffee-coloured eyes remaining serious, and a thread of tension pulled at Emily's insides.

'I need you to fire your accountant,' he said.

She went completely still. 'Excuse me?'

'Jeremy Turner.'

Feeling a flicker of something close to anger, she snapped, 'I know my accountant's name. What I don't know is why you're telling me to fire him.'

'He's a liability.'

She stiffened, everything in her rejecting that statement. 'Jeremy has been with The Royce for more than thirteen years. I trust him implicitly.'

'That's a mistake.'

The certainty in his voice sent a prickle of unease down her spine. 'How would you know that?'

'I know that Jeremy Turner got drunk in a cocktail bar several weeks ago and talked to someone about your father's financial problems.'

Shock stole the air from her lungs for a moment. Jeremy had been drunk? Had been talking about her father's private affairs *in a bar*? Divulging information she had shared with him in confidence? She leaned back. Her hands shook and she fisted them in her lap. 'To whom?'

'It doesn't matter.'

'It does to me.'

Ramon expelled a breath. 'To a woman with whom I'm acquainted.'

Acquainted? As in, lovers? For some reason the idea

turned the taste in her mouth bitter and she promptly redirected her thoughts. She tried to think of a reason Ramon would fabricate such an allegation and drew a blank. He had no reason to lie, and she had to admit it did make a horrible kind of sense. Why else would he have suddenly set his sights on The Royce, if not because he knew they were vulnerable?

A sense of betrayal knifed under Emily's ribs. She hadn't socialised with Jeremy beyond the occasional work-day lunch, but for the last few years she'd considered him a close colleague. A confidante, of sorts.

She rubbed her forehead. 'I'll talk to him.'

'No.' The hard edge in Ramon's voice brought her gaze sharply back to his. 'Turner goes,' he said. 'No compromise.'

Even as she nursed a sense of hurt over Jeremy's misdeed, Emily balked at such a merciless stance. 'He has a right to put his side of the story forward, surely?'

'It's irrelevant.'

'He exercised poor judgement—'

'He shared personal information about his employer with a stranger. That's indefensible.'

Jaw flexing, Ramon stood, the ruthless businessman emerging from behind the easy charm. The glimpse of arrogant intractability should have repelled her. Instead her pulse quickened, her heart pumping faster.

'I need to be able to trust the people who work for me,' he added. 'As should you. There's no room for soft hearts in business, Emily. Not everyone deserves a second chance.' There was a quiet ferocity in his voice that suggested he truly believed it. 'Cut him loose,' he finished. 'Or I will.'

His ultimatum delivered, he turned and walked out before she could articulate a protest.

Emily dropped her head in her hands.

She'd awoken this morning grimly resigned to yesterday's outcome and consoled herself with the thought that at least this week couldn't get any worse.

She laughed bitterly.

More fool her.

Emily didn't have to fire Jeremy in the end.

He resigned.

As soon as she walked into his office and confronted him, his face crumpled with guilt and he tendered his resignation with immediate effect.

Regret made her chest ache, but Jeremy's confession had tied her hands—made it impossible for her to plead his case with Ramon.

And, though it pained her to admit it, maybe Ramon was right. Maybe she was too soft. Too forgiving. How many times had she dug her father out of trouble, only for him to disappoint her and mess up again?

She paused outside his office. Or was it Ramon's now? She'd hoped it might be hers one day, but the future unfolding was very different from the one she had imagined. Was he even in there? She hadn't seen him since the meeting with the department heads and it was after three o'clock now. She took a deep breath, knocked twice and opened the door.

He looked up from behind the big mahogany desk that used to be her grandfather's.

So he had settled in.

The knot of resentment in Emily's stomach hardened. He looked perfectly at home, as if he had every right to be there, and she hated that he did.

She closed the door and he leaned back in the enormous leather chair as she crossed the office. He'd removed his suit jacket and tie—a liberty acceptable only in the privacy of the offices, given the strict formal dress code of the club—and he looked good in just a shirt, the tailored fit of the white fabric emphasising the breadth of his shoulders and a strong, well-proportioned physique that looked more suited to a rugby pitch than the office.

She stopped in front of the desk, squeezed all inappropriate thoughts of his body out of her head and placed her hand on a chair back for support. 'Jeremy's gone,' she said, intending to sound matter-of-fact, but to her horror a faint quaver hijacked her voice.

Ramon's eyes narrowed, telling her he hadn't missed it. He studied her until heat crawled around the back of her neck. 'Sit down,' he said.

'No. I only came to tell you—'

'Sit down, Emily,' he repeated, more firmly this time, and she closed her mouth and sat, even as she scorned herself for being so meek.

Rising, he turned to a shelf on the large bookcase behind him and picked up two crystal tumblers in one hand and a heavy vintage decanter in the other. He set the tumblers on the desk. 'First time firing someone?'

She watched him pull the stopper from the decanter and pour a shot of her father's whisky into each glass. 'I didn't fire him,' she said. 'He resigned.' But she knew that was just semantics. If Jeremy hadn't offered his resignation, she'd have been forced to terminate his employment.

Ramon slid one of the tumblers across to her.

'Why are we drinking?'

'Because you look as if you need it.'

She glanced at him sharply. Was he offering comfort? Or attempting to avert what he thought might be an emotional crisis?

Grabbing the tumbler, she swallowed the whisky and winced as it burned on the way down.

'Better?' he asked after a moment.

'Not really.' Although the warmth spreading through her stomach had a rather soothing effect. She met his gaze.

His eyes reminded her of hot, molten caramel—rich and tempting, but dangerous if you dipped your finger in too soon. She cleared her throat. 'I suppose you've fired plenty of people.'

'Three.' He sat, knocked back his whisky and put the glass down. 'Trust me, it's not something that brings me pleasure.'

So they had that in common at least. His words from this morning came back to her.

Not everyone deserves a second chance.

Did that harsh belief stem from personal experience?

'Emily.'

With a start, she realised he had spoken. 'I'm sorry?'

'I said you have a good team here,' he said. 'Dedicated. Professional. And they respect you.'

Warmth spread through her chest, though she told herself that was from the whisky, not his unexpected praise. 'Thank you,' she said. 'They're all extremely dedicated. Most of them have been here since my grandfather's time.'

And Emily had worked hard to earn their respect. She was young, but in the three years before her grandfather's death she had worked at ground level in every department including the kitchens to prove she was serious about learning the business. No one had been able to accuse her of looking for a free ride because her surname was Royce. Even her grandfather, who had rarely given praise, had remarked on her commitment. Of course, he had gone on to say her commitment to hard work would stand her in good stead for marriage and motherhood. In his mind, her greatest obligation to the family was to provide him with at least one great-grandson who would one day inherit his precious club and his wealth. He'd even rewritten his will in a sly effort to influence that outcome.

It'd been a wasted effort, of course. Emily had no intention of being ruled by a clause in a will.

Ramon spoke again and she tried to focus. What was wrong with her? One shot of whisky and her mind was all over the place. Or was it the effect of the man sitting opposite?

'My CFO will have one of his team pick up the slack until you've recruited a new accountant.'

'Oh...' She nodded slowly. 'Okay. Thank you.'

'I have a contact at a top recruitment firm here in London,' he said. 'I'll email his details to you. Once you start the process, keep me updated.'

Feeling off-kilter and not sure why, she simply nodded. 'All right.'

'And keep Friday night free for dinner.'

'Fine—' *Wait.* 'What?' she said.

'Dinner,' he repeated.

She blinked at him. 'With whom?'

'With me,' he said smoothly.

Emily opened her mouth and closed it again.

'Is that a problem?'

Yes. For too many reasons to list, not least of which was that she was smart enough to know she was out of her depth with this man. He had more sex appeal than anyone she'd ever met. Dealing with him in a professional setting required every ounce of composure she possessed. Outside of the office, she wouldn't stand a chance of remaining immune.

'I thought you'd be going back to New York by the end of the week,' she said.

He gave a slow smile that made her shift in the chair. 'Eager to be rid of me, Emily?'

'Of course not.' But a hot, incriminating blush burned her cheeks. 'I'm aware you have businesses all over the world, that's all. I assume you don't stay in one place for long.'

'Not unless something holds my interest.'

The heat in her face spread down her neck. He was talking about women. She didn't know how she knew that, she just did. Maybe it was the look in his eyes—the gleam that was making her feel as if *she* were the current object of his interest. Which was, she reminded herself, how every playboy operated. They were automatically programmed to flirt. To pull out their charm like a magic wand and zap a woman's defences. It was why men like Ramon—and her father—were never short of female companionship. Not that she'd seen her father in action with the ladies for herself. But the string of glittering, vacuous women who'd come and gone over the years spoke for itself.

'I'm not sure dinner is a good idea.' She shifted again, her skin feeling sticky under her blouse. 'Yesterday...' She trailed off, waiting awkwardly for him to catch her drift.

His brows rose. 'Yesterday...what?'

At the gleam in his eyes, she pressed her lips together. *He knew what.* She glared at him, her face growing hotter. 'You almost kissed me.'

As soon as the words came out she wished they hadn't. Mentioning it gave the impression she'd been thinking about it and that would only feed his ego. Of course, she *had* been thinking about it, which made everything—this conversation included—ten times more excruciating. She wanted to groan. How had they gone from the serious topic of firing people to this?

Unlike her, Ramon didn't appear at all discomfited. 'Which is why we should have dinner.'

She frowned. 'I don't understand.'

'We're business partners now.' His tone was patient. 'We have a relationship—'

'A professional one,' she cut in.

'Yes. Which would benefit from putting the tension—and events—of the last two days behind us and starting with a clean slate.'

Meaning, he wouldn't try to kiss her again? The thought provoked a sinking sensation she couldn't explain. Ignoring it, she raised her chin in challenge. 'By having dinner?'

He shrugged. 'It's a good way to relax and talk. To get to know one another.'

Put like that, it didn't sound completely unreasonable. But caution kept her wary. 'We can talk here. In the office.'

'Or we can enjoy a meal without work-day interruptions and you can give me an opportunity to show you one of my clubs.' His lips curved in a half-smile. 'Perhaps even improve your opinion of them.'

That made her pause—from guilt as much as anything. She'd not been very complimentary about his clubs.

In truth, she was intrigued.

His properties had a reputation for unrivalled luxury, and she'd read that A-list celebrities booked up to a year in advance to hold their private soirees in his West End club. His latest venture, in Paris, was meant to be even more glamorous and exclusive.

She puffed out a breath. She'd run out of arguments, or at least any that were valid. Telling him she couldn't have dinner with him because he made her feel hot and bothered was hardly an option. She stood up. 'Fine. A *business* dinner,' she said, putting a clear emphasis on 'business'.

One evening. She could grit her teeth and bear it, couldn't she? And, when it was over, he would disappear, to New York or Spain or Dubai or wherever, and Emily would get on with doing what she did best.

Running The Royce.

Two days later, standing in her bathroom, Emily applied a final coat of mascara to her lashes, stepped back from the mirror and gave her reflection a critical once-over.

She couldn't remember the last time she'd devoted this much effort to her appearance.

She smoothed the front of her dress with both hands. It was a safe choice. The scooped neckline revealed only a hint of cleavage and the hem stopped just above her knees. The midnight-blue fabric clung softly to her body and the subtle shimmer woven through it kept it from being boring. It was classy enough for an exclusive venue, but not attention-seeking.

She uncapped a tube of tinted gloss and slicked it over her lips. She'd gone for more make-up than usual, enhancing her grey eyes with soft, smoky colours, and lightly rouging her cheeks.

Recapping the gloss, she looked at her hair and felt a stab of uncertainty. Her curls were shiny, well-conditioned, but they were thick and unruly. She should have left them in the neat chignon she'd worn to work.

She pulled open a drawer filled with hair clips and bands as her doorbell chimed from the hallway.

With a fresh bout of nerves making her hands unsteady, she glanced at her watch.

Six-fifty p.m.

He was ten minutes early.

And standing at the front door of her flat, she thought with a flash of unaccountable panic.

Quickly, she slipped her bare feet into a pair of high-heeled navy sandals and went to the door.

Her renovated flat was on the top floor of a converted three-storey Victorian mansion. She had told Ramon to text her when he arrived and she would meet him on the street. She paused by the hall table and checked her phone. No message.

Maybe a neighbour was calling and it wasn't Ramon. How would he have gained access? Unless Mr Johnson, her elderly ground-floor neighbour, had forgotten to lock the main door again.

Taking a deep breath, she calmed her spinning thoughts and opened the door.

And forgot to breathe out.

Ramon stood there and he was…

Oh.

He was breathtaking…tall and powerful and a bit edgy-looking, dressed entirely in black. He wore a jacket, no tie, an open-necked silk shirt and he hadn't shaved, leaving a dark five o'clock shadow on his lean jaw that served only to magnify his sex appeal. He looked relaxed, yet lethal—a heady combination that turned her knees watery and her insides hot.

She steadied herself with one hand on the door, slowly growing aware of Ramon conducting his own appraisal—of her.

His gaze travelled all the way down to her coral-tipped toes and back up to her face.

Their gazes locked and Emily couldn't misinterpret the dark, appreciative smoulder in his hooded brown eyes.

Heat saturated her skin.

This was business, she reminded herself, not an evening of pleasure, but the electrifying hum of physical awareness didn't lessen.

And then his gaze shifted to her hair, moving over the wild mass of honey-blonde curls that more often than not defied her efforts to tame them. Which was why she always, always restrained her hair in a tight chignon for work.

Wishing again that she'd left it up, she tugged the end of a thick curl. 'It's a little wild.' She sounded almost apologetic. 'I was going to put it back up. If you wait a minute—'

Ramon caught her wrist before she could turn away. 'Don't.' His voice was deep, gruff. 'Your hair is beautiful.'

Her heart gave a little jolt, as if his touch had cranked up the voltage on her awareness and fired a tiny electric charge through her body. 'Actually, it's a nightmare,' she said, brushing off the compliment and ignoring the small dart of pleasure that pierced her.

He released her, and though it was fanciful she imagined she could still feel the warm imprint of his fingers on her skin.

'I like it.' His lips curved and she wondered how many women had fallen prey to that lazy, sensual smile. 'Are you ready?'

Because it was too late to back out, she made herself nod. 'I'll just grab my bag.'

Reluctant to invite him in, she left Ramon at the door while she slipped her phone and a few other essentials into a silver clutch and grabbed the velvet wrap she'd left on her bed when choosing her outfit.

On the landing, she stopped to lock the door and glanced at Ramon. 'This wasn't necessary, you know. I told you, I could have met you at your club.'

'Are those the kind of men you normally date?'

She looked at him sharply and felt heat creep into her cheeks. It had been a long time since any man had taken her on a date. 'Excuse me?'

'The kind who are happy to let you traipse across the city alone at night?'

Hearing his sharp tone, she turned to him. 'This isn't a date.' She slipped her keys into her clutch. 'And we might be business partners, but I don't think my personal safety falls under your purview.'

She headed towards the stairs and Ramon fell into step beside her.

'Perhaps not,' he said. 'But it would be very inconvenient if something happened to you.'

She shot him a sidelong glance. His profile looked stern, but there'd been a teasing lilt to his voice.

'I'm quite capable of looking after myself.' She had,

after all, been doing it for a long time. 'Believe it or not, I'm even rather good at it.'

'Yet you live in a building that isn't secure.'

As they started down the stairs, Ramon cupped her elbow and the brush of his fingers was warm, light and not entirely unwelcome. After six years she was familiar with the carpeted stairs that led to her beloved home, but she normally navigated them in the ballet flats that lived in her work bag for the specific purpose of her week-day commute. Descending in four-inch heels felt somewhat more precarious.

'The main door is usually locked,' she defended, and made a mental note to have another word with Mr Johnson. 'My downstairs neighbour is elderly. Sometimes he disables the self-locking handle if he's bringing in more than one load of shopping then forgets to unlatch it.'

'You should have an alarmed access system with an intercom for visitors.'

In spite of herself, Emily's mouth twitched. 'This is Wimbledon. Not the Bronx.' Something occurred to her then. 'How did you know which flat to come to?' The converted mansion housed five residences, two each on the ground and middle floors, and hers taking up the entirety of the top floor.

'You mentioned you lived at the top.'

She thought for a moment. Yes. She might have—when they'd had the conversation which had started with her telling him she'd make her own transport arrangements and ended with him overriding her. Ramon de la Vega, for all his easy charm, was not a man accustomed to hearing no.

Outside, a sleek, black sedan of European design waited by the kerb with its driver sitting patiently behind the wheel. Ramon guided Emily into the back and then joined her from the other side. His big frame made the enclosed space, with its tinted windows and luxurious leather, feel disconcertingly small.

Emily tugged at the hem of her dress, which had ridden up as she'd slid onto the soft leather, and cast around for a conversation starter. 'Tell me about your club,' she said, settling on a topic that felt safe.

'The London club?'

'Of course.' Wasn't that where they were going? 'I read somewhere that the waiting list for membership is estimated at five years long.'

'At least.' His tone wasn't boastful, just straightforward, matter-of-fact. 'We have a strict limit of a thousand members at any one time.' He went on to describe a range of high-end facilities, including restaurants and bars, a health spa and a grooming salon, fitness amenities and luxury accommodation for members who lived abroad.

Emily felt a touch of envy as she listened. Ramon had a clear vision for his clubs and the freedom to pursue it. She, on the other hand, was hamstrung by a conservative membership that was allergic to the very whiff of change and anything that might be remotely perceived as bucking tradition.

A short while later, when the car stopped and the purr of the engine ceased, Emily realised she'd lost track of time as well as their whereabouts. She glanced out through the tinted window beside her, expecting to see the night-time bustle of London's vibrant West End, and stilled.

She snapped her head back around to look at Ramon. Anger vibrated in her voice when she spoke. 'You have exactly three seconds to explain why we're sitting on a runway next to a plane.'

His expression was calm. 'I'm taking you to Saphir.'

Confusion blanked her mind for a moment, then understanding crashed in.

'We're having dinner in *Paris*?'

Three things seemed to converge on Emily at once. Shock, panic and a tiny, treacherous streak of excitement.

She shook her head. 'That's crazy. I... I can't.'

'Are you afraid of flying?'

'No.'

'Then what's the problem?'

She sent him a furious look. 'The problem is that travelling to another country for dinner is...is *insane*.'

'The flight is less than an hour.'

She gripped her clutch tightly in her lap. 'I don't care. You misled me. You said we were having dinner at your club.'

'I didn't say which one.'

'Lying by omission doesn't excuse you.' She set her jaw. 'Anyway, this is all pointless. I don't have my passport.'

He reached inside his jacket and withdrew something.

Eyes widening, heart pumping hard, she snatched the passport off him and checked inside it. She looked up, incredulous. 'How on earth did you get this?' It should have been sitting in a safe in her office.

'Marsha,' he said.

Emily threw him an appalled look. 'You should be ashamed of yourself.'

No doubt he had layered on the charm in order to coerce young Marsha's help. The poor girl wouldn't have stood a chance in the path of all that concentrated testosterone.

Emily shoved the passport into her clutch, snapped it closed and stared straight ahead. She could see the back of the driver's head through the glass partition, but if he'd overheard their conversation he gave no sign. 'Take me home.'

'After dinner.'

Ramon climbed out and walked around the car to her side. When he opened the door and stared down at her, she crossed her arms and refused to budge. He waited, and the seconds ticked by until she started to feel childish. Finally, muttering a curse under her breath, she got out. 'For the record, I don't like surprises.'

'Everyone likes surprises.'

The amusement in his tone grated. 'I don't. And I still think this is crazy.'

He closed the door and she leaned against the car for support, as if it were an anchor in a choppy sea—a safe, solid object that would keep her grounded, and stop her doing something stupid. Something she might regret. Like getting on that damned plane.

'It's just dinner, Emily.'

His voice had a deep, soothing quality, but it didn't help, because it wasn't just dinner. Not for her. Not when she stood there contemplating a giant leap out of her neatly ordered comfort zone. She eyed the plane. It was a small, sleek private jet. 'Is that yours or did you charter it for the evening?'

'I bought it yesterday.'

'Very funny.'

'I'm serious.'

She turned her head to look at him. There was no mockery on his face. She looked at the plane again. A uniformed male attendant stood at the foot of the steps, patiently waiting. 'This is very...spontaneous,' she said weakly.

'That's a bad thing?'

'Yes.' She held her wrap and her clutch against her chest in a death grip. 'I'm not very good at spontaneous.'

'Try it.' His deep, sinful voice coaxed. Enticed. 'You might like it.'

She might.

And where would that leave her?

Already she felt a gazillion miles out of her depth with this man, but it was everything else he made her feel that terrified her.

Never had she felt so physically attracted to someone before. The one intimate relationship she'd had had left her feeling deeply discontented, believing in the end she just wasn't that into sex, but Ramon…

He made her think about sex.

She, who guarded her space and preferred not to be touched, had caught herself more than once thinking about his big hands and his beautiful mouth and how they might feel on certain parts of her body.

She forced herself away from the car.

Thoughts were just thoughts, weren't they? Harmless unless translated into action, and that wasn't going to happen. Theirs was a professional relationship and she was too sensible to breach that boundary. She wasn't controlled by her desires. Not like her father.

It's just dinner.

She thought of all the women who would give their eye teeth to fly in a billionaire's private jet to Paris for dinner and then straightened her shoulders. 'Let's not stand around all evening, then.' She set off towards the plane. 'I'm famished.'

CHAPTER FIVE

RAMON HAD BEEN labelled 'reckless' from the day he'd been old enough to clamber out of his cot and send his mother and the entire household staff into a frenzied hour-long search of the house and grounds. As a fearless, rebellious child he'd become the bane of his parents' lives, unlike his brother, who'd never once defied authority or set a foot wrong.

As an adult, Ramon had learned to curb his impulses. The tabloids portrayed him as a playboy and his reputation wasn't entirely undeserved. But he didn't pursue pleasure with a careless disregard for the consequences, like some of his peers did. Risks, when taken, were calculated, impulses acted upon only if there was no potential for harm.

And he was no longer fearless. He understood the pain of loss. Understood that when you hurt people, when you took something precious from them, there were no words or actions that could undo the harm. No way of turning back the clock.

Tonight, as he took Emily's hand to help her from the limousine outside Saphir, Ramon understood something else. He understood that, for the first time in a long time, he had miscalculated.

Because he had believed he could keep his relationship with Emily professional. Had told himself that tonight was simply an elaborate attempt to break down her barriers and smooth the way for a more harmonious partnership. That, plus the opportunity to bring her to Saphir and showcase the best of his portfolio.

But he had failed to factor into his calculations the possibility that Emily would look the way she did tonight. Or that his body would end up humming with a raw, irrepressible desire he'd find impossible to quell.

He didn't want just to break down her barriers.

He wanted to rip off the dress that clung so seductively to every lush curve and dip of her body and haul her off to bed.

'Wow.'

She stood beside him, her face upturned, her gaze trained on the club's white stone entrance and the soaring, double-tiered archway bathed in subtle blue light. She'd loosened up in the last hour, maybe in part due to the champagne they'd consumed on the plane, along with canapés to tide them over, or maybe thanks to the small talk they'd settled into once her anger with him had subsided.

'Welcome to Saphir.' No sooner had he spoken than a pop of white light flashed in his periphery.

Blinking, Emily looked around, spotting the photographer a second after he did. 'Was he taking a photo of *us*?'

Ramon gestured to a security guard. 'Ignore it,' he said, guiding her inside with a hand pressed to the small of her elegant back. He nodded to the concierge as they entered the high-ceilinged granite and glass reception area. 'Security keeps the paparazzi at bay, but they're like flies. Swat one away and a dozen more appear. Unfortunately Saphir has become their new favourite haunt. This way.' He turned her down a hallway lined with contemporary art work and illuminated sculptures, many of which he'd handpicked in consultation with his designer. As they approached the restaurant, a willowy redheaded hostess whose name he couldn't remember greeted him with a deferential smile, relieved Emily of her wrap and escorted them through the restaurant's lively interior to a table in the private alcove he had specifically requested.

Emily took in their surroundings then looked out of the floor-to-ceiling window to an internal courtyard where sculptured water features and luxuriant plant life created an exotic, colourful haven. 'This is beautiful.'

Ramon signalled to the redhead, who pressed a button, and then the wall of glass beside them slid back.

A smile spread over Emily's face. 'I feel like I'm sitting in paradise!'

Her reaction was unguarded, her smile so beautiful, so real, that Ramon felt its impact like a burst of warmth in his chest. He was trying to process the feeling when a waiter materialised with menus, the champagne he'd pre-ordered and two *amuse-bouches* served in shot glasses with delicate glass spoons.

'*Foie gras*, figs and apricot,' the waiter explained. He uncorked the champagne, filled their flutes then melted away again.

After one mouthful of her *amuse-bouche*, Emily made an appreciative humming noise in her throat that Ramon was fairly sure he could feel in his groin.

'That is delicious.' She scraped the glass clean and savoured her last mouthful. 'Who's your executive chef?'

'Levi Klassen.'

Her grey eyes, which had a softer look about them tonight, rounded. 'The Dutch chef?'

'You know him?'

'I know of him. Our executive chef at The Royce speaks highly of him.'

He finished his own *amuse-bouche* and acknowledged it was exceptional. As he'd expected. He only hired the best. 'Perhaps we can have them collaborate on a menu some time.'

'Really? That would be amazing.' She turned her attention to the menu on the table. After a quick scan, she asked, 'Are the desserts on a separate menu?'

'Yes.'

'Oh.' She sounded disappointed.

He lifted an eyebrow. 'Problem?'

'I always check the desserts first.' She glanced up and must have seen the question on his face. 'So I know how much room to leave,' she elaborated.

Ramon tried to think of a time he'd taken a woman to dinner and watched her do more than pick at a lettuce leaf or a piece of white fish. He found himself smiling.

Her eyes narrowed. 'Have I amused you?'

'Surprised me,' he admitted. He caught the waiter's attention and sent the man for a dessert menu.

'Because I like to eat dessert?'

He shrugged. 'I don't often dine with women who admit to having a sweet tooth, let alone indulge it.'

'That's because supermodels live on diet pills and fresh air,' she said pertly and, given that a number of beautiful but rake-thin models had come and gone from his bed over the years, he was hard pressed to defend himself against that comment.

Fortunately, their waiter returned and saved him from having to. He sipped his champagne and watched as Emily studied the list of desserts, amusement mingling with a hot flare of curiosity. What other passions besides her sweet tooth did she hide beneath that beautiful, reserved exterior?

She put down the menu. 'Okay. I've made up my mind.'

The waiter noted their selections and then Emily settled back in her chair. 'The membership secretary put four new applications on my desk today.' She spoke quietly, her gaze fixed on her champagne, her long, slender fingers sliding idly along the delicate glass stem. 'I noted all four are board members of the Vega Corporation. I also saw that Lord Hanover has stamped his endorsement on all of them.' She glanced up, her expression difficult to read. 'How did you manage that?'

The same way he accomplished any major business win—by doing his homework, being prepared. 'In negotiations, there's a simple rule of thumb for getting what you want.'

She gave him a thoughtful look. 'Knowing what the other party wants?' she correctly guessed. She tilted her head, her magnificent honey-gold hair catching shards of reflected light from the modern chandelier above their heads. 'And Lord Hanover?' she asked. 'What does he want?'

His palms itched with a strong desire to bury his hands in those lustrous curls and explore their silken texture. He tightened his hand on his champagne glass. 'His son-in-law is chasing a major multi-billion-dollar construction contract in Saudi Arabia.'

Her gaze turned speculative. 'And…?'

'And he's hit a wall of red tape.'

'Ah. And you happen to have some connections that might smooth the way?'

He nodded, impressed. Emily was intelligent—he knew that—but she was also perceptive. Shrewd. 'My former Harvard roommate and friend to this day is a Saudi prince.'

Her eyes widened fractionally. 'Well…' After a moment, she lifted her champagne. 'Congratulations. Lord Hanover is very influential. Gaining his support is a smart move.'

He heard a trace of something in her voice. Not resentment—it was more wistful than bitter. Envy perhaps? 'Does it bother you that your shareholder status can't be revealed?'

She swallowed a mouthful of champagne and shrugged. 'Not really. It's just the way things are. There'd be an uproar if it was.'

'How can you be certain?'

She put her glass down. 'Because two years ago, three of our members proposed that women be permitted to join the club. It went to a ballot but things got very heated beforehand and some members threatened to leave if the proposal passed. It didn't…obviously.' She arched an eyebrow.

'That was their response to the idea of women joining their club. Can you imagine the reaction if they knew a woman *owned* their club?'

'And the proposers?'

'Ostracised. All three left within six months.'

It was outrageous but not surprising. Lord Hanover and his peers were prominent in the club and chauvinism was still rampant in their ranks. Ramon could imagine which way their votes had gone. 'So why did your grandfather leave half the business to you?' he asked. 'He must have known it could risk the club's stability.'

She took a moment to answer. 'Because my father has always been the way he is. Addicted to the high life, less so to responsibility. I guess my grandfather didn't trust his own son.'

'But he trusted you?'

Another shrug. 'He knew I was sensible. Devoted enough to do whatever was best for The Royce.'

'Including keeping your ownership secret.'

'Yes.'

So her grandfather had taken a calculated risk. Ramon could appreciate that strategy. And yet the old man had placed a tremendous burden on his granddaughter's shoulders. 'Surely people...the members...would expect that you'd eventually inherit the club from your father anyway?'

'Not necessarily. My father was only forty-six when his father died—fifty-three now. He could still remarry, have other children...other legitimate heirs.'

'Was that what your grandfather expected?'

'I think my grandfather stopped having expectations of my father a long time ago.'

'And you?'

She frowned. 'What do you mean?'

'What expectations did he have of you?'

Her lips twisted. 'My grandfather expected me to marry and start popping out babies—preferably boys—before the age of thirty. He only ever intended my ownership of The Royce to be a short-term guardianship.' She blinked and her mouth suddenly compressed in a tight line, as if she'd said more than she'd intended to and regretted the lapse. She shifted in her chair. 'I'm sure he turned in his grave many times this past week.'

'You think you've let your grandfather down?'

Her expression was tight. 'No offence, but the Vega Corporation owning fifty-one per cent of his precious club is not an outcome he would have endorsed.'

Ramon frowned. 'Would he have considered the alternative less desirable?'

Her gaze met his then slid away. 'Of course.'

'So the only person at fault is your father,' he said, but she looked unconvinced, and he wanted to reach across the table, grab her by the shoulders and give her a good shake. Either that, or drag her onto his lap and kiss the anguish from her face.

The latter held infinitely more appeal.

Her gaze came back to his, held for a moment, and awareness thickened the air between them. He saw the flicker of her eyelids, the surge of tell-tale colour in her cheeks, and knew she was just as conscious of their chemistry as he. Heat skated through him, but then the waiter arrived with their starters and Emily dropped her gaze. Lingering by the table, the waiter began to explain the different culinary elements on their plates. Ramon went to wave him off until he noticed that Emily was listening intently. He sat back and let the Frenchman finish, then watched her pick up her knife and fork and take a sample, sliding a sliver of beef carpaccio into her mouth. 'You're a foodie,' he observed, forcing his gaze away from those soft, perfectly shaped lips.

She glanced up. 'If that means I appreciate good food, then yes, I suppose I am.'

He picked up his own cutlery. 'Do you dine out often?'

She shook her head. 'Only occasionally.'

Her answer pleased Ramon more than it should have. He'd already learned from young Marsha—who had a talkative streak he'd shamelessly exploited—that Emily had no significant other and preferred working to socialising. But, workaholic or not, Emily Royce was too beautiful to escape male notice. If she'd said yes to his question, he would've imagined her being wined and dined by men with a great deal more than food on their minds, and that was sufficient to turn his thoughts inexplicably dark.

'I suppose you eat out all the time,' she said, 'With all the travelling that you do.'

'When the mood takes me.' Which, admittedly, was often. Dining alone rarely appealed and, no matter where in the world he was, he never wanted for a willing companion. Lately, however, his palate had become jaded, the abundance of food, wine and women failing to distract him.

This past week in London was a prime example. Twice he'd gone out with his friend Christophe only to return to his suite before midnight, alone. Not that he'd encountered a shortage of enthusiastic women, but none had held his interest. It'd left him restless and frustrated. Pursuing pleasure was a means of distraction. The alternative—boredom—was dangerous. It invited reflection, and looking too deeply inside himself never revealed anything good. That was why he never stood still for long. Why he always looked for his next challenge, whether in the boardroom or the bedroom.

Refocusing, he took a mouthful of rare, tender venison and, following Emily's lead, paused for a moment to savour the flavour and texture of the food. It was, he appreciated as he swallowed, outstanding.

'Good?'

Realising he'd closed his eyes, he opened them and looked straight into Emily's. 'Exceptional,' he said, dropping his gaze to her mouth, knowing he'd give up the rest of his meal in a flash for one taste of those luscious lips. There would be no boredom with Emily, he decided. Not with all those hidden depths to explore. She would challenge him in bed, just as she did in the office. Lust churned through his veins, hot and savage, triggering a flood of explicit thoughts as tempting as they were dangerous.

'May I ask what percentage of your revenue is generated by your food and beverage department?'

He looked at her, her question making a mockery of the desire raging through his body. She was talking business while he pictured her naked and spread beneath him. He wondered if he'd misread the signs of attraction and then he saw how tightly she gripped the handles of her cutlery. How short and shallow her breaths were and how the pulse in her throat flickered visibly. No. He hadn't misread anything. She was fighting for control of her body, just as he was doing. With brutal determination, he concentrated his thoughts and came up with a number that sounded correct.

And then she asked another question, something about the occupancy rate of Saphir's suites, and he understood that she was attempting to keep things impersonal. Preventing the undercurrent of sexual tension from pulling them under.

Right then his body wanted anything *but* impersonal. And yet his brain conceded that restraint was the wisest action. Emily didn't strike him as the kind of woman who indulged in casual affairs. If they slept together, and her expectations went beyond the physical side of things, she'd only end up disappointed. Or, worse, hurt.

Still, keeping his mind focused and his urges restrained proved a challenge throughout the rest of their meal. When Emily's dessert finally came, he sat with his double-shot espresso in front of him and watched her devour every last morsel of the rich, decadent dark chocolate soufflé. At the end she licked her spoon clean, the tip of her pink tongue catching one last smear of chocolate, and Ramon suppressed a groan. He could feel his body responding. Feel a stirring of the old, impulsive recklessness he knew better than to indulge.

Emily looked up and froze, the spoon in her hand suspended halfway between her mouth and the plate. 'Ramon...'

Hearing her say his forename for the first time—and in that husky, slightly breathless tone—sent a small shock-wave of heat through him that mingled explosively with the lust. He dragged his gaze from her mouth and locked onto those silver-grey eyes.

'Stop,' she whispered, her eyes wide and pleading, and he didn't feign innocence.

There was no point.

He knew his desire was stamped on his face and he wouldn't pretend it didn't exist. His reputation as a player was well-earned but he didn't engage in cat-and-mouse games. When he set his sights on a woman he pursued her without pretence. He wouldn't deny the truth, to Emily or to himself.

And the truth was, he wanted her.

She'd had too much champagne.

Emily put down her spoon and lowered her gaze from Ramon's. She couldn't watch his eyes stare at her mouth a moment longer. Not because she felt scandalised by the brazen interest in his heavy-lidded gaze, but rather because of the wild curiosity pulsing through her. The shocking temptation to lean across the table, part her lips and invite him to take what he wanted in spite of having just now implored him to *stop*.

Oh, yes. She'd had too much to drink.

And it was time to be sensible. Time to steer the conversation back to safer ground.

Except she'd tried that, hadn't she? And it hadn't worked. Worse, now she found herself not wanting to behave sensibly at all. Not yet, at any rate. She was dining in Paris in plush, exotic surroundings with a man who made her think about sex! She was, quite literally, miles removed from her normal, familiar world and she didn't feel like herself. She felt like Cinderella, and she wasn't ready for the ball to end.

She lifted her lashes and looked at him. 'Show me your club,' she said before good sense prevailed and spoiled her fun. What harm could prolonging the evening cause? Tipsy or not, she wouldn't do anything foolish. Thinking about kissing Ramon was one thing—acting on the impulse quite another.

He held her gaze, the look in those toffee-coloured eyes dark and deliciously potent.

Warmth blossomed in her stomach. Knowing he would kiss her if she let him filled her with a heady sense of feminine power she'd never experienced before.

He pushed his empty espresso cup aside. 'What would you like to see?'

'Everything.'

His lips spread in a slow smile. 'Then everything it is.'

Their tour of Saphir took almost a full hour. The club was enormous, far more extensive than Emily had imagined and utterly, unapologetically luxurious. They started with the recreation complex, where a full-service health spa and bathhouse operated twenty-four-seven alongside a yoga studio, squash courts, a huge swimming pool and a gymnasium. Despite the late hour, a handful of men and women were sweating it out on the state-of-the-art machines and the sight of their toned, sculpted physiques made Emily uncomfortably conscious of all the calorie-laden food she'd devoured at dinner.

Even more impressive than the recreation wing were the entertainment facilities. In addition to the restaurant where they'd dined, and two other eateries, the club boasted a champagne and caviar bar, a glamorous nightclub and the gorgeous Blue Lounge with its live jazz ensemble, sophisticated cocktail menu and cerulean silk-lined walls.

Emily tried to pay attention to what Ramon was telling her but she absorbed only half of what he said. She couldn't concentrate. The champagne still fizzed in her bloodstream and the sexual awareness that had shimmered like a desert heat wave across the dinner table all evening seemed only to grow more intense. By the time they stepped into another lift to travel to yet another floor, Emily felt as if she were caught in the grip of a blistering fever—one that was burning up her mind as much as it was her body.

She couldn't stop looking at him. Couldn't stop thinking that he really was the most beautiful man she'd ever seen. His bone structure was nothing short of magnificent, his face a perfect landscape of hard, contoured angles. And his mouth…

'Emily.'

The warning in Ramon's tone only vaguely registered. She felt giddy, drunk not on champagne but on the pheromones drenching her senses, and the speed of the lift shooting them skywards wasn't helping. She stumbled forward, and she couldn't honestly say if she'd done so by accident or on purpose. Ramon caught her, just as he had that day in her father's office, but this time she was prepared for the impact of hard muscle, the swathe of masculine heat, that instantly engulfed her. Their gazes tangled for breathless seconds, and when the lift doors whispered open neither of them moved.

'Are we getting out?' Her voice was husky. Alien. Not at all her own.

The doors started to close and Ramon reached his hand out to halt them, his other hand remaining on her hip. 'That's your call.'

'Why mine?'

'Because this is the penthouse.'

She blinked. The feverishness in her blood made the act of thinking a challenge. Or maybe it was the intimate press of her curves against his hard body, the hot imprint of his hand on her hip, that scrambled her brain. 'The penthouse?'

'A private suite.'

His gaze probed and she needed only a second to interpret the question blazing in his eyes. Only a second longer for the curiosity she'd failed to stem to flare brighter, wilder, in her veins. If she waited one more second, sanity would intervene and she'd be saved. Saved from doing something foolish, reckless and totally out of character.

And then she'd go home to London and never know how it felt to be kissed by a man as beautiful as Ramon.

She didn't wait. She rose up on tiptoes, the sweet lure of anticipation combined with a surge of heart-pounding adrenalin giving her the courage she needed to press her lips to his.

Her first impression was of warmth. Her second, of how firm and perfect his lips felt against hers. She pressed harder, heard a rough sound like a harsh, stifled exclamation climb his throat, and then his mouth opened over hers and suddenly they were kissing, really kissing and... *Lord.* It was everything she'd imagined and more. Passionate. Molten. Consuming.

One strong arm looped around her waist and suddenly her feet floated off the floor. Their mouths still fused, he walked them out of the lift. When her toes touched the floor again and his mouth slid off hers, a sound that was half-protest, half-plea fell from her parted lips. She opened her eyes and got a fleeting impression of plush surroundings and muted lighting before her gaze centred on Ramon. His other arm came around her, encircling her fully as he dragged her close, and she didn't flinch. Didn't try to escape despite the unfamiliarity of being held.

His gaze roved her face, settled on her mouth. 'Do you know how long I've thought about doing that?'

She stared up at him. Her lips tingled, aching for the return of his. 'Since Tuesday?'

He shook his head, one corner of his sexy mouth lifting. 'The first time we met.' He tugged her closer and coils of heat kindled in her belly. 'You were so cool. So superior.' He lifted a hand and brushed the pad of his thumb over her lower lip. 'I wanted to kiss the prim, haughty smile you gave me right off your beautiful face.'

Somehow, through the thick haze of desire shrouding her senses, her mind summoned a sliver of indignation. 'And I wanted to slap yours.'

He laughed, unabashed, and then as swiftly as it had arisen his amusement vanished and the dark, smouldering look that made her stomach swoop was back. He removed her clutch from her hand, her wrap from over her forearm, and dropped the items onto a sleek, red lounge chair. His jacket followed and then he returned to stand before her.

Heart racing, Emily pressed her palm to the centre of his chest. When she spoke her voice belonged to someone else. Someone she didn't recognise. 'What happens in Paris stays in Paris.'

Another of those slow, sensual smiles slanted his mouth. 'As the lady wishes,' he murmured, and wrapped his fingers around her wrist. He raised her hand to his mouth, kissed her knuckles then turned her palm up and bit the base of her thumb.

Emily's breath caught on a soft gasp. The sharp press

of his teeth followed by the velvet slide of his tongue was unexpected—and surprisingly erotic. Her spine loosened, her legs went weak, and then he was scooping her into his arms, holding her effortlessly against his broad chest, as he strode through the suite. Seconds later he set her feet down and she barely had time to register they were in a bedroom before he was kissing her again, the heat of his mouth on hers even more explosively potent than before. Wantonly, she slid her arms around his neck and revelled in the earthy scent of him, the hot, bold stroke of his tongue against hers and the branding heat of his palms through her dress as they took possession of her hips.

His hands slid downwards, cupped her buttocks, and a low groan rumbled up his throat. He pulled her against him hard, pelvis to pelvis, giving Emily her first taste of the sheer strength and size of his erection. Before she could acknowledge the dart of apprehension in her stomach, his fingers hooked into the soft, clingy fabric of her dress and tugged upwards. 'Lift your arms,' he commanded against her mouth.

Willingly she obeyed, stretching her arms above her head, and he dispensed with the dress with a speed and ease that suggested he was well-versed in the art of removing women's clothing—a thought Emily refused to dwell upon as she stood before him in nothing but her heels, her cream satin underwear and her pearl necklace. She reached for him, partly to disguise her self-consciousness, and partly because she craved the return of his heated body against hers.

But he took a step back. 'Patience, *mi belleza*,' he said throatily, his accent more pronounced now, and she dropped her arms helplessly back to her sides. His gaze trailed over her. Hot. Intense. 'I have seen you naked in my mind many times,' he said. 'I want to know if my imagination did you justice.' He started to move, walking around her in a slow, deliberate circle, his unhurried appraisal of her near-naked body setting fire to every inch of her exposed flesh.

Her legs trembled, barely supporting her. She closed her eyes. 'Ramon…'

'I like hearing you say my name.' His voice came from behind her and she felt the silk of his shirt brush her shoulder blades. Still he didn't touch her. 'Say it again.'

She swallowed. 'Ramon.'

'Yes, Emily?'

Excitement made her heart pound, the tension and build-up of anticipation proving unbearably sexy.

Without warning he drove his hands into her hair, his fingers spearing deep and tangling in the mass of soft curls. He tugged her head back against his shoulder and put his mouth against her ear. 'What do you want?' he rasped.

'I want you to touch me.'

'Where?' His voice was rough, laced with satisfaction and a dark note of carnality that made her insides quiver.

'Everywhere,' she whispered, and felt a deep shudder move through him.

His hands came around her waist and just the hot slide of his palms across her naked midriff triggered a rush of liquid heat between her legs. He pressed an open-mouthed kiss to her bare shoulder and she arched her back, her breasts aching with an instinctive need that he answered by cupping his hands under them and dragging his thumbs over their tips.

She moaned, luxuriating in the sensations his touch was evoking. But she wanted more. She wanted skin against skin. Blindly, she grabbed at the straps of her bra and yanked them down, knocking his hands away in the process.

'Sí, mi belleza.' His voice rumbled with approval. 'That's right. Show me what you want.'

She did. She seized his hands and moulded them to her

bare breasts, her back arching again as he rolled her hardened nipples between his thumbs and forefingers. A little cry of pleasure escaped her, then he was kissing her neck, and she could feel his erection nudging her bottom, teasing her curiosity until she could no longer bear to stand passive. With a boldness that ordinarily would've shocked her, she reached back and palmed his groin, and even through his trousers she could feel how thick he was. How hard. *For her*.

That heady sense of feminine power surged again, throbbing in her veins like a potent aphrodisiac. 'More,' she croaked. 'I want more.'

Shifting his weight, he swung her off her feet, took three long strides and set her down on the edge of an enormous bed dressed in soft, luxurious linens. His dark gaze locked on hers, he stepped back, tugged his shirt out of his waistband and began unbuttoning it.

Her mouth filled with moisture and she stared up at him, mesmerised by the prospect of watching him strip down to nothing right in front of her.

With deft hands he peeled off his shirt and dropped it on the floor, and Emily's eyes widened.

He was utter perfection, his torso lean and chiselled, his skin like golden satin over ridges of steel. She wanted just to sit there and look at him, take the time to indulge in a leisurely inspection, as he'd done with her. But he toed off his shoes, dropped to his knees in front of her and plunged one hand into her hair, tugging her forward so that her face was close to his.

'How much more?'

She licked her lips. 'All of it.'

Eyes gleaming, he leaned in and claimed her mouth with a searing kiss that promised her she would get exactly what she'd asked for. Then his lips travelled down her throat, trailing hot, open-mouthed kisses over her sensitised skin until he reached the hard tip of her right breast.

She arched towards him before he'd even taken her nipple into his mouth. And when he did...it was exquisite, the pleasure almost unbearable. Her hands flew to his head of their own accord, her fingers streaking into the thick, dark strands of his hair, holding him to her as he mercilessly sucked her nipple into a tight, ultra-sensitive point. And then he lavished the same attention on her other breast and she dropped her head back, wondering if she might die from the blistering heat she could feel building inside her like an out-of-control inferno.

Her bra was still strung around her ribs and he unhooked it, threw it aside then pushed her back on the bed and dragged her knickers off with such efficiency, she had no time to feel hesitant or shy. But when he grasped her knees, eased them apart and lowered his head, her body tensed.

Pausing, Ramon glanced up from between her legs, hunger, heat and a clear, white-hot intent burning in his eyes. 'You wanted it all,' he reminded her thickly.

Yes...but she hadn't been thinking about oral sex. She'd never gone there before. The ex-boyfriend with whom she'd had her one, uninspiring sexual relationship had never initiated it and neither had she. And, while she was guilty of having entertained X-rated thoughts about Ramon's hands and mouth, she hadn't considered how it might feel to have his mouth on her *there*.

But, heaven help her, she wanted to know.

She relaxed her muscles, inviting him to do as he pleased, and the first stroke of his tongue elicited a shocked gasp and sent a bolt of red-hot sensation through her that made her body jerk against his mouth. With a broad hand flattened over her stomach, he anchored her to the bed and her breath seesawed on another gasp as he gently parted her with his fingers, giving his tongue deeper, more intimate access.

Oh, God.

She'd never known anything like it before. Had never experienced this tight, quickening sensation in her body. Had never imagined she would enjoy being pleasured in this way. He slid a finger inside her, finding a spot with his fingertip that seemed to set off an electric current deep within her core. She felt taut, tingly, as if her body were a high-voltage wire coiling tighter and tighter around his finger. He pushed deeper, flicked his tongue, and before she understood what was happening she came, every muscle in her body tensing with surprise and the sudden, unexpected eruption of pleasure.

As her limbs went from rigid to limp, she panted his name, once, twice, and he raised himself over her, his smile a study in male satisfaction. 'That's right, *dulzura*,' he murmured, tracing a line between her breasts with the tip of one finger. 'Get used to saying my name. You are going to scream it many times before we are done.'

CHAPTER SIX

EMILY WOULD HAVE told him how cocky he sounded if her flesh wasn't already crying out again for his touch.

She'd never experienced an orgasm like that before, yet he'd coaxed her to that sensational, mind-shattering peak with seemingly little effort.

He dropped a kiss on her mouth then levered himself to his feet, unbuckled his belt and pulled his zipper down, his gaze all the while tracking her naked, climax-flushed body.

Suddenly conscious that she was sprawled on the bed like some open-legged, sacrificial offering, Emily quickly closed her thighs and clambered backwards until she encountered the pillows. For a moment she thought she saw amusement flicker over his handsome face, but then he pushed his trousers and underwear down, kicked them off and straightened.

The air deserted Emily's lungs in a rush. Ramon de la Vega was a big man in every conceivable way and, though she was inexperienced—her sexual history confined to one partner—she knew she was small down there. Tight. Her pelvic muscles clenching with just a touch of apprehension, she watched him extract a condom from the bedside drawer, tear open the foil and roll on the sheath.

He climbed onto the bed, pulled her beneath him and kissed her, and this time she took full advantage of the opportunity to touch him, sliding her hands across the smooth skin of his shoulders, over his chest with its light smattering of hair and down the hard, ridged muscles of his abdomen. Apprehension giving way to need and excitement, she reached lower, curled her hand around his hot, rigid length and felt him tense. She tightened her hold and he growled something in Spanish against her mouth.

His knee came between her legs, pushing her thighs apart, and when he disengaged her hand from his shaft and then touched her just as intimately she could tell she was slick by the way his finger easily slipped into her. He added a second finger, stretching her a little further, and she gasped as he found the same hypersensitive spot he had earlier. A moment later he withdrew his fingers and the head of his erection replaced his hand. He stilled, poised above her, eyes locked on hers. 'Say my name.'

A tiny shred of stubbornness pushed to the fore. 'Kiss me first.'

His eyes glinted, one corner of his mouth lifting in a 'two can play that game' smile. Deliberately avoiding her mouth, he kissed her neck, finding the soft, sensitive place with his tongue that made her back arch in response. Then he pushed inside her, a strong, steady thrust that went only so far before her body resisted.

'*Dios*...you're so tight.'

He pushed in a little further and she stiffened, her body demanding a moment to accustom itself to the intimate invasion. Eyes closed, she dug her hands into his shoulders and willed her internal muscles to relax.

'Emily?'

Hearing concern in his voice, she opened her eyes, looked at him and saw a stark mix of lust and uncertainty in his expression. 'It's been a long time,' she whispered and felt her cheeks redden at having revealed that small intimate truth. She shifted and drew her knees up and back, and suddenly her body yielded and he slid all the way in, so deep and so completely they both gasped aloud and shuddered.

Groaning, Ramon buried his face in her neck and ground out more words in Spanish.

And then he rode her hard, a sheen of sweat gathering

on his skin, his magnificent body rippling above hers as he drove them both towards climax with breathtaking skill.

Emily clung to him, each powerful thrust of his body into hers pushing her closer to the edge. She tried to hold on, sensing he was close, wanting him to come at the same time as her. But there was no stopping the intense burst of pleasure that hurtled her high into the stratosphere. White light splintered behind her eyelids and then she did what she'd refused to do before.

She cried out his name.

Again. And again. And again.

Ramon hit the 'end call' button on his phone and padded through to the bedroom. It was after one a.m. and, since Sleeping Beauty had appeared dead to the world, he'd decided to make some calls in the living room.

He studied her sleeping form. Emily was an outrageous bed hog and the discovery both surprised him and amused him. She was so contained most of the time, so controlled, he had assumed she would sleep in a similar fashion—either curled into a tight ball or flat on her back, hands folded neatly on her stomach. Instead, she lay sprawled across two-thirds of the mattress, her arms flung wide and her long legs half-in, half-out of the tangled covers. She was totally naked except for the silver chain and pearl that hung around her neck, and her tumble of golden curls, damp still from their shower, spilled across the pillow, begging him to bury his hands in them.

His body stirred, lust pooling with the memory of how many ways he'd enjoyed her body in the last two hours.

She'd blown his mind. Revealed a streak of passion and daring underneath her natural reserve that he'd relished exploring. Her inexperience had surprised him but pleased him too, satisfying some dark, proprietorial part of his male ego he hadn't realised existed. He'd planned to take his time with her and he had up to a point. But the second her body had accepted him, pulling him into the heart of her tight, satin heat, he'd lost control.

And then he'd lost control in the shower too. He'd carried her in with the intention of doing no more than soaping the sweat from their bodies, and instead he'd lifted her against the tiles and plunged into her, the roar of pleasure in his veins obliterating all thought until she'd whispered urgently in his ear, telling him not to come inside her. He'd withdrawn immediately, shocked that he'd forgotten to protect them—even more shocked that for one reckless, fleeting second he'd wanted to bury himself inside her again and say to hell with the risk.

He'd stood panting, torn between lust and good sense until, with a bold, saucy look that'd stopped his breath, Emily had dropped to her knees, wrapped her fingers around him and taken him in her mouth. He'd tried to summon a protest but his attempt had been half-hearted at best, and in a matter of seconds she'd brought him to the edge of completion.

Ramon had slept with countless women in countless places, but standing in that shower, with his hands braced against the walls, staring down at Emily's flushed, satisfied face, had been the single most erotic experience of his life.

Her words from earlier came back to him.

What happens in Paris stays in Paris.

At any other time, such an edict would have suited him down to the ground. What self-professed playboy wouldn't want to hear words that relinquished him of any unwanted strings or emotional commitments?

And relationships without strings were Ramon's golden rule. It was how he'd lived his life for the last twelve years and how he intended to carry on. Forming attachments was something he avoided for good reason. You couldn't hurt people if they didn't get close.

The thought of hurting Emily made him feel physically ill. She was tough, but he sensed her outer armour shielded an underlying vulnerability. Their conversations hadn't touched on family, but he recalled reading some tabloid bio on Maxwell that had talked of his wife having died in childbirth.

How must it feel, knowing the woman who'd given you life had lost her own while bringing you into the world? He couldn't imagine it, yet *he* knew a worse pain. The pain of knowing his actions, his choices, had led to another person's demise—not once, but twice.

His hand tightened around his phone. He had no business comparing Emily's life to his own. Unlike him, she had done nothing wrong. She wasn't responsible for her mother's death.

He thought of his mother, Elena, and her difficulties with conceiving and carrying a child to term. Having Ramon after adopting Xavier must have been quite the shock. To their credit, his parents had shown no favouritism, treating their sons with equal affection, but no doubt it'd been a great irony for them that Ramon—their own flesh and blood—was the one who'd proved a disappointment. Who had shamed the family. His mother was a good woman, but he wouldn't blame her if she never found it in her heart to forgive him.

He ran his gaze over Emily's face, wincing at the small patches of redness where his stubble had grazed her skin. He felt a tightness grip his chest. He'd known her for less than a week yet he knew she was strong and principled—a good woman, like his mother. Was that why she made allowances for her father? Or was it because she had no one else? Her grandfather was dead, she had no siblings and there didn't seem to be any extended family on the scene. Aside from Royce, who hardly qualified as a contender for Father of the Year, was Emily alone in the world?

The tightness intensified and with it came a vague sense of unease. Since when did he speculate on the personal lives of his lovers?

Yet he knew he couldn't class Emily as one of his casual flings. His relationship with her was primarily a professional one and tonight he'd crossed a line he shouldn't have crossed. He'd been reckless, allowing his base desires to govern him, and he knew he should be regretting it right now, but he wasn't. Instead, he was thinking about pulling the sheet away, easing her thighs apart and tasting her again. He was thinking that one night, a few brief hours, wasn't enough time to do all the things he wanted to do with her...*to* her. And he was thinking that, if their time together had to be confined to Paris, then perhaps this one night wasn't long enough. Perhaps they needed the whole weekend.

Her eyes opened and she blinked drowsily, stretched her gorgeous limbs and smiled up at him with lips pink and swollen from his kisses. 'Ramon?'

'*Sí, mi belleza?*'

'What time is it?'

'Late—or early, depending on your view.'

She rose onto her elbows. 'Do we need to go? Is the plane waiting for us?'

He put his phone on the nightstand. 'No. I've stood the pilot down for the night.'

A flicker of anxiety showed in her face. 'Will he be available to take us back first thing in the morning?'

Ramon climbed onto the bed. 'He's available when I want him to be available.' He pushed the tangled sheet off her and palmed the soft mound of honey-blonde curls at the apex of her thighs. Slowly, he ran a fingertip down her sensitive flesh and her soft gasp made his groin tighten. 'Tender?'

'Only a little.'

He gave a slow smile then moved his hand and made her gasp again. 'In that case, I'll be gentle.'

Bright morning sunlight streamed through the lounge windows of the penthouse and for the first time in Emily's life she truly appreciated the sentiment behind the expression 'the cold light of day'.

She pulled the belt of the fluffy white bathrobe tighter around her waist. 'No,' she said and felt an immediate rush of relief, because the other word she could have uttered— the big, fat, resounding *yes* that was even now attempting to crawl up her throat against her better judgement—could not, under any circumstances, be allowed to escape. 'I can't stay another night. I need to go home to London this morning.'

And I need you to put some clothes on, she almost added, although thankfully only his chest was on display. He wore his dark suit trousers from last night but they weren't belted or zipped properly and they sat too low on his hips. She knew if she let her gaze drop she'd see more of his flat, muscled stomach than her composure could handle at present.

Unaware of her internal struggles, he poured coffee from a silver pot into two china mugs. 'Is there something you need to return for today?'

'Yes,' she lied, accepting the coffee he handed her without meeting his eye. Her *sanity*. That was what she needed to return for. Because clearly she'd lost it somewhere between here and London and she could really do with getting it back before the wanton, needy creature he'd unleashed in her decided that staying in Paris with him was more appealing than returning home.

She took her coffee over to the big floor-to-ceiling window and stared out at the stunning view of the city.

Perhaps the light of day wouldn't have seemed so harsh right now if she hadn't emerged from the bedroom at just the wrong time. If the man who'd been wheeling a heavily laden breakfast trolley out of the lift hadn't glanced at her and she hadn't seen, in the moment before he blanked his expression, the speculative glint in his eyes. He'd been judging her, eyeing up the drowsy, bed-rumpled woman who'd slept with his boss—and, given she was guilty as charged, could she really blame the guy for looking at her as if she were a two-bit slut?

She swallowed, self-disgust rising in her throat like bile. She'd set aside all manner of caution and self-preservation and let curiosity and pure physical lust take control.

Oh, God.

All these years of despising her father's behaviour and now she couldn't even claim the moral high ground.

She gripped her mug between her hands. She couldn't spend another night in Paris with Ramon. Just thinking about the things they would do together made her skin flush with heat and her body tremble with a deep-seated longing she couldn't quash. He was like a dangerous, addictive narcotic. She'd had her first hit, experienced the ecstasy of the high, and now she was craving another.

Could addiction take root so quickly?

She shook her head. Crazy thinking. She was out of her element, her comfort zone, and she'd just done something completely out of character. Something that—even now with self-condemnation dragging at her stomach—had felt wrong and yet impossibly right at the same time.

Good grief. No wonder she was feeling disoriented.

'Emily…' Ramon's arms came around her from behind and she stiffened so suddenly her coffee spilt, the hot liquid scalding her thumb.

Cursing softly, he took the mug away and returned with a napkin.

She patted her hand dry. 'Sorry.'

'For what? For flinching when I touched you just now, or for what we did last night?'

Hearing an edge to his voice, she fisted the napkin in her hand. What could she say? That she wasn't used to having someone put their arms around her? She wasn't. She was more comfortable when people kept their distance, though not because she didn't crave human contact. Contrary to the nasty things her ex had said after she'd ended their relationship, her veins didn't run with ice water. But when you hadn't been hugged much as a child, when you had never experienced the physical manifestation of a parent's unconditional love, you were hardly going to blossom into a touchy, feely adult.

And as for last night…her and Ramon…that hadn't been about affection, or emotion. It had been about sex.

Nothing else.

She drew a deep breath. 'I think last night was a mistake.' His eyes rapidly narrowed and she hastened to add, 'I'd had too much champagne. I… I was tipsy.'

His face darkened. 'Are you saying I took advantage of you?'

'No! Of…of course not,' she stammered, instantly regretting her feeble excuse. 'But…my judgement was impaired.' She twisted the napkin between her hands and cringed inwardly. She was making a hash of this. 'I… I wasn't thinking straight.'

'Are you drunk now?'

She blinked. 'No.'

'Are you thinking straight?'

Hardly. How could she think straight with his bare, muscled chest and powerful shoulders dominating her field of vision? 'Yes.'

Moving with lightning speed, Ramon grabbed the belt of her robe and gave it a single hard yank.

Before Emily had time to react, the sides of the garment gaped open and exposed her naked breasts.

She made a small, startled sound and tried to tug the robe closed but his arm was already snaking under the soft terry towelling and circling her waist like a band of reinforced steel.

He hauled her against him, plunged his other hand into her loose, bed-tousled curls and cupped the back of her head.

Her breasts tingled, her nipples hardening into treacherous points of need. 'Ramon—'

His mouth came down on hers. Hot. Forceful. A teensy bit brutal. Somewhere in her reeling mind she wondered if she should struggle, try to bite him, perhaps. She didn't. Instead, she curled her hands over his shoulders, arched her body like the wanton creature he'd turned her into and opened her mouth under his. He backed her against the solid glass window, his kiss growing more fervent, more demanding, and she didn't notice he'd released her head until she felt his hand sliding between her legs. A single finger thrust inside her, right into the centre of her wet, pulsing heat, and she gasped against his mouth.

He lifted his head, withdrew his finger and, holding her gaze, very deliberately put it into his mouth. He sucked, extracting his finger slowly, and then licked his lips. His smile was utterly, wickedly shameless. 'That doesn't taste like a mistake to me.'

Outrage surged, instantly tempering the hot pulse of desire between her legs.

How dared he smash through her defences and mock her in a way that was so...so *erotic*?

She banged the heels of her hands against his chest, twisted out of his grip and yanked the robe closed. 'I'm going to get dressed,' she told him, holding her chin high, injecting a hard, chilly note into her voice. 'And then I'd like to go home please.' Her throat feeling tight all of a sudden, she secured the belt around her waist and strode towards the bedroom.

'Emily.'

Civility overriding the urge to ignore him completely, she stopped and turned, just as a brown paper package bound with string landed at her feet.

'Clothes,' he supplied before she could ask. 'So you don't have to worry about the 'walk of shame'.'

He turned away to the breakfast tray and Emily stared at his back. Then she picked up the package, blinked away the sharp sting of unexpected tears and shut herself in the bedroom.

By the time the London limo driver turned into her quiet neighbourhood street, a headache pounded in Emily's temples and she felt as if her nerve endings had been wrapped in razor wire.

Ramon sat beside her on the back seat, silent and brooding, as he had been for most of the journey. They were both angry. Both upset. Which only reinforced Emily's belief that they'd made a terrible mistake. Jeopardised their professional relationship for—*what?*—a bit of short-lived gratification?

She wiped a clammy palm over her thigh. The jeans she wore fit perfectly, as did the sleeveless, pale blue top and matching cardigan. Even the underwear was the right size. Every item she'd found in the neatly wrapped package had been new, the tags still attached. Emily was appreciative but she didn't want to think too hard about whomever had bought and delivered the clothing and what they must have thought of such a task. Or maybe they hadn't thought anything. Maybe they were used to running such errands for their boss.

The idea made her feel slightly ill.

The limo stopped. Ramon said nothing, so she quietly gathered up her things.

'Are you staying in London?'

He turned his head and looked at her and electricity arced between them, as red-hot and incandescent as ever. Anger, it seemed, had only intensified their chemistry.

'No. I'm returning to New York.'

'Good.' She prayed the word sounded more convincing to his ears than hers. 'I think it would be wise if you stayed away for a while. Gave us both some…space. We can conduct any business by email and phone.'

A muscle flickered in his jaw. 'I'll come to *our* club in person whenever I deem fit.'

Stiffening at his arrogant tone, she opened her mouth to offer a pithy retort and found she had nothing. 'Goodbye, Ramon,' she said instead, ignoring the sudden dull ache beneath her breastbone, and climbed out.

He said something but Emily didn't catch it, his words muffled by the thud of the limo door as she slammed it closed.

CHAPTER SEVEN

SIX WEEKS.

That was how long it was before Ramon finally returned to London, although it had taken considerably less time for him to conclude that his morning-after behaviour in Paris had been reprehensible.

Abominable.

He hadn't reacted well to rejection. Yes, Emily could have handled the situation with more grace than she had, but his own behaviour had lacked any degree of decorum. He wasn't unfamiliar with self-contempt and regret, but until that weekend those particular demons had not sat so heavily on his soul in a long time.

So he'd respected Emily's wishes and stayed away, keeping their communication to a minimum.

But six weeks was long enough. He was done with the polite, impersonal emails. The short, stilted phone calls. She still hadn't hired a replacement accountant and he wanted to know why. If she was keeping the position open in the hope that he would grant Turner a pardon and allow her to invite the man back, she was courting disappointment.

He walked down the carpeted corridor on the executive level of The Royce and saw Marsha sitting at her desk. At his approach, her eyes widened and she jumped up as if she'd been stuck with a cattle prod. 'Mr de la Vega! I didn't know we were expecting you.'

'You weren't.' He unleashed a good-humoured smile and gestured to the closed door of Emily's office. 'Is she in?'

'Er...no.'

'When will she be back?'

She blinked then stared at him.

'Marsha?' he prompted.

'I… I don't know.'

He frowned. 'What do you mean, you don't know?'

'I mean…she's not in today. She's sick…' Marsha bit her lip. 'At least, I think she's sick… She rang yesterday morning and said she was taking the day off—which is very unusual. And then today…she left a message on my phone early this morning, saying she'd be in before noon, but I haven't seen her yet.'

He glanced at his watch. 'It's after two p.m.'

Marsha wrung her hands. 'I know.'

'Have you tried calling her?' he demanded.

'Twice. I left her two messages. She hasn't called back.'

An icy sensation hollowed out his gut. That didn't sound like the dedicated, conscientious Emily Royce he knew.

'Call me if you hear from her,' he commanded and turned on his heel.

Emily opened her eyes.

Someone was pounding on her door. Or was it the pounding in her head that she hadn't been able to shake for two days that she could hear?

Her doorbell chimed, the sound piercing in the silence of her flat, and Emily groaned. It was a week day and her neighbours should all be at work, except for Mr Johnson, who was retired. But he had never climbed the stairs to visit her. Of course, he could have forgotten to lock the main entrance again, in which case the person banging on her door could be a stranger.

She groaned again, closed her eyes and snuggled deeper into the softness of the sofa.

'Emily!'

She froze, the sound of her name being barked on the other side of the door forcing its way into her stress-addled mind. She knew that voice. Deep, masculine…

'Emily!'

She sat up—too fast, apparently, because her stomach performed a sharp lurch and roll.

Ramon was at her door.

The knowledge sent a rush of heat over her skin followed closely by a cold wave of dread.

He knows.

She swallowed hard and fought down the flare of irrational panic with a forced dose of sanity.

Of course he doesn't know.

She'd only found out for herself a little over a day ago, though she'd had her suspicions for almost three weeks before visiting her doctor.

The doorbell pealed again, repeatedly, as if he were leaning on it, and she threw off the light cotton throw she'd curled under and urged her legs to move. When she opened the door a moment later, the thought came to her, much too late, that she looked a mess.

The fact that Ramon looked both powerful and sexy in his immaculate three-piece suit made her feel hot and unaccountably irritable at the same time.

She dragged her attention from his body, blotting out images in her head that she'd tried hard for the last six weeks to forget, and focused on his face. A deep frown marred his brow.

'Are you all right?'

'Yes.'

'I knocked for ages.'

'I was asleep.'

His gaze tracked over her grey tee shirt and black yoga pants then returned to her face. Her very pale, make-up-less face. 'Are you unwell?'

'Yes—no...' She shook her head. Tried to bring some semblance of order to her thoughts. 'Why are you here?'

'I went to the club,' he said. 'Marsha thought you might be sick. You haven't returned her calls.'

Confusion descended. She glanced at her watch and her heart lurched. It couldn't be almost three o'clock! It'd been only ten a.m. when she had decided to take some pain-killers and lie down for half an hour before heading into work. She'd slept for almost five hours which, now that she thought about it, wasn't all that surprising given she hadn't slept a wink during the night.

She put her hand to her forehead, guilt surging. 'Oh, no. Poor Marsha.' She turned towards the hall table where she'd left her phone. 'I need to call her.'

Not waiting for an invitation, Ramon stepped inside and closed the door. 'That can wait,' he said, taking hold of her shoulders and turning her to face him.

Emily tensed. His touch had been seared into her memory ever since Paris, but memory was no match for the reality of having his hands on her body, even in a non-sexual way. Her heart raced and she felt warm, a little lightheaded.

His gaze scoured her face. 'Something's wrong,' he stated, his voice firm with certainty. 'What is it, Emily?'

Fear gripped her throat and for a moment she couldn't speak. Revealing her condition was something she had planned to do in her own time, when she had managed to come to terms with it herself. She'd wanted to put careful thought into how she would tell him, but now he was here and she no longer had that luxury. She had to tell him now, because the alternative was to lie, and she couldn't do that. Not about something so important, so potentially life-changing.

She swallowed, her throat painfully dry. 'I think you'd better come in.'

His hands dropped from her shoulders, and she knew a moment's regret, because their weight and warmth had felt oddly steadying in the midst of the tumult occurring in her body and mind.

But soon, *very* soon, he would share the tumult. And then he might not feel so inclined to offer support.

Her stomach churning, she led him through to her lounge. Like the rest of her flat, it was light and spacious, and decorated by her own hand, the palette of soft creams, pale lemons and blues intended to create an elegant, soothing space that invited one to relax. She loved this room, but she was conscious now that in less than nine months' time the cream carpet and pale colour scheme would be terribly impractical.

She stood by the sofa, thought about offering him tea or coffee—or something stronger—then decided against it. She doubted he would stay for long.

'I'm pregnant.' Saying the words out loud made her knees do a little wobble, but she stayed standing, even as a renewed bout of nausea rolled through her.

In the middle of the room, Ramon went as still as a statue, and his face… A small, detached part of her mind was fascinated by the way the colour slid right out from under his skin, leaving a pallor that made it look as if someone had tipped a bucket of whitewash over him.

Emily wrapped her arms around her middle. Waited for him to say the words she imagined most men came out with in this situation.

Is it mine?

The seconds ticked by in heavy silence, and she felt as if she were a character in some tacky scene from an over-dramatic soap opera. The final line of dialogue had been delivered and the actors had paused for dramatic effect before the show cut to a commercial break. The random thought nearly tore a hysterical giggle from her before she caught herself. She closed her eyes. What was wrong with her? Nothing about this was funny.

'Have you confirmed it with a doctor?'

It took her a moment to realise it wasn't the question she'd expected. That he wasn't doubting that he was the father. Wasn't insulting her by suggesting there were other men to whom she could point the finger. 'Yesterday,' she said, her throat growing thick with something awfully like gratitude.

A glazed look entered his eyes and she knew he was processing. 'We used protection.'

Emily had said those same words to herself, over and over. It hadn't changed the outcome. She shrugged. 'Condoms aren't foolproof,' she offered. 'And maybe…the shower…?' Their gazes locked, the sudden, scalding intensity of his transmitting loud and clear that he hadn't forgotten the things they'd done to each other under the steaming water.

Ramon looked away, dragged his hand over his mouth and breathed in hard, his nostrils flaring. 'Give me a minute,' he said abruptly, and walked out of the room.

Emily stared after him, her breath locking in her chest as realisation struck and her stomach curled into a hard, familiar knot of resignation. Ramon was walking away, doing exactly what she'd expected him to do, exactly what she had known he would—so why was a silly sob pushing its way up her throat?

She slapped her hand over her mouth but she was too slow and the sob escaped, making a loud, choked, hiccupping sound. A *humiliating* sound.

Ramon appeared in the doorway, his brows clamped together. 'Emily?'

She jerked her hand down. 'Just go.' Somehow she managed to inject some backbone into her voice. 'I'm fine. I don't need you to stay. This is my problem to deal with.'

He stood looking at her for a long moment, then he stalked across the room and her heart surged into her throat. He looked angry but, as he drew closer, the hard lines bracketing his mouth resembled determination more than fury. He stopped in front of her, lifted his hands and framed her face. The warm pressure of his palms against her cheeks made her pulse skitter. 'I am not leaving,' he said. 'I am going downstairs to dismiss my driver and then I'm coming back here so we can talk.'

She stared at him in stunned silence.

'Do you understand me, Emily?'

Her brain told her a simple 'yes' would suffice, but her throat suddenly felt too tight to speak. So she simply nodded. And then she sank onto the sofa, watched him leave and waited for him to return.

Ramon braced his palms on the wall outside Emily's flat and sucked in one lungful of air after another.

He didn't need to go downstairs. A simple text message to his driver had done the job. But he'd needed an excuse to grab a moment alone, to get a handle on himself—on the turbulent emotions storming through him.

Dios.

He wanted to run. To somewhere. To anywhere. As fast and as far away as his legs would carry him.

How the hell had this happened?

Stupid question. He knew how it had happened. He'd been reckless. Unthinking. And now he was the father of an unborn child.

Another unborn child.

Another innocent life to destroy.

His breath shuddered out of him. He wasn't meant to be a father, or a husband. Husbands and fathers were supposed to protect the people close to them and Ramon had already failed that test on a spectacular scale. He kept people, his family included, at arm's length for a good reason: to protect them from *himself.*

He swallowed hard and straightened, a grim sense of determination rising in him, pushing through the turmoil, calming both his thoughts and his breathing. It was the same determination that had seen him do his family and friends a favour by walking away from them twelve years ago, except this time Ramon wouldn't be walking away. How could he? He'd been presented with an opportunity to protect his unborn child—an opportunity he'd been denied all those years ago. He'd barely processed Emily's revelation, but he had enough clarity of mind to recognise that he was being given a rare second chance. A chance to do something right...this time.

He pulled out his phone, called Marsha and told her Emily had the flu and wouldn't be back for at least two days.

When he re-entered the flat she was sitting on one end of the cream sofa where he'd left her. Her hands were clasped on her knees, her grey eyes big and unblinking. They grew even larger when she saw him as though, in spite of his assurances, she hadn't truly believed until that moment that he'd return. That she'd assumed he would desert her filled him with too many emotions to examine. He removed his suit jacket and draped it over the back of an armchair.

'It's yours,' she said.

He turned to her. 'Pardon?'

'The baby.' Her fingers fiddled with the pearl around her neck. 'It's yours.'

He sat beside her, clasped her chin and forced her gaze up when she tried to look away. 'I know.'

Her tongue came out to moisten her lips in a nervous gesture that he shouldn't have found arousing in the circumstances—but he had lain in bed and thought about those lips on many nights during the past six weeks of self-imposed celibacy, and they were just as lush and pretty as he remembered.

He dropped his hand. 'I'm sorry, Emily.'

'What for?'

'For the way I behaved in Paris. I wanted another night with you. When you refused, I didn't like it,' he confessed. 'I was out of order.'

She shrugged. 'I'm not proud of my behaviour, either. And, since we're making apologies...' colour seeped into her pale face '... I didn't sleep with you because I was drunk.'

He knew that, but the part of his male ego she'd wounded six weeks ago appreciated hearing it all the same. He lifted his hand again and traced the elegant arch of one cheekbone with his thumb. 'You look tired,' he remarked. 'And pale. Have you eaten today?'

She shook her head, her long, untethered curls tumbling about her shoulders. 'I've been a bit ill.'

'Are you drinking plenty of water?'

'Some...not as much as I should.' She stood up, her plain tee shirt and stretchy black leggings emphasising that she'd lost weight.

He frowned. Just how ill had she been?

'Actually, I could kill a cup of tea,' she said. 'I'll make us a pot.'

'Sit.' He rose to his feet. 'I'll do it.' Her eyes widened and he adopted an affronted air. 'You don't think I can make tea?' he challenged.

A faint smile crossed her features. 'I'm sure you're very capable. But it's my kitchen and I know where everything is. And I've done nothing all day... I need to move.'

He let her go without further protest, then sauntered to the window, thrust his hands in his pockets and studied the street below. He let his thoughts run to practical matters. The building wasn't wired with a security system and that bothered him. The neighbourhood seemed respectable but good neighbourhoods weren't immune to crime. The building's current security measures were flimsy and not helped by her downstairs neighbour who repeatedly left the main entry unlocked. Ramon had walked straight in today, just as he had six weeks ago.

And the stairs…three flights of them. Should pregnant women climb stairs every day?

He heard movement behind him and turned. Emily carried a wooden tray bearing a blue china teapot and matching cups. He waited for her to place the tray on the coffee table before he spoke. 'You can't stay here.'

She looked up, one hand gripping the handle of the teapot. She frowned as if he'd spouted something unintelligible. 'Excuse me?'

'Come and stay with me at Citrine.'

'Your West End club?'

'Yes. I'm using the penthouse. I can make it available for us long-term.'

Slowly, she put the teapot down and straightened. 'Why?'

'Because it's safer. And closer to work for you.' He paused. 'Not that you'll want to do that for much longer, of course.'

She stared at him. 'What are you talking about?'

He pulled his hands from his pockets and reminded himself that she was tired and stressed. Most likely not thinking straight. 'Emily,' he said patiently, walking towards her. 'Your life is about to change. Permanently. We need to consider what's best for you and the baby.'

'What's best for me,' she said, her voice rising a notch, 'is to stay in my own home.'

'It's not secure here.'

'This is a decent neighbourhood!'

He put his hands on her shoulders to calm her, but she shrugged him off and took a step back.

'Bad things happen in good neighbourhoods all the

time,' he said. 'And what about the stairs? How do you think you'll cope with those in six months' time?'

She put her palms to her cheeks. 'Ramon—just slow down for a minute. Please.'

'Emily. We need to talk about these things.'

She shook her head.

'Make some decisions,' he pressed. 'Think about the future.'

'Oh, my God.' She scrunched her eyes closed. 'Next you'll be suggesting we get married.'

Her tone was incredulous and Ramon clenched his jaw, jamming his hands back into his pockets. Marriage ranked right alongside fatherhood on his list of undesirable scenarios, but he'd be lying if he said the idea hadn't crossed his mind in the last twenty minutes.

When he remained silent, she opened her eyes and gave him a blunt look. 'I'm not marrying you.' She picked up the teapot and started pouring as if she hadn't just plunged a knife into the heart of his male pride. 'And besides...' She set the pot down and straightened again. 'Don't you think all these suggestions are a little premature? I'm only six weeks along and—' She hesitated, biting her lip for a moment, her gaze lowering. 'Miscarriages aren't uncommon in the first twelve weeks of pregnancy,' she finished quietly.

This time her words cut deeper than his pride and he felt their impact like a cold blade under his ribs. The sharp reminder of history only strengthened his resolve. 'I know,' he said, deciding then and there on a more ruthless approach. 'I've lost a child before.'

The look of shock on Emily's face was swift and complete. Her hand flew to her stomach. 'Oh, Ramon... I'm so sorry. That must've been awful.'

He picked up a cup and took a mouthful of black tea, welcoming the hit of warmth in his stomach. 'It's ancient history,' he said, replacing the cup. 'But, yes, the experience was difficult. My girlfriend miscarried and I was helpless to prevent it.' It wasn't the full story but hopefully enough to elicit Emily's sympathy. With a hand on her slender waist, he guided her to the sofa, handed her her tea as she sat and pressed home his advantage. 'You're clearly not well,' he observed. 'And you could have some challenging months ahead. Why stay here alone when there's an alternative?'

She shook her head, her jaw taking on a stubborn tilt. 'I'm fine.'

'You're pale and weak.'

'I'm in shock,' she defended. 'I haven't known about this for much longer than you have. And I have a bit of morning sickness, that's all.'

He sat down beside her. 'Your mother died in childbirth.' He delivered the words as gently as he could, but still her face drained of what little colour it possessed. Ramon himself wasn't unaffected by the statement. The thought of Emily dying evoked a dark, volatile emotion that tore through his chest.

Her hand rose to her throat and he saw her fingers tremble as they closed around the pearl. When her gaze met his, the naked appeal in her eyes reached into his gut like a fist and squeezed. 'Can we just slow this down?' she implored him. 'Take one day at a time? Please?'

He inhaled a deep breath. 'Slow' wasn't how he preferred to do things but he knew that pushing Emily too hard in her current state would be counterproductive. Which meant a change of tack was required. He expelled his breath, making a swift decision. 'Of course,' he said, then got to his feet and pulled out his phone.

She frowned. 'Who are you calling?'

'Someone who'll arrange to have my things packed and brought over.'

Her eyes rounded. 'I beg your pardon?'

'If you stay,' he said, 'then so do I.'

She stared at him and then she flopped against the sofa and slapped her hand over her forehead. 'Oh, my God.' Her laugh held a touch of hysteria. 'You're really *not* leaving.'

Calmly, he hit the number for the concierge at Citrine and put the phone to his ear.

Emily glowered at him.

He glowered back. 'Drink your tea, Emily.'

Emily awoke with a violent shiver. She felt cold. She lifted her head and saw she'd thrown the duvet and sheets off some time during the night. She'd had a hot flush, she suddenly remembered. Was that a symptom of early pregnancy? Or was it more to do with the man who was sleeping in the spare room across the hall?

She squinted at her clock. Four a.m.

Sighing, she dragged the duvet over her and stared at the ceiling. None of this felt real. The pregnancy. Ramon being in her home. A future looming that was nothing like the one she'd envisaged.

Not that she'd ever devoted much time to pondering her future beyond running The Royce. Marriage and children weren't things she'd allowed herself to dwell upon. Doing so had filled her with an unsettling yearning. A feeling of emptiness she could only banish by burying herself in work.

And there was nothing wrong with that. Nothing wrong with being a career woman. Not every girl got to marry the perfect man and have the perfect family, the perfect life. Look at her mother—she'd married a charming, handsome man who'd turned out to be a philandering pleasure-seeker and then died having his child.

A metallic taste surged in her mouth.

Oh, no. Was she going to be sick?

She tossed the covers off, sat up and waited for a moment to see if the nausea would pass. She should grab her robe or a sweatshirt, she thought. She and Ramon were sharing her only bathroom and she was wearing only knickers and a cotton…

She clapped her hand over her mouth, ran from her room and reached the toilet just in time.

Ugh. She hated this. *Hated* it.

She retched again and, as she tried to scrape her hair away from her face, felt a warm, firm hand touch her back.

Ramon didn't say a word. He just knelt behind her, relieved her hands of her hair and waited for her to finish.

'I'm done,' she croaked a long, humiliating minute later, and he helped her to her feet and gave her space to clean herself up at the basin.

When he scooped her up she acquiesced with a shameful lack of protest and, despite her mental exhaustion, she was acutely conscious of everything as he carried her back to her room. His strong, muscular arms. His clean, soapy scent. His hard, tee-shirt-covered chest under one of her hands.

She shouldn't have liked any of it.

She liked all of it.

He sat her on the edge of her bed and pressed a glass of water into her hand. 'Drink.'

'You're very bossy,' she muttered.

He crossed his arms over his chest. 'And you're very mouthy for someone who's just been hugging the toilet bowl.'

It was difficult to find a dignified response to that, so she sipped her water instead. Her throat hurt. And so did her head. Although she figured that wasn't from throwing up so much as it was a side-effect of the relentless racing of her mind over the past forty-eight hours.

She put the glass on the nightstand. Her hand trembled, but it was nothing compared to the uncontrollable shaking inside her. 'I'm not sure I can do this,' she said, fear and uncertainty crashing in like a fast-moving tidal wave she couldn't outrun.

He dropped to his haunches. 'Do what?'

'Have a baby,' she whispered.

His shoulders tensed, a stark expression descending over his features, and her heart clenched as she realised he'd misinterpreted her words. 'No,' she said hurriedly, cursing herself silently. 'I don't mean that. I don't want to get rid of this baby, Ramon.'

How could she have forgotten what he'd told her? That he had lost a child? The revelation not only shocked her but cast him in a different light. It was easy to look at Ramon and see only the confidence and charm. But he had suffered something devastating. That kind of loss had to leave a scar. She inhaled a deep breath. 'I mean... I don't know *how* I'm going to do this. I feel...'

'What?'

She shrugged, reluctant to articulate such a weak emotion. 'Scared,' she admitted, and glanced away.

Slipping a finger under her chin, he returned her gaze to his. 'I think you can do anything you set your mind to, Emily Royce.'

His tone was firm, his vote of confidence unexpected, and a burst of warmth blossomed in her chest.

But was he right?

She knew nothing about motherhood. Nothing about the bond between mother and child. She'd never had her own mother to bond with. No aunts or grandmothers or female role models. Just her strict teachers at boarding school and her grandfather's housekeeper, the humourless Mrs Thorne. Emily didn't doubt she would love her child—and she would do so fiercely—but would her child love *her*?

As a daughter she was hardly worth loving; her father had demonstrated that time and again through his rejection of any close bond with her. Who was to say she'd prove any more lovable as a parent?

And then, as if her insecurities weren't enough to unsettle her, there was her mother's death to consider. The frightening reminder of life's utter fragility.

What if childbirth put Emily at a similar risk?

She felt the prick of tears and mentally rolled her eyes. *Great.* Another symptom of pregnancy. She wondered if she could also blame her newly discovered condition for the heavy, achy sensation in her breasts or, like the hot flush, did that have more to do with the man hunkered beside the bed and the desire that flooded her body every time she looked at him?

'I'm tired,' she said, lowering her gaze before her eyes betrayed her. The man had just held her hair as she hurled up the last contents of her stomach. He was unlikely to find her attractive right now. 'Thanks for checking on me.' She curled onto her side and pulled the duvet up to her chin. 'I'm going to try to get some more sleep.'

Ramon stood up and she closed her eyes, listening for the tell-tale sounds of him leaving her room and going back to his. But the absolute silence told her he hadn't moved. Her heart thudded in her ears, and then she felt his hand brush gently over her hair. Felt his lips press a soft, feather-light kiss on her temple. 'We'll do this together, Emily,' he said, his breath fanning warmth across her cheek. 'You're not alone now.' And then he padded out of the room.

As the door closed Emily's chin wobbled dangerously and she tucked her face into the pillow. Yesterday, walking into her empty flat after visiting her doctor, she'd felt very alone but had told herself it didn't matter.

She was used to being alone.

You're not alone now.

She drifted off to sleep, that last conscious thought wrapping around her like a warm, comforting cocoon.

CHAPTER EIGHT

ON THURSDAY EMILY returned to work even though Ramon had wanted her to stay home and rest for the remainder of the week—a preference he'd expressed for the umpteenth time in her kitchen last night. She'd been preparing a simple meal for them and he'd not long been back from a meeting in the city. He'd loosened his tie and collar, rolled his shirt sleeves up his bronzed, muscular forearms and planted his palms on the kitchen island as arguments and counter-arguments had bandied back and forth.

For a brief time Emily had felt as if they were an ordinary couple in the midst of a minor domestic dispute. The thought had left her feeling slightly breathless and flustered, not because it was outlandish or repellent, but rather because it'd sent a flare of unfamiliar warmth through her chest.

No one had ever cared about her enough to argue with her over her choices before.

He cares about the baby. Not you.

The insidious thought elbowed its way into her head and she frowned at her computer screen.

Of course he cared about the baby. And that was all that mattered, she assured herself. He was accepting responsibility for the child they'd conceived and Emily wasn't hoping for anything more. Certainly not marriage or any long-term commitment beyond his being a loving, supportive father to their child. If her grandfather had been alive he would have demanded that she wed, but the eccentric, formidable Gordon Royce was no longer here, and not even the outrageous financial incentive laid out in his will could persuade Emily to consider a hasty, loveless marriage. No. She and Ramon would take a sensible, modern-day approach and work out some kind of shared custody arrangement. Ultimately they would lead separate lives while keeping things amicable for the sake of their child.

She clicked her mouse and opened a file on her computer. *Work.* That, if nothing else, would give her a sense of normality, of being in control. And, given that her home and her independence were being seriously encroached upon, she needed to feel in control. Right now she was humouring Ramon, allowing him to assert his dominance because she suspected that underneath all that machismo he, too, was afraid. Who wouldn't be after experiencing the devastating loss of an unborn child? It was why she was willing to tolerate his over-the-top concerns for her safety and wellbeing—for now.

But he couldn't camp in her spare room for the next seven and a half months. It wasn't practical for either of them. He had an office and a home in New York. Clubs and resorts around the world. A jet-setting lifestyle she couldn't imagine him curtailing for long. And she needed her space. Her equilibrium restored. She could barely think straight with all of that potent, simmering testosterone floating about her home.

Which was why she'd been so desperate to return to work. She needed some distance. Some perspective.

A knock sounded on her office door.

'Come in,' she called, glancing up with a twinge of guilt. A closed door sent a message to her staff that she was unavailable. In fact, it was only closed because she'd been making a list of gynaecologists to consider and hadn't got round to re-opening it.

She pasted on a smile that slid off her face the moment the door opened and Ramon stepped in. Exasperated, she glared at him.

He closed the door. 'If I didn't know you were secretly thrilled to see me, *querida*, I'd take offence at that scowl on your face.'

The endearment combined with his dry wit made her heart skip a beat. She sat back in her chair. 'I thought you had meetings all day at Citrine?' She eyed him in his dark pinstriped suit and wondered how many female mouths he'd left watering in his wake that morning. 'Don't you have other places to be besides checking up on me?'

One dark eyebrow lifted. 'Such as?'

'I don't know… New York? Paris? The Arctic Circle?'

He sauntered over and lowered his big frame into a chair in front of her desk. 'You know, you're cute when you're not throwing up.'

She sent him a withering look. 'That's not funny.'

The twitch of his lips suggested he thought otherwise. 'How are you feeling?'

'Fine. As fine as I was feeling an hour ago when you called and asked the same question.'

'Nausea?'

'Better.'

'No more vomiting?'

'Not since this morning.' When yet again he'd knelt on the bathroom floor and held her hair as she'd wretched into the toilet, then carried her back to bed before returning to the spare room. The fact she'd almost grabbed onto him at the last second and implored him to stay in her bed with her was something she'd deliberately avoided dwelling on today. 'Honestly,' she said. 'I'm fine.'

He frowned. '"Fine" is not a term I would apply to someone who is throwing up several times a day.'

'It's just morning sickness. It won't kill me.' She thought of her mother and ruthlessly quashed the inevitable surge of fear.

'Or it could be *hyperemesis gravidarum*.'

She blinked. 'Excuse me?'

'Severe morning sickness,' he said. 'Which could be harmful to both you and the baby.'

She stared at him. 'How do you even *know* that term?'

'It's in one of the booklets on your coffee table. The ones you said your doctor gave to you.' His eyes narrowed. 'You have read them, haven't you?'

She shifted in her chair. 'I'm working my way through them.' It was close to the truth. She'd made a start and then given up when she'd felt overwhelmed by the sheer volume of information. She'd educated herself on the basics—what she should and shouldn't eat, which supplements to take— and that was all she could cope with for now.

'Good.' He stood up. 'Let's go.'

She frowned. 'Where?'

'To lunch.'

She shook her head. 'I'm not hungry.'

'You have to eat, Emily.' His tone grew stern. 'For you and for the baby.'

The knowledge that he was right—she couldn't live entirely on crackers and herbal tea—grated against an instinctive urge to rail against the web of control he was slowly weaving around her. She wasn't accustomed to having her decisions made for her...and yet she understood that he had the best interests of their baby at heart.

And that, she reminded herself once again, was all that mattered right now.

Her baby.

Their baby.

She retrieved her handbag from a drawer and stood. 'Very well,' she said, the prospect of trying something other than crackers for lunch not as unappealing as she'd made out. She missed food. Missed her ordinarily healthy appetite.

Before Ramon opened the door, she placed her hand on

his forearm. 'I haven't told anyone yet,' she said. 'Not even Marsha. I'd prefer we keep the pregnancy a secret until I've passed the first trimester.'

'Of course.'

She felt the muscles in his arm tense under her hand and quickly let go. 'You haven't told anyone?'

'No.'

'Not even your family?'

His mouth tightened fractionally. 'No one, Emily.'

Sensing she'd ventured into sensitive territory, she left the subject alone, yet as they exited the club through a discreet side entrance she couldn't help wondering about his family. She'd assumed he would want to tell them almost straight away about the pregnancy but clearly that wasn't the case. For a moment she thought that was strange and then it occurred to her that she was the last person qualified to make that kind of determination.

What did *she* know about family?

Sadly, not a lot.

On Saturday morning Ramon flew to Paris to meet with a team of engineers at Saphir. Apparently there was some structural issue with the enormous swimming pool in the recreation centre and a dispute with the original installation company that was sufficiently serious for him to involve himself.

He'd urged Emily to go with him, but she'd refused. Returning to Paris, to the same place where they'd shared their one night of incredible, mind-blowing sex, would do neither of them any favours. Sharing her home with him, sleeping in separate rooms while every night she yearned for his touch, was challenging enough without stirring up memories safer left buried. Reluctant to leave her alone even for a single night, Ramon had argued, and their heated exchange had acted like lighter fluid on an already blazing fire, ramping up the sexual tension that'd simmered below the surface of their every interaction in the last five days.

Tired and irritable by the week's end, Emily had told herself she was looking forward to his absence.

Now, after twenty-four hours without his overwhelming, charismatic presence in her home, she had to admit the truth.

She missed him.

Which was lunacy. How could you miss someone who'd been a fixture in your life for less than a week?

She frowned into the bowl of brownie batter she was mixing by hand with a solid wooden spoon. Allowing herself to grow dependent on Ramon would be a mistake. Whatever form their relationship eventually took, he would be there for their child, not for her. And that suited Emily just fine. She needed him to step up and be a father—a better one, hopefully, than Maxwell had been to her—but she didn't need him to be anything else. Not in the long term.

Curbing her thoughts, she focused on her baking. This morning, for the first time in a week, her nausea had been short-lived and mild enough to avoid a sprint to the bathroom. Taking advantage of the unexpected reprieve, she'd gone for a walk in the autumn sunshine, picked up some fresh produce from a local market, indulged in an early-afternoon nap and then awoken with a fierce, irrepressible craving for chocolate.

She stopped stirring, dipped her finger into the batter for a taste test and closed her eyes as she let her taste buds reach a verdict. The balance of the dark chocolate and the vanilla was perfect. Sliding her finger out of her mouth, she hummed her approval.

'*Dios.*'

Emily almost screamed with fright at the deep, gruff

voice that echoed through her kitchen. She flattened her palm over her racing heart and turned.

Ramon stood in the doorway, one powerful shoulder propped against the frame, the compact leather holdall he travelled with sitting on the hardwood floor at his feet. In a casual open-necked shirt and thigh-hugging jeans, he looked rugged, gorgeous and a thousand times more mouthwatering than any brownie batter.

A rush of need tightened her belly. 'I thought you weren't getting back till later!'

His gaze slid over her, leaving a trail of heat in its wake. 'Why are you cooking in your underwear?'

Her cheeks burned and she silently cringed. Her pink knickers were the old, practical cotton ones she wore for comfort, and she knew without looking that her stretchy white camisole did little to conceal the fact she was bra-less. She resisted folding her arms over her breasts. 'I went for a nap.'

He straightened. 'Are you unwell?'

She stopped herself from executing an exasperated eye roll. 'No. I was just tired. When I woke up I was craving something sweet and... I was hot...' It was her only excuse for not having thrown her clothes back on after her nap. She cast him an accusing look. 'Why did you creep in?'

One corner of his mouth lifted. 'I didn't "creep". I came in quietly in case you were resting.' He pushed away from the door frame, his gaze trailing over her again, and there was something very deliberate about the way he looked at her. 'So you're feeling okay?'

She swallowed, her mouth gone dry. 'Yes.' Was her imagination running wild or was the gleam in his eyes almost predatory? She cleared her throat. 'Did you get the problem with the pool sorted?'

'*Sí.*'

He moved closer and her skin started to tingle. She pressed her back against the edge of the bench. 'Will you need to return next week?'

'No. Did you miss me, Emily?'

Struggling to keep her breathing even, she shrugged. 'Not really.'

One dark eyebrow rose. 'Not at all?'

He moved another inch closer and her limbs weakened. 'Maybe a tiny bit,' she relented.

He braced his hands on the counter either side of her. 'I missed you.'

His voice was low and gravel-rough, and a pulse of excitement flickered in Emily's throat. She sent her tongue out across her lower lip to alleviate its dryness and heard his breath catch. Raw desire flared in his eyes, and the look of intense arousal on his face, the palpable throb of leashed energy from his big body, was enthralling. Intoxicating. He wanted her, and his patent hunger called on some deep, primitive level to her own equally ravenous desire.

'What are you making?'

She saw his mouth move, saw those sensuous lips form the words, but couldn't comprehend the question. 'What?' she asked faintly.

He tipped her chin up, forcing her gaze to lift from his beautiful mouth. 'What are you making?' he repeated.

This close, she could see the tiny individual pinpricks of the dark stubble along his jaw, feel the impact of the raw heat radiating off him. It shimmered in the air, saturating her skin, slowing the blood in her veins to a sluggish, sensual beat.

She managed to articulate a response. 'Chocolate brownies.'

'Doesn't chocolate contain caffeine?'

As if drawn by the pull of a powerful magnet, her gaze returned to his mouth.

'Are you going to lecture me,' she challenged huskily, 'or kiss me?'

Ramon slid his mouth over Emily's and drank in her sweet taste like a man savouring his first sip of water after days trapped in a merciless desert.

Except his deprivation and thirst had lasted for weeks, not days, and this last week had proven by far the most torturous.

Four nights of sleeping in her spare room. Four nights of doing the right thing. Four nights of struggling to dampen the hot embers of desire that constantly threatened to burst into flame and incinerate his restraint, along with his questionable attempts at chivalry.

And the mornings... The mornings were their own special brand of hell. Each time she was sick, a gut-wrenching combination of powerlessness and disgust tore at him. *Self*-disgust because, even as he carried her back to bed after a bout of illness, his body stirred with an untimely lust he had no ability to switch off.

Last night in Paris had offered no reprieve. And not only because of the constant, gnawing concern about her welfare that he knew in some part of his brain was irrational and extreme. He'd stayed in the same suite they'd shared seven weeks before and realised too late his mistake. Every inch of the place, from the living room, to the bed, to the shower, had teased hot, erotic images from his memory until desire had pounded through him so relentlessly he'd had to rely on his hand to achieve a degree of release.

Flying back today, he'd been as grimly and ruthlessly determined as ever to keep his lust banked and his hands to himself—and then he'd walked in and found her standing in her underwear in the kitchen, with her glorious mane of hair flowing loose over her shoulders and her finger in her mouth like some provocative magazine centrefold.

God forgive him.

He was only human.

Her hands in his hair, her soft body moulded to his, she moaned against his lips, a low, needy sound that ramped up the heat in his body and assured him that she was a willing, enthusiastic participant. Reluctantly, he dragged his mouth from hers. If he didn't press pause he'd end up taking her right there against the kitchen bench, or on the floor. He gathered her into his arms, strode from the kitchen and halted in the hallway.

Intuiting his quandary, she whispered in his ear. 'My room.'

Seconds later he lowered her onto her bed and ripped off her scant attire in between pressing hot, urgent kisses to her mouth and throat. When he had her completely naked, he groaned. Her creamy skin was smooth and flawless, her breasts as perfect as he remembered, perhaps even a little fuller. He drew one of her rosy nipples into his mouth and she arched up, drove her hands into his hair and encouraged him with little mewls of delight that intensified the throb of his desire.

She tugged at his shirt, her fingers fumbling with a button. 'Not fair,' she panted. 'I'm the only one naked.'

To which he gave a low chuckle, reluctantly left her side and quickly dispensed with his clothing. Naked, he returned, straddling her legs so he could admire the view while tracing the curves of her body with his hands.

Her stomach was flat, no sign of the life growing inside her evident as yet. But knowing it was there—knowing they'd created it together—flooded him with a fierce sense of possessiveness far more potent than any fear he'd wrestled with in recent days.

The child inside her was his.

She was his.

He leaned over and kissed Emily's stomach, glancing up as she lifted her head. Their gazes locked and it seemed in those few seconds, with only the sounds of their breathing and the drum of his heartbeat filling his ears, as if something unspoken and powerful passed between them. He dragged his gaze from hers before the strange pressure in his chest could intensify, then went lower, down to the sweet, feminine centre of her body. Gently, he parted her and found her wet and swollen. He slipped his finger inside her, loving the way she panted and writhed.

'Come for me, *mi belleza*,' he commanded, then licked once, and she climaxed almost immediately.

'Ramon!'

Gasping his name, she dove her fingers into his hair, gripping his scalp as he sucked and licked, extending her orgasm until her keen cries of pleasure became soft whimpers and her whole body went limp. He rose up between her legs, his body taut with tension, his muscles trembling from the effort required to contain his need. He was afraid that, if he plunged into her now, he'd lose control and take her too hard and fast. *Dios.* Was it possible to hurt the baby?

He rolled onto his back and took her with him so that she sat astride him. Grasping her hips, he positioned her above his erection. This way she'd have control. She seemed to understand because she reached down, wrapped her fingers around his aching shaft and guided the tip to her entrance. For a second he tensed, automatically thinking, *Condom*, then realised they didn't need one. He closed his eyes and couldn't stop a rough cry ripping from his throat as she sank onto him, encasing him in a sheath of silken heat.

Teeth gritted, he kept his pelvis as still as possible, allowing Emily to set the pace and decide how deep to take him. She began to move, her tight, wet heat sliding up and down his shaft, and Ramon's consciousness narrowed until there was nothing but her sitting atop him, her face contorted with pleasure as she wantonly rode him.

Nothing else filled his head.

No concerns.

No fears.

Just their stunning, mind-blowing chemistry and the shattering pinnacle of a climax more powerful than any he'd ever experienced.

'I've made an appointment for us to see a gynaecologist on Tuesday.'

Emily's head rested on Ramon's chest. She blinked drowsily. His deep voice had registered but she had trouble processing his words. Possibly something to do with the post-coital haze shrouding her brain, she thought with a bloom of lazy satisfaction.

A smile pushed its way onto her mouth. She'd always thought the notion of multiple orgasms was a fallacy, just as she'd always believed she would never be someone who enjoyed sex very much.

Now she knew better.

On both counts.

She thought about the brownie batter, abandoned on the kitchen counter, and smiled again. Who needed chocolate when you could have...?

Suddenly her limbs went from languid to rigid. 'What did you say?' She tried to sit up but his arms tightened, keeping her locked against his side. 'Let me go,' she demanded.

'No.'

His abrupt refusal sent a pulse of anger through her. 'Why not?'

'Because you're about to get upset.'

'I'm already upset,' she snapped.

'All the more reason to stay here and calm down.'

Furious, she struggled against him, but he was too strong, his arms like bands of solid steel, his big, muscular thighs trapping one of her own. 'Fine,' she bit out after a moment of angry panting and mental cursing. 'At least let me look at you properly.'

He loosened his hold, just a fraction—enough for her to twist around. The movement brought her breasts into full contact with his chest, and she ignored the puckering of her nipples, the strum of heat in her belly. They were both naked still, the sheets tangled around their feet, the air heavily scented with sex. She looked at him expectantly, and he blew out a breath.

'You were taking too long to decide on a specialist,' he said. 'So I made the decision for us.'

'Us?'

'Yes, Emily. Us.' He propped a hand behind his head, his biceps bunching impressively, and stared down the length of his nose at her. The strong, proud quality of that particular appendage reminded her that many generations of Spanish aristocracy ran through his blood. 'It's my baby too.'

His tone chided, and she felt uncomfortably as if she'd been slapped on the wrist. 'But it's my body,' she countered. 'I should get to choose who looks after it.' The fact she hadn't done so yet was beside the point. Damn it, she was pregnant. She was allowed to be indecisive.

'And when were you planning to make your decision?'

'Soon,' she prevaricated.

'Well, now you don't need to. I've done you a favour.'

'No, you haven't. You've swooped in and taken control again as if—' She stopped and drew her bottom lip between her teeth.

'As if I'm the child's father?'

A tense silence descended. She couldn't argue with that simple truth. Then again, she wasn't in a terribly rational mood. She set her jaw. 'I'm not going.'

He scowled. 'You will.'

'I won't.'

'Now you're being childish.'

'What are you going to do?' She gave him an arch look. 'Spank me?'

He growled and moved so fast she was spread-eagled on her stomach before she'd taken her next breath. A large, heavy palm in the centre of her back kept her playfully pinioned to the mattress with her bottom helplessly bared.

She twisted her head to glare at him. 'Don't you dare!'

His grin was wicked and devastatingly sexy. He didn't spank her—she hadn't really thought he would—but he did hold her down, run his hand up the inside of her thigh and do things with his fingers, and later his tongue, that made her whimper, plead and promise to do absolutely anything he commanded.

Afterwards, they lay together again, Emily's cheek pressed to his chest, one arm flung over the hard, beautifully sculpted surface of his abdomen.

'Which gynaecologist?'

He told her the name and her eyes widened. He had chosen a Harley Street specialist. One she had struck from her list of potential private ob-gyns because the cost was too prohibitive and he was bound to have a waiting list.

Clearly, there were certain benefits to be reaped when the father of one's baby was a billionaire.

Her gaze drifted to the pearl necklace lying on the nightstand. Feeling hot and sticky earlier, she'd taken it off before her nap and forgotten to put it back on.

The pearl was the only possession she had of her mother's. Surprisingly, her father had given it to her. He'd left it in a small velvet box on her bedroom dressing table in her grandfather's mansion a few days before her sixteenth birthday, while she'd still been at boarding school. There'd been a handwritten note with it—nothing elaborate, just three short sentences in her father's untidy scrawl:

This belonged to your mother.
She would have wanted you to have it.
Happy Birthday.
Maxwell

Not *Love, Dad.*

Just *Maxwell.*

Her throat tightened. She'd heard people say you couldn't miss something you'd never had, but Emily knew that wasn't true. She'd never known her mother, but she had missed her desperately throughout her life. When Emily was ten, Mrs Thorne, in a rare moment of compassion, had given her two photographs of her mother and she had cherished them, looking at them often and longing to know more about the woman with the wild blonde curls and the pretty smile. But Mrs Thorne, when asked, had said she hadn't known Kathryn very well and had told Emily to ask her father.

It had taken Emily six months to work up the courage to broach the subject during one of his infrequent visits, and then Maxwell had brushed her curiosity aside.

Closing her eyes, she held her breath and listened to the sound of Ramon's heart beating. It was strong and powerful, much like the man himself. How had she ever drawn parallels between Ramon and her father? They weren't cut from the same cloth. She saw that now.

If her mother had had someone like Ramon by her side during her pregnancy, ensuring she received the proper care and attention, would she have lived?

Emily would never know the answer. She would never know her mother and she could do nothing to change that. But she could do everything within her power to ensure *her* child would grow up knowing its mother.

'I'll go to the appointment on Tuesday,' she said softly, and he kissed the top of her head.

'Gracias, mi belleza.'

CHAPTER NINE

MR LINDSAY, THE Harley Street specialist, was a mild-mannered, softly spoken man to whom Emily warmed at once despite the nerves jangling in her belly in the hours leading up to the appointment. As an expectant mother she felt as if she should be more excited about her first prenatal visit, but it simply made a situation she still grappled to cope with all the more stark and real.

Mr Lindsay smiled from the other side of his big desk in his big, plush medical suite. 'Do you have a rough idea of when you conceived?'

Emily felt her face flame. Was it normal to know the exact date you'd conceived? Or did that scream *one-night stand*?

Just as she opened her mouth to stammer out an answer, Ramon smoothly intervened, supplying the date and then adding, 'We think it was around then, at any rate.' From the chair beside hers, he gave her a warm, encouraging smile. 'It's hard to say exactly, isn't it, *querida*?'

She nodded, returned his smile and tried to transmit a 'thank you' with her eyes.

She was glad he was there—a turnaround from this morning, admittedly, when she'd told him she'd prefer to come alone. A waste of breath, of course. He'd been adamant about attending with her, and no argument had come close to changing his mind.

Mr Lindsay did a swift calculation and pronounced a due date, and Emily's breath locked in her lungs for a moment. In just under thirty-one weeks her baby would be born. Suddenly, it all felt very real.

And very frightening.

She tried to focus, answering Mr Lindsay's questions to the best of her ability. After a while her head spun. The checklist was exhaustive. Medications, supplements, health conditions...

'Any family history of miscarriages or complications with pregnancy?'

Emily froze. She'd anticipated the question, but now the time was here the words jammed in her throat. A chill rippled over her skin—a whisper of the fear she'd tried until now to ignore—and she shivered. The seconds stretched and her silence grew awkward, embarrassing, but still she couldn't unlock her voice. And then Ramon reached over and closed his fingers around hers, stilling their shaking. He squeezed, his touch firm. Reassuring. She looked down at their joined hands, the panic abating, then inhaled deeply. 'My mother died in childbirth,' she said.

Mr Lindsay looked up from his notes. 'Your birth?'

'Yes.'

His expression was grave. 'I'm very sorry,' he said. 'Do you know the details?'

'Not really. I think it might have been pre-eclampsia.'

He scribbled a note, then put his pen down and clasped his hands together on his desk. He stared directly into her eyes. 'Emily, it's perfectly natural given your history to feel some fear about your pregnancy,' he said, 'but I want to assure you both—' he glanced at Ramon, then back at Emily '—that you'll be receiving exceptional care throughout every stage of your journey. We'll take extra precautions, with frequent check-ups and regular testing, and keep a close watch on your blood pressure.' He smiled reassuringly. 'We'll do a physical exam and an ultrasound today to check everything is fine,' he continued. 'There won't be much to see, however. It will be another six weeks at least until we can determine your baby's sex.'

'Oh.' She blinked. Did she want to know her baby's sex

before it was born? She glanced uncertainly at Ramon. Would it matter to him if their child was a girl or a boy? It didn't matter to Emily. And the crazy clause in her grandfather's will certainly didn't sway her one way or another. Gordon Royce had been a fool to attach such an outrageous condition to a large part of his legacy. Even if she had a boy she wouldn't accept the money. It could go to charity for all she cared. 'I don't think I want to know that anyway,' she said. 'I mean—' she glanced again at Ramon '—I'd rather it was a surprise, if you don't mind.'

He shrugged. 'Of course.'

Half an hour later, her first prenatal check-up was over. Ramon had sat in the waiting room while she'd undergone the exam and the ultrasound. She emerged and smiled at him. His coming with her today had shifted something and their connection felt less tenuous, less fragile. It was something Emily hadn't experienced before—a close connection with another person. It gave her hope. Hope that her bond with her baby would be strong. That she'd be a good mother. *That her child would love her.*

Ramon held her hand as they stepped out into the warm autumn sunshine. Outside, they paused on the pristine Mayfair pavement, waiting for his driver to arrive. Emily looked up at him, at those gorgeous, perfectly landscaped features, and her heart performed a slow somersault in her chest. She opened her mouth, wanting to thank him, to tell him how much his support meant to her today, but a bright pop of light stopped her in her tracks.

'Mr de la Vega! Who's the lady? Is she knocked up? Is it yours?'

The lone paparazzo fired off another round of shutter clicks. Scowling, Ramon turned Emily into him, cupping the back of her head and pressing her face protectively into his shoulder.

'When's the kid due?'

Ramon swore under his breath, and then their car pulled up and he was bundling her into the back of the sleek black sedan. The second they were safely ensconced, the driver sped off. Heart pounding, Emily sucked in a shaky breath and cast a stricken look at Ramon.

His face was thunderous.

'You'll marry her, I assume.'

The statement carried a faint air of command. Ramon gritted his teeth. If he could have reached down the phone line and strangled his brother with his bare hands, he would have. There were never any grey areas with Xavier. Life was comprised of black and white.

Right and wrong.

Do or don't.

Right now Xav was urging him towards the 'do'. More specifically, the words 'I do'.

'I'll make that decision when I'm ready.'

A short silence. 'You *are* taking responsibility for the child?'

Ramon ground his teeth a little harder. Xav's opinion of him really did scrape the bottom of the barrel. 'Of course,' he bit out.

He curled his hand into a fist on the desk top and absently cast his gaze over the office that had belonged to Maxwell Royce. In recent days Ramon had staked a more permanent claim on the space, using it as his main base from which to work while in London. He leaned back in the chair, his mind working overtime as it had for the past twenty-four hours. Perhaps he should stake a more permanent claim on the man's daughter as well. It wasn't as if he hadn't already entertained the idea many times over.

'Mamá and Papá are upset they had to find out this way.'

Ramon couldn't help but hear the implicit criticism in his brother's voice. The unspoken words.

You've hurt them. Again.

'Why did you not tell us?' Xav demanded.

'We haven't told anyone. It's too soon. The pregnancy was only confirmed last week.'

'Did you not think the photos would surface?'

He'd thought, *hoped*, they would make a small, scarcely visible splash. Certainly here in England that had been the case, thanks to a minor royal and her very public skirmish with law enforcement dominating the tabloids. Spain was a different story, however. Every gossip site had picked up the photograph of him and Emily standing outside a Harley Street gynaecologist's clinic. In addition, the shot taken of them outside Saphir in Paris over seven weeks ago had surfaced.

'The photos are unfortunate,' he said tightly.

A heavy sigh came down the line. 'Hector's been on the phone. He's on his high horse again. He says the board will have some natural concerns about the potential for negative reaction from our more conservative shareholders.'

'Tell Hector he can go scr—'

'I did.'

Ramon leaned back in his chair. His cool, diplomatic brother had told Hector where to go? That was a conversation he would have liked to witness.

'But he has a point.' Xav's voice was weary. 'This kind of publicity could have a negative impact on both the business and the family.' He was silent. 'Marry the Royce woman and make this right, Ramon. It's what Mamá and Papá will expect. Make them happy. Don't bring disgrace on the family.'

He didn't add the word 'again', but he didn't need to.

The inference was loud and clear.

* * *

'I made you some tea.' Marsha walked across the office and placed a mug of steaming liquid on Emily's desk. 'It's ginger,' she said. 'For the nausea.'

Emily managed a grateful smile. 'Thanks.'

'Can I do anything else?'

'No. Thank you. You're doing plenty. Have there been many more calls?'

A scowl formed on Marsha's pretty face. 'Those tabloid journalists are scum,' she declared. 'Honestly, the things they have the nerve to ask—' She broke off, perhaps seeing Emily's silent wince. Quickly, she added, 'But they're not worth fretting over. And they're not getting anything from me but a "no comment".'

Emily nodded, gratitude surging again. From the moment her pregnancy had become fodder for the tabloids, her assistant had been a godsend. Seventy-two hours of online speculation and gossip had taken its toll, however, and it seemed even Marsha's sweet, patient disposition was being tested.

Emily waited until the younger woman had left before dropping her head in her hands. Humiliation swamped her. This was not how she'd wanted her pregnancy revealed to the world. It was embarrassing and intrusive, and she didn't want even to think about the impact it could have on The Royce. So often she'd swept her father's scandalous behaviour under the carpet, condemning him for his irresponsibility and lack of discretion. Not once had she ever imagined that *she* would cause a scandal.

At least they hadn't made the front page of the papers, although the online gossip sites were having a field day. Emily had fought her curiosity until a moment of weakness had struck. She'd regretted the impulse as soon as she'd clicked on the photo of her and Ramon standing outside the clinic. It made her want to crawl into a very deep hole and never come out. The paparazzo had snapped them just as she had looked up at Ramon, and the expression on her face…

Oh, God.

A fresh wave of humiliation struck. The photo made her look besotted. Infatuated. *In love.* Which was ridiculous. Yes, they were sleeping together—something she knew they'd have to stop doing eventually—but she wasn't in love with him. How could she be? She didn't know the first thing about love.

'Emily.'

She jerked her head up, an immediate shiver running down her spine. She mightn't love Ramon, but his deep voice nevertheless held the power to elicit a swift, visceral response. He moved from the doorway, a mouthwatering mix of raw masculinity and sharp, sophisticated style. He didn't own a single suit that didn't fit his broad frame to utter perfection. The casual look he sported in the evenings in her home was the one she'd come to prefer of late, however. Faded jeans, tee shirt and bare feet. Until recently, she hadn't realised how sexy a man's feet could be.

'Emily?'

She started. 'Sorry?'

'I asked if you're all right.'

'Of course.' A lie. She was a mass of tension and nerves.

'Do you have much more work to do?'

Bereft of her usual focus and energy, she looked at the report on her desk. The one she'd stared blankly at for the last hour. She glanced at her watch. It was only four o'clock. 'A bit,' she said.

'Finish up and come with me.'

She frowned at his commanding tone. 'Where?'

'It's a surprise.'

'You know I don't like surprises.'

His smile was gentle enough to melt her insides. And her resistance.

'Humour me,' he said.

An hour later Emily stood in the centre of an enormous living room on the lower floor of a beautiful late nineteenth-century mansion in Chelsea.

'What do you think?'

Slowly, she turned and looked at Ramon. He stood in front of the big window that overlooked the large fenced-in front garden, rays of late-afternoon sunshine highlighting the rich, glossy mahogany of his hair. His jacket was undone, his tie was loosened and his hands were thrust casually into his trouser pockets.

Emily wasn't fooled, however.

Every hard inch of him radiated tension.

She gazed up at the moulded ceiling and the beautiful, intricate glass chandelier above her head. 'It's stunning.' More than stunning, she thought. Even unfurnished, the three-storey, seven-bedroom residence was breathtaking.

Having grown up in her grandfather's mansion north of London, she wasn't unaccustomed to large houses. But, while the interior of her grandfather's home had been characterised by dark wood and heavy, oppressive furnishings, this house was light and airy, its preserved period features interspersed with touches of contemporary luxury that gave it an elegant, timeless appeal.

And the kitchen!

Emily had salivated over the walk-in pantry, the giant stove, the hand-crafted cabinetry with oodles of storage space and the massive custom-designed granite counter-tops offering plenty of room for culinary experimentation.

Her heart had soared with excitement, and then just as quickly had dropped.

This was a 'for ever' home. The kind where kids grew up

and couples grew old. Where families laughed and argued and loved and cried. Where children and grandchildren came back for Christmases and birthdays and boisterous reunions—the kind you saw in movies or read about in books that guaranteed you a happy ending.

It wasn't the sort of home a billionaire playboy considered buying.

Sadness weighted her down. 'Ramon,' she whispered, a wealth of feeling and helplessness pouring into that single utterance of his name.

His gaze held hers and she thought maybe he understood. Thought he might be experiencing some of the same turmoil she was. He crossed to where she stood and curled his hands over her shoulders. She wanted to press a finger against his lips so he couldn't say the words, but her limbs were frozen, her breath locked in her chest.

'Marry me.'

She closed her eyes. 'I can't.'

He was silent a moment. 'You're saying that because you're scared.'

She lifted her lids. 'Aren't you?'

A muscle worked in his jaw. 'Yes,' he confessed, the word seeming to drag from the depths of his throat. 'But fear isn't a reason to avoid doing the right thing.'

She drew a deep breath. 'Is that what we'd be doing? The right thing?'

His brows lowered. 'Of course.'

'How do you know it's the right thing?' she challenged softly.

His eyes hardened a fraction. 'Providing our child with a stable home with both parents isn't the right thing?'

She swallowed. He painted a nice picture. And, if she let herself, she could easily indulge the fantasy. Imagine them living here as husband and wife, raising their child in this beautiful home. 'Is this what you want, Ramon? A life of domesticity? Tied down with a wife and child?'

His jaw flexed. He dropped his hands from her shoulders. 'I'm thirty years old. Most men settle down eventually.'

Her chest grew heavier. 'I'm not asking what other men do. I'm asking if it's what *you* want. If Paris hadn't happened,' she pressed. 'If I wasn't pregnant, would you be thinking about giving up your bachelor lifestyle?'

'But you are pregnant, Emily.' His voice turned a shade cooler. 'With *my* child.' He paced away, turned back. 'Would you relegate me to the role of part-time father? Someone who breezes in and out of our child's life whenever the custody arrangement tells me I can?'

Emily felt her face blanch. That was exactly the kind of arrangement she'd assumed they would agree upon. But Ramon's description made her blood run cold. Made her think of all the times she'd curled up on her bed as a little girl and cried, believing her daddy didn't care enough to visit her.

A fluttery, panicky feeling worked its way up her throat. 'But what about us?'

He moved closer, eyes narrowing. 'What do you mean?'

'I mean...' she hesitated, colour seeping back into her face '...us—our relationship. You're talking about a long-term commitment. Or at least until our child has grown and left home. That could be twenty years, Ramon. Twenty years of commitment to our child...and me. Twenty years with no other...' She hesitated, her chest suddenly constricting.

'Women?' he supplied.

She lifted her chin. 'I won't tolerate that kind of relationship.'

'Marriage,' he corrected. 'We're talking about marriage, Emily. And, yes, I understand the full implications of such a commitment. For the record—' he grasped her chin and locked his gaze on hers '—I won't tolerate that kind of marriage either.'

She blinked. A part of her wanted to believe him. Another part of her said it didn't matter if she believed him or not, because all of this was hypothetical.

Besides, pledging his faithfulness now, when they were still burning up the sheets, was easy. How would his vows hold up when she was heavy and listless with his child, or exhausted from juggling the demands of motherhood and a job?

He clasped her shoulders again. 'We're good together, *querida*. Are you denying that?'

'Lust is hardly a foundation for marriage.'

The hard line of his mouth softened. 'But it's a good starting point, *sí*?'

Love was supposed to be the starting point for marriage, she thought. But then what did she know?

She stepped back, forcing his hands to drop. 'It's a beautiful house,' she said, casting a final look around the room. 'But I... I just need some time to think.'

Emily didn't stop thinking. Not for a single waking minute. For the next forty-eight hours, her mind spun and her stomach churned and Ramon waited on her answer with barely leashed impatience.

At two a.m. on Sunday morning she sat on the cushioned window seat in her lounge, staring out at the moonlit night, her mother's pearl tucked in her hand. She laid her other hand over her stomach and knew instinctively the bond she had feared mightn't grow between her and her child was already there. She could feel it with each beat of her heart. A strong, deep connection unlike anything else she'd ever known. It filled her with a fierce resolve to nurture and protect. To do whatever was best for her child. To give it the best life possible and shield him or her from the same bitter hurts and disappointments she'd suffered as a child.

Breathing deeply, she rose and went back to bed. Ramon lay on his back, the white cotton sheet bunched around his waist, his bare chest rising and falling. The sound of his deep, steady breathing was familiar and somehow comforting. She slipped off her robe and climbed between the sheets.

Ramon stirred, his arm lifting so she could curl into his side. 'Emily?' His voice was a sexy, sleep-roughened rumble.

'I'm fine.' She snuggled close and leaned on her elbow. 'Ramon?'

He caressed her hip. *'Sí?'*

'Yes,' she said softly.

He went still. And then he deftly turned her onto her back. He didn't say anything. He just stroked his fingers over her hair. Her cheek. Her mouth. And then he kissed her. Long, deep and hard.

CHAPTER TEN

'ARE YOU CLOSE with your brother?'

Ramon glanced up from his laptop. Emily sat in the seat opposite him in his private jet. In a pale blue trouser suit, with her hair caught loosely in a band over one shoulder, she looked beautiful and flawless in spite of the vomiting spell that had struck shortly before their departure for the airport. Ramon had regarded the sudden resurgence of her nausea as sufficient excuse to cancel their trip to Barcelona, but she had refused to let him postpone the weekend.

Five days had passed since she'd agreed to marry him, three days since he'd placed the enormous radiant-cut diamond on her finger. Two days ago he'd notified his family and afterwards released an announcement to the press. Yesterday, he'd closed the deal on the house in Chelsea.

With each step he'd waited for a sense of panic to set in. Instead, he felt a deep, unmitigated satisfaction. A growing certainty that he was doing the right thing.

He answered Emily's question. 'Not especially.'

'Oh.' She sounded surprised. 'Xavier's adopted, right?'

'Yes. But that's not a factor in our relationship. We have different personalities, that's all. Sometimes we clash.' He closed his laptop, noting Emily's hands fidgeting in her lap. 'You're nervous,' he observed.

'A bit. I'm afraid the whole family thing is rather alien to me.'

Little wonder, he thought. She'd grown up with an absentee father and no mother. By her own account, the closest thing she'd had to a maternal influence as a child had been her grandfather's housekeeper, who she described as an austere woman whose one saving grace had been teaching Emily to bake and cook.

'Have you heard from your father?'

She shook her head, her mouth turning down, and Ramon knew a fierce desire to find Maxwell Royce and hurt him. The man's daughter was pregnant and engaged and he hadn't bothered to return her calls. Out of courtesy, Ramon had left a message on his phone the day before the engagement was made official, but Royce hadn't responded.

'Why The Royce?' he asked, voicing a question that had been lodged in his brain like an annoying burr for weeks.

'What do you mean?'

'You're smart, dedicated, hard-working. You could have done anything,' he said. 'Chosen any number of professions. Why carve out your career there?'

Colour swept her cheeks. 'When I inherited half of the club, I had no choice but to step up.'

'But you devoted yourself to The Royce long before then.'

She frowned. 'It's my family's business.' A defensive edge crept into her voice. 'Why wouldn't I get involved?' Her expression became shuttered. Averting her face, she looked out of the window at a bank of solid cloud, effectively ending the conversation. But, slowly, her gaze came back to his. 'Actually, there's more to it than that...' She hesitated, her throat moving around a tight swallow. 'I think, in the beginning, I was looking for some kind of connection.'

'To your father?'

'Yes. And to my grandfather. I wasn't close to either one of them, but they were the only family I had. Working at The Royce gave us some common ground. I suppose I wanted to prove myself. To earn their respect. Their attention.'

Ramon felt a tugging deep in his chest. No young person

should have to earn attention from a parent. His dislike of Maxwell Royce strengthened.

'What about you?' she asked, swiftly diverting the focus from herself. 'You gave up an architectural career to join your family's business. Do you miss being an architect?'

'Yes and no,' he hedged. 'I often have a hand in the design and renovation of the clubs and properties under my purview, so I still get to dabble.'

'It must be amazing to have a creative talent.' Her voice was wistful.

'You don't see yourself as creative?'

'Not really.' She wrinkled her perfect nose. 'The most creative I get is baking.'

'I like it when you bake.'

She gave him a pert look. 'Correction. You like it when I bake in my underwear.'

He couldn't hold back a grin. On impulse, he reached for her left hand and pressed a kiss on her knuckles—just above the glittering diamond that proudly proclaimed to the world she was his. A smile softened her face and his mood lightened. Perhaps, with Emily by his side, he wouldn't find this weekend with his family too painful.

Emily sensed a dark storm of tension building within Ramon from the second the jet's wheels touched down in Barcelona. During the flight he'd been happy to talk and their conversation had distracted her from her nerves. Now, as they travelled in the back of a chauffeur-driven SUV to his parents' villa, he was silent and brooding.

Did he not get along with his family? The thought sent a shaft of dismay through her. If his relationship with them was strained, how would they receive *her*? Would they welcome her as a daughter-in-law? Or would she be the scarlet woman who'd trapped their son into marriage by getting herself pregnant?

She looked at the enormous rectangular diamond that glittered on her ring finger. Set in platinum and flanked by two sapphires and clusters of smaller diamonds on either side, it was a beautiful piece of artistry which had drawn a shocked gasp from her when he'd slipped it onto her finger. But after three days it still felt heavy and unfamiliar on her hand—as alien and disconcerting as the experience of meeting his family was going to be.

Her stomach threatening to rebel again, she rummaged in her handbag for a piece of crystallised ginger and popped it in her mouth.

Twenty minutes and three pieces of ginger later, their driver turned off the road and drove between two massive gated pillars. A long tree-lined driveway dappled with early-evening sunlight eventually opened onto lush, colourful gardens and led to a circular courtyard at the front of a magnificent two-storey villa. Before the vehicle had stopped, the villa's big front door swung open and a slender, casually dressed woman emerged.

She was beautiful. A generation older than Emily, but still trim and fit-looking in white trousers and a simple sleeveless burnt orange top. Dark chin-length hair streaked with the odd strand of grey was tucked behind her ears, revealing a stunning bone structure that bore such a striking resemblance to Ramon's, Emily knew at once that this was Elena de la Vega, his mother.

She smiled broadly as they exited the vehicle, then stepped towards her son, her arms extended. She spoke to him in Spanish and Emily didn't understand the words, but she heard affection in the older woman's voice, and saw the shimmer of restrained tears in her eyes. Her emotion, so visible and patently heartfelt, made Emily's chest squeeze. But when mother and son embraced, Ramon was stiff, the hug he gave his mother awkward-looking in spite of Elena's obvious delight at seeing her son.

Emily had no time to dwell on the odd dynamic. Elena turned, clasped Emily's hands in both of hers and squeezed. 'And you are Emily,' she declared, her English accented but perfect. Her eyes shone, a rich shade of caramel-brown like her son's. 'It is a great pleasure to meet you.'

'And you, Mrs de la Vega.'

'Elena,' she insisted. 'My goodness, you are beautiful.' She touched Emily's cheek, her eyes glistening again. 'Come.' She motioned them towards the villa. 'Vittorio has been feeling breathless today so he's resting in the salon before dinner. But he is looking forward to seeing you both.'

As they headed indoors, Ramon placed his palm in the small of Emily's back and murmured in her ear. 'My mother can get a little over-emotional.'

'It's fine,' she whispered, wondering why he felt the need to apologise. Elena de la Vega was delightful.

Vittorio de la Vega turned out to be a tall, commanding man who looked reasonably well, despite the heart problems Ramon had briefly mentioned on the plane. He greeted his son with a firm handshake, then welcomed his future daughter-in-law with an infusion of warmth similar to his wife's, if less effusive. After kissing Emily on both cheeks, he politely enquired about their journey, then offered her a choice of non-alcoholic beverages. The subtle deference to her pregnancy made her blush, but she saw no outward sign of judgement or disapproval.

'Have you set a wedding date?'

Elena posed the question the moment they were all settled on comfortable sofas in the beautiful, high-ceilinged salon.

'Elena,' Vittorio gently chided. He sent Emily an apologetic look. 'You must forgive my wife. She can be very excitable.'

Elena flicked an elegant hand, unperturbed. 'I've recently discovered I'm getting a daughter-in-law *and* a grandchild. I think a little excitement is perfectly acceptable.' Her warm smile encompassed both Emily and her son. 'You'll want to get married before the baby arrives, yes?'

'When we decide on a date, you'll be the first to know, Mamá,' Ramon said.

If Elena found her son's tone a little too sharp, she gave no indication. She addressed Emily. 'Your mother must be very excited.'

Emily stiffened, her gaze shifting to Ramon. Had he told his family nothing about her? He covered her hand with his and rubbed his thumb over her knuckles, his eyes offering a form of apology. To Elena, she said, 'My mother died when I was born. I never knew her.'

'Oh, my dear.' Dismay clouded the older woman's eyes. 'I'm so sorry.' She was silent, as though taking a moment to respect the depth of Emily's loss. Then, 'I would not wish to intrude but, if you need help with planning for the wedding or the baby, I would love nothing more. You may already know that Ramon and Xavier don't have a sister, so I've missed out on all the exciting girl things. I would have loved a daughter...' Her gaze flicked to her son. 'But when Ramon came along, he was our miracle. We couldn't have expected another.'

Ramon didn't say anything, but the slight tightening of his hand over hers betrayed the sudden flare of tension in his body. She glanced at him again, but his face was impassive. Unreadable. Hiding her confusion, she smiled at Elena. 'Thank you. I'd appreciate that. I think I'm going to need all the help I can get.' And then, because Ramon's ill humour was starting to unsettle her, she remarked on the splendour of the villa and asked Elena for a tour.

Less than an hour later, they sat down to dinner at one end of a long table in a sumptuous formal dining room.

'Xavier couldn't join us tonight,' Elena said, her tone apologetic. 'But he'll be here tomorrow.'

Vittorio poured wine for the table and a sparkling grape juice for Emily. 'Have you been to Barcelona before?'

'No. This is my first time in Spain.'

Elena clapped her hands together. 'Oh! That's very exciting. You have so much to see! Ramon, where will you take her first?'

For the first time since they'd walked off the plane, a relaxed smile curved his mouth. 'Barri Gòtic,' he said.

'Ah. Marvellous,' Elena enthused. 'The old city is magnificent.'

From then on the conversation remained light and flowed throughout the meal. With her nausea gone and the tension dissipated, Emily was able to enjoy the fabulous food served over three courses to the table by a trio of discreet, efficient waiting staff. As the evening grew late, however, she found herself stifling a series of yawns.

'I believe my fiancée needs to retire.'

Ramon's statement elicited a small start of surprise from Emily. Was he really so attuned to the subtleties of her body language? And there she'd been, thinking her efforts to hide her tiredness had been rather stellar.

'Of course.' Elena cast her a sympathetic look. 'You must go and rest. We will have plenty of time over the weekend to talk.'

Upstairs, the suite she and Ramon had been allocated was enormous and just as resplendent as the rest of the villa. Emily dropped onto the end of the majestic four-poster bed, sighed and kicked off her low-heeled sandals. 'Your parents are lovely, Ramon.'

He stripped off his shirt and she admired the impressive expanse of hard muscle and smooth skin. She didn't think she'd ever tire of gazing at his magnificent body. He was truly breathtaking. He toed off his shoes and unbuckled his belt. 'They're good people.'

Emily dragged her gaze away from his taut, flat stomach and that tantalising downward arrow of dark hair. 'But…?' she said softly.

He paused. 'But what?'

She hesitated. 'Did I just imagine the tension earlier?'

He shrugged. 'No family is perfect, Emily.'

Brows tugging together, she opened her mouth to ask why he was being cryptic, but he turned away, shed the rest of his clothing and then straightened to face her.

Emily's mouth dried.

Not only was he standing naked before her…he was erect. Proudly, gloriously erect. Liquid heat pooled between her legs.

Struggling to remember the gist of their conversation, she forced her gaze up. 'Is this your best attempt to avoid talking?'

One corner of his sinful mouth curled. He tipped her chin up. 'Sleep or sex, Emily?'

If she said sleep, he would leave her alone. Respect her need for rest. But suddenly rest seemed very overrated. And her nausea hadn't recurred in several hours. What was the expression? Make hay while the sun shines? She arched an eyebrow. 'Conversation isn't an option?'

'No.'

'Well, in that case…'

She reached out, curled her fingers around his hot, rigid length and took him into her mouth.

Showing Emily the sights of Barcelona proved a more pleasurable experience than Ramon had anticipated.

Rising early on Saturday, he borrowed one of his father's cars and took her on a scenic coastal drive before heading into the centre of the city. They parked up and strolled along grand boulevards and winding cobblestone streets, and he realised it'd been many years since he'd allowed himself to enjoy the energy and vibrancy of the city he'd loved as a boy. Whenever he returned for business he kept his visits as short as possible. Now, as he pointed out iconic landmarks and showed her some of the city's greatest architectural gems, he realised his designer's eye had missed the unrivalled beauty of Barcelona with its mix of contemporary, Gothic and mediaeval design.

Barri Gòtic, the Gothic quarter, was still a tangle of old, narrow stone alleyways and unique, interesting storefronts. Emily loved it and insisted they explore. When their stomachs growled for sustenance, he chose a traditional tapas bar with art nouveau murals on the walls, lively jazz music and a reputation for outstanding food.

Whether from pregnancy or the excitement of discovering a new city, Emily glowed. She was beautiful—and she had charmed his parents, as he hadn't doubted she would. His mother already adored her. More than that, her presence had been a balm of sorts, gradually easing the tension in him. The burning shame and brutal guilt he relived every time he saw his parents and which, even after twelve years, made looking his mother in the eye almost impossible.

He reached across the table and tucked a curl behind her ear as she bit into another savoury croquette. So far today, no nausea. In fact, her appetite was exceptionally healthy, not unlike her appetite in bed last night...

'Ramon?'

Jerked from the memory of her lush mouth on him, he smiled at her, but her attention was elsewhere.

She frowned, looking over his shoulder. 'There's a young man over there staring at you.'

Twisting round, he followed the line of her gaze.

And felt his stomach muscles clench into a sudden, violent spasm.

Jorge.

His spine turned to ice. He blinked, trying to shake the crazy notion from his head. It couldn't be Jorge. Jorge was dead. Ramon knew this. He had watched him die twelve years ago.

The lookalike stood up, started stalking towards their table and a swift bolt of recognition cleared the confusion from Ramon's head.

Slowly, he rose. 'Mateo.'

Mateo Mendoza glared at him with fierce, undiluted hatred blazing in his black eyes. He spoke in Spanish, his voice a low, belligerent snarl. 'You've got a nerve showing your face around here, de la Vega.'

Keeping his cool in the face of the younger man's hostility, Ramon tried to remember how old Jorge's brother had been when he'd last seen him. Twelve? Which would make him twenty-four now.

Another man, roughly the same age, appeared at Mateo's back. He put his hand on his friend's shoulder and murmured something, but Mateo shook him off.

Ramon threw a glance at Emily. A look of startled alarm had settled on her face.

Dios.

He didn't want her to witness this. Didn't want her in the middle of a situation he might not be able to control. Body tensed, alert, he focused his attention on Mateo. 'Whatever you want to get off your chest, Mateo,' he growled, 'this is not the place.'

The younger man drew his right arm back and Ramon knew he was about to put his weight behind a punch. He could have ducked, blocked the blow; he was bigger and stronger, so he could take the other man easily. Instead, he braced his shoulders and took the full impact of Mateo's fist on the left side of his jaw. It hurt like hell, making a cracking sound like a gunshot inside his skull.

Emily shot to her feet. 'Ramon!'

'Sit down, Emily,' he gritted out. He didn't want Mateo's attention on her.

'I will not sit down!' she cried. 'What on earth is going on?'

Eyes narrowed, chest heaving, Mateo trawled his gaze over her, a sneer twisting his lips.

Ramon fisted his hands. 'Did that make you feel better, Mateo?' he asked drawing the other man's attention.

Slicing another look at Emily, Mateo jabbed a finger in Ramon's direction. 'This man is a murderer,' he spat in English, and then his friend grabbed his arm and roughly dragged him out of the bar before the burly staff member who was weaving through the tables reached them.

His heart racing, Ramon apologised for the disturbance, paid the bill and added an extra-large gratuity, then took Emily by the elbow and walked her into the street.

In a high-pitched voice, she demanded, 'What on earth was that about?'

Retaining a firm hold on her arm, he headed in the direction of the car. 'Keep walking, Emily.'

'Why did you let him punch you?'

'Because he was angry and needed to vent.'

'By *hitting* you?'

'I deserved it.'

'What do you mean?'

He realised she was panting and slowed his stride a little. 'I'll explain later.'

'He said you were a murderer.'

Ramon clenched his teeth and winced as renewed pain shot through his jaw. 'I heard what he said.'

'Are you going to tell me what he meant?'

'Later,' he repeated.

She fell silent but he sensed her gaze darting back to him, again and again, questioning. Confused. In the car, a thick, heavy silence enveloped them, Emily's rigid posture telegraphing her anger.

He cursed under his breath.

Coming to Barcelona had been a mistake.

When they reached the villa, he stopped the car outside the front steps and kept the engine idling. 'Go inside, Emily.' He felt the weight of her gaze on him, but he looked straight ahead, his hands clenched on the steering wheel.

'Where are you going?'

He didn't know. But he needed some space. He couldn't deal with her questions right now. 'Go inside,' he said hoarsely. 'Please.'

She got out and slammed the door, and he gunned the engine and drove off.

Dinner that evening was a tense, awkward affair, the empty chair beside Emily a painful reminder of the awful incident at the tapas bar.

She still had no clue what the confrontation had been about, but she knew one thing with utter, unequivocal certainty.

Her baby's father was *not* a murderer.

She wished he would come back and tell her that himself. But she hadn't seen him since he'd sped off in a cloud of gravel and dust and brooding testosterone.

Anxiety gnawed at her, diminishing her appetite for the lovely meal in front of her. Question after question tumbled through her head. Where was he? Was he okay? Why hadn't he called? Had he been involved in an accident? Why hadn't he returned for dinner?

Had he abandoned her?

Reading her anxiety, Elena said gently, 'He'll be back.'

The man seated across from her gave a derisive snort. 'This is typical of him to run off.'

Xavier's voice vibrated with anger and Emily gripped

her knife and fork, everything within her rebelling against the notion that Ramon had 'run off'.

He wouldn't desert her. Not here. Like this. He could have run at any time in the last three weeks, starting from the moment she'd told him she was pregnant. He hadn't. And she refused to believe he'd done so now.

'I am sorry you had to witness what you did this afternoon.' Xavier spoke to her. 'My brother—'

'Xavier.' Vittorio interrupted his son. 'Emily deserves an explanation, but I think it must come from Ramon.'

Xavier's expression tightened, his intense, somewhat superior gaze flicking back to Emily.

Like his younger brother, he was devastatingly handsome, but far more formidable. Although they weren't genetically related, nature had graced them both with strong, broad-shouldered physiques and stunning facial structures. The most striking contrast Emily could see was their eyes. Where Ramon's were expressive and warm, Xavier's were a cold, hard grey. Not unlike her own, she supposed, though hers were several shades paler and a lot less piercing.

She suppressed a shiver.

Had she been wise to tell them what had happened? When she'd gone inside, bewildered and upset, Xavier had been there with his parents and Elena had seen her stricken expression and immediately put a comforting arm around her. Before Emily had thought better of it, she'd spilled the details of the entire incident.

Distracted, she toyed with the food on her plate.

And then the sound of a car engine and gravel crunching outside had everyone surging to their feet.

Xavier threw down his napkin and stormed out first, a fierce scowl on his face.

Vittorio strode after him.

Emily made to follow, but Elena placed a restraining hand on her arm. 'Give them a few minutes,' she advised.

'My boys have tempers. There might be some fireworks.' She looped her arm through Emily's. 'Walk with me on the terrace.'

Emily didn't want to walk. She wanted to go to Ramon. She wanted to check with her own eyes that he was all right. *She wanted the explanation she was owed.*

No sooner had they stepped onto the terrace than the arguing commenced outside the front of the villa. Raised male voices carried clearly on the still evening air and she heard Xavier, then Ramon, and his deep, familiar baritone made her heart clench in her chest. Vittorio wasn't as loud—the mediator between his sons, she assumed. They spoke in rapid-fire Spanish, frustrating her attempts to understand. And then their voices grew muffled, suggesting they'd moved into the house and closeted themselves in a room.

Emily's breath shuddered out, a deep sigh of despair. 'I don't understand any of this.'

Elena hugged Emily's arm as they strolled. 'I'm afraid things have been strained in our family for a long time. Ramon has struggled to move on from the past—from the mistakes he made as a boy—and he believes that, because he hasn't done so, we haven't either.'

Emily looked at her. 'But you have?'

'Of course. I love my son. I always have. I never stopped loving him—he simply stopped allowing himself to *be* loved.'

Why? Because he believed he didn't deserve love? A deep ache spread through Emily's chest.

Elena sat down on a cushioned rattan sofa and urged Emily to sit beside her. 'Everything will be fine. You'll see.'

Emily wished she shared the older woman's optimism. 'What did Xavier mean—when he said it was typical of Ramon to run off?'

Elena shook her head. 'Pay no attention to what Xavier

says. He is hard on people—himself included.' She wrapped her hands around Emily's. 'Ramon is a good man. He will be a good father. Already I see changes in him I never would have imagined.'

Her heart missed a beat. 'Really?'

Elena smiled. 'Really.' She squeezed Emily's hands. 'Sometimes all a man needs is the love of a good woman.'

Love.

Emily's heart began to race.

Did she love Ramon?

These last few days, she had started to think she might, and the idea overwhelmed her with a wild, conflicting mix of wonder and fear.

'I've only known you for twenty-four hours, Emily,' Elena continued, 'but I am a good judge of character. I believe you have a kind, forgiving soul. And I believe my son can learn from you.' She cupped Emily's cheek with her palm. 'He fears responsibility, but not for the reasons you might think.'

'Emily.'

Ramon's voice stopped her breath in her lungs. In unison, she and Elena rose and turned.

Rumpled, dishevelled and still breathtakingly handsome in the khaki trousers and black tee shirt he'd worn throughout the day, he strode across the terrace.

He held his hand out to her and, after a brief hesitation, she slipped her hand into his.

His grip was firm as he turned to his mother, his demeanour stiff. 'I apologise for my absence, Mamá.'

Elena reached up and kissed her son's cheek. 'Apology accepted. Now, go. Talk with Emily. You owe her an explanation.'

CHAPTER ELEVEN

KEEPING HER HAND firmly in his grip, Ramon led Emily into the gardens, along a lighted pathway and into a secluded alcove. Hedges and fragrant rose bushes provided privacy and, to one side, an ornate stone bench sat beneath a high, vine-covered arch.

His blood still beat furiously in his veins from his run-in with Xav.

His brother could be so sanctimonious. So self-righteous, at times.

He let go of Emily and she lifted her hand to his face. 'Ramon...your jaw.'

He seized her wrist and pulled her hand down before she could touch him. 'It's just bruised.'

Frowning, she jerked her wrist free, then hugged her arms around her middle. 'Where have you been?'

He heard the hurt in her voice and his self-hatred burned brighter. Deeper.

But he'd needed the time alone. Time to bring his emotions under control. Time to work out how to explain—how much to tell her.

All of it, his conscience cried.

'I hadn't planned to miss dinner,' he said. 'There was a road accident—' Her eyes widened and he quickly added, 'Not me. Tourists.' A group of three young Australian holidaymakers who'd run their camper van off the coastal road and flagged him down in distress. 'I stopped to help and waited until the emergency services arrived.'

Even upset and pale, Emily was beautiful. The mint-green knee-length dress she'd donned for dinner was fresh and feminine, showcasing a figure that was starting to show subtle signs of pregnancy. Her hair was captured loosely at her nape and he knew an overwhelming desire to sink his hands into those lustrous curls, bury his face in them and breathe deeply until her scent overtook his senses and his mind was filled with nothing but her.

He jammed his hands in his pockets and nodded towards the stone bench. 'Sit, Emily.'

Her chin came up, and for a moment he thought she might refuse. Then she sighed and sat down.

He took a deep breath. 'The young man in the tapas bar today was Mateo Mendoza,' he said. 'He's the younger brother of Jorge Mendoza, my best friend during my teens.' He drew another breath but his chest was so tight his lungs wouldn't expand properly. 'When we were eighteen Jorge drowned in a boating accident. Mateo blames me for his brother's death.'

Emily stared at him, wide-eyed. 'Why?'

'Because it was my fault.'

She shook her head. 'I don't understand.'

'It was a reckless teenage escapade. There was alcohol involved. And the boat wasn't seaworthy.' He clenched his jaw against the surge of hated memories. The vision of Jorge's pale, blue-lipped face as he slipped beneath the surface of the ocean, beyond Ramon's desperate reach.

Emily turned her palms up, imploring. 'Ramon. Please. I still don't understand.'

'I was the ringleader,' he bit out. 'And it wasn't the first time I'd led Jorge on some reckless pursuit. His parents had already spoken to mine, expressing their concern.'

She was silent. Then, 'Isn't that what all teenage boys do? Push boundaries? Do reckless things?'

Her attempt to minimise his culpability only fuelled his guilt. She'd heard only half the story. He doubted her sympathy would withstand the rest. He forced himself to go on. He just wanted it out now. Over with.

'I had a girlfriend at the time. Same age, eighteen. After Jorge's funeral, she tried to comfort me but I was in a bad place. I didn't want comfort, so I pushed her away, ended the relationship. I was blunt,' he confessed. 'Cruel, even.' He paused, emotion rising, threatening to engulf him. His throat felt hot and thick. 'She was upset. She went out with her friends and overdosed on a party drug. In the hospital, it was discovered she was five weeks' pregnant.' Shame burned his insides, hot and searing. 'She lost the child.'

'Oh... Ramon...' Emily stared up at him, her features illuminated by silvery moonlight. 'Did she know she was pregnant?'

'No.'

Emily stood up, took a step towards him. 'Which means you didn't, either.'

He frowned. 'That doesn't exonerate me.'

'Of what?' she challenged. 'Ending a relationship? That's not a crime, Ramon.'

He hardened his jaw. 'My actions were callous and ir-responsible.'

'That doesn't make you a murderer.'

'I killed my best friend and my unborn child,' he grated.

She placed her hands on his shoulders. 'You don't really believe that. *I* don't believe that. You were just a teenager.'

'I was old enough to know better. I was reckless. Care-less with the lives of the people I cared about. I hurt Jorge's family. I hurt my girlfriend's family. I hurt *my* family.'

Emily moved closer and he wanted to push her away. Urge her to protect herself. Protect their child.

From *him*.

'You're a good man, Ramon.'

'You don't know that.'

'Yes,' she argued, tilting her chin up. 'I do. When I told you I was pregnant, you could have run. You could have abandoned me. You didn't. You're standing by my side. By our child's side.'

'Don't paint me as a saint, Emily,' he warned. 'I'm not.'

'You're not a monster, either.'

He pinched the bridge of his nose and then remembered it was Xav's favourite gesture and dropped his hand.

'Come to bed,' she said, her voice soft. 'You look exhausted.'

Expelling a heavy breath, he lifted his hand and pushed a stray curl back from her face.

'That's my line,' he growled.

She smiled. Then she caught his hand, interlaced her fingers with his and led him back to the house.

The next day, by mutual agreement, they embarked on their return journey to London sooner than originally planned. Elena was disappointed, but she understood they both wanted to put Saturday's incident behind them and have some time alone to process it.

As their bags were loaded into the SUV that would take them to the airport, she drew Emily aside and embraced her in a tight hug. 'Whatever happens, you and your child— my grandchild—are now part of this family,' she said. 'You will always be welcome here.'

Emily fought hard to stem a rush of tears. In a different life, a make-believe life, she would have grown up with a kind, compassionate mother like Elena. She could only hope she'd be as good a mother to her own child. 'Thank you.'

Elena gripped Emily's arms and gave her a firm look. 'For what it's worth, I believe you and Ramon are going to be fine.'

Not wanting to burst the older woman's bubble, Emily forced a smile. Yesterday, wandering hand in hand with Ramon through the old city, talking and enjoying each other's company as they'd explored the intricate labyrinth of winding streets, she might have agreed. Today, doubt, fear and uncertainty had stripped away any fledgling sense of happiness and hope. Already she could feel an unsettling shift in Ramon, his mood when he'd woken this morning taciturn, remote.

She swallowed, her throat tight. 'How can you be so sure?'

Elena pressed her hand to Emily's cheek. 'Because my son has been running for twelve years,' she said. 'Now he has a reason to stop.'

The journey to the airport was dominated by silence, and as soon as they were in the air Ramon opened his laptop and Emily buried her nose in a magazine.

She didn't absorb a single word.

Instead, her mind replayed every line of every conversation she'd had over the weekend with Ramon and with his mother.

You have a kind, forgiving soul.

Did she? She'd never thought of herself as a particularly benevolent person before.

Her mind skipped to her father who'd been AWOL for weeks now and hadn't returned any of her calls.

Was he all right?

She snuck a glance at Ramon, still focused on his screen, and knew he'd be angry if he knew she was worrying over her father's welfare. Her tenuous relationship with Maxwell frustrated Ramon. He didn't understand why she didn't simply sever all connections with her father. She couldn't blame him. Most days she didn't understand it herself.

Where *was* Maxwell? Holed up with a woman somewhere? Deep in some gambling den, perhaps, losing whatever possessions and money he had left to his name?

A familiar feeling of despair washed over her. When it

came to winning her father's attention, she'd never stood a chance against the lure of the high life. For Maxwell, women and high-stakes poker games had proved far more appealing than the responsibilities of fatherhood.

Why had he never settled? Was he running from something? The way Ramon had been running for the last twelve years?

As soon as they'd landed and transferred from the plane to a chauffeured black sedan, Emily fished her phone from her bag. She hadn't checked for messages in more than twenty-four hours. She powered the phone on and held her breath, waiting. Praying.

Seconds later, the air left her lungs on a little exhalation of surprise.

On the screen was a text from Maxwell.

Ramon sent her a questioning look. 'Is something wrong?'

She shook her head. 'No,' she said, and slid her phone back into her bag.

Emily chose a small, quaint restaurant nestled in one of Mayfair's quiet side streets, just a few blocks from The Royce, in which to meet her father. Their phone call, three days previously, had been brief, just long enough for Maxwell to ask if she'd be willing to meet with him and for Emily to agree. He'd turned the choice of time and place over to her and told her to text him the details.

She paused outside the restaurant.

Would he turn up?

She stepped inside and Maxwell rose from a table in the rear corner, gesturing to catch her attention.

A dart of surprise shot beneath Emily's ribs. She was ten minutes early, yet he was here waiting for her.

Dry-mouthed, her hands clammy, she propelled her legs forward and made her way over.

Maxwell stayed on his feet, hands by his sides, waiting until Emily had seated herself before taking his chair again.

'You look well, Emily.'

'So do you.'

She couldn't hide her surprise. There were no hollows carved into his cheeks, no dark shadows beneath his eyes. His complexion was healthy, and the whites of his eyes weren't bloodshot. He looked as if he'd spent a month at an exclusive health spa.

'I've been in Switzerland,' he said, as if her expression had broadcasted her thoughts.

'For two months?' The query came out more sharply than she'd intended. But she'd not had a scrap of communication from him until his recent message. It wasn't unusual for him to disappear for weeks on end, but two months was the longest he'd ever gone incommunicado.

'Yes,' he said quietly. 'I was at a private rehab clinic. For gambling and…other addictions.'

Shock suspended Emily's breath. Her gaze went automatically to the table top. There was no whisky tumbler, she realised. No bottle of expensive wine. Just a carafe of water and two glasses.

A waiter approached and Maxwell raised a hand. 'Could we have ten minutes, please?'

When they were alone again, she said, 'I don't know what to say, Maxwell.'

He shook his head. 'There isn't anything you need to say. But, if you're prepared to listen, there are some things I'd like to say to you.'

Emily nodded; she didn't trust herself to speak. Her mouth was too dry, her throat too tight all of a sudden.

'I'm sorry, Emily. I know those words are inadequate,' he said, his voice thick, a little uneven. 'But I want you to know that I am sorry. For everything. You deserved better than me for a father.'

His gaze held hers and she felt as if it was the first time her father had ever looked at her.

Really looked at her.

The ache in her throat intensified. She *had* deserved better.

Silence cloaked them for a long moment.

Finally, her voice barely above a whisper, she said, 'Why? Why was it so hard to love me?'

A wretched look crossed his face. 'I wanted to. More than you'll ever know. And I thought maybe I could...after those first few years had passed. But then you started to look so much like her.' His gaze moved slowly over her face, her hair. His look of anguish deepened. 'I couldn't let myself do it. I couldn't risk that kind of pain all over again. If anything had ever happened to you...it would have been like losing Kathryn a second time.'

Her lungs locked again. 'You loved her?'

'More than anything else in this world.' His voice was raw. 'Losing her was the worst thing that's ever happened to me.'

Emily stared at him. The revelation tore through every belief she'd had about her father. 'I... I had no idea.'

A deep frown etched his brow. 'That I loved your mother?'

'How could I have known? You always refused to talk about her.'

'Because it was too painful.'

She rubbed her forehead. 'But...all the women...'

His face reddened. 'When your mother was alive, I was faithful to her, Emily. She was my soul mate. She was irreplaceable... So, after she was gone, I didn't try. I just...'

He let the sentence hang, and Emily thought she understood. He'd resigned himself to casual, meaningless flings because he didn't believe he could love again—or was too afraid to try.

She sucked in a deep breath. Then asked the question she was most afraid to ask. 'Did you blame me for her death?'

Maxwell's chin dropped, agony and shame driving his gaze away from his daughter's. 'Yes.'

The stark admission felt like an all-over body blow, as if someone had dropped her straight into the path of a speeding truck. A part of her understood the psychology of it. Grief could make people irrational. Warp their view of things. Still, it hurt. 'Do you still feel that way?'

His gaze jerked up. 'My God…no. Emily…' He shook his head. 'The fact you look so much like her is still…difficult. But no. It wasn't your fault.'

Her eyes stung, and she blinked back the tears. 'You made me feel unlovable.'

His expression was bleak. 'I don't know how to make that up to you. But I'd like a chance to try.'

'Will you tell me about her?'

'If that's what you'd like.'

Emily thought she'd like that very much.

She took a long sip of water, soothing the burn in her throat. Then she put the glass down and gave him a shaky smile. 'You're going to be a grandfather.'

Maxwell swallowed. 'So I understand. Congratulations, Emily.' He reached across the table and covered her hand briefly with his.

Emily's heart contracted.

The gesture was a long way from a hug.

But it was a start.

When Emily left the restaurant over an hour later, the black sedan and driver that Ramon had insisted she have at her disposal waited on the other side of the street for her.

The driver emerged and opened her door and she sank gratefully into the soft leather.

'Home, Ms Royce?'

'Yes. Thank you.'

Closing her eyes, she let her head fall back against the seat. Her father's unexpected attempt to connect had left her feeling quietly optimistic, but it also heightened the sense that her life was changing at a more dramatic pace than she could handle.

She looked at her watch and sighed. It was barely eight o'clock and she already craved the comfort of her bed.

A comfort she'd soon relinquish, she reminded herself with another flare of unease.

Tomorrow at ten a.m. she would meet with an interior designer at the house in Chelsea to discuss colour schemes and furnishings. Within the month, she and Ramon would be living in their new home and her beloved Wimbledon flat would be rented out to strangers.

Ramon wanted her to sell it.

Emily had refused, then enquired pointedly if he planned to sell his penthouse in Manhattan.

The stand-off had only sharpened the tension between them these last few days.

After thanking and dismissing her driver, she dragged her feet up the stairs and opened the door to her flat, relieved to be home, but also aware of a flutter of trepidation.

Ramon had been deeply unhappy about her meeting with her father and his mood before they'd left for work this morning had been dark and intractable.

Much like his mood every day since their return from Spain, she thought gloomily.

She flipped on a light and put her bag and keys on the hall table before walking through to the lounge. Darkness blanketed the room and suddenly she remembered Ramon had said he was entertaining a business associate at Citrine this evening. Her mind moving to thoughts of hot chocolate and bed, she turned on a lamp—and felt her heart lunge into her throat.

'My God! Ramon!' She clapped her hand over her breast, staring at him as he turned from the window. 'You scared me half to death. Why are you standing in the dark?'

He moved into the lamplight and Emily saw from his face that his mood had not improved from this morning. He still wore his work attire, although his tie and suit jacket had been discarded, and his shirt collar loosened. 'How was dinner with your father?'

His tone was clipped and Emily stifled a sigh. She was exhausted, her emotions drained; she couldn't talk about her conversation with her father, not right this minute, standing here in the middle of the lounge. 'Interesting,' she said, turning towards the kitchen. 'I'm making hot chocolate. Would you like some?'

'I had an interesting meeting, too.'

Reluctantly, she stopped.

'I ran into Carter,' he said.

She frowned. 'Carter…?'

'Ray.' His voice carried an edge of impatience, as though he thought she were being deliberately obtuse. 'Your lawyer.'

'Oh.'

'He offered his congratulations on our engagement and the baby.'

'That's…nice,' she said, the skin at her nape beginning to prickle.

'Asked if we knew yet if it's a boy or a girl.'

The prickling spread into her throat, then her chest, making it difficult to breathe. 'Ramon…'

'Said if we're expecting a boy,' he barrelled on, as if she hadn't spoken, 'you should notify him so he can prepare to activate your inheritance as soon as the child is born.'

Her breath stopped altogether. *Oh, God.*

He stepped forward, his jaw clenching. When he spoke again, his voice was soft. Dangerous. 'What did he mean, Emily?'

She forced herself to breathe. Told herself it wasn't a big deal. Not to her. Surely it wouldn't be to Ramon?

'There was a...a clause in my grandfather's will. A ridiculous clause,' she added. 'It bequeathed a sum of money to me if certain...stipulations were met.'

His eyes narrowed. 'What kind of stipulations?'

She swallowed, embarrassed. 'If I marry and produce a male heir by the age of thirty.'

She heard his sharp inhale.

'How much?'

'S...sorry?'

'How much money, Emily?' he snapped, and she jumped, unaccustomed to him raising his voice.

'Two million pounds,' she croaked.

'*Dios.*' For a second, incredulity wiped the anger from his face. 'And if you don't?'

'I forfeit the inheritance. The money goes to charity.' She shifted her feet under his hardening stare. 'I'm sorry I didn't tell you about it sooner, but it's not important to me, Ramon. It was my grandfather's eccentric attempt to ensure his legacy eventually passes to a male heir. I couldn't care less about that money.'

The hard gleam in his eyes remained. 'Does your father know about the clause?'

She hesitated. 'Yes.'

'And what did he want tonight?' The cynical twist of his lips made his implication shockingly clear.

She took a step back from him, her insides wrenching. '*No.*' The word burst from her, almost a shout. She gave her head a vigorous shake. 'You're wrong.'

He grasped her wrist, halting her retreat. 'Don't be naive, Emily,' he said tersely.

'I'm not being naive. You're being twisted and cynical. And unfair!' She tried to pull free but he held fast. 'You have no idea what happened between my father and me tonight.'

'Then tell me.' He tugged her close and cupped his other hand under her jaw, forcing her gaze up to his. 'Convince me he hasn't crawled out of the woodwork after two months hoping to benefit from your potential windfall.'

'That accusation is disgusting.' Her voice trembled with outrage. His scepticism cast an icy pall over her optimism. Worse, it filled her head with horrible, stomach-shredding doubts. 'My father has been in a rehab clinic for the last two months, if you must know. He's getting himself together. And yes—' she stared at him defiantly '—he wants to reconcile.'

He gave a low, grating laugh. 'Like I said, *querida*. Naive.'

His mocking tone drove a dagger of hurt into her thundering heart.

Ramon never spoke to her like this.

Not the Ramon she knew.

Not the Ramon she loved.

But he'd not been the same man since Spain, had he? The awful incident with his friend's brother had affected him on some deep level, somewhere far beyond the limit of her reach.

'I don't think this…this *mood* of yours is about my father at all,' she challenged. 'I think it's about you.'

As though she were suddenly radioactive, he released her and stepped back. 'What the hell does that mean?'

'It means you don't believe you're worthy of forgiveness, so you don't think anyone else is either.'

A savage frown furrowed his brow. 'Forgiveness must be earned, Emily.'

'Is that what you've been doing, Ramon? Earning forgiveness these last twelve years?' His expression darkened but she forged on. 'Is that why you gave up your architectural career to join the family business? Why you set your sights on The Royce? Is it all about earning brownie points so your family forgives you?'

'Emily.' His voice was a low growl.

She ignored the warning. 'Do you know what the crazy thing is? You have amazing parents who love you, but you're so busy keeping them at arm's length you haven't noticed they forgave you a long time ago.'

'Enough!' He slashed his hand through the air. 'This *is* about your father. And I forbid you to see him.'

Disbelieving laughter tore from her throat. 'You can't stop me seeing my father, Ramon.' Before he said anything else that further shredded her heart, she spun on her heel and stormed into the kitchen.

Ten seconds later, she heard the front door slam. The sound echoed through the empty flat and through her chest like the final, crippling thrust of his knife into her heart.

Ramon found a pub in the local village, wedged himself into a dimly lit corner and nursed a glass of single malt until his temper had cooled.

Dios. Why was she so stubborn? So blind? So willing to give her father yet another chance?

Maxwell was a gambler. Was it not obvious to her that he was playing an angle? Playing *her*?

Protectiveness surged, fierce and overwhelming. He believed her about the money not mattering to her. If it had, she would have wanted to know their child's sex as soon as possible, yet she had told the specialist she'd prefer to wait until the birth.

But not to question the timing of Maxwell's desire to reconcile was insanity.

Perhaps they *should* find out the baby's gender. It would

put the matter to rest. If it was a girl, and Maxwell's enthusiasm for connecting with his daughter suddenly waned, it would dispel any illusions.

And break Emily's heart at the same time.

He pushed his empty glass away and rose, regret scything through him.

He'd seen the look on her face when he had questioned Maxwell's motives. He knew the sour mood he hadn't shaken off since their disastrous weekend in Barcelona had lent his tongue a harsh, uncharacteristic edge. He'd hurt her. Which went against the grain of everything he was trying to achieve.

And then she'd lashed back.

I think it's about you.

His feet pounded the pavement, frustration congealing in his gut as he stalked the streets back to the flat. She'd seen him with his family for all of thirty-six hours and thought she understood him.

She understood nothing.

Nothing.

When he arrived, she was waiting up, sitting in the window seat she favoured for quiet reflection. Her glorious golden hair flowed loose and a pair of flannel pyjamas swamped her delectable curves. He suspected the attire was a deliberate attempt to discourage him from intimacy. It didn't work. He wanted to bundle her into his arms. Carry her to bed and make passionate love to her until the hurt and anger on her face dissolved into something else.

His desire only deepened his frustration. Intensified the sense he was waging a losing battle within himself. Every part of him felt at odds. His emotions. His instincts. His desires.

He wanted to protect her. From her father. From the world. From anything and anyone who dared to threaten the wellbeing of her and their child. But he also wanted to distance himself from her. Protect her from himself. From his inherent ability to hurt the people he loved.

And Ramon had come to suspect that what he felt for this woman was raw, terrifying, unadulterated love.

'I can't marry you, Ramon.'

He blinked, her statement skating over his thoughts, taking a moment to register. 'What?'

She uncurled from the cushions, stood and faced him. 'You told me I wouldn't have to do this alone.'

He shook his head, confused. 'You don't. I'm here, Emily.'

'Are you?' She stared at him, her eyes gigantic pools of anguished grey in her pale face. 'Because these last few days, it's felt as if you've been somewhere else. As if you've erected a wall I can't see over, or through.'

'That's not true.' His denial was abrupt. Hoarse.

'It is,' she disputed. 'And this business with my father—with the inheritance—it's all just a smokescreen for the deeper issue.'

Exasperation had him throwing up his hands. 'Not this again.'

'Yes, Ramon. *This* again. You have to forgive yourself and move on.' She took a deep breath. 'I learned something about my father tonight. He's been running for a long time. Choosing the lifestyle he has because he's afraid to love and lose again, the way he lost my mother. I think you're running too, Ramon.'

Her comparison with him to Maxwell cut to the bone. His nostrils flared. 'I'm here, Emily,' he repeated. 'I haven't run since the day you told me you were pregnant.'

'Not physically.' She stepped forward, pressing her hand against the centre of his chest. 'But in here…you're afraid. Afraid to get too close to people in case you hurt them.'

'You're talking nonsense,' he gritted out.

The look of utter sadness crossing her face sliced a

sharp, unbearable pain through his chest. She dropped her hand. 'I'm in love with you, Ramon,' she said, and the words robbed his lungs of breath. 'You're the father of my baby and you're a good man. I want to marry you, share a home, raise our child together. But I can't be with you if you're going to be emotionally distant, the way you are with your family. I—we—' she placed her hand over the gentle swell of her belly '—deserve better.'

She twisted the diamond and sapphire engagement ring off her left hand.

'Emily...'

'I've put your things in the spare room. You can stay to-night—or not. Up to you. But I want you to leave tomorrow. Take some time and decide if you're ready to stop running. Until then—' she put the ring on the coffee table '—I think you should hold onto this.'

CHAPTER TWELVE

So far Emily had waited five days, and they'd been the longest, most misery-filled days of her life.

She missed Ramon. Every hour. Every minute. Every second of every day.

The weekend had been the worst. The home she usually adored had felt cold and soulless, and even an afternoon of baking had failed to stir any joy.

And now, back in the office, seated at her desk and staring listlessly at her screen, work wasn't proving the distraction she'd hoped for either.

Her stomach churned with doubt and fear.

She'd taken an enormous risk by confessing her love to her baby's father then sending him away.

Had she made a terrible mistake?

She hadn't wanted him to stay away. She'd wanted him to go and take a long, hard look inside himself and then come back to her.

And tell her he loved her.

Because she wouldn't settle for less. For too many years she had pined for love. She couldn't waste the rest of her life pining for his. He'd always have a place in their child's life—she'd never deny her child its father—but she could not marry a man who didn't love her.

Emily's phone pinged. Shutting off her thoughts, she delved into her bag and pulled out her phone.

And froze.

Her heart climbed into her throat.

Ramon.

His message was short.

A car is waiting outside for you. See Marsha on your way out.

She frowned at the screen. He'd made her wait five days and these were the words with which he'd chosen to communicate with her first? Hands shaking, she texted back.

It's 3.30 p.m. on a Monday. I'm working.

His response was immediate.

Finish early.

Heart pounding, she chewed her lip, then forced her thumbs to work again.

Where am I going?

It's a surprise.

I don't like surprises.

Humour me.

She stared at the screen for a long moment, her tummy taut with indecision. When the phone pinged again, she jumped.

Please.

She hesitated, but her resistance was already melting, her desire to see him too powerful, too overwhelming. Releasing a pent-up breath, she fired back an 'OK'.

Outside the office, Marsha rose from her desk, her cheeks flushing pink. 'I'm sorry,' she said, holding out Emily's passport. 'He said I wasn't to warn you.'

A flicker of excitement and hope skimmed through Emily's stomach before she quickly dampened the hazardous feelings. She had no idea what he'd say to her when she saw him. She'd be a fool to allow hope to soar only then to find her heart painfully crushed.

Still, the fluttering in her stomach grew more intense during the ride to the airport. Not even the short, sharp jab of disappointment she felt when she boarded Ramon's plane and saw he wasn't there could diminish the jittery feeling of anticipation for very long.

The male flight attendant brought her an orange juice. 'It's nice to see you again, Ms Royce.'

She managed a smile. 'And you. Umm… Could you tell me where we're going, please?'

His polite expression didn't alter. 'Paris,' he said. 'We should be there in fifty-five minutes.'

By the time Emily climbed out of the back of a shiny limo in front of Saphir, her mouth was bone-dry and her palms so damp she had to repeatedly wipe them down the front of her simple black dress. A smiling concierge greeted her, escorted her inside and led her to the same lift she'd ridden with Ramon three months earlier.

She stepped in and gripped the handrail.

Only three months?

It felt like a lifetime ago.

The lift bore her swiftly upwards and when she stepped out into the penthouse, feeling breathless and a little light-headed, he was there.

Her feet stumbled to a stop.

Clean-shaven and wearing dark trousers and a pale blue open-necked shirt, he looked as vital and bone-meltingly beautiful as he had on that fateful late summer night when he'd brought her here.

Their gazes locked and she began to tremble, desire and

nervous excitement pin-wheeling through her in a potent, knee-weakening mix.

Then, abruptly, he pulled his hands from his pockets and strode towards her, his steps long and purposeful. He halted in front of her and cradled her face in his hands, and just that simple touch catapulted her senses into overdrive.

'Did you miss me, Emily?'

Oh, so much. She feigned a shrug of indifference. 'Not really.'

His eyes gleamed. 'Not at all?'

'Maybe a little bit,' she whispered.

They both faintly smiled. It was the same exchange they'd had in her kitchen more than three weeks ago when he'd returned from Paris—moments before they'd had scorching hot sex in her room.

'I missed you.' He drew his thumbs across her cheeks, lowered his forehead to hers.

Emily felt her insides melting. Felt little tendrils of hope weaving around her heart. She dropped her bag, lifted her hands and curled them over his strong, masculine wrists. 'Where have you been?'

He raised his head. 'I went back to Spain.'

'What for?'

His hands lowered, settling around her waist, drawing her close. 'I had some ghosts to lay to rest. Some people to visit.'

'Including your parents?'

'Including my parents.'

Emily's thoughts flickered to Elena and her heart swelled with gladness for the other woman. 'And did you make any discoveries?'

'A few.'

His heart pumping at a fierce pace, Ramon studied the exquisite features of the woman who had boldly declared her love for him, then sent him packing and told him not to return until he'd figured himself out.

She'd shocked him to his core. Flipped him into a brutal tailspin of anger and disbelief.

And fear. Mind-bending, gut-wrenching fear—because he'd known he couldn't lose her.

'I learned,' he said, 'that sometimes a man must confront his past before he can put it behind him.'

Soft grey eyes searched his. 'And have you?'

'*Sí, querida*. I have.'

Tears filled her eyes then and, though he had no wish to see her cry, he took them as a good sign.

'Who else did you visit?'

'Many people,' he confessed.

He had started with his old girlfriend, with whom, once he'd tracked her down, he'd had the conversation they should've had twelve years ago before he'd fled Spain. He'd found Ana in a stylish home in Madrid, married with two small children, and happy. She'd moved on and she bore Ramon no ill will. Next he'd visited Jorge's parents in Barcelona, whom he'd not seen since the funeral, and discovered they didn't share their youngest son's antipathy towards Ramon. Jorge's mother had hugged him, cried for a moment, then invited him in. Matteo, they'd said, was a troubled young man, and they'd been appalled to hear of the incident in the tapas bar.

The next day he'd gone to see his brother, and then he'd returned to his parents' villa, where, for the first time in a long time, he'd looked his mother in the eye and embraced her in a hug that had lifted her feet clean off the ground.

Finally, he'd come back to London and had a long, frank conversation with Maxwell Royce.

It'd been an intense, cathartic five days, and at some point he'd tell it all to Emily, but not now. That was the past. Right now his interest lay only in the future.

'Want to know what else I learned, *querida*?' he asked softly.

She nodded, and he reached into his pocket, pulling out the black velvet box containing her engagement ring.

'I learned that I'm tired of running...' He plucked the ring from its bed, lifted her left hand and slid the cool platinum band with its striking setting of diamonds and sapphires onto her finger. 'And that I want to be the man—the *only* man—who loves you for the rest of his life.' He pressed his lips to her knuckles. 'I love you, *mi belleza*. Will you do me the honour of becoming my wife?'

Eyes glistening, she wound her arms around his neck, her delicious curves pressing into his body. 'Yes,' she said, and a groan of relief mingled with desire tore from Ramon's throat.

Gathering her close, he claimed her mouth in a kiss that was almost savage in its intensity.

Long minutes later, when their breath-deprived lungs cried out for air, they broke apart.

Surrendering to the feverish need to stamp his possession on her in every way possible, he swung her into his arms and headed for the bedroom.

As he lowered her onto the bed, she captured his jaw in her hand and murmured, 'Why Paris?'

He laid his hand over her stomach, the small bump which he couldn't wait to see grow filling his palm. 'This is where we began. Where we created our child.' He trailed his lips along her jaw, down her neck. 'It will be a special place for us always, *si*?'

Her eyes filled again. 'I love you, Ramon.'

Fierce emotion flooded him. 'Say it again,' he demanded roughly against her throat.

Her laughter was pure. Sweet. 'I love you.' Insistent hands tugged his shirt tails from his trousers. 'Your turn,' she whispered.

He slid his hand under her dress, his questing fingers moving over heated, quivering skin. 'I love you, *mi belleza*.'

She arched under his touch.

'Show me,' she urged.

And he did.

EPILOGUE

WITH A GLASS of chilled Prosecco in her hand, Marsha slipped away from the lively gathering taking place in the big, sunny back garden of Emily and Ramon's Chelsea home and crossed the bright green lawn towards the house.

She stepped into the kitchen and her gaze fell on the home-made custard tart over which Emily was grating fresh nutmeg. 'Yum! That looks delicious.' She shifted her attention to the large kitchen table where Emily and Ramon often shared their meals instead of in the formal dining room. This afternoon, savouries and cakes and slices and tarts crowded the table's surface. 'I can't believe you did all of this yourself.'

'I had some help from my housekeeper,' Emily confided.

Marsha's eyebrows rose. 'You have a housekeeper?'

'A part-time one,' she said. 'Ramon insisted. It was either that or a nanny and I refused the latter.'

Marsha put her glass down on the bench and cast her gaze around the gorgeous designer kitchen. 'I miss you at work but I can't blame you for not rushing back.' She gave a wistful smile. 'Do you think you'll ever return?'

Emily's shrug was non-committal. 'I haven't decided yet,' she admitted, her feelings on the matter mixed. The club and her role there had been her life for so many years, and she'd expected to miss it, but she had other priorities now. Priorities that filled a void she hadn't realised existed and which meant a great deal more to her than The Royce.

A small, plaintive wail pierced the air and Emily's maternal instincts went on instant alert.

Elena de la Vega entered the kitchen, making shushing, soothing sounds to the tiny bundle in her arms. 'I think my granddaughter has already tired of her christening party,' she said to Emily, her lovely face awash with pride and pleasure as she handed over her grandchild.

Emily smiled her thanks. 'I'll feed her and settle her for a nap and then I'll be out.' She glanced at Marsha. 'Would you do me a favour and let everyone know they can help themselves to food?'

She climbed the elegant curved staircase and made her way to the light-filled nursery, an intense joy ballooning in her chest as she gazed down at her daughter.

Kathryn Georgina de la Vega—Katie, to her parents— had arrived ten weeks ago, exactly three months from the day her parents had wed in a beautiful church in Barcelona. The wedding and reception, attended by hundreds of guests, had been a larger, more elaborate affair than Emily had wanted, but the de la Vegas were a prominent family in Spain, and she'd quickly understood her hopes for a small, private ceremony were unrealistic. Plus, Elena's enthusiasm for the planning had been both irrepressible and contagious. Emily hadn't had the heart to restrain her.

She'd invited Marsha and her management team to the wedding and, to her surprise, they'd all come, but the person whose presence had mattered to Emily the most had been her father's. He'd given her away and as he'd walked her down the aisle in her stunning gown of ivory silk and French lace, cleverly styled to hide her baby bump, she'd been fairly sure she'd seen a tear shining in his eye.

Of course her relationship with her father remained a work in progress. Twenty-eight years of hurt wouldn't heal overnight. But they were moving in the right direction and even Ramon was thawing towards him, especially now the inheritance issue had been temporarily sidelined.

Emily finished nursing then drifted to the window with Katie nestled in her arms, humming the tune of the Spanish lullaby Ramon crooned to his daughter every night.

Chatter and laughter floated up from the garden, along with the squeals and shouts of their neighbours' children—Joshua and Maddie—who chased each other through the trees at the rear of the property. Amidst the clusters of people Marsha chatted with Maddie and Joshua's mother, Tamsin, who'd become a friend to Emily, while Elena, a natural-born conversationalist, talked with Marsha's boyfriend and Tamsin's husband. Seated in the shade of a large oak tree, Vittorio and her father conversed and, further away beneath a different tree, Ramon and his brother appeared deep in conversation.

Whatever they spoke about it must have been serious, for the expressions on their faces were intense.

Emily still marvelled that Xavier, an incurable workaholic, had taken time out of his demanding schedule to visit London.

Suddenly Ramon looked up and caught her eye through the glass and her breath hitched. Her husband seemed to possess a sixth sense where she was concerned; rarely did she get to observe him without his noticing.

She watched him grip his brother's shoulder, say something and then stride across the lawn towards the house. By the time he walked into the nursery, she'd settled their daughter down to sleep and returned to the window. He leaned over the cot, kissed a rosy little cheek and then moved behind his wife, sliding his arms around her middle.

She leaned her head against his shoulder, her gaze focused on the figure of his handsome, enigmatic brother, standing alone beneath the tree now. 'Is everything all right with Xav?'

Ramon kissed the top of her head. 'He's fine.'

'He doesn't look fine,' she said. 'He looks…lonely.'

Ramon gave a soft snort. 'My brother isn't lonely.'

'How do you know?'

He turned her in his arms and looked down at her. 'How

about more focus on your husband and less on his brother?'
he growled.

Emily hid a smile. Her husband's occasional displays of
jealousy always amused her. 'Fine,' she whispered, conscious of their daughter sleeping. 'Let's join our guests,
then.'

She went to move but his arms tightened, locking her
in his hold. He dropped a kiss on her mouth that stole her
breath with its tenderness, then raised his head. 'Happy?'
he queried softly.

This time she let her smile show. How could she be
anything else? She had a family, people she loved, people
who loved *her*. And she had this beautiful home that was
already filling with love, laughter and joy.

Their 'for ever' home.

She wrapped her arms around his neck and kissed him.
'Blissfully.'

* * * * *

HEIR TO A DARK INHERITANCE

MAISEY YATES

To Jackie Ashenden, my writing lifeline and lover of my dark heroes. Thank you for always encouraging me.

PROLOGUE

ALIK VASIN DOWNED the last of the vodka in his glass and waited for the buzz to make it to his brain. Nothing. It was going to take a lot more alcohol tonight. To have some fun. To feel something.

Either that, or it was going to take a woman. And since that was next on his agenda, he figured he might as well skip the alcohol.

Alik pushed away from the bar and wove through the crush of bodies on the dance floor. The music was so loud there, the bass so heavy he could feel it in his blood. There would be no way to have a conversation with anyone in here. Which was fine by him. He wasn't looking for a talk.

It didn't take long for him to spot a woman who wasn't looking to talk, either.

He approached the blonde skirting the edges of the dance floor. She smiled. Ah yes, he'd found the evening's entertainment. No doubt about it.

He moved closer and she extended her hand, her fingers brushing his chest. Forward. He liked that. She might even be the kind who wouldn't want to wait to get to the hotel room.

His pocket buzzed and he reached inside and wrapped his hand around his phone. In his experience, women didn't like being thrown over for a phone call, but if his checking it chased her off, another one would come along in just a few moments. If he didn't want to go to bed alone tonight, he wouldn't.

He took the phone from his pocket and saw a number he didn't recognize. Anyone who managed to contact him from a number he didn't know was important.

He held his finger up, an indicator he wanted the woman to wait. She might. She might not. He didn't really care.

He answered the call just before pushing the door open and put the phone up to his ear as he stepped out onto a crowded street in downtown Brussels. A group of women walked by and offered him inviting looks. He might keep an eye out for which club they went to, rather than going back to the blonde waiting for him inside.

He put the phone up to his ear. "Vasin."

And suddenly the cobblestones didn't feel so steady under his feet. He had to wonder if the vodka had finally started working. If it was the cause of the buildings appearing to close in around him. Of the tightness in his chest. If it was making him hear things. If he was imagining what the woman on the other end of the line was saying.

But no. He wasn't. Yes, he was Alik Vasin. Yes, he had been in that region of the United States more than a year earlier.

He stood still for a moment, waited for the earth to right itself beneath his feet. Everything fell away in pieces. The clubs. The women. And he could no longer remember why he was there, on a dark street in Brussels.

There was only the phone call.

Adrenaline shot through his veins. The jolt he'd been missing all night. He would not freeze up. He was not that kind of man. He acted.

Alik hung up and stuffed his hands in his pockets, walking quickly away from the club, his steps heavy and loud on the cobblestone. He had to get to the airport. Had to get to a lab so he could get confirmation.

He took his phone out of his pocket, searching for Sayid's number. His friend would know what to say. Would know what to tell him.

Because it wasn't the vodka. It was just the truth. He knew it, deep in his bones.

He was a father.

CHAPTER ONE

"DID YOU REALLY THINK you could keep my child from me?"

Jada stopped on the courthouse steps, the hair on her arms standing on end, the back of her neck prickling with cold sweat. It was the voice of her most dreaded nightmare. A voice she'd never heard before outside of her dreams, and yet she knew that it was him.

Alik Vasin.

A stranger. The man with the power to come in and rip the beating heart from her chest if he chose to do so. The man with the power to devastate her life.

The father of her daughter.

"I don't know what you're talking about," Jada said, inching up the stairs that led to the courthouse. But she knew. She absolutely knew, and apparently he did, too.

"You had the court date changed."

"I had to change it," she said, defiant, confident in her lie. It didn't feel wrong, or even like a lie, not when she'd told it to protect her child. Jada had spent her life behaving, following the rules, but there were no rules for this situation. There was no right, no wrong. There was only need. The need to keep Leena with her.

"And you thought that since I had to travel halfway around the world on short notice, I would be forced to miss it. Too bad for you I have a private jet."

He didn't look like the kind of man who owned a private

jet. He didn't look like a man ready for a court hearing. He was wearing low-slung jeans, held onto his lean hips with a thick belt. He had a rumpled button-up shirt on that somehow looked all the better for being wrinkled, the sleeves pushed up past his elbows, revealing muscular forearms. And aviator sunglasses. Like he was some sort of rock star or something.

He turned his hand and adjusted the buckle on his watch, revealing a dark tattoo, an anchor, on the underside of his wrist. She wondered, briefly, how much something like that had hurt. She wondered what it said about him. He was danger personified, and just looking at him made a shiver course through her body.

On the plus side, his blatant lack of regard for convention made her feel more and more confident about her chances. She'd had Leena in her custody for a year, after all. And this man, her father, had no claim on her beyond the genetic.

Blood was certainly thicker than water, but dirty diapers trumped blood. And she had changed more than her share of those over the past year.

He looked at his watch. "Looks like I've made it with time to spare. I'll be back in a moment."

"Don't rush," Jada said. She took a seat in one of the chairs that lined the door outside of the family courtroom. She wished she could hold Leena right now, but Leena was with the social worker. Jada's arms felt empty. She picked her purse up from the floor, her phone out of one of the pockets, opened an app and played it mindlessly. She just needed to keep her hands busy. And her mind vacant.

"Good. I didn't miss anything."

She looked up and a swear word rushed out of her mouth. He looked…it wasn't fair how he looked. He was in a black suit, open at the collar, everything fitted perfectly to his well-muscled physique. The dark fabric poured over him like liquid, flowing with his movements, revealing strength, power. He looked like the sort of man who got what he wanted with the snap of a finger. The kind of man who had women falling at his feet with a glance.

He'd gone from rumpled traveler to James Flipping Bond in ten seconds flat.

Although, Bond was always fighting the Russians, so maybe he was more of a Bond villain.

"I see you decided to dress for the occasion," she said.

He'd removed the sunglasses, and for the first time she could see his eyes. They were somewhere between blue and gray, like the sea during a storm.

"It seemed the thing to do," he said, his lips quirking up into a smile. He seemed entirely unruffled, as if the outcome of this didn't matter to him at all. It meant everything to her. This, Leena, was her entire life. All she had left.

"It seemed the thing to do? Well, I suppose it's good that going out for Chinese food didn't seem the thing to do at the moment instead. Is that all she is to you? Just...is this just an experiment for you? Why did you even bother to show up?"

"She's my daughter," he said, his tone betraying no emotion, no concern. Just stating a fact. "That means I must claim responsibility for her."

"Responsibility? Is that what she is to you?"

She caught a hint of steel in his eyes. "She's my blood. Not yours."

Jada snorted and crossed her arms beneath her breasts. "I've only raised her from the time she was born. What do I matter?" She didn't know where this strength was coming from. She only knew she had it, and she had to use it. There was no one standing behind her. No one on her side. No one but herself.

"I didn't know about her," he said.

"Because her mother thought you were dead. And why did she think that? Did you tell her you were going off on some secret mission? That's the sort of thing a man like you might say to get a woman into bed."

"If I told her that, it was true," he said.

She blinked. "If? You don't remember?"

He shrugged. "Not specifically."

And then her brain caught up with the rest of his claim. "And you *were* on a mission of some kind?"

"How old is the child?"

Jada blinked. "You don't know?"

"I know nothing about this," he said. "I got a phone call while I was in Brussels, telling me that if I didn't come and claim a child I didn't know I had by a certain date, I would lose my rights to her forever. Then I went and got testing done to confirm that I am in fact the father, and I am, just so you know. Then yesterday I got a letter saying my parental rights would be terminated and she would be adopted to someone else if I failed to come to a hearing that had been moved to today."

"She's one. She just had her birthday." Just the two of them in Jada's little house, on the same street where she'd lived for eight years. "Where were you a little over a year and a half ago?"

His mouth twitched. "Near here. I was in Portland seeing to some business."

She put her hands on her hips. "Ah. Business."

"I can't talk about the exact nature of it."

Disgust filled her. He was the sort of man she'd been blessed never to have had any interaction with. She'd married too young and her husband had been completely decent. She didn't think men like this, men who bed-hopped with zero discrimination, were real outside of terrible movies. "I can guess. I've been caring for the results of that *business*."

One brow shot upward. "Just an added bonus to my trip. I'm not a sex tourist."

Jada blinked, heat rushing into her cheeks. "You are direct, aren't you?"

"And you are prickly. And extremely judgmental."

And not accustomed to people who were so comfortable talking about their bad behavior. He seemed to wear it like a badge of honor. "You're here to take my child from me— what reaction did you want me to have to you?"

He looked at their surroundings. They were the only two people in the antechamber. "I didn't anticipate being stuck in the lobby with you, I have to say."

"And yet you are. Answer me this…what does a man who travels the world, doing Lord knows what, want with a baby? Do you have a wife?" She hoped not, all things considered.

"No."

"Other children?"

"Not as far as I know," he said, a smile that could only be described as naughty curving his lips. "Clearly these things can surprise you."

"Not most people, Mr. Vasin," she bit out. "So, why do you want her?"

It was a good question. One Alik didn't know the answer to. All he knew was that if he turned and walked away, if he never met her, never made sure she was cared for, if he left her to fight her way through life as he'd had to do, then there would officially be no hell hot enough for him.

Forgetting about the phone call had crossed his mind. Not making it to the hearing had crossed his mind. But with each thought had come a twinge in his chest, a brand on a conscience he hadn't known he'd possessed.

He didn't particularly want her. But no matter what, he found he couldn't leave, either.

He gave the only answer he had. "Because she is mine."

"Hardly a good reason."

"Why do *you* want her so badly, Ms. Patel?" he asked, returning her formality. "She is not your child, no matter how you feel."

"Is that so? Blood relation, even to a stranger, is more

important than the care that's been given? Is that how you see it?"

Alik looked down at the woman in front of him, all fire and passion. Beautiful, and if it was any other situation, his thoughts might have turned to seduction. Black, glossy hair, golden skin and honey-colored eyes, combined with a petite and perfect figure, made her a very tempting package.

Though, at the moment she was also a dangerous one. She was tiny, barely reaching the middle of his chest and yet she did not fear him. She seemed ready to physically attack him if need be.

Not in the way he would like, he imagined.

"It is not an emotional matter," he said. "It is black-and-white in my eyes. I am her father. You are not her mother."

She drew back, a cobra preparing to strike. "How dare you?"

"Mr. Vasin? Ms. Patel?" A small woman in a black jacket and slacks opened the door and poked her head out. "We're ready for you both."

As Mr. Vasin is here and clearly of sound mind, and, having submitted to a paternity test, has proven to be the father, we have no reason not to release his child into his custody.

Jada replayed the last ten minutes of the hearing in her mind, over and over again. The judge was sorry, the caseworkers regretful. But there was simply no reason why Leena shouldn't be with her father. Her *billionaire* father, as it turned out, which she knew had bearing on the ruling regardless of what anyone said.

How could it not? Jada was a housewife with no spouse to support her. Her only source of income came from her late husband's life insurance settlement and as generous as it was, it wasn't a billion dollars.

That, combined with the irrefutable proof of his paternity, when it was made clear that he had been wronged, the victim of a misunderstanding, had meant Jada hadn't had a case. Not in anyone else's mind. In hers, she had the only case that mattered. But no one else cared.

And now, Leena was with this Alik Vasin, in a private room so the two of them could get to know each other. Have an introduction. They couldn't let Jada take Leena with her. She was a flight risk. Another thing everyone was very regretful about.

Jada leaned against the wall in the empty hallway and gasped for breath. No matter how much air she took in she was still suffocating. Her chest was locked tight, and she tried to breathe in, but her lungs wouldn't expand. She wondered if her heart had stopped beating, too.

Her knees shook, gave way, and she slid down the wall, sitting with her legs drawn up to her chest, not caring that she was in a skirt, not caring if anyone saw. She hated that this feeling was so familiar. That it slipped back on as easy as an old pair of jeans. Shock. Grief. Loss.

Losing Sunil had been hard enough. Unfair. Unexpected. No one planned to be a widow at twenty-five. Coming to terms with it, with being alone, when she'd leaned on her parents, and then her husband, for all of her life, had been the hardest thing she'd ever gone through. She was still going through it.

Losing Leena on top of it…it wasn't fair. How much was one person expected to lose? How long before she was simply gutted, left empty, with nothing and no one to care for her? No one to care for. And then what was she supposed to do with herself?

Her shoulders shook and a sob worked its way up her throat, her body shuddering with the force of it. People were walking by, trying not to stare at her as she dissolved, utterly and completely, in the hall of the courthouse.

And she didn't care. What did it matter if a bunch of strangers thought she was losing her mind? She might very well be. And if they felt uncomfortable being in the presence of her grief, she didn't care. It was nothing compared to trying to live inside her body. Nothing compared to contending with the pain she was dealing with.

"Ms. Patel." That voice again.

She looked up from her position on the floor, and saw the man, the man who had taken her baby from her. There was only one thing that stopped her from going for his throat. Only one thing stopping her from opening her purse, finding her mace and unleashing her fury on those stormy gray eyes.

Leena.

He was holding a squirming Leena in his arms. And she was squirming to try to get to Jada. She could only stare at her daughter for a moment, hungry to take in every detail. To remember every bit of her.

Jada scrambled to her feet and extended her arms. Leena leaned away from Alik's body, and he had no choice but to deposit the fussing, wiggling child into her arms.

Jada clung to her daughter, and Leena clung to her. Jada closed her eyes and pressed her face into her daughter's silky brown hair, inhaled her scent. Lavender shampoo and that sweet, wonderful smell unique to babies.

She didn't feel like she was drowning now. She could breathe again, her heart finding its rhythm.

"Mama!" Leena's exclamation, so filled with joy and relief. And Jada broke to pieces inside.

"It's okay," she whispered, more for her benefit than her daughter's. "It's okay." And she knew she lied. But she needed the lie like air and she wouldn't deny herself.

"She does not like me," Alik said, his voice frayed. For the first time since she'd seen him, he was betraying his own discomfort with the situation.

"You're a stranger," she said.

"I'm her father." He said it as if a one-year-old child cared about genetics.

"She doesn't care if you're related to her or not. Not in the least. I am her mother as far as she's concerned. The only mother she knows."

"We need to talk."

"What about?"

"About this," he said, his voice slightly ragged, a bit of that smooth charm of his finally slipping. "About what we need to do."

She didn't know what he meant, but she knew that right now she was holding Leena, so the rest didn't matter.

"Where?" she asked.

"My car. It is fitted with a car seat."

"Okay," she said. Going with him should feel strange; after all, she didn't know the man. But the court had found no reason he couldn't be a fit father. That meant they were going to send her baby off with this man, by herself. So she was hardly going to hesitate over getting in his car with him, all things considered.

She swallowed hard. There was no one else to do this. She was the final authority here, the only one who could change things. And she would take every second with Leena she could get.

She followed him out of the courthouse and down the steps. He pulled out his phone and spoke into it. She wasn't sure what language he was speaking. It wasn't Russian, English or Hindi, that much she knew. A man of many talents, it seemed.

A moment later a black limousine pulled up against the curb and Alik leaned over, opening the back door. "Why don't you get her settled."

She complied mutely, putting Leena, who was starting to nod off after her traumatic afternoon, into the seat and then climbing in and sitting in the spot next to hers. She hadn't wanted to take any chances that he might drive off while she was rounding the car. Paranoid, maybe, but there was no such thing as too paranoid in a situation like this.

She was momentarily awed by the luxuriousness of the car. She'd ridden in a limo after her wedding, but it hadn't been anywhere near this nice. The seats lined the interior of the limo, leaving the middle open. There was a cooler with champagne in it.

That made her bristle. Had he been planning on celebrating his victory over champagne? A toast to stealing her child away? She wanted to hit him. To hurt him. Give him a taste of what she was dealing with.

"What is it you wanted to speak to me about?" she asked, her voice sharper than she intended.

He closed the door behind him and settled into place. "Drink?"

"No. No drink. What is it you wanted to talk about?"

"How did you meet the child's mother?"

"Leena," she bit out. "Her name is Leena."

"What sort of name is that?"

"Hindi. She's named for my mother."

"She should have a Russian name. I'm Russian."

"And I'm Indian, and she's my daughter. And really, aren't you some kind of arrogant, thinking you can come and just take my child away from her home, away from her mother and then, on top of it all rename her?"

His dark brows shot upward. "I will not rename her. It is not a bad name."

"Thank you," she said, cursing her own good manners. She shouldn't be thanking him. She should be macing him.

"Now," he said, straightening, his posture stiff, like he was about to start a business meeting, "how did you meet Leena's mother?"

"Just…through an adoption agency. She told me the baby's father was dead and that she couldn't possibly raise the child on her own. It was a semi-open adoption. She was able to choose the person she wanted to take her. It wasn't easy for her." She remembered the way the other woman had looked after giving birth, when she'd handed Leena to Jada. She'd looked so tired. So sad. But also relieved. "But it was right for her."

"And the adoption?"

"Normally they're finalized within six months of placement. In Oregon the birth mother can't sign the papers until after the birth, which makes it all take a bit longer. And we were held up further because…because while she listed the birth father as dead, it wasn't something that was confirmed. She had your name, but there was no record of your death, and neither could you be found to sign away your rights. And it hadn't been long enough for you to simply be declared absentee."

"And then they found me."

"Yes, they did. Lucky me."

"I am sorry for you, Jada. I am." He didn't sound it at all. He sounded like a man doing a decent impression of someone who might be sorry, but he personally didn't sound sorry at all. "But it doesn't change the fact that Leena is my daughter. I can't simply walk away from her."

"Why not? Because you're just overcome by love and a parental bond?" She didn't believe that for a moment.

"No. Because it is the right thing to do to care for your children, your family. Leena is the only family I have."

At another time she might have felt sorry for the man. As it was, she felt nothing.

"Caring for her would mean having her with me," she said.

"I can understand how you might see it that way." He looked out the window. "She does not like me. She cries when I pick her up. And frankly, I don't have the time to be a full-time caregiver to an infant."

"Then why did you come?"

"Because the other alternative was having nothing to do with her, and that was not a possible solution in my mind."

"So what does that mean then? You're just going to hire nannies?"

"That was my thought. I was wondering if you would like to take a position as Leena's nanny."

"You what?"

Jada couldn't believe the man was serious. The nanny? To her own child? An employee of the man who was stealing everything from her?

Leena was her light in the darkness. She was everything to her. Being her mother had become the entirety of Jada's identity. And her daughter had become her whole heart.

And he wanted her to be an employee. One he could fire at a moment's notice. A termination he could delay until a later date. A date he saw fit.

"Did you just ask me to be the nanny to my own daughter?"

"As a court ruling just declared, she is not your daughter."

"If you say that one more time so help me I will—"

"It is up to you. Hang on to your pride if you wish, but I'm offering you a chance to see your daughter. To be a part of her life still."

"How can you do this to me?" she asked, the words scraping her throat raw. Everything in her hurt. Everything. He had come in, taken her newly repaired life and shattered it all around her again, and she didn't know how she would reclaim it. It had taken so long to rebuild, to repurpose, to find out what she would do, who she would be.

She'd loved her husband, but he couldn't give her children. And every time other options came up, he shut down. It was a reminder, he'd told her, of all he could not give her. Of what she would have to get from someone else. No, there would be no artificial insemination. She wouldn't carry another man's baby. Adoption had been something he'd said they'd consider, but he never truly had. All the brochures she brought him, all the links to websites she sent him, went ignored.

When the dust had settled after her husband's death, it had been the thing she'd latched onto. She wasn't a wife anymore, but she could be a mother.

And now he was ripping it from her hands. Leaving her arms empty.

"I'm not doing anything to you. Leena is my child and I am claiming her, as is the responsible and right thing to do."

"You have a warped sense of right, Mr. Vasin."

"Alik," he said. "You can call me Alik. And my sense of right seems to match that of the justice system, so one might argue that it is you with a warped sense of justice."

She blinked. "My sense of justice involves the heart, not just laws written on paper, unconnected to specific people and events."

"And that is where we differ. Nothing I do involves the heart." She looked at his eyes, black, soulless. Except for that moment in the courthouse when he'd been holding Leena. Then there had been emotion. Fear. Uncertainty. A man who clearly knew nothing about children.

And he wanted her to be the nanny. He wanted to assume the position as Leena's father and demote her to staff. This man who had been living his life, a full complete life apart from Leena, now wanted to come and take the heart from her.

"She's all I have," Jada said, her voice trembling, emotion betraying her now "All I have in the world."

"So you say no because of pride?"

"And because I am not my child's nanny! I am her mother. The idea of simply being treated as though I'm paid to be there..." It hit at her very identity, who she was. She had been Sunil's wife, and then she had become Leena's mother. She couldn't be nothing again. Not again.

"I would pay you to be there. I can hardly ask you to forfeit whatever job you might have and come be her nanny for free now, can I?"

"How can you..."

"I will of course allow you to live in whatever house I install her in. It will be simpler that way for all involved. I have a penthouse in Paris and one in Barcelona. A town house in New York, though I suspect you would find it rather too busy...."

"And what about you? Where will you be in all of this?"

He shrugged. "I will go on as I have. But you have no need to worry about Leena. As the judge pointed out when he opened up my file—I am a wealthy man."

"Somehow all of your wealth and power doesn't impress me very much, not when your idea of raising a child is to install her in a house somewhere in the world while you leave her with staff!"

"Not just any staff. You. You would be very well-trusted staff."

"You bastard!" No. She wouldn't do it. She couldn't do it. Couldn't allow this man who didn't even want to live in the same home as his daughter to come in and steal everything she had built for herself. For Leena.

"No," she said, the word broken, just like everything inside of her.

"Excuse me?"

"No. Stop the car."

She didn't know what she was doing. Until the moment the car pulled up to the curb and she looked at Leena, and back at Alik. She thought again of the fear in his eyes as he'd held Leena at the courthouse. Of the way Leena had struggled to escape his arms.

And she knew.

"No." She opened the door to the car. "I am her mother. You can't simply demand a change of job title. If you think you're her father because of a magical blood bond then you go and you take care of her."

Her heart was in her throat, her stomach pitching violently. But it was her hope. Her only hope. And it was all born out of some insane idea that what she'd witnessed in this hard, inscrutable man's eyes was truly fear.

And if she was misreading him, there was every chance she would lose her child forever.

But if you don't, he'll always have the power. He has to know that you're right. That he needs you.

She closed the door to the limo, the gray sky reflected in the tinted windows, obscuring Alik, obscuring Leena, from view. Panic clawed at her, tore her to shreds inside.

She turned away and closed her eyes, trying to breathe. She couldn't. A sob caught in her chest. And then Jada started walking away. And she just prayed that Alik would follow.

CHAPTER TWO

ALIK HAD FACED DOWN terrorists hell-bent on blowing him into pieces and scattering his remains in the ocean. He'd dogged his way across enemy lines, into an enemy camp, to save the life of a friend. He'd spent hours calculating tactical strategies for nations at war, finding the smart way to get in and win the battle.

None of it had shaken him. A welcome burst of adrenaline, the rush of having survived, he got all of that from it. But never fear.

He felt it now. Staring down into the dewy eyes of his child. Her little face crumpled and she let out a wail that filled the inside of the limo.

"Don't go yet," he said to his driver. "Don't go."

Leena cried, louder and louder, and Alik had no idea what he was expected to do. He looked out the window, and he didn't see Jada. She was gone. Somewhere into the shopping center they were near, he imagined, but he didn't know where.

Unless she'd hailed a cab and simply left them both. It didn't seem like something she would do, but he admitted, willingly, he knew nothing about emotion. About mothers who stayed with their children.

Jada wasn't even Leena's mother. But he was her father.

He didn't know how to comfort a child. He didn't have a clue as to how to go about it. No one had held him. No one had sung him songs or rocked him until he stopped crying. It was very possible he had never cried.

Leena on the other hand, did. Quite well.

He had always intended to hire a nanny, and when he'd gone out into the hall he'd felt, for the first time in his memory, like he was in a situation he could not control. And when he had seen Jada slumped against the wall, crying into her hands, he knew he'd found the solution.

But then she'd left. She wanted more, and he had no idea what more it was she wanted.

Alik had given up on emotion long ago. His body had put all of that into a deep freeze, protecting him from the worst of his experiences while growing up. And by the time he hadn't needed the protection anymore, it was far too late for anything to thaw.

He experienced things through the physical. Sex and alcohol, and, in his youth, various other stimulants, had done a good job of providing him with sensation where the frozen organ in his chest simply did not.

It was how things were for him. It was convenient too, because when he had to carry out a mission that was less than savory, whether on the battlefield, as he'd once done, or in the boardroom, as he did now, he simply went to his mind. Logic always won.

And after that, there was always a party to go to. He'd learned how to manufacture happiness from his surroundings. To pull it into the darkness that seemed to dominate his insides and light the way with it, temporarily. A night of dancing, drinking and sex. It created a flash, a spark in the oppressive dark. It burned out as quickly as it ignited, but it was a hell of a lot better than endless blackness.

Except he didn't feel vacant now. He felt panicked, and he found it wasn't an improvement. Without thinking, he undid Leena's seat and pulled her into his lap. She shrieked and jerked away from him, and with that came a punch of something—emotion, pain—to his chest that nearly knocked him back.

As afraid as he was, she was just as scared. Of him.

"Mama! Mama mama mama." The word, just sounds really, came fast and furious, over and over, intermingled with sobs.

He tried to speak. To say something. But he had no idea what to say. What did you say to a screaming baby? He'd never wanted this. Never imagined it. He truly might have turned away if not for Sayid. If not for the conversation they'd had when he'd left Brussels.

"You have to claim her, Alik. She is your responsibility. You have so many resources at your disposal, so many things you can provide her with. She is your blood, your family."

"I have family without blood," Alik had said, a reference to Sayid's family, to whom he had sworn absolute allegiance.

"A family by choice. She is your family. You are bound to her. To dishonor something so strong would be a mistake."

"No, my only mistake was coming here for the weekend instead of heading down to Paris or Barcelona to get laid."

"Running is your specialty, Alik," Sayid had said, his tone deathly serious. "But you can't change what is by running. Not this time."

His friend was right. Alik lived his whole life moving at a dead run. But he was never running *from* something. Nothing scared him that much. But he wasn't really running to something, either. He was simply getting through as quickly, as loudly and recklessly, as possible.

He found it was the loud and reckless things in life that offered the most return in terms of what they made him feel. And he was hungry for feeling. For tastes of what years of existing in survival mode had denied him.

Maybe that, more than Sayid's comments, had been the deciding factor in why he'd come. That or watching the other man's life, watching all of the change it had brought about for Sayid to acquire a wife and children.

Either way, when he'd decided to come after his daughter, he hadn't made the decisions hesitantly or lightly. No, there had been no instant bond between them, but he had hardly expected that. Alik had never bonded to people instantly. Sometimes he simply never did.

Sayid was the exception, and then later, Sayid's family. But he'd been twenty-eight when he'd met his friend, who was more a brother to him than anything else, and it had been his first experience of caring for another human being.

It still didn't come easily to him. But swearing his allegiance? That came as simply as seeing whose name was on the check. It always had for him. Even now that he'd moved into the business of tactical, cutthroat corporate raider, rather than tactical, cutthroat mercenary and overthrower of governments, that fact remained true.

His loyalty could be bought, and once he was purchased, he would defend those he was loyal to till death if he had to. And then, when the job was done, he would break the bonds as easily as they'd been forged.

Again, Sayid was the exception. A job gone wrong, turned into a rescue mission to save the life of the sheikh, even when everyone else had given up, had made their bond unbreakable.

He would simply choose to cultivate that bond with his child. She had bought his loyalty with her blood, a check that could never simply be cashed, could never just disappear.

That meant, no matter what, he would defend her. Fight for her, die for her.

Or pound the streets as long as it took, looking for the woman she called mama.

"I will protect you," he said to her, looking at her red, tear-streaked face. "That is my promise."

His daughter was unimpressed with the vow.

He pushed the door to the limo open. "Wait here," he said to his driver.

He got out, holding Leena, who was squirming and screeching against his chest. People were staring at him, at them. He was used to being able to fly under the radar when he wanted to. Used to making a scene only when he wanted to. But he had no control over this scene.

How a tiny child could assume total control over things with the ease most people breathed astounded him. He walked down the sidewalk, cursing the rain, and the knots of kids in skinny jeans smoking cigarettes and blocking his way.

Cursing his total lack of control.

There was a clothing store, a pizza place and a coffeehouse along the main drag of the shopping center, and he was willing to bet that Jada hadn't gone far.

He pushed open the door to the coffee place and saw her there, clutching a mug in both of her hands, looking ashen and in shock.

He crossed the coffee shop, wiggling baby attempting to impede his progress, and stopped in front of her table.

"Tell me then, Jada Patel, if you do not take the position as my nanny, what will you do?"

She looked at him, the relief that washed over her so strong it was tangible. And yet she didn't move to take the baby from his arms. Didn't try to relieve him.

She didn't respond. She simply looked at him with eyes that conveyed a depth of emotion he hadn't known was possible to feel.

"You don't seem to have a very strong sense of self-preservation," he said, shifting the baby in his arms. "I have offered you a chance to come and live with my daughter, to continue caring for her. You've as much as admitted that you have nothing here if you don't get to keep her. You have no husband. No girlfriend or other sort of lover, obviously. They would have come to the hearing with you, offered support."

She looked down into her coffee mug. "No. I don't have a husband."

"Then you have nothing to leave behind."

She looked away, her eyes glassy, reflecting the gray sky outside the coffee shop's window. "Leaving here isn't the problem." She looked back at him. "What assurance do I have that you won't simply fire me one day? Cast me out onto the street without any warning some day five years down the road and put me in the position of losing her then? I couldn't bear it. I can't bear it now, so part of me wants to take the chance, but I am giving you all of my power, the power over my life if I take the position, and I don't like it at all."

"I don't blame you. I wouldn't like it, either, and yet I see very little in the way of other options."

Jada fought the panic that was rising inside her. Panicking wasn't going to help. She had to think. Had to figure out what to do.

She wished, so desperately, that there was someone she could ask. Her friends…she could hardly stand to be around them. They just looked at her with sad eyes, touched her like they were afraid she was cracking, breaking like a piece of delicate glass. And they'd all thought her crazy when she'd decided to adopt.

Her parents had been gone for so long now. Her father when she was a teenager, her mother six years after that.

And then there was Sunil. She would have turned to him, would have asked him what to do. After he'd died, she'd felt like she was drifting. Unable to think, unable to make a decision. The only thing that had gotten her out of bed every day was the knowledge that he would have wanted her to. He would have told her that there would be something else for her. Something good. And while he hadn't been enthusiastic about adoption during their marriage, she knew he wouldn't have wanted her to be alone.

The something good she'd been waiting for was Leena.

From the moment she'd seen Leena, tiny and pink, swaddled in a blanket with her hospital cap fitted snugly over her mop of brown hair, Jada had known she would give her life for her daughter.

Becoming Leena's nanny wasn't even close to giving up her life. But it wasn't the thought of leaving home that frightened her. She had no home without Leena anyway. It was the fact that, at Alik's pleasure, at his whim, he could still tear her daughter away from her at any moment.

She would have no parental rights. She would be nothing more than hired help, waiting for the ax to fall. Loss, when it came suddenly, was hideous. But living her life knowing that any day could bring it would be unbearable.

"So what you need is more security?" he asked. "Something that would feel legal and permanent?"

"Yes, something that would feel more stable, so that I wasn't wondering if you were simply going to sweep through one day and decide I was no longer needed."

She looked at him, into those stormy gray eyes, and a shiver ran through her body. He had a kind of easy grace, a relaxed posture that made him look like he was at ease with the world, with his surroundings.

But what she saw in his eyes just then proved that he was lying to the world. He was ice beneath the exterior.

"You are the kind of woman," he said, "who would never sell her allegiance." The way he said it, with a mix of wonder and admiration, surprised her. "You remind me of someone I know."

"That's all very well and good, but it doesn't solve my problems."

"And I now live to solve your problems?"

"I think we both can see that no matter how tough you play, you have no idea of what you're doing with a child."

"I can hire someone else."

"And you think that would make her happy? Does she not notice when I'm gone?"

That hit him. Square in the chest. A strong, sudden burning of loss. He'd been two or three when he'd been left at an orphanage in Moscow. He didn't remember his mother's face. Or her voice. Or where he'd lived before then. But he remembered loss. Loss so deep, so confusing and painful.

"She would notice," he said, because there was no lying about that. Something had to be done. He knew now he stood in a terrible position. That of abandoning his child, or tearing his child away from the only woman she'd ever known as her mother.

He was trapped.

"You need to come up with a solution we can both be satisfied with."

Jada didn't know how she'd kept from bursting into tears. She was on the edge of breaking completely. But she had to be strong. She had to show Alik that he wasn't in charge. She had to take back control somehow.

This was her life. The life she was creating for herself, and he didn't get to own it. She'd had enough of being jerked around by fate or whatever it was that had reached down and disordered everything. She was done with that. Done with feeling like a victim. Done with allowing life to make her one.

Alik looked down at Leena, his discomfort obvious, then looked back at Jada.

"What do you need?" he asked, his voice frayed, his expression that of a desperate man.

"I need security," she said. "I need to be her mother, because no matter whether you understand it or not, that's what I am, and that's what a child needs. A mother, not a caregiver, not an absentee father. Someone who is there with her. Always."

He looked at her for a moment, black eyes completely

unreadable, his handsome face schooled into a mask. "You think something of permanence would be best for Leena."

"Yes."

He nodded slowly. "I may have a solution to your problems. You don't like the idea of my simply...how did you put it? Dumping my child off somewhere in the world with nothing but staff. You think she should have a family, a real family."

"Everyone should."

"Perhaps, but it is not reality. Still, if I could find a way to make that happen for her...having a family is very important, yes?"

Jada nodded, her throat tightening. "Yes."

"I would hate to deny my child anything of importance."

She wanted to scream at him that he was denying his child her mother, and yet she knew it would do no good. He simply didn't seem to understand the connection she felt for Leena. He didn't seem to understand love. And losing control wouldn't win this battle. When he pushed, she had to push back.

"Perhaps then, I should take a wife," he said.

Pain crashed through her. He still didn't get it.

The thought of another woman filling her position, of another woman being the caregiver for her daughter, made her see red. And she knew that was selfish, and she didn't care.

"That easily?" she asked. "That easily you'll just find a wife? One who will care for Leena like she's her own child?"

"I've already found her," he said, gray eyes fixed on her.

She felt the chill from his eyes seep through her skin, making her tremble. "Have you?" she asked, not sure what he was going to say, only that she wasn't going to like it. Only that it was going to change everything.

"You didn't like my offer of coming to be my nanny. Would you like to be my wife?"

CHAPTER THREE

"Do I want to be your...wife?"

He'd said it so casually, so utterly void of emotion that she was certain she must have misheard him.

"Yes," he said. "As you've made it clear, my offer of nanny is unacceptable. And you are right—without you, the child is unhappy."

"Leena," she bit out again, frustrated by his insistence on detachment.

"I know her name." He bent and handed her Leena, a rush of love washing over her as she felt her daughter's weight in her arms. He started to pace beside the table in front of her. "It's a simple thing, one that will protect both us and my daughter legally. You will be able to adopt her and, should we divorce, which I have no doubt we will, unless we find each other so unobtrusive that the marriage simply never gets in our way, we will be able to work out a shared custody agreement."

"I...it is *possible* for an unmarried couple to work out an adoption. It's more difficult...there needs to be a clear emotional involvement, but..."

"And why make it more difficult? This will be much more simple. Proving a legal connection is much simpler than faking an emotional one, don't you think?"

Yes, she did think. She was sure he was right. It would protect her. It would make her Leena's mother. It would give her the adoption she wanted. But…but there was this man, this stranger. And he was asking to be her husband.

For the second time in her life, everything had changed in one day. She tried, she tried desperately, not to remember the day three years ago when she'd gotten a call from Sunil's office saying he had been sent to the hospital.

Tried not to remember what it had been like, driving there, feeling shocked, dazed. Then seeing him in the bed. He'd looked so sick. Like he was a man barely clinging to life.

Because that was what he had been. And only a few hours later, he'd lost his grip on it.

And her perfect world had crashed down around her. Three years spent rebuilding, trying to pick up the pieces, and Alik Vasin had come along and broken it all again.

"You can't just get married for those kinds of reasons," she said. Her lips felt cold, her entire face prickly.

"Why not? Can you think of a better reason?"

"Love," she said. It was the craziest thing she'd ever heard. And the worst thing was, she didn't know if she could say no.

She looked at Leena and her heart lodged in her throat. If she said no, would this be the last she saw of her? Would she never see her grow? Hear her speak in sentences? Watch her go from a baby, to a child, to a teenager and finally, a young woman? All of her dreams, ash at her feet. Again.

Unless she said yes. She was the one who had demanded more. And now that she was getting the offer, could she really say no?

He frowned, one shoulder lifting. A casual dismissal. "Marriage has never meant very much to me. Marriage is a legal covenant, and it protects a lot of legal rights. That to me makes legal issues the most logical reason to marry."

"I don't even know you."

"I'm not asking you to know me, I'm asking you to marry me. Then my daughter will have a mother and a father. She will be cared for in every way that counts."

Jada blinked, trying to catch up with Alik's logic. Trying to understand it. He sounded so certain, and he moved so quickly, she could scarcely process one thing he'd said before he'd moved on to something else completely.

"How can you simply suggest something like this so… calmly?"

"Because it doesn't matter to me whether you're my nanny or my wife. Nothing will change, and it will offer you the protection that you desire."

"And why is it so important to you to give me that?"

"Additional stability for my daughter. And…" He hesitated. "Her attachment to you is very strong. She…seems to love you. I would hate to cause her any pain."

The way he said it was odd, as though he didn't truly understand either emotion he spoke about. Like he was trying to say the right things, or forcing himself to think the right things, but wasn't quite managing it.

It was crazy. Totally and completely. But she had nothing left here, not without Leena. No reason not to accept the insane offer.

You don't know him.

No, she didn't know him. But if she didn't go, her daughter would. Without her there to protect her. No. That couldn't happen. It wouldn't. No matter the cost.

Unbidden, she thought of her own wedding day, more than eight years ago. She'd been so young. So full of hope for the future. And so very much in love.

Marrying Alik, making him her husband, she felt like it made a mockery of that. Felt like she was putting Alik in a place that should be reserved for another man. The man that she'd loved with all of her heart.

Oh, Sunil, please forgive me.

She didn't know if he would have been able to. She wasn't sure if he'd truly understood her desire to have children. If he'd realized how deep it went. Or maybe he had, and he simply couldn't acknowledge it, because for him, it would mean facing how much he'd failed her. But she'd never seen it that way. She would have been happy, even then, to adopt.

Still, just for a moment, she wished she had him back so she could lean on his strength. Feel his arms around her, in comfort, just one more time.

It was a strange disconnect, though. If she still had Sunil, she wouldn't have Leena. And she needed Leena.

Truly, marrying Alik was marrying for love. For the love of her child.

Then another thought occurred to her. One that made her feel scared and hot at the same time. She didn't know if it was angry heat, embarrassed heat, or something else entirely. It was the something else entirely that really worried her.

"You said there would be very little difference between my position as nanny and my position as wife. Were you planning on sexually harassing me as your staff or are you planning on keeping your hands off me if I'm your wife?"

"It is of no matter to me. If you want sex, I'm more than willing to give it."

The thought made a rash of heat spread over her skin. The way he said things like that, so bald and open, was something she just didn't understand. She wasn't a prude, but she wasn't going to start offering sex to a stranger either, as if it wasn't a bigger deal than choosing between pizza or dal for dinner.

"If *I* want sex?"

"You make it sound strange. Don't you like sex?"

She nearly choked. "I...I don't... It's not a recreational activity."

"Perhaps not to you." The smile that curved his lips told her he, indeed, thought of it as such, and she felt her toes curl in her shoes. Oh, good grief, he wasn't that hot. He was inappropriate. "Either way, the choice is yours. If you want it, I am willing."

"And if I don't?" she asked.

"As I said, it is of no matter to me. I'm not intending to pledge my faithfulness either way."

"You're not?" she asked, annoyed by that for some reason. Perhaps because in this plan, Alik seemed to be giving up nothing, while for her, everything was changing.

"I have a short attention span where women are concerned. My life is not conducive to relationships."

"I don't know that anyone's is. That's why people work at their marriages, you know?" For all that she'd loved her husband, they'd had their problems, but everyone in a long-term relationship did.

"Do you want my faithfulness?"

She half snorted half laughed. "Hardly."

"Then why make an issue of it? I won't demand yours, either. So long as Leena is cared for, I can't be bothered by what you do or who you're doing it with."

"Did you honestly just question whether or not I will care for Leena? I've been doing it for the past year—it's hardly going to change now. It's all I want to do. She's what I want."

"And because of that you have no interest in relationships?"

"I had a relationship," she said, feeling, for some reason, like claiming Sunil as a husband, considering the conversation, might cheapen it in some way. "He was all I ever wanted in a man, and he's gone now. That part of my life is gone. Over. Leena is my life now."

"Very noble of you."

"Hardly. I just know that I already had what a lot of people spend a lifetime looking for. No one gets that lucky twice."

He skipped over her words, as though he hadn't even been listening. "As I said, I don't care either way."

She felt numb. Light-headed. There was only one answer she could give.

"I will have to collect my things," she said, her words detached, as though they were being spoken by a stranger.

"I can send someone to do that for you."

Of course he could. He was a billionaire and all. "When would the marriage take place?"

"As soon as possible. In fact, I know just the place to have the wedding."

"Wedding?" she repeated, knowing she sounded dull.

"Of course we will have a wedding. We want it all to look authentic. For Leena's sake if for no other reason."

Just like that, she was treated with a welcome burst of anger. She stood from her chair, Leena still in her arms. "And your being seen with other women won't seem abnormal to Leena? I hope to God it does."

"She won't know about it," he said.

"How?"

He smiled, bright white teeth against tanned skin. "I'm a ghost, Jada. You don't read about me in the news, and there's a very good reason for that."

"You don't read about me in the news, either, and the reason is that I'm boring."

"Oh, I am not boring, and if the press ever got wind of me? I would be a headline." Coming from another man it would have sounded like bragging. Like he was talking himself up. But Alik said it like he was stating the most mundane of facts. And it made her believe him. "As it is," he continued, "they know nothing about me, and I intend to keep it that way."

A shiver ran up her back, the hair on her neck standing on end. "You have a high opinion of yourself and your media appeal."

Granted, he would have media appeal in spades. Even if it was just because he had model good looks. She looked at him harder. No, perhaps he didn't have a model's good looks. Models usually possessed some sort of androgynous beauty, while Alik was hard. A scar ran through the center of his chin, one marring the smooth line of his upper lip. His hands were no better. Rough, looking as though the skin on the backs of them had been, at some point in his life, reduced to hamburger, and had since healed badly.

She hadn't noticed at first. She'd been too bowled over by his presence in general to take in the finer details. And now she was wondering exactly who this man was. This man she'd agreed to marry.

She had a feeling that she didn't really want to know.

"I'm simply realistic," he said. "However, anonymity suits me. It always has."

"Well, that's good, because it suits me, too."

"Glad to hear it." He picked up his cell phone and punched in a number. "Bring the car to the front of the coffee shop. And map the route to the airport."

"The airport?" Panic clawed at her, warring with despair for the position of dominant emotion.

"There is no need to wait, as I said."

"So, where are we going then? Paris? Barcelona or that town house in New York?" She tried to feign a bravado she didn't feel. Tried to find the strength she needed to survive this new pile of muck life had heaped onto her.

"Tell me, Jada, have you ever been to Attar?"

Attar was Alik's adopted country. The only country he'd ever sworn a willing allegiance to. As a boy, pulled off the streets of Russia, he'd been asked very early on to betray his homeland, his people.

And he had done it. The promise of food and shelter too enticing to refuse. His conscience had burned at first, but then it burned past the point of healing. Singed beyond feeling.

Over the years he'd belonged to many nations. Taken the helm of many armies.

Attar was the one place he loved. The one place he called home. Sheikh Sayid al Kadar and his wife Chloe were a big part of that.

As his private jet touched down on the tarmac, waves of

heat rising up to envelop the aircraft, Leena woke with a start, her plaintive wails working on his nerves.

He'd never been especially fond of children. Yes, he tolerated Sayid and Chloe's children, had sworn to protect them, but he hardly hung out to play favorite Uncle Alik, regardless of the fact that Sayid was the closest thing to a brother he'd ever had.

But then, he didn't anticipate spending too much time with his own child. The thought made him feel slightly uncomfortable for the first time, a strange pang hitting him in the chest. He wasn't sure why.

Because you know what abandonment feels like.

He shook off the thought. He wasn't abandoning Leena. He was shaking up his entire damned life to make sure she was cared for. And he was doing her a kindness by staying away.

"Welcome to Attar," he said. "We're on the sheikh's private runway, so there's no need to wait."

"The sheikh?"

"A friend of mine." His only friend.

"Well, I guess you are sort of newsworthy," she said.

She had no idea. His relationship with Sayid was only the tip of the iceberg, but he hardly intended to tell her about his past. He had no need to. They would marry, he would install her in the residence of her choice and then he would carry on as he had always done.

He made a mental note to put Leena's birthday in his calendar. He would attempt to make visits around that time. Failing that he would send a gift. That seemed a good thing to do. And it was a bloody sight better than abandonment.

He put his sunglasses on, prepared to contend with the heat of Attar, a heat he had grown accustomed to over the past six years. He suddenly realized that Jada and Leena weren't.

He pulled out his cell phone. "Bring the car up to the jet, make sure it is adequately cooled." It was strange, having to consider the comfort of others. He rarely considered his own comfort. He would have charged out into the heat and walked to where the car was, or walked on to Sayid's palace himself.

He grimaced. He didn't especially want to go straight to Sayid's palace. He would have the driver take him to his own palace.

"Wait until the car pulls up," he said to Jada.

"Why?" she asked.

"This is not the sort of heat you're used to."

"How do you know?"

"Unless you've spent years in a North African desert, it's not the kind of heat you're used to. I assume you have not?"

"Not recently," she said, her tone stiff. It almost struck him as funny, but he had the feeling if he laughed vulnerable body parts might be in danger.

"I thought you probably had not."

When he saw the sleek, black car pulling near the door of the plane, he gave the pilot the signal to open the door. The moment it started to lower, a wave of heat washed inside the cabin.

"You weren't joking," she said.

"No, I wasn't." The stairs were steep, and he wondered if a woman as petite as Jada could manage a wiggling one-year-old on her way down.

"Give her to me," he said.

"Why?"

"Do you want to try and negotiate those with her in your arms? If so, by all means." His discomfort with the situation, with the prospect of holding the child again, made his voice harder than he intended.

"And what makes you think you'll do better? You aren't experienced with babies. What if you drop her?"

"I have carried full-grown men down mountainsides when they were unable to walk for themselves. I think I can carry a baby down a flight of stairs. Give her to me."

Jada complied, but her expression remained mutinous.

"After you," he said.

She started down the steps and into the car, and he followed after her. There was a car seat ready in this vehicle, his orders followed down to the letter. There should also be supplies for a baby back at his home. Money didn't buy happiness—he knew that to be true. He doubted he'd felt a moment of true happiness in his life. But money bought a lot of conveniences, and a lot of things that felt close enough to that elusive emotion.

He much preferred having it to not having it. And a good thing, too, as he'd sold his soul to get it.

"Where are we headed?" she asked when the car started moving.

"To my palace." He looked out the window at the wide, flat expanse of desert, and the walls of the city beyond it. This was the first place he had ever felt at home. The desert showed a man where he was at, challenged him on a fundamental level. The desert didn't care for good or evil. Only strength. Survival.

It had been a rescue mission in this very desert that had nearly claimed his life. And now it was in his blood.

"You have a palace?"

"A gift from the sheikh."

"Extravagant gift."

"Not so much, all things considered."

"What things?" she asked.

He didn't know what made him do it, but he unbuttoned the top three buttons on his shirt and pulled the collar to the side, revealing the dark lines of his most recent tattoo. The one that covered his most recent scar.

Her eyes widened. She lifted her hand as though she was tempted to touch, to see if the skin beneath the ink was as rough and damaged as it looked. It was. He wanted her to do it. Wanted her to press her fingertips to his flesh, so he could see just how soft and delicate she truly was against his hardened, damaged skin.

She lowered her hand and the spell was broken. "Is that part of that newsworthiness you were talking about?" she asked.

"Some might say."

"It looks like it was painful."

"Not especially. I think the one on my wrist hurt worse."

"Not the tattoo," she said.

He chuckled, feeling a genuine sense of amusement. "I know."

They settled into silence for the rest of the drive. Jada stared out the window, her fingers fluffing his daughter's pale hair. He wondered if she looked like her mother. Her birth mother. He could scarcely remember the woman.

Based on geography he had a fair idea of who she was, but he ultimately couldn't be certain. A one-night stand that had occurred nearly two years earlier hardly stuck out in his mind. He'd had a lot of nights like that. A lot of encounters with women he barely exchanged names with before getting down to the business of what they both wanted.

He wondered if a normal man might feel shame over that. Over the fact that he could scarcely recall the woman who'd given birth to his child. Yes, a normal man would probably be ashamed. But Alik had spent too many years discovering that doing the right thing often meant going hungry, while doing the wrong thing could net you a hotel room and enough food for a week. He'd learned long ago that he would have to define right and wrong in his own way. The best way he'd been able to navigate life had been to chase all of the good feelings he could find.

Food and shelter made him comfortable, so whatever he'd had to do to get it, he had. Later on he'd discovered that sex made him feel good. So he had a lot of it. He was never cruel to his partners, never promised more than he was willing to deliver. And until recently, he'd imagined he'd left his lovers with nothing more than a smile on their face and a post-orgasmic buzz.

That turned out not to be strictly true. It made him feel unsettled. Made him question things it was far too late to question.

His palace was on the coast of Attar, facing the sea. The sun washed the sea a pale green, the rocks and sand red. And his home stood on the hill, a stunning contrast to the landscape. White walls and a golden, domed roof that shone bright in the midday heat.

Here, by the sea, the air was more breathable. Not as likely to burn you from the inside out.

"This is my home," he said. "Your home now, if you wish."

He wanted to take the invitation back as soon as he'd issued it. There was a reason he'd not mentioned the Attari palace in his initial list of homes Leena might live in. The heat was one reason, but there was another. This was his sanctuary. The one place he didn't bring women. The one place he brought no one.

Not now. Now he was bringing his daughter and the woman who was to become his wife. For the first time in his memory, he seriously questioned the decisions that he'd made.

CHAPTER FOUR

JADA COULD SCARCELY take in all of her surroundings. She clutched a sweaty, sleeping Leena to her chest and tried to ignore the heat of her daughter's body against hers, far too much in the arid Attari weather, and continued through the palace courtyard and into the opulent, cool, foyer.

"This is…like nothing I've ever seen."

"I felt the same way when I first came here. To Attar. It is like another world. Although, it's funny, I find some of the architecture so similar to what you find in Russia, but with dunes in the background instead of snow."

"Do you keep a home there?" she asked. She realized suddenly that it was not in the list of places he'd named earlier.

"I do," he said. "But I don't go there."

"Why?" The question applied to both parts of the statement. Why would he keep a home he never went to? And why would he not go there?

"I have no need to revisit my past."

"And yet you keep a house there?"

"Holding on to a piece of it, I suppose. But then, we all do that, do we not?"

"I suppose," she said. She flexed her fingers, became suddenly very conscious of the ring that was now on her right finger. She'd removed her wedding ring about a year after Sunil's death. And then a few months later she'd put it back on, but on her other hand. A way to remember, while acknowledging that the marriage bond was gone.

A way to hold on to a past that she could never reclaim. She knew all about holding on to what you couldn't go back to.

"I asked that my staff have rooms prepared for you and Leena. Rooms that are next to each other. I will call my housekeeper and see that she leads you to them."

"Not you?"

"I don't know where she installed you," he said, his total lack of interest almost fascinating to her. She wondered what it would be like to live like him. No ties, no cares. Even when it came to Leena, he seemed to simply think and act. None of it came from his heart and because of that there was no hesitation. No pain.

But there was also no conviction. Not true conviction. Not like she felt when she'd made the decision to come here, knowing that, no matter the cost she couldn't turn her back on her child.

As attractive as his brand of numbness seemed in some ways, she knew she would never really want it. There was no strength in it. Not true strength. It was better to hurt for lost love, and far better to have had it in the first place. Even in the lowest point of her grief she wouldn't have traded away her years with her husband. Even facing the potential loss of Leena, she would never regret the bond.

"Well, then how am I supposed to find you in this massive palace if you don't know where I am and I don't know where you are?" Everything about Attar was massive. The desert stretched on forever, ending at a sea that continued until it met sky. The palace was no less impressive. Expansive rooms and ceilings that curved high overhead. It made her long for the small coziness of her home. For the buildings back in Portland that hemmed them in a bit, the mountains that surrounded those.

Here, everything just seemed laid bare and exposed. She didn't like the feeling.

"I hardly thought you would want to find me," he said.

She had thought so, as well, but the idea of not being able to find the only person she knew in this vast, cold stone building didn't sit well with her at all.

"Better than getting lost forever in this fortress you call a home."

He looked up, his focus on the domed ceiling. Sunbursts of gold, inlaid with jasper, jade and onyx. "A fortress? I would hardly call it that. I have spent time in fortresses. Prisons. Dungeons."

"I don't need to know what you do in your off time," she snapped, not sure what had prompted her to make the remark.

A slow smile curved his lips. "But what I do in my off time is so very fascinating. I'm sure you could benefit from a little off time yourself."

Her body reacted to the words with heat, with increased heart rate and sweaty palms. Her body was a filthy traitor. Her mind, on the other hand, came to her rescue. Sensible and suitably outraged.

"I already told you, I'm not going there with you. I've agreed to marry you, but I'm not sharing your bed. This marriage won't be real." It couldn't be real. She'd had a real marriage. A marriage filled with laughing and shouting and making love, and this, this union with a stranger, no matter that it was legal, would never be that.

There had been security in her marriage. Even at the low points, there had been an element of safety. Alik possessed nothing even slightly resembling safety. He was a law unto himself, much like the desert she found herself stranded in.

He crossed his muscular arms across his broad chest, one eyebrow arched. "On the contrary, this marriage will be very real in every way that counts."

Her skin prickled. "What does that mean?"

"All marriage is, is a legal document. But then, that's what adoption is, *da?* So you have to collect the proper legal documents to get your life in order. That's how I see it."

"That's not what marriage is."

"And you're an expert."

"Yeah," she said. "I am."

He stopped talking, his gray eyes locked with hers. "I do not claim expertise in that area. But all I'm saying is, it will be as real as it must be in order for you to make a permanent claim on Leena. That is all you require."

"Yes. Although I'm still a little unsure about why you're helping me."

Alik was, too. In some ways. In others…it made sense. It was what a family looked like. A mother and father, married. That was the traditional way of it. It was everything he'd never had, and he'd suffered for the lack of it. He would not allow Leena to suffer similarly.

And it was what Sayid had done. He had married Chloe in order to secure the future of his nephew and it had all turned out very well for him.

Of course, Alik wasn't counting on love and more children. He was in no danger of it, in fact. Love was something he had never managed to feel. Loyalty, yes. A bond of brotherhood with Sayid. But otherwise…no, love was certainly not on the table for him. It had been torn from him, the day his mother had left him in an overcrowded orphanage.

There could be no love but…perhaps a sort of facade of legitimacy. He hadn't been a soldier for hire in a long time. And since then, he'd parlayed his experience as a military strategist into the business world, and he'd been a huge success. But there were events, functions where people brought spouses or at least dates.

He'd never had an actual date. He didn't take women out, he met them out. At parties, clubs, and then he took them to bed. To whatever hotel room was closest. To the backseat of his car. He'd never been particular.

But things were changing. His life was changing. He'd long since abandoned some of the more self-destructive exploits of his youth. The truth was, being a soldier for hire had afforded him a lot of money. And in combination with being a man who didn't care whether he lived or died, it was a very dangerous thing.

Now though, things were different. He was ready for them to be, in some ways. He wondered if this was the thing that might finally reach the frozen block in his chest where his heart should be.

He'd spent years serving the lusts of his flesh, allowing his body to feel the things his heart simply could not.

He looked at the child in Jada's arms and he wished for a connection. For something. A recognition of her as his blood, as his family.

And there was nothing. No magic bond.

He gritted his teeth. "Yes, I think having you as a wife actually suits my purposes well. I've had a career change in the past few years and it will sometimes be good for me to have a wife to attend galas and things of that nature with me."

"Galas?"

"Yes."

"I didn't sign on to attend galas. I signed on to be a mother to my own child." He noticed that she adamantly continued to refuse to call Leena *his* child, "and to be left alone in one of your penthouses. In a location of my choosing, if I remember correctly."

"Perhaps I have changed what I expect. I ought to get something additional out of the deal, don't you think? And since sex isn't on offer I think the least you can do is put on a ball gown and hang on my arm at business functions."

She lifted her chin, lioness eyes glittering with deadly intent. "Whatever you wish, of course."

Such a dangerous acquiescence. He could tell she meant none of it, but that she was willing to play along with anything at this point. Anything to keep Leena close to her.

That realization made his chest burn, as though her conviction was so strong it had lit a spark within him. His child deserved that. This intense protectiveness, born of love, that Jada wore so proudly. And Leena would not get it from him. He could not give it.

All the better that Jada would be in residence.

"Somehow, I don't believe that," he said. "But I don't require your obedience."

"Don't you?"

He shrugged. "No. Where's the fun in that? I prefer women who like a challenge."

"I prefer you not think of me as a woman."

He looked over her petite figure. Small, perfectly formed breasts, gently rounded hips. "It's a bit late for that. It's the curves. They give you away."

She lifted her chin, golden eyes burning with fire. "I'm ready to see my room now."

"Then I shall call Adira."

Jada had been forbidden from putting her own things away by Alik's very stern head of the household. There were people for that sort of thing, and she was not to trouble herself. That extended to Leena's things. Both of which had arrived, inexplicably, only hours after they did.

Alik had made good on his every promise so far, which made it truly difficult to hate him too much.

Leena was his daughter, after all, and regardless of how she felt about his behavior, about how irresponsible one had to be to get into such a situation, she couldn't deny that he was Leena's father.

How could she deny Leena a chance to know him? That Jada had been the one to love her and care for her did make her more important in her estimation, but the biological connection between Alik and Leena wasn't nothing.

The morality of the entire situation was sticky and horrible.

Jada sank onto her bed and watched Leena, toddling around the exterior of her blanket before sitting down a little bit too hard, her movements wobbly and clumsy. She didn't cry. She just clapped her chubby hands.

Jada slid off the edge of the bed and clasped one of Leena's hands in hers, ran a finger along the little dimples that disguised her knuckles. The price for this, for being with her daughter, wasn't too high.

There would never be a price too high. If she hadn't agreed to the marriage, to coming here with him, then she would have lost her child forever.

And if she'd agreed to be the nanny, she would have lost the position that was rightfully hers. After the doctors, she'd been the first person to hold Leena. She'd been the one who'd spent countless sleepless nights pacing the halls with a squalling child in her arms.

She was Leena's mother in every way that mattered. Marrying a stranger, leaving her home, her country, it was a small sacrifice for moments like these, and every moment in the future.

Leena was her life. Nothing else mattered.

"Settling in, I see."

Jada turned and saw Alik standing in the doorway. She hadn't heard him approach, hadn't heard the door to the bedroom open. He was almost supernaturally stealthy. It was a bit unnerving. But then, the man was unnerving in general.

"Yes. We are. I don't think Leena is fazed at all by the different surroundings."

"I think it would be different if you weren't here."

She blinked, not expecting the compliment. Not expecting him to understand. "You're very right about that."

"I made some calls. I was able to secure us a marriage license and it's all in order for the ceremony to take place this weekend."

Her throat tightened, her mouth going dry. "I imagine your connection with the sheikh helped on this one."

"It didn't hurt."

Why was the room spinning now? It seemed like it was spinning. "This morning, I woke up and got ready to go to the courthouse to finally get this adoption finalized. I thought, there's no way he'll get here in time and they'll just rule him as absentee. Now, I'm in a foreign country with a man I barely know, and I'm marrying him in three days." She said it all out loud, like it might help make it real. And if it wasn't real, maybe speaking out loud would wake her up from this bizarre dream.

"And this morning," he said, his voice quiet, "I got word that the hearing date had been changed and I went to a court-house in another country, to make sure that I didn't lose the chance of ever seeing my own child. Knowing if I missed it, I may never even get a chance to look at her."

For the first time, she realized that Alik's life had been upended, too. Even if the upending was a result of his own actions. "I suppose we've both had a strange day."

He straightened. "To say the least." The gravity was now absent from his tone. "One of the strangest I've had, and if you were aware of my past history you would know that's saying something."

"I get that vibe from you."

"Do you?"

"Nothing about you seems typical."

Not even close. He was like a predatory animal in human form. Easy grace and harnessed power. But with the ability to spring into action and tear out someone's throat in the blink of an eye. He'd looked at home in his denim and rum-pled shirt, tattoos on display, and just as comfortable in a custom-tailored suit. He was a man who shifted identities as easily as breathing.

"I suppose not," he said. His words were oddly flat.

"So what is it you do?" she asked.

He looked surprised. For the first time since all of this had happened, since she'd met him, he actually looked caught off guard. "What do I do?"

"For work. For money. Other than…having sheikhs be indebted to you and gifting you palaces, that is."

"Right now? I'm a tactical expert. I go into corporations and help with strategies. How to take out the competition. Plans to increase productivity and profit. Whatever they need."

"Taking out the competition?"

A half smile curved his lips. Wicked. *Wicked* was the only word for that smile of his. "It's a clever little take on what I used to do, but that's another story."

"And do you do this for everyone? At some point aren't you working both sides?"

"Sometimes. But I am always one hundred percent loyal to whoever is paying for my services at a given time. It suits me. I don't want to man a massive corporation—I prefer to be a free agent. This allows me to move as I please."

"Given the financial information mentioned at the hearing you do very well at this."

"I do all right," he said.

Yeah. Eight figures of all right, but she wasn't going to say that. It was crass to talk about money, at least that's what her parents had always said.

"I'm just…I'm very tired," she said.

He looked down at Leena. "Will she sleep for you or shall I send one of my staff to help you?"

She felt drained suddenly. Incapable of doing anything but crawling into bed, pulling the covers over her head and trying to forget the entire day had happened. Trying to forget that this was her life.

She recognized this. Shock. Grief in a way. It was the loss of the life she'd planned for her and Leena.

"She'll be fine," she said. No way was she letting her daughter out of her sight. In fact, she doubted she'd even be using the adjoining room for her. She had a feeling she'd just pull the crib in and place it by her bed.

"As long as you're certain."

"I need her with me."

"Of course," he said. It was strange how he said it. His words lacked emotion. They lacked understanding. As though he didn't really get why she might need Leena close.

"I guess we'll talk more tomorrow."

"Yes. We will need to discuss wedding plans."

"I don't care about them," she said. "Hire someone else to do it."

"I was planning on it, but still, someone will have to come take your measurements. For your dress."

"Of course." She imagined he would put her in a Western-style wedding gown, which she found she actually preferred.

She'd had her big Indian wedding with Sunil. Worn the red sari she'd dreamed of since she was a little girl. Her extended family had all been there, her mother. She'd still had her mother then. It had been everything she'd wanted.

She would not let this wedding, this farce, infect the memory of *her* wedding. She needed this to be something else. Something different. A wedding that had no personal significance to her at all. Something that didn't feel like part of her.

"I want a white dress," she said.

"Tell the stylist when she comes tomorrow."

"I will."

As long as she kept it separate, someone else's wedding and not hers, maybe she could survive it.

CHAPTER FIVE

THE NEXT DAYS PASSED too quickly. No matter how hard Jada wished time would stand still, it simply wouldn't. And before she knew it, the day of the wedding arrived.

Why were they even having a wedding? For Leena, she knew, and then of course for Alik's peers. Wedding photos would be necessary for both.

It would be small, she'd been assured. Only Sayid and his family. Sayid, she'd found out, was the sheikh of Attar. So, only the sheikh. No big deal.

Jada felt like she would throw up.

She clutched the bouquet of lilies to her chest and looked down at the flowing, white fabric of her gown. She'd asked that everything be white. A total contrast to her first wedding, which had been filled with color, food and music.

She would have this feel as different as possible. As much like something other than her wedding as she could manage.

It wasn't working right now. Wasn't working to tame the butterflies that were rioting around in her belly.

There were more staff seeing to the wedding than there were people in attendance. It was almost funny. Between the photographer, the kitchen staff, the decorators, the coordinator and the minister, it was rather amazing.

They didn't have music. Her cue to walk up the aisle was when she could see Alik standing at the head of it. She peered

MAISEY YATES 57

around the gauzy curtain that separated the stone veranda from the walled gardens.

She could see him there. In a suit. No tie, the collar unbuttoned at his throat.

She almost turned and ran. But then she saw Leena. Leena in her little white dress, her chubby legs hanging over one of the chairs that had been set up around the altar area.

Chloe, Sayid's wife, was keeping an eye on her, along with her two children.

And that right there was why this was happening. It was why she was getting ready to walk down the aisle toward a man she didn't know. It was why she was going to do it with her head held high.

Because for Leena, she could do nothing less.

"You can do this, Jada," she whispered.

Then she swept the curtain aside and started down the aisle.

Alik wasn't certain what he'd expected to feel. Nothing, actually, that was what he'd expected to feel. That was the status quo after all.

But when he saw Jada, headed toward him, a white gown fitted over curves, white flowers pressed tightly against her chest, her dark hair covered by a frothy veil, he felt something.

Heat streaked through his veins, hot as fire and just as dangerous.

Lust.

He was well familiar with lust. But Jada was not a woman he wanted to feel any lust for. Keeping their arrangement purely on paper was essential. To the peace of his household, to the way he conducted his life.

Lust was something he simply couldn't afford.

And yet it was there, an insistent ball of heat in his gut. And when Jada came forward and placed her small, soft hand in his, golden and perfect against his own battered skin, it only stoked the flames.

She looked up, her eyes wide, as though she felt it, too. And was no happier about it than he was.

He had intended for her to have no effect on his life. And that was how it would remain. He kept that in the forefront of his mind as he spoke his vows. Repeated it mentally. No matter the words they spoke today, here at the altar, it would not change what he had planned.

It would not change his life.

But what if it does? That thought pushed against the ice blockade around his heart. And he shoved it away.

There was no kiss during the ceremony. It was not traditional to kiss publicly in Attar, and he felt that they should adhere to that part of the custom. He was exceedingly glad they had done so now.

As if a kiss could affect you?

After all he'd done, it should not have the power to do so. But he wondered. Wondered what it would do to him to touch his lips to hers. They were full, soft. So perfect looking. And he wanted a taste badly enough to know he'd made the right choice to exclude it from the ceremony. He'd bet she tasted like passion. Like emotion so deep he'd never reach the bottom.

He was used to women as jaded as himself, or at least halfway to that point. But Jada was not that woman. He had to wonder…if he touched her, would it burn with heat like her eyes? Would it have the power to burn away the scars over his own emotions and set them all free?

The thought both intrigued and repelled him. It was a foolish thought. There was nothing that strong. Not even the fire of Jada's passion.

The wedding ended very quickly, and for that, he was grateful. The moment the pronouncement was made, that they were husband and wife, Jada left his side and went to where Leena was sitting, pulling the child into her arms.

He wondered if he would ever be able to do that so easily. If he would ever do it the way she did, out of necessity. If only that sort of connection, that sort of understanding could be transferred through a kiss.

But then what would be left of you if you lost your armor? Do you even know if there's anything underneath?

No. He didn't. And he had no intention of finding out.

Sayid came up from where he'd been sitting and joined Alik where he was standing, both of them watching their respective wives and children. That moment confirmed he had done right. His heart would not give him confirmation. It simply wasn't capable of it. But in his mind he knew, it was right.

"What have you done, Alik?"

"I did as you said I should do. I went and claimed my child."

"And the woman?"

"She is the woman who was trying to adopt Leena. I could hardly rip the child from her arms." Though that had been the original plan. Strange to think of it now. Strange to think he'd imagined it would work. To take Leena from Jada, when it seemed like they were a part of each other.

"Was she?" Sayid asked. "I did not realize there was someone who had been caring for her."

"Yes. Would that have changed your advice?" Alik was worried it might. That even Sayid would think Jada was better suited to the task.

"Not necessarily. How is it she ended up agreeing to marry you?"

"I told her to. It keeps her with the child. It creates a proper family. I did the right thing."

"You uprooted them both from their country. You forced a woman who has only known you for four days to marry you."

"Is it so different to what you did with Chloe?"

Sayid shot him a deadly look. "It was different."

"Not in the least."

"I had feelings for her when we married."

"I know," Alik said, mildly amused by the memory. He'd incurred the wrath of his friend by implying he'd been less than gentlemanly with the other man's wife in their brief time alone at his seaside palace.

"And you don't have feelings for this woman?"

"Of course not, Sayid, I barely have feelings." He flashed his friend his most practiced grin, the one that had gotten him out of more trouble than most people had ever been in.

"So you think."

"So I know."

"You told me once, Alik," Sayid said slowly, "that you saw no point in making vows you couldn't keep."

Alik shifted, the memory rushing back to him, making him uncomfortable. Because that was just what he'd done today. He'd made vows he had no intention of keeping. He had every intention of continuing on as he'd always done.

"I also told you that I avoid making vows whenever possible. Today, it was not possible." He looked over at Jada. She was sitting, holding Leena in her lap. Her golden skin had a gray tinge to it and her lips were chalky pale. She was miserable. The realization sent a pang straight to his chest. Strange. "This is different. She knows what this is."

"And you think that's enough? You think what happened here today, the words you spoke, you think those won't matter?"

"It is not the same as a normal marriage. It is to protect my daughter. To protect Jada's rights, which she insisted on. This makes sense."

Sayid laughed. "One thing you'll discover soon, my friend, is that women and children rarely make sense."

"I know about women."

"Yes, you do. But you don't know about wives."

* * *

Jada was sitting in her room, watching Leena sleep. Sayid and Chloe had lingered for a while, but as nice as they were, Jada had been happy to see them go. She was tired of being on show. Tired of playing the part of, if not happy bride, then at least contented bride. It was too much and the strain was starting to break her.

This whole thing might break her. She was afraid it would.

There was a light knock on her door. "Come in."

The door opened, and Adira appeared. Alik's head of the household was spare with her smiles but today, she offered Jada one. "Mr. Alik has requested that you join him for a late dinner."

"I..." With Adira looking at her like that she hardly felt like she could refuse. "What about Leena?"

"I will stay on this floor. If she cries, you will be fetched immediately." Adira was being friendly, but she had the air of a woman who brooked no nonsense, and would not be disagreed with. She reminded Jada a bit of her own mother.

"Thank you," she said.

She stood from her position on the bed and wondered if she should change again. She'd stripped off her wedding dress the moment she was up in her room, and had traded it out in favor of a simple sundress. She'd longed for the comfort of her sweatpants but it was way too hot to indulge herself.

No. She wasn't going to change. It didn't matter what she wore to see Alik.

Her husband. A vision of Alik swam through her head and panic assaulted her. No. She closed her eyes and thought the words again. Her husband. And she willed an image of Sunil to appear. Alik was not her husband. Not truly.

She swallowed hard and patted the sleeping Leena once on her rounded belly before offering the housekeeper another smile and walking out of the room.

As she drew closer to the dining area, her heart started

beating harder, faster. And she started remembering the wedding. The moment when Alik had taken her hand. His fingers had been rough on her skin, and hot, so hot. The heat had seeped through her skin, shot through her body, pooling in her stomach.

It had been so very like…

No. She wasn't even going to think it. He didn't turn her on. Yes, he was a handsome man, in his way. Well, *handsome* seemed wrong. *Handsome* sounded banal and safe. Vanilla. And Alik Vasin was anything but that.

He was scarred, rough. Dangerous. And in that danger, there was a magnetism that defied logic. That was unlike anything she'd ever experienced. Ever.

She blinked. Just thinking that felt like a betrayal. Not just to her marriage, but to who she was. She wasn't the kind of woman who lost her head over a hot man. A hot man she didn't even like. She idly wiped her palm on her skirt, trying to rid herself of the feeling of his flesh against hers. Trying to get rid of the heat.

It didn't work.

She walked down a curved staircase and a long hall, the high-gloss black floors casting a ghostly reflection in front of her. The palace was like a maze, and the week she'd spent there, mainly huddled in hers and Leena's rooms, hadn't been enough to make it feel familiar.

The one good thing about the size of the palace was that it made avoiding Alik simple. And all things considered, avoidance had been high on her list of priorities.

Her problem was simply that it had been too long since a man had touched her. Too long since she felt any sort of attraction or arousal. She simply hadn't been interested. She still wasn't, but it was nothing more than a body/brain disconnect. Nothing to get worked up about. She was still in control.

She took a shaking breath and walked into the dining room. Alik was sitting there, at the head of the table. The only light in the room was coming from flickering candles, set on the table, casting sharp shadows onto Alik's face.

She'd just been thinking that he looked dangerous. She'd had no idea. Until now. His cheekbones looked more hard cut thanks to the flickering flames, his jaw more angular. Harder. And his eyes, they just looked hollow.

That, right there, should have been enough to erase the heat.

And yet, for some reason, her palm burned all the more.

"Do you feel rested?" he asked.

"I'm not really sure." She twisted her wedding band, the one on her right hand. Not the one she'd been given today. A reminder. Of what was real, and what wasn't.

Then she took a seat somewhere in the middle of the long, opulent banquet table. Sitting at the other end made her look like a coward. And she was a coward so she wasn't going to go sit next to him.

"I thought I should make sure you ate. You touched nothing at the lunch after the wedding."

"I was too nervous to eat."

"You seemed very calm."

"I've learned not to show too much emotion on the outside."

"Except that day at the courthouse."

She remembered vividly how she'd sat down and cried on the floor. She wasn't even embarrassed about it. The thought of losing her daughter deserved that level of emotion. "Restraint was the last thing on my mind."

"Was everything at the wedding to your taste?" he asked.

"No," she said. "It wasn't. And that was my plan."

"Your plan?" He looked over at her and frowned. "Come sit closer to me. I'm not shouting down the table at you for our entire meal."

She complied reluctantly, again, because she didn't want

to look like a coward, scooting toward him until there were only two chairs between them.

"Better?"

"Yes. Now tell me about this plan."

In order to tell him, she would have to talk about Sunil, and she'd been avoiding that. Because it seemed wrong to talk about him to Alik, the man she'd just made her husband. It was too complicated. Too confused.

"I... This was my second wedding."

"Was it?" His response wouldn't have sounded out of place if her previous statement had been "it was nice and warm today."

"Yes. I didn't want this one to resemble *my* wedding. This wasn't my wedding. Not in that way."

He turned the wineglass in front of him in a slow circle. "And what happened to your first husband?"

Leave it to Alik to ask so bluntly. Social niceties were not something he gave deference to. Although, she found she almost liked it. At least he asked for what he wanted to know. At least he spoke, even when the words were unpleasant.

Now *that* thought, the comparison she was making to her husband, that was a betrayal. She shut it down as quickly as it started.

"Sunil had a lifelong heart defect. At least that's what his doctor told me later. It had gone undetected until, one day his heart...stopped. He was at work. They took him to the hospital, kept him on life support for a while. But he never came back. He just slipped away."

"How long has it been?" he asked.

"Three years."

"You loved him?"

"I love him," she said. "Very much. Not...not in the same way, obviously. But, he will always live in my heart."

A knot of emotion formed in her chest, and she welcomed it. It was safer than the heat that had been blooming there only moments before. Much safer than any of the new, raw emotions she'd experienced in the past few weeks.

"I have never lost anyone I cared for like that. I can imagine it must be difficult for you."

For you. As if it wouldn't be for him. "You've never lost anyone you cared for?" She thought of her parents, of her husband. "You're very fortunate."

"I've never really loved anyone," he said, his tone cold, frightening in its flatness. "One good thing about that is it keeps you from loss."

"What about your parents?" she asked.

"I never knew them. My mother left me at an orphanage when I was two, probably nearly three. My date of birth is a best guess made by the woman working at the facility at the time I was brought in. My name was given to me in much the same way. I don't share my surname with anyone I'm related to. From there, when it became overcrowded I was put out on the streets."

"I...I'm sorry."

"No need to be."

Two servers came in and placed a tray in front of both her and Alik before leaving the room as quietly as they'd entered.

"It must have been hard," she said.

"It was all I knew. And as I think you must know, it's impossible to waste time feeling sorry for yourself when there is life to be lived."

She did know that. It had been one of the things that had made her most angry when she'd been at the lowest point in her grief. That life had gone on. That she'd still had to go to the grocery store, still had to eat. Pay bills. There had been no time to drown in her grief the way she'd really wanted to.

Now she saw that for the blessing it was.

"That's very true."

"I have been thinking," he said, his subject change sudden. "You should take my name. As should Leena."

"What? Why?"

"You don't want a different last name than your daughter, do you?"

"No...I hadn't...I hadn't considered it."

"You gave her her first name, and I will not change it, but I want her to carry my name. She is my only family. And you should carry it, as well."

"I don't..." Patel was her husband's name. Except, Sunil wasn't her husband anymore. Alik was. "I'm not sure I can do that." After what he'd just told her, about the orphanage worker who had chosen his name, she understood why it would matter to him.

But she couldn't do it. Not now. Changing her name was like changing herself, and she couldn't allow it. Couldn't allow this, couldn't allow Alik that sort of power.

"It is the most logical thing to do."

"I know," she snapped. "But I've just been so damn logical for the past week, that my heart has taken a beating and I'm not sure I can do this, too. I made you my husband today. That place belonged—belongs—to the man I loved. And if I take your name, then I have to get rid of his."

"It is no matter to me," he said, his tone hard. "It's entirely up to you. I thought you might like our family to share a name."

"A family? Is that what we are?" She hated herself for saying it. After what he'd just said, she knew she was stabbing at him, but she honestly couldn't stop herself.

"The closest thing to one I've had." Again, his voice carried that sort of detached weightlessness. As if none of this meant anything to him. As if he was simply relaying facts. The man seemed to live entirely in his head.

No, that wasn't really true. Because there was something else about him. Something darker, much more frightening. Something earthy and sensual that came from a place deep inside of him. He was a man very much connected with his body, too.

And she didn't like how much her own body seemed to be intrigued by that.

"I will think about it. It doesn't have to be done right away. I can do it anytime."

"Of course. In the meantime though, I will give Leena my name."

"Leena Vasin," Jada said quietly. And she looked at the man across from her again, at the stubborn set of his jaw, the shape of his brow. She saw it then, for the first time. How had she missed it?

Leena looked so very much like her father. The expression she made when she was grumpy especially, favored the stern look on his face now.

"It suits her," Jada said, surprising herself when she said it. Surprised by how much she meant it.

Leena was Alik's daughter. There was no denying it or ignoring it. And she was glad in that moment that he was in her life. She was sure the feeling would come and go, but right now, she was glad that Leena had a father. Her father.

"Do you know," she said slowly, "she looks like you?"

Alik's eyes were obscured by shadow and it was impossible to see what he was thinking. "Does she?" His voice was inscrutable as ever. There was no way to get a read on his emotions. No way to know what he thought about that revelation.

"Yes. When she's about to throw a tantrum she gets a little crease between her eyebrows, just like you. And her eyes have more green in them, but they also have that gray that yours have."

"I hadn't noticed," he said.

"Neither had I until just now."

Alik looked down at his wineglass again. "We should eat before it gets cold."

"Yes," she said. She wasn't conscious of what she was eating, and the moment the plates were clear she couldn't actually remember what they'd been served.

"Would you like me to show you back to your room?"

Jada hesitated. It was dark now, no helpful light filtering in through the windows to guide her way. But the idea of traversing dark corridors with Alik didn't exactly make her feel extra safe.

It made her stomach feel tight, made it hard to breathe. Still, she didn't want to stumble around the palace for longer than necessary.

"Yes. Please, if you wouldn't mind."

Alik rose from his seat and Jada was reminded just how large he was, how imposing. Every inch the master of the castle. She didn't know why she found it so fascinating. Didn't know why she found him so fascinating.

He moved past her with that effortless grace of his. The deadly silence of a predator. It didn't seem possible that a man who was so large, so tall and broad, could be so quiet when he moved.

She followed him out into the dark hall and a shiver ran over her body, creeping up her arms, her neck. "Got a flaming torch you can tear off the wall and use to light our way?"

Alik paused and turned, his expression cast into shadow. The shivery feeling got a bit more pronounced. He extended his hand and placed it flat on the wall, and then...the lights came on. And the expression revealed on his face could only be called *smart-assed*. "I could do that," he said, "but it would be so much easier to simply find the light switches."

"That would have been nice to know about earlier, so I wasn't walking through this medieval heap in the dark."

He turned away from her and started down the hall again, his back, wide and muscular, filling her vision. "Why on earth would I live in a place that didn't possess modern conveniences? I've been homeless. I've been in prisons. I've done my time without modern luxury, and I find it isn't my favorite."

"You've been in jail? How is it that the court deemed you a more fit parent than I am?"

"I don't think it was a question of who was more fit, so much as who was more related. But, if it soothes you, the court didn't see any criminal record."

"How is that possible?"

"First of all, I doubt the Russian Mafia keep a record of every snot-nosed street kid they've locked up for a few days to teach a lesson to. Second, I'm skeptical that any of the guerrilla military factions I found myself on the unfriendly side of reported my prison time to the United States—or any government. Also, records and things like that may have been sanitized by some grateful rulers and the occasional victorious revolutionary."

She stopped in her tracks and he kept on walking. "Wait a second. What is it you used to do?"

"What I do now for corporations? I used to do that for governments. Or, as I said, revolutionaries. Whoever offered the money."

"You were a mercenary." For the first time, she realized that the little prickle of hair on her arms, that vague sense of danger, wasn't ridiculous. Alik Vasin was, or had been, a very dangerous man. And she had just married him.

"I suppose that's the job title, though I was never too bothered about being specific with that. Didn't exactly fill out tax forms. But that's another thing I won't be advertising to the courts."

Jada curled her fingers into fists, her nails digging in her palms. "I don't imagine there's a box to check for that on official forms."

"Not so much."

"How did you...how did you get into something like that?" She was curious, even though she knew she shouldn't be.

What she should be, was running away, and yet, for some reason, though that feeling of danger emanating from him remained, she wasn't afraid of him.

"I told you, I was an orphan. I crossed paths with the Russian Mafia quite by accident one day when I was picking pockets. After teaching me a sufficient lesson," he said, one long finger drifting over a scar that ran the length of his jaw, "the man I had attempted to rob asked how I'd done it so well. You see, he didn't feel me lift his wallet. He was told by his guards, who were walking behind him. Who I was walking in the middle of."

"What did you say?"

"I explained to him my process. The way I waited for the crowds on the street to be at a certain peak, how I waited for my mark to be at a certain point in their stride. And I told him, that when I was about to go for the grab, everything slowed down, and it was just effortless. He liked that."

"And he had you picking pockets?"

"Hardly. But I was twelve and what he saw was the mind of a strategist. He was right. I had a gift for seeing all angles of a scenario, except, of course, in the instance where they caught me. I missed seeing that he had guards with him. That's always bothered me."

"It has?"

"No one likes to lose. Anyway, that was the start of my career in organized crime. They helped me hone my abilities and then they exploited them. Until I became too recognizable in Moscow. Until I got tired of playing the game. This was when I was maybe sixteen or so. But I left them with a lot of money in my pocket, though I have to say I'm not overly keen on wandering the streets in my hometown alone. I don't trust how far that goodwill we parted with extends."

"Then what?" In spite of herself, she was fascinated. She should be scared, but she wasn't. Not really.

He started walking again and she jogged into place behind him to keep up. "Then, I found out I had a reputation. A man found me when I was in Japan and asked me to do a job. To help a militia overthrow a very oppressive government."

"And you helped them."

"The price was right. I'm not a charity."

"But you did the job."

He nodded once. "I did. And I did it successfully. After that, word spread."

"And that's what you did after that? Hired yourself out as a...weapon?"

"For some years."

"And then?"

"I had a mission here in Attar. To try and secure the borders. And for the first time, the mission went wrong. Sheikh Sayid was taken captive." It was the first time she'd heard even a glimmer of true emotion in his voice. "And though I was offered another check, another job, I knew I couldn't leave him there."

"You cared for him."

"I was the head of the mission—if it went wrong it was on me. When I take money to aid a certain faction then I am loyal to that faction until the job is done. The job wasn't done."

"And you cared for him."

"Sayid is the most honorable man I have ever met, in a life spent surrounded by men who would sell their grandmothers for a chance at their version of glory. It was refreshing to meet someone who had nothing but loyalty to his family, to his country, no matter what he could achieve elsewhere. Sayid was taken into captivity because he deviated from the mission. Because he stopped a woman from being assaulted by two soldiers. I would not have done the same in his position, because at that time in my life, all I saw was the mission. The plan. And Sayid made me look past that for the first time."

Jada felt something shift around her heart. Dear heaven, she wasn't starting to understand this man, was she? She'd grown up in a comfortable, middle-class home in the U.S. Born to parents to who had risked everything, left their homeland, to build a better life for their children. How could she understand a man who had spent his life alone? A man who had witnessed, and very likely committed, terrible acts of violence? It made no sense.

And yet, for some reason, she felt she did understand. She wasn't sure why, or how…if it came back to hormones and the fact that he was just muscular enough to lull her into a stupor.

Except, her hormones weren't centered around her heart, and that was definitely where a good portion of the feelings were coming from. She felt for him. Sad, happy that he'd found Sayid. And the real danger lay in the fact that she wanted to know more. That she was curious about him. About what was beneath the layers of rock that he kept between himself and the world.

Because there were layers. All shields were up with this man, no question. As he'd relayed the story of his desolate childhood, his life as a mercenary, there had been no emotion. Until the mention of Sayid.

"And that's how you ended up with a palace in the desert?"

"That is the long version of the story, yes. The short version is, a sheikh gave me a palace. Women like that one, usually," he said, giving her a careless wink before turning away, taking a right at the curved staircase that would lead them back to her room.

"I'm sure they do. What do they think of the whole ex-mercenary thing?"

"Oh, I don't go spreading that one around."

"What do you tell them you do?"

"They don't usually ask."

"They don't?"

"No," he said.

She had to take two stairs at a time to try and keep up with his long stride. At only five three, she wasn't exactly long legged, and she guessed he was more than a foot taller than she was. "What do they ask?"

He stopped and turned to her and she didn't manage to stop her stride in time, putting herself right in front of him, her eyes level with the center of his chest. "They don't usually talk this much," he said, eyes intent on hers.

She sucked in a shuddering breath, suddenly finding it hard to stand straight. She'd never been so close to a man who was so...so much. That's what it was. Alik was just too much. Too masculine, too unrefined, too sexy. Oh, he was much too sexy. He was also too immoral, too unemotional and too much a stranger for her to be going weak-kneed over him.

Yet again, her body didn't seem to care much for the common sense take on things.

"I see."

"Do you?" he asked, his head cocked to the side.

"Y-yes."

Why wasn't he moving? She couldn't back up, then she would betray that she was unnerved by his closeness. She was, but he didn't need to know that. He needed to move on up the stairs so that she could breathe again. So that her body would feel like it belonged to her again.

"You don't approve," he said, turning away and continuing up the stairs.

The knot that had been building in her chest frayed and loosened, releasing a gust of air from her lungs. "I'm not judging," she said.

"You are judging."

"Only a little. Because clearly, Leena as evidence, you have some control issues when it comes to women."

"I do not have control issues," he said.

"Really?" They reached the top of the stairs and Alik didn't turn on any lights.

"Really," he said, crossing his arms over his chest. "Saying I have control issues implies that I fail at stopping myself from conducting liaisons with women when the simple truth is, I give in willingly. Unless I'm on duty, I don't see the point in abstaining."

"I don't even know what to say to that. And I don't believe that that's sufficient evidence that you don't have an issue with control. I find you self-indulgent."

"I am extremely self-indulgent. And also quite indulgent of my partners. But it still doesn't speak to a lack of control." He took a step toward her, and she took one away from him. Her back came up against the wall and her breathing stopped altogether.

"I think it does," she said, unwilling to back down.

"Oh, Jada, if I had a lack of control—" he advanced on her again, and she found herself without anywhere to flee "—you would know."

"I would?" She cursed her mouth. It was part of the mutiny against common sense her body was currently executing while her brain looked on in horror.

"I would have kissed you by now. I would have pulled you into my arms and tasted your lips, your throat. I would have put my hand on your breast, felt your nipples getting hard beneath my fingers. Then my tongue."

She turned her head to the side. It was the only way she could force herself not to look at him, the only way to keep herself from being drawn into his web.

He chuckled and she looked back. He had moved away from her, continuing on down the hall. "Lucky for you," he said, "I have no such control issues."

Insults flooded her mind, insults that wanted badly to escape and fly at his head. However, for some reason, now she had some sort of handle on her self-control and she couldn't speak them. A cruel joke.

It took her a moment, but she could finally speak again. "I wouldn't let you."

"I'm not so sure that's true," he said, stopping at a door

that looked very much like the rest of the doors to her. "This is you."

"So it is," she said, still not convinced. Everything looked the same to her and this place was like a maze. "And I *wouldn't* let you."

He looked at her, and she felt every heated word he'd said pouring into her. Felt it beneath her skin, promises of sensual pleasure that went well beyond her experience.

She didn't know where that thought had come from. She knew about sex and she'd had plenty of it. She seriously doubted that there was sensual pleasure she somehow hadn't reached. Sex was all fine and good, but not, in her experience, something to make you lose your mind. And there was no way the experience would be better with Alik. She'd loved her husband, after all, and she didn't even like this man.

Love made sex better, surely. Love was what she'd waited for. Love and marriage, and there had been no one since. Because emotion was more important than desire and she understood that. She almost pitied Alik for not getting it.

And she pitied her poor, traitorous body its increased heart rate and sweaty palms. She was above all that. She knew better than to be drawn into it.

"If you say so," he said. "Have a good night."

"I will." *Alone.*

"I will see you tomorrow."

She didn't want to see him tomorrow. She wanted to pretend that in the morning, all of this would evaporate. But she'd been hoping that for days now, and still, every morning she woke up in a palace in a foreign desert country, the sea crashing outside of her window.

And while, on paper, that all sounded fine, the inclusion of Alik Vasin made it feel decidedly less so.

CHAPTER SIX

THERE WAS NO GOOD REASON for Alik to remain in Attar, and remain celibate. None at all. And yet, here he was, still tethered to his palace and, in effect, to the woman and child who were occupying it.

It had been a strange couple of weeks. It had, at first, been easy to justify that he was staying to ensure he didn't subject the child to another move too quickly after the first one. Then he'd had to wait for the adoption paperwork to come for Jada so he could sign anything he needed to sign and they could get everything sent in. Then, he thought he shouldn't leave them here. It was too remote. He would feel more comfortable, a bit like less of a marauding bastard, if he installed them in one of his more urban homes.

So that Jada could walk or drive where she needed to go. So that they didn't have to worry about sandstorms or any of the other dangers in the desert. And there were so many.

Alik paced the length of the balcony that looked out over his pool. That pool was one of the dangers. As was a balcony. He would have to be sure everything was secured.

He hadn't known there were so many dangers in the world until he'd brought a child into his life. Laughable though the thought was, since he was a man who had faced death more times than most. But thinking of danger in the context of himself didn't bother him in the least.

But that soft, small, helpless little girl who now lived in his home? Thinking of her in danger twisted his insides.

And there were so many dangers to a person that small. The floors in the palace were too hard. The stone a hazard for a toddling child's forehead.

Alik strode back into his room and down the stairs. Jada was sitting in the dining room, holding Leena in her lap. Leena had her chubby fist wrapped around a piece of banana.

"Babies are impractical," he said.

Jada arched one dark eyebrow. "How so?"

"They are too small. It's unreasonable."

"Do you think so?" she asked, her eyes glittering with amusement. It irritated him.

"Yes."

"You should have seen her when she was a newborn. She weighed six pounds. She was no longer than your forearm."

He looked down at his arm. "That is entirely unreasonable."

"But so cute."

"They are also loud. Too loud for something so small."

"The better to keep track of them."

"That is practical."

Jada smiled, and Alik felt a strong tug in his gut. More impractical even than babies, was his attraction to his new wife. She was beautiful, so it was no real surprise that it existed. It was the insistence of it. The total, consuming nature of it. He wasn't accustomed to giving a woman more than a passing assessment and, if she was willing, acting upon the attraction, or walking away if she wasn't.

Although, in his memory there had been no unwilling women. Women typically responded to him. It was almost predictable. The kind of predictable he would never complain about. Perhaps that was the difference. Jada didn't want him, or rather, didn't want to want him, with a vehemence that emanated from her petite frame.

It was unusual. And not as deterring as he would have liked it to be.

He should stay well away from her. That he felt the desire to kiss her, to steal some of that passion from her, was warning enough that she was the sort of woman he should never touch. The level to which she tempted him should be warning enough.

"I'm glad you find something about your daughter to be practical," she said.

"It wasn't a commentary on her, but on all new humans. The head size is also of concern to me."

"Of concern to you? Think of how concerning it is for women—we have to give birth to them."

"You didn't."

He realized the moment he said the words, that they had been wrong. He had never spent much time being concerned with whether or not his words were hurtful or right. He'd never had to. He wasn't in the habit of making much in the way of conversation with anyone. Only Sayid had his ear.

Otherwise, in the rooms filled with the most people, there was rarely anything to say. In clubs everyone was too busy dancing, letting the music move through their bodies and erase everything else. Failing that, there was the alcohol chaser—he was a big fan of those.

But there wasn't conversation. And as he'd always seen himself as being smooth, adept, he was shocked to discover that conversing with women was not his strength. Which made it an even bigger shame that sex with Jada was off the table. Because, in the bedroom at least, he would satisfy her, of that he was certain.

"That was a jackass thing to say," she said, standing up, Leena held firmly against her chest.

Frustration bubbled up in him. He wished he could understand things like this. Emotion. He'd spent the better part of his life faking it, expecting that one day it would take root down inside of him, but it hadn't. It left him feeling at a disadvantage in these types of situations. And he hated feeling at a disadvantage.

"I know," he said. Because he did know, even if he didn't understand why.

"Then why did you say it?"

"I was merely making an observation."

"Don't make observations like that."

"Explain to me then, why it was the wrong thing to say."

She looked shocked, and angry. Her dark brows were locked together, eyes glimmering with golden fire. "You need it explained to you? Why your need to undermine me as Leena's mother is offensive? I didn't marry you to be treated like the help. I married you so that my position as Leena's mother would be unquestionable. To you and to everyone else. So your comments about how I didn't give birth to her only serve to take that sacrifice and make it meaningless!"

"How is it made meaningless by a comment? I didn't physically destroy the marriage license, or any of the adoption paperwork, and that is what gives you your status."

Logic. He would try and use logic to defuse the situation.

Judging by the stormy look on her face, it didn't work.

"That's your problem, Alik. You see things in black-and-white. You see them as blood or paperwork without taking the heart into the equation, and you can't do that." She turned and walked from the room, leaving him standing there alone.

Why the hell hadn't he left? He could get some peace and quiet. Stop worrying about Leena bumping her head on the stone floors.

He could find a woman. He could go and get laid and stop obsessing about Jada.

He took his cell phone out of his pocket and dialed his personal assistant. "Luca, forward my calls. I will be here in Attar working for the foreseeable future."

He punched the end call button and sat down at the table.

He put his palm on the table and into a spot of mushed banana. He grimaced. "Coffee!" he shouted, not caring he sounded demanding. He had to have control over something.

Because he seemed to have lost control over a hell of a lot since Jada Patel had entered his life.

Leena was sound asleep, and Jada found she envied her daughter. Leena didn't have any cares. She slept soundly and with a clean conscience, while Jada paced around in the dark feeling overheated and guilty. And a little dirty.

She should be upset at Alik. She *was* upset at Alik. But what she shouldn't be was attracted to Alik, and she found that no matter how stupid and offensive the things that came out of his mouth were, the feelings didn't go away.

They hadn't been instant. Not anywhere near it. She'd been too angry with him, had hated him too much initially. She wasn't sure she liked him a whole lot more now, but being in proximity with him had given her time to notice what she hadn't at first.

And that was basically a chiseled jaw, flawless muscle structure and eyes that seemed to see straight through her. Or at least straight through her clothes. Which, again, should be much more offensive than it was.

She huffed and walked out of her bedroom, closing the door gently behind her, and heading down the stairs, out to the garden area. The palace was still hard for her to navigate, less so now that she'd realized it had light switches. The memory made her smile and she forced herself to stop. No dreamy, smiley-type memories of Alik.

It was manufactured. Because if she went further with that memory, she would come to the crude, awful things he'd said to her in the hall. About kissing her. Touching her.

Her body heated. With rage, she was sure. Because it had been crude. Not exciting.

She pushed open the ornate double doors that led out to

the pool and the gardens. She paused and headed toward the pool, which was set into the balcony, overlooking the ocean.

She stopped when she heard the sound of water in motion, closer than the waves below. And she had to wonder if she'd come here on purpose, hoping a little bit that she might find him.

He hadn't seen her yet, though. There was no way.

She could just barely make out his shape. He was gliding through the water, a dark shadow in the brightly lit pool. Like a shark. She had to stop comparing him to predators—it was giving her a complex. Making her feel hunted.

Another rash of heat spread through her. What was wrong with her? Where was sensible, practical Jada?

"Jada." His head was above the surface now and he was treading water, his eyes fixed on her.

"How do you do that?" she asked.

"If I was not good at sensing when people were present, I would be dead by now."

"You say that with such certainty."

"I am certain of it." He swam to the edge of the pool, planting his palms firmly on the side and levering himself out of the water.

She watched the play of his muscles, water sliding down over the dips and hollows. Her throat felt suddenly dry and she realized she was thirsty. That brought to mind the image of her sliding her tongue over his skin, collecting the drops and...

She blinked. "I couldn't sleep," she said. "Obviously neither could you."

"Not so much." He reached down and took a towel from one of the chairs that lined the pool, dragging it over his broad chest. Her eyes followed the motion.

She could see now, more clearly, the tattoo on his chest, and when he raised his arm to brush the towel over his short dark hair, she saw another one, words, running the length of his bicep.

"What do they mean?" she asked.

"This one?" he pointed to the inside of his wrist, the black anchor. "Nothing. I was very drunk that night."

"And the one on your chest? It's written in Arabic, isn't it?"

"Yes. I got it after that hideous injury healed. I don't often complain about pain, but that one hurt." He paused. "It was after Sayid was taken captive. He was in prison for a year. That's how long it took us to find him. A year of intel, of threats and whatever else we could do to convince his enemies to reveal his whereabouts. I got it just before we executed the mission to rescue him. It's a common proverb here, something parents say to their children. 'At the time of a test, a person rises or falls.' I knew that when I went in after Sayid, I would rise or fall with him. Luckily, we lived."

"Yes, luckily."

White teeth flashed in the darkness, one of his naughty smiles, she was sure. "You don't sound overly thrilled about me coming out of it alive, Jada."

"I wouldn't wish death on you. Not on anyone. I'm glad Leena has a father." Though she wished Leena could have a father more capable of loving her. Alik cared, she could see that. There was a fierce protectiveness that ran through his actions with his daughter, but there was no tenderness. He almost seemed afraid of her. Afraid to touch her.

She thought back to their earlier conversation about babies and wondered if he was worried that she'd break beneath his touch.

"You just wish it wasn't me," he said. There was emotion beneath his words, and she was startled by it. She was used to cool detachment from him, from a logical approach to things that simply couldn't be reasoned out, in her opinion.

She shook her head. "Not necessarily."

"She would be your husband's daughter, if he were still alive."

She closed her eyes and fought a wave of sadness as it washed over her. Typical of Alik to say, with overwhelming casualness, the most hurtful thing. And to not even realize or understand it. No, Sunil wouldn't have been Leena's father. Because with him, she wasn't sure adoption would have ever happened. Thinking about that just confused her. Hurt her.

"But he's not." She opened her eyes again. "He's not here. He's not her father. And I've moved on from that."

"You have moved on?"

She blinked, knowing her next words would be a lie. "Yes."

"How? Explain to me how you have moved on? You have had other lovers?"

She hadn't even been on a date. Hadn't looked at another man. Hadn't wanted to. Until Alik. And since she'd met him she still didn't *want* to look at another man, she was just finding it difficult not to. "No. I was focused on the adoption."

"Then how is it you've moved on?"

"How do you move on?" she asked. She knew he wouldn't know. He didn't understand things like that. Things like emotion and pain, things like what it meant to love someone. "I mean, really. That part of my life is a part of me. It's who I am."

"And what do you mean by that?"

"I spent most of my adult life being his wife. Learning how to live with him, as you do with any marriage. Cooking food just how he liked it."

"Making love how he liked it?"

Her cheeks burned. "That too."

"And what about what you like?"

"Marriage is compromise," she said. "You give, your spouse gives. You form a new shape to accommodate them. And then when you lose them…"

"The changes don't make sense?"

She nodded slowly. "Something like that."

"She would, perhaps, be better off with your first husband than with me."

His tone was rough now, an edge to it.

"I don't resent your place in Leena's life," she said, realizing that it was true.

"I think you do."

"No, Alik. I only resent your place in my life."

"I see. And what about it do you find so objectionable?"

"You're my husband," she said, her voice cutting itself off, choking itself out. "And you shouldn't be."

"Tell me honestly, did you ever plan to marry again?"

"No."

"Then why does it matter what title I have. You are all about the heart, Jada, in which case, to you, no matter if I'm your husband on paper, the fact that I'm not your husband in your heart is all that should matter."

But it did. She wanted to scream it. Wanted to shout it to the heavens so he would understand. It mattered because only one man should ever have had the title. It mattered, but it shouldn't. She knew that.

Signing a document wasn't what forged a bond between people, and yet…there was something. Husband was still a meaningful position whether she wanted it to be or not. That was the real problem. Not that she felt nothing, but that she was starting to. And maybe it was down to Leena, to their connection with her.

That she could handle. Yes, they should feel bonded over Leena. They both wanted what was best for her and had acted in her best interest. So of course, they would feel a connection. Not that he did—she doubted Alik was bothered with her at all. But with her maternal instinct and all, it was logical she would feel something.

And that was all. She was sure of it.

"I don't know how you can be so calm about it. This is hardly how I saw my life going."

"Maybe then, that is the difference between you and me. I didn't see my life going anywhere."

"What does that mean?"

"Every day I got up and didn't count on making it back to my bed that night to sleep. I lived every day like it would be my last one, and sometimes I made an attempt to make it my last one. Oh, not actively, but safety has never been high on my list of priorities. So it's very hard to be disappointed at how your life has turned out when it's a surprise that you're still living at all."

His words chilled her down to her bones, and at the same time, the fire that was blazing in his eyes ignited her soul. She had always planned, always worried. Had always held life close to her chest like the precious gift that it was. And she had gotten so much pain, so many carefully laid plans utterly destroyed. What would it be like to be covered in a layer of armor as thick as Alik's? Would things roll off? Would life feel easier? She imagined that it might. Things had been so hard for so long she could hardly imagine what it might be like to have it just be simple for a while.

Alik's life certainly wasn't easy—it wasn't even terribly happy and yet he seemed so much more at ease with all of it.

"Failing that," he said, his voice getting rougher, deeper, causing everything in her to respond to it, "I could always try and make you feel more married to me."

He took a step toward her and she knew what was going to happen. She also knew that she should tell him to stop. That she should be good and sensible. That she should ignore the rapid beat of her pulse, and the tightening in her stomach. That she should embrace logical thought, and reason.

But she didn't. She just stood and watched him advance, her throat dry, her breath coming in harsh, shallow bursts.

Why wasn't she running? Why wasn't she telling him no?

Because I don't want to.

He hooked his arm around her waist and pulled her up against his body. Water from his bare skin soaked through her cotton top, the chill making her nipples tighten. She wasn't wearing a bra because she'd been dressed for bed and now she was unbearably conscious of the fact and, heaven help her, grateful.

He cupped her chin with his thumb and forefinger, forced her to meet his gaze, and a flame burst to life inside of her. She wanted, so much it was painful, the need hot, raging, threatening to destroy everything if it wasn't met.

The tip of his thumb touched her lips, and she opened her mouth, tasted the salt on his skin from the water drops. She sucked on him, gently, and a rough growl came from deep in his chest. He tightened his hold on her and pulled her in tight, and in one fluid motion, he dipped his head and started kissing her.

Deep, sensuous, his tongue sliding against hers, tracing the line of her lips, before delving deep again. She'd never been kissed like this. So hard, so desperate. She didn't know where the hunger had come from. And then she had to wonder if it was coming from her.

This kiss was different because she had never wanted like this. Had never craved a man in quite this way.

She flattened her palms on his chest, his skin slick, hair roughened and hot beneath her hands. And she could feel his heart, throbbing fast and hard, proof that he felt it, too. That he felt the intensity like she did.

He lowered his hand and palmed her butt, drawing her in closer, bringing the V at the apex of her thighs into contact with the hard evidence of his desire. She moved her hands off his chest and looped them around his neck, forking her fingers through his hair, holding him tight.

His hand slid upward and then down the waistband of her sweatpants, beneath her underwear. She gasped when his callused palm cupped her skin, and she sighed when he squeezed her tight, amping up the tension, her need, making her ache for him.

He pushed his other hand beneath her top, found her breast, squeezed her nipple tight before sliding his thumb over it. She arched into his touch, raking her nails over his back and letting her head fall back. He took advantage of her exposed throat, pressing hot, openmouthed kisses to her skin.

He pushed his hand up higher and managed to strip her of her top in one easy motion, then he kissed her mouth again, deeper, harder, and she couldn't think. Couldn't remember why she'd ever wanted to run from this. Couldn't remember why she was here or even who she was. All she knew was that she wanted more. Whatever he would give, she wanted more.

He moved his hand down from her butt, pushing it between her thighs, sliding his fingers between her slick folds. If she could have thought, she would have been embarrassed over just how obvious it was that she wanted him, over just how ready she was, so fast. But she couldn't think past the burning pleasure that was arcing along her veins.

One finger slid over her clitoris and she pulled her mouth away from his, a strangled cry, too loud in the still of the night, escaping her lips, pushing against the haze of fantasy she'd built up to block out reality.

And then it hit her, with full, hideous force. She was half-naked, outside, with a man she barely knew and she was about to let him have sex with her.

She pulled away from him, gasping for air, looking around frantically for her shirt. She ran through a litany of curse words just under her breath while she bent to retrieve her top and tugged it over her head.

"What happened?" Alik asked.

"What happened? You kissed me and then thirty seconds later you were stripping me naked and…touching me."

"Are you going to pretend that you didn't like it?" he asked. "Because I have a low tolerance for things like that."

"I don't do things like this."

He looked at her, slow, appraising. Making her hot all over again. "Maybe you should, because you're very good at it."

She frowned, wrapping her arms around herself, a shiver racking her frame. "What's that supposed to mean?"

"That I enjoyed kissing you. And touching you. And I would very much enjoy taking it to its logical conclusion."

"But to what end?" she asked.

He frowned. "Orgasm, what else?"

She let out a short, frustrated growl. "Is that all that matters to you? Not if we mess up what we're trying to build for Leena, but having an orgasm?"

"Why would it mess anything up?"

"Are you truly so obtuse?" She examined the look on his face, totally blank, totally unruffled, and she suddenly started to understand. "It would honestly make no difference to you, would it?"

"What we do in the bedroom would be separate from how we raise Leena."

"But sex isn't separate from a relationship—it's woven through it. You can't simply ignore it during the day."

"Why not? I don't see how sex is connected to the day to day. It's a release, an adrenaline rush. My favorite way to get one, in fact, but it hardly affects what I do with the rest of my time."

"And that's why we can't. Because I can't separate it. Because I know what it can mean. How close it can make people. And you never will."

"I don't feel I especially need to know it."

"I know, Alik. And that's another problem." Jada crossed her arms beneath her breasts and walked back into the house, making a concerted effort not to look back at him. That might look like longing. It might look like she regretted the decision to stop. And she didn't. She couldn't.

This kind of thing might be fine for some people. It might be fine for Alik, but it wasn't her. Love was stronger than lust; it was more important. No matter how much she might think she wanted Alik, that was just physical. And the physical wasn't all that important.

She liked the physical, but you couldn't cuddle up with the physical afterward. And it wouldn't sit and have pancakes with you in the morning. Wouldn't hold you when you cried. The physical was only good for one thing, and she just didn't live her life that way.

It wasn't her.

Of course, that meant she would be living the rest of her life feeling very physically unsatisfied. Because she wasn't doing love again. And without love, she wasn't doing sex.

She bit her lip, fighting against a wave of unresolved arousal, and tried not to think about how very much she'd wanted to cast off her inhibitions and live life like Alik, if only for one night.

Alik prowled the length of his office, his entire body on red alert, an adrenaline high on a level he'd never experienced outside of the battlefield.

What was wrong with him? And what was wrong with her? Clearly she'd wanted him, so what was the point in denying it? It made no sense to him.

He pushed his hands back through his hair and noticed that his phone was blinking. He snatched it up off his desk. "Vasin."

"I expected to get voice mail."

"I was awake. What is it?"

"This is Michael LaMont. We spoke a few weeks ago."

"I remember," Alik said, gritting his teeth. As if he would forget.

"I was wondering if you'd given any more thought to taking up my cause?"

"Your ailing company? Yes, I have."

"And have you made a decision?"

"Not as of yet." He looked out the window, down at the pool, and his body tensed.

"I would love it if you could come to Paris for a while. See the sights, my company, take in an opera. Bring your wife if you like, or bring someone else if you need a break."

A break was exactly what he needed. Some time away. Parisian clubs and Parisian women. "Sounds like a plan, LaMont. I'll be there tomorrow. It's past time I got out of Attar."

Past time he got away from Leena, Jada and all of the ways they upended his life. Past time he took another woman to his bed and purged his system of this...this unreasonable desire for Jada. She was under his skin, and he could not allow it.

They would stay here in Attar, and he would find the man he'd always been in Paris. Alone.

CHAPTER SEVEN

"Instruct the servants on how to pack for you. We're heading to Paris in two hours."

The pronouncement seemed to shock Jada, but it shocked Alik a whole lot more. He had been planning on coming into the dining room to tell her that he would be gone for a week, and that she and Leena would stay here until his return. But that wasn't what he'd ended up saying.

"Two hours?" Jada's mouth, the mouth that he knew tasted like the most decadent dessert, rounded into a perfect O.

"Yes. I am on a time frame and you don't want to stay out here in the middle of this godforsaken desert by yourself, do you?" Frustration at himself made him sound harsher than he'd intended.

"I don't know. The alternative is going to your godforsaken bachelor pad in the middle of a French city, where you will also be—am I right?"

"You are coming with me. I am not leaving you here. It is an issue of safety."

"How is it an issue of safety? We're quite fine out here. All the modern conveniences. Light switches, even, as you pointed out."

"I do not like the idea of leaving you alone."

"Alik, you have a staff of about a hundred out here. I think we'd be fine."

"Are you honestly arguing with me about going to Paris?

No woman would do that. What is wrong with you?" She made no sense to him. Trying to get out of a trip to Paris, turning down sex when she clearly wanted sex. The woman was inscrutable.

"What is wrong with me? I'm finally coming to terms with the fact that this is my life, finally finding a routine, and now you want to uproot me."

"The plan was never for you to stay here."

"I know."

"It was also the plan for you to come with me and be my date at business functions if it was required. It is now required and you will do as I tell you." He was lying. And for some reason his conscience, which until thirty seconds ago he hadn't known he possessed, twinged a bit.

"I did agree to that, Alik, you're right. But I didn't agree to submit to your every command, so you can get off your high horse and chill for a moment. If I have to be ready in two hours I'd better go figure out what I need now."

"Never mind that...I will have the servants see to it. Did you just tell me to...chill?"

"Something wrong with your hearing? I did. And you need to."

"No one talks to me that way."

"Does anyone talk to you for longer than five minutes at a time, Alik? Anyone other than Sayid, who I'd venture to say could give you a serious run for your dominance and is probably not bothered by you in the least."

"Not very many people do, and do you know why, Jada?"

She set Leena down on the floor, on her blanket and stood, arms crossed beneath her breasts. "Why, Alik? Please do enlighten me."

"Because people who are smart are afraid of me. They know that even if I'm smiling at them, I could turn on them at a moment's notice. If money passes into my hand and my allegiance is asked to be changed, it will be changed. That is why people are afraid of me. And they should be."

"I'm not afraid of you, Alik."

"I think you are."

"You think wrong."

"I don't think wrong, Jada, I know you're afraid of me. Oh, perhaps you aren't afraid of me harming you in any way, and you should not be. For all my sins, I have never hurt a woman or child, and I never would. There is a line in the sand that even I won't cross. But I think you're afraid of what might happen if I get too close. Of what might happen if I touch you. Kiss you again."

He took a step forward, watching as her pupils expanded, making her eyes appear darker, more seductive, watching her pulse throb at the base of her throat, revealing just how unnerved she was. Revealing just how turned on she was, he suspected.

"Yes, you're afraid of that," he said. "So afraid of my touch." Nearly as much as he was coming to fear hers. What it did to him. But in keeping with his character, the more dangerous something seemed, the more he wanted it.

He extended his hand, intent on cupping her cheek, feeling her silken skin beneath his fingertips and Jada jerked back like she'd seen a snake.

Jada was mainly horrified that she'd wanted to lean into his hand, that she'd longed to feel his skin against hers again. That she wanted more than what she'd gotten last night when she should really hope nothing like it ever happened again.

He was wrong, though. She wasn't afraid of him. She was afraid of herself.

"Just because I don't want it, doesn't mean I'm afraid."

"You do want it, though," he said.

"No." She bent down and scooped Leena up into her arms. "I don't. I have too much going on in my life, and frankly, so do you. We have a daughter. We have a daughter together. That means we have to be able to parent together."

"I told you, I doubt I will be doing much in the way of parenting."

"I think you will," she said, challenging him. The way he'd challenged her. "I think you're going to have to. Leena isn't an accessory to add to your home. She's not a vase that has been in your family for generations that you're owed based on lineage—she's your blood. Not a thing you hold rights to."

"It is not for my own sake that I thought to avoid her, but for hers. Don't ask why, because you know the answer."

She did. She knew why. Alik said the worst things at the worst possible times, and that was when he wasn't trying to hurt anyone. He just seemed to be missing that place inside of him that should be filled with emotion and empathy. He was void there.

The realization, the image of an empty hole in his chest where his heart should be, made her own heart feel pain. It wasn't fair. Alik had never had a chance. He had never had love or family. He'd grown into the man he was thanks to circumstances, but even though so much of it wasn't his fault, it didn't make it any less difficult for him to deal with. It didn't make it any less real.

"I know you might not know this," she said, "since you didn't know your parents, but children are able to forgive a lot of shortcomings. Because they are born loving you, trusting you. At the moment, you have that love, that trust. No matter what you say, no matter what you intend to do, no matter how distant you want to be, you will be Leena's father. And if you never try, she will have a lifetime of pain, disappointment and the breaking of that bond. Because she has that bond, Alik."

"She doesn't seem to like me," he said, looking down on Leena's head.

"She does. And she will more as she gets older. She'll love you, Alik. You will be her hero. It's how a little girl looks at her father. It's how I looked at mine. He died when I was seventeen, and it was such a shock. He'd seemed invincible to me. Superman. I always felt safe with my father around."

"How did he die?"

"My parents were older. I was a late-in-life surprise for them. I came sixteen years after their last child, my much-older brother. They were wonderful, and I didn't get enough time with them. But my father... He taught me what to expect from a man in terms of treatment, simply by treating me like a princess. I would never have settled for less, because without words he showed me what it was I deserved. You have the chance to do that for her. Or not."

"I need to go and ensure all is going as it should with the packing."

"Of course," she said.

Alik turned and walked out of the room, and a flood of emotion washed through her with such ferocity she was afraid it might bring her to her knees. She didn't feel hopeless, though, not as hopeless as she had a moment ago.

Because when Alik had turned to go she'd seen emotion in his eyes. She'd seen fear. He didn't want to let Leena down, and whether he knew it or not, he was on the road to loving her. And with that, more would follow. She had to hope so.

Right now, she just ached for him. For the man who was lost in a situation that made no sense to him. Alik was alpha, controlling and extremely capable. He had money and power, charisma to spare when he chose to apply it. But Alik didn't understand love, and in this situation, that made him infinitely more helpless and less equipped than she was.

When it came to emotion, she held the power, while he stood, defenses down, with nothing.

She kissed the top of her daughter's head and closed her eyes, repeating a promise in her mind, over and over again.

I will help your father learn to love you. Because you deserve nothing less.

* * *

She'd been on one of Alik's private planes before, but that didn't mean she was immune to the glamor of traveling in that kind of style. Not after a lifetime of flying economy. And after suffering, happily, with the inundation of luxury, brought on by having a bed available for a flight, she was completely floored by her first glimpse of Paris.

She'd been to India, with a stopover in Frankfurt, on a visit to see her in-laws once, but beyond that, she was hardly a world traveler. Seeing so many sights in person that she'd seen immortalized in movies was a truly surreal experience.

And after being treated to her first vision of the Eiffel Tower, she was shocked even further by the location of Alik's town house. It was sleek and spare inside, the perfect foil for the view it afforded. Out one side was an alley, with a cobbled street and small, crowded shops. The patisserie, the boulangerie and various cafés with pastries guaranteed to go straight to her hips. And on the other side was the tower itself, the base of the iron structure filling the view from the kitchen windows. And from the bedrooms, you could see the rest, glittering in the darkness, iconic and surreal.

No, not even the luxury of Alik's private plane could have prepared her for it. As if a palace in Attar hadn't been sufficient to prove what sort of man Alik was, to demonstrate the sort of power he had, the opulent home in the heart of Paris drove the point home.

"Your room is here," Alik said, "Leena's is down the hall. The master is on the top floor."

"Only the master?"

"And my office, but yes."

Alik was a man of total self-indulgence. That, also, should have been clear by now. For some reason, she was understanding it slowly, in increments. Perhaps because it was so very different from the way she did things. From who she was.

She should be disgusted by his attitude. Instead, she found

she was fascinated by it. Not many people were so honest about how selfish they were. Alik owned it, enjoyed it. He'd made a life that was purely for himself and he seemed happy in it.

As happy as Alik could ever be.

That thought made her sad. Reminded her that sometimes having whatever you wanted didn't add up to a satisfying life.

"So what are our plans while we're here?"

Alik put a hand in his pocket and leaned against the door frame of the bedroom. "Tomorrow night my potential client is providing us with tickets to the opera, before I meet with him the following day."

"Opera? I've never been." And she shouldn't want to go. Not with Alik. It was shockingly like a date. Because you couldn't bring a one-year-old to the opera.

"Then it shall be a culturally enriching experience for you," he said, his eyes not focused on her, but on a point somewhere past her head.

"What about Leena?"

"I have secured an au pair for the duration of our stay."

"Have you?" she asked, anger—welcome, blessed anger—spiking in her. "And what are her references? Shouldn't I have been consulted?"

"Adira took care of it, and I trust her as much as I trust anyone." She noticed he didn't say he trusted her completely. Simply as much as he trusted anyone. Because Alik didn't trust. Another piece of him to add to her puzzle. She shouldn't be working on an Alik puzzle.

No, she should be. Because she was trying to figure out how to help him have a real, positive relationship with Leena, and in order to do that she would have to understand him.

"Still, in the future, I would like to be consulted."

"Of course, my princess, whatever you desire," he said on a slow drawl, his tone mocking.

"She's my daughter. I've rarely left her alone." And she

shouldn't be leaving her now. She should tell Alik no. Tell him she didn't want to go to the opera.

But she did. And it had been a long time since she'd been out. Since she'd done something she wanted to. Something for herself.

"She will be fine. She'll be sleeping for most of the time we're gone, as she is now."

"I know," she said. "I mean, I do know but...kids make you worry."

Alik frowned. "Yes, they do. That is a universal feeling, then?"

"Yes. Everyone worries about their kids."

A slow half smile curved his mouth. "And so do I."

Even as they were preparing to leave for the opera, Alik wondered why he'd issued the invitation to her. He could have asked another woman. Could have gone to a club the night before and met someone to take out.

Better still, he could have given it a miss entirely. Opera wasn't his thing. But he had asked Jada. And he found that he actually wanted to take her.

Maybe because he was sure it was something she would never do for herself. And she looked tired, something he was certain was partly his fault.

And no matter what she'd said to him, she hadn't moved on. She was still grieving her husband; even he could see it, and he scarcely understood that emotion or any other.

That was how he found himself waiting at the base of the stairs in his town house, his heart beating a little faster than normal, waiting for her to join him. Waiting for his first sight of her in the dress he'd selected for her to wear.

That was another unusual thing. He'd never concerned himself with putting clothes on a woman before. In the past, he'd only been worried about taking them off. He was hardly a connoisseur of fashion, female or otherwise. But he'd seen the dress in a boutique window that afternoon on his way through the city and he'd known he had to have it for her.

As if on cue, he heard the sound of high heels on marble floor, and he looked up. And then it became hard to breathe. Hard to swallow.

The rich, crimson fabric made Jada's golden skin glow, the strapless, scooped neckline of the dress revealing a teasing glimpse of her full, perfect breasts. Her waist was small, the gown fitted there before gently flowing away from her hips in waves of chiffon. And when she took her first step down the stair, the fabric parted and revealed its secret, and a hint of Jada's shapely legs.

"The slit is too high," she said, walking down toward him, her hair, glossy black and wavy, shimmering beneath the lights as she moved.

"It is not high enough," he said, unable to take his eyes off her.

She stopped on the last step, the top her head still barely reaching his eyebrows. "I never wear clothes like this. It's very revealing."

"I know. And it's perfect."

"That's a very male perspective."

"I'm very male."

She blinked. "Granted."

"So then it should come as no surprise to you."

"I would love to have refused to wear it on principle, but I don't have other opera dresses lying around, and regardless of the fact that I feel like it puts far too much of me on show...I do like it." A reluctant smile tugged on the corners of her full mouth.

"I knew you would. Or rather, I knew I would, and that was all I cared about."

"So you dressed me for your own pleasure? A bit selfish, but then, that's to type I suppose."

"Feel free to enjoy me for your own selfish pleasure, Jada, if it helps."

He didn't think he imagined the slight coloring of her cheeks, the tinge of pink in her skin. She paused for a moment, her head cocked to the side, black hair sliding over her shoulder like an ink spill. "You look very nice. I've never seen you with a tie."

He raised his hand to the knot of midnight-blue silk. "It is an opera," he said, lowering it again.

"Yes, but you showed up at the courthouse in jeans."

He turned around and opened the front door. "I changed before the hearing."

"Yes, you did."

The car he'd ordered was idling outside. He put his hand up when the driver started to get out, and opened the door for Jada himself. "After you," he said.

She slid into the car and he got in after her. She was looking down, a strange expression on her face, then she looked back at him. "I haven't been on a date since…you know since when."

"Is this a date?" he asked.

Her eyes widened. "Not really, but…well, it sort of is."

"I'm not certain I've ever really been on a date," he said.

"That can't be true," she said, looking out the window at the passing view as the car started moving. He watched where she watched, taking in the lights smearing across the darkness as they drove on. She was seeing the city for the first time. It was interesting to see it through her eyes, to see it with wonder and excitement.

"I don't date women, princess. I sleep with them."

"I see," she said, her words clipped.

"You find me crude. I understand that, but I also don't lie."

"I do appreciate that."

"But, for the purposes of tonight," he said, not understanding quite why the words rolling around in his head were giving him pleasure, only that they were, "we are on a date."

"I think I can handle that if you can."

"I have dodged enemy gunfire, and on more than one occasion, not dodged it entirely, so I think I can handle going on a date with my wife."

His words hung in the air. They'd seemed louder than anything either of them had said before. And they seemed to just float there.

He had never called her that before. Never referred to her as his wife. Because while he considered them married in the eyes of the law, he'd never thought of her with the title attached.

So maybe she was right. Maybe marriage was more than paper, even to him. But it didn't explain why he'd suddenly called her his wife.

"It's okay," she said as the car slowed. "I'll let it go if you will."

He nodded, aware that in the dim lighting she might not have seen.

The car came to a complete stop and again, he halted the driver, getting out and then rounding to Jada's side to open it for her.

He extended his hand and clasped hers in his. She felt so good, so soft and warm. And then he didn't let go. "Since we're on a date," he said, leading her up the lit, white stairs that led into the opera house.

They walked in and the lobby was filled with people, glittering from head to toe in designer gowns, tuxes and enough gems to fill the vaults of the World Bank.

Alik watched Jada's eyes as they walked through the opulent entryway. And he took notice of the high-gloss, caramel-colored marble floor, the pillars, the ceiling. Took notice of the chandelier, hanging low above them, dripping with crystals.

It had been a long time since he'd been impressed by such things. A long time since he'd even bothered to notice. When he'd been a boy, taken into the organized crime business, he'd been stunned by the glamor, by the wealth. And at some point, he had gotten used to it, and it had become tarnished by the kinds of activities he knew were often involved in the acquisition of such things.

Funny how, though he'd inhabited the world for most of this life, he had never loved it. Had never felt entirely settled in it.

Through Jada's eyes, things seemed glittery again. Strange. Interesting. And wonderful in its way.

"We're up here," he said, gesturing to the curved staircase that led away from the crowd.

"Don't tell me you have some sort of private box."

"The royal box," he said. "Actually, it's the box the last Tsar of Russia and his wife used to use when they visited Paris and got a craving for theater. It was designed specifically for them, and I think our host found himself quite clever putting me in this particular box."

"Tsar Alik. It's not so bad."

"Tsarina," he said, bowing slightly to her, gratified by the flush of pink in her golden cheeks. He took her hand in his and led her up the stairs, into the booth. A heavy velvet curtain in a robin's-egg blue was held back by thick, velvet ties. Matching curtains were tied back around the front part of the box, keeping the far recesses of it obscured to any curious onlookers.

"The thing about these sorts of boxes," he said, putting his hand low on her back and guiding her inside, "is that you don't have the best view of the stage. You are in front, which is prestigious, and if you sit in the center, you are on stage yourself. We even have our own curtain. People will look up here and wonder who we are. And that is what they're designed for."

"Very ostentatious," she said.

"Very. But it's what people do with money."

"It's not what you've done with money," she said, taking a seat in one of the plush chairs, her fingers tracing the carved wood on the edge of the arm. "You're hardly in the news, if you are at all."

"Because attention has never mattered to me," he said, taking his seat next to her.

"What does matter to you?"

It was a good question. As a kid, he had wanted to survive. To get up and live to see another day. As an adult, he'd grown tired. Had pushed back at life, challenged it. Now that he had Leena, things had changed again. "Life to me has often just been something I was doing. I was not dead, which meant I lived, which meant I was obligated to act. I never loved my life, was never so concerned with it as some people. So I went on dangerous missions no one else would take, rode motorcycles too fast, jumped out of airplanes."

"You had a death wish, you mean?"

"Not so much. But there I was, alive. And I was trying to…feel it."

"By courting death?"

"Makes a sick sort of sense, doesn't it?"

She looked away from him, down at the filling auditorium. "Yes. It does. What is the name of the show?"

"*La Traviata.* She dies at the end."

Jada shot him a deadly glare. "Spoiler alert!"

"It's hardly a spoiler…it's opera. She always dies in the end." He leaned back in his chair, and Jada fell silent. They sat like that until the house lights dimmed, until the curtains below opened.

And the music started. And Jada was on the edge of her seat, her eyes rapt on the stage below them. While she watched the singers, he watched her, watched her shoulders tense, watched her expression contort dramatically when something would happen.

She was so beautiful to him then. So unguarded. He knew that was how people saw him. As unguarded. Perhaps he was, but it was simply because he'd never had anything to protect. He was too numb to hurt.

Jada was so soft inside. She had so much light in her, so many delicate intricacies to her that would be so simple, and so cruel to destroy. It made him worry for her. Made him feel all the more fascinated by her.

By the time intermission came, he found he could hardly breathe, and it had nothing to do with the performance happening on stage.

Jada relaxed, leaning back in her chair. "This is wonderful," she said.

"Yes," he said, his throat tight for some reason, "it is."

She stood and stretched, arching her back, her breasts rising, pushing against the fabric of the gown. Her tension might have dissipated with the halting of the production, but his had not.

He felt like something was going to burst inside of him. Like he was suddenly aware that there was a dam inside of him, a great stone wall holding back the potential for torrential destruction.

And he had to stop it. Had to shore it up with something. Something simple. Something he understood. He stood, his hand shaking, his heart thundering.

Jada looked at Alik and froze. She realized, in that moment, what it was like to be a gazelle, stalked by a predator. Except, she wasn't going to run. She didn't know why, only that she wouldn't.

The opera was mesmerizing. It was all feeling, feeling put to music, so rich and affecting. And even though she didn't understand the words, it transcended language. It went down deep inside of her, tapped into a well of emotion, a well of need, that she hadn't known was quite so immense.

And now Alik was looking at her like he wanted her. More

than wanted, like he needed her. There was something dark and deadly in his eyes now. Something desperate. And she liked it, responded to it. It was different than the flat nothingness she usually saw there, different than that blasted, false, shallow front he usually put on.

In that moment, as his eyes met hers, everything fell away. Her present, her past. There was nothing but Alik, nothing but the intense, terrible ache he made her feel.

This was frightening. This was real. And it was enticing. A black flame dancing in front of her, so beautiful she couldn't look away, so dangerous she knew she had to. But she wouldn't.

Instead, she reached out her hand and prepared to touch the fire.

CHAPTER EIGHT

JADA'S FINGERS MADE contact with Alik's heated skin, and a shiver went through her body. She was burned, heat arcing through her, raging in her veins, but she wasn't hurt. And she didn't want to take her hand away. Didn't want to turn from the path she was walking down now.

And then the moment of calm was over. Alik growled, taking her into his arms and pushing her behind the curtain, against the wall. And then he was kissing her. Deep. Hard. Hungry and desperate and everything she'd ever fantasized about. Everything she'd never known to fantasize about.

"Alik," she whispered, a plea. For him to stop. For him to keep going.

He kissed her neck, her bare shoulder, his hand resting at the base of her throat, gentle, arousing. He spoke to her, low and rough, in more than one language, as if his brain couldn't settle on one in that moment. Gratifying, since she was no less confused. No less lost in the sensations that were rioting through her.

His other hand rested on her hip, his fingers curling, bunching the thin material of her dress up into his palm, widening the slit that ran up to her thigh. He brushed her bare skin with his fingers, tugged the fabric to the side.

"Alik," she said again, a warning this time.

"No talking," he said, kissing her lips.

She didn't want to talk. She wanted to kiss. So the order

seemed fine enough to her. Except there was a reason she was supposed to stop him; she was sure there was. But she couldn't remember it, and even if she could, she was sure that right now she wouldn't care about it.

She just kissed him back, sucking his tongue deep into her mouth, feeding off his hunger, letting his desperation fuel her own. She tugged at the material on his suit jacket, pushed it from his shoulders.

He growled and his hand tightened at her throat, then eased, fingertips sliding down, so gentle, tracing her collarbone, curving over the swells of her breasts. She sucked in a sharp breath, her nipples puckering beneath the crimson fabric, aching for him, for his touch.

"Tell me," he said, pressing a kiss to her neck.

"Touch my breasts," she said, not sure why it was so easy to tell him what she wanted. Only that, in that moment, there was no time for embarrassment. There was no time for hesitation, for flirtation. She was on the edge of something, something she couldn't put words to, and she knew that only Alik could take her over.

Alik obeyed her command, his hands coming down to cup her, thumbs teasing her through the gown's bodice.

She tugged at his tie, loosening it, not bothering to pull the knot out completely. There wasn't time. Music swelled in the background and she didn't care. Because her need wasn't satisfied yet.

For the past three years this part of herself had been dormant. Buried. Lost. She hadn't experienced desire, hadn't burned for the touch and kiss of a man. She hadn't let herself remember what it was like, not truly.

And now she was on fire, the sensation so hot, so painful and beautiful, that she had to embrace it, had to follow the path, even if it led to total ruination. This was beyond the desire she knew. Past reason. Beyond herself.

He lowered his head and kissed the top of her breast, his

tongue tracing the line of the dress. She forked her fingers through his hair, held him there for a moment.

The hand at her hip moved, fingers teasing at the edge of her panties, dipping beneath the silken fabric, sliding through her slick folds. A low moan escaped her lips, swallowed by the music coming from below.

"You're so good at this," she said, her words broken.

He said nothing, a low chuckle vibrating against her chest as he licked and kissed his way back to her mouth, fingers pushing deeper, sliding over her clitoris. He dipped one inside of her and she bucked against him, hungry for more, hungry for everything.

She held on to the front of his dress shirt, her face buried in his chest while he worked her body with his skilled hands. An orgasm built in her, and he brought her to the edge, then pushed her away from it, his rhythm maddening, enough to turn her on more than she'd ever been in all her life, without giving her the release she craved.

"Alik, now," she said, her hands gliding down his muscular chest, to the buckle of his belt, undoing it quickly, then his pants.

He pushed them partway down his hips, freeing himself.

She took his heavy length into her hand, squeezing gently. He was a very big man, and without making comparisons, she could honestly say she'd never seen a man quite like him. But she wasn't nervous. She was too needy for that, too desperate. She knew what she wanted, and she knew he could give it to her.

He reached down and picked his coat back up, digging through the interior pocket and producing his wallet, then a condom. She could have wept with relief. At least one of them could think. She was well beyond it.

"Let me," she said, taking the packet from his hand and tearing it open, rolling it onto him quickly.

He pushed her panties to the side and put his hand on her

thigh, opening her to him, positioning her. He teased her entrance with the head of his erection. The breath hissed through her teeth as he filled her slowly, completely, perfectly.

She arched into him and he slid his hand around to palm her butt, pulling her more tightly against him, pushing inside of her farther. She kissed his mouth, her hands on his back, holding on to him tightly as he thrust into her, driving them both toward completion.

She was so close, had been since he'd first touched her, but now she wanted it to last. Wanted that moment of him being in her to go on. Because it was so delicious, so incredible, far beyond her experience.

It was lust and desire, a perfect storm of physical need being met, of the need being exceeded.

He thrust deep, hard, her body pressed tightly against the wall, Alik, hot and delicious in front of her. She was surrounded by him, lost in him.

And when she reached the peak, as it built, so strong, so fast, she fought it. It was too much, too much too quickly. She was sure she couldn't survive it. It was too big, too far beyond anything she'd ever known. The sensation, the pressure, felt like too much for her body to contain, too much for her to withstand.

Then it broke over her, like a burst of stars inside, white hot and bright, overpowering, beautiful. It consumed her, burned through her like a flash fire. All she could do was cling to Alik.

She felt the moment he found his release, felt his muscles go tight, his body still, felt the shiver of pleasure that worked its way through him, the pulse of his erection deep inside her setting off a series of aftershocks.

And then she was back on earth. Back in the real world. The music didn't seem so distant, the background no longer fuzzy.

And she realized what she had done, with who and where.

"Oh no." She pushed against his chest, her hand coming up to cover her mouth.

"What?" he asked, his voice hushed.

"We just…" She looked around, tried to see if anyone was watching them. She couldn't see anyone from her position behind the curtain, only the edge of the singers on the stage, and they were completely involved in their performances. "We're in public, Alik," she hissed.

And she'd just had sex with another man. A man she didn't love. It didn't matter that he was her husband on paper because in truth, he was a stranger. If she was going to be with someone other than the man she'd loved, there had to be a better reason than blinding lust.

It made a mockery of everything she believed in. Of the values she wanted to teach her daughter. Of everything she'd always thought about herself. Of what she'd shared with the man she loved. Only with him.

And she had done it all with an audience below.

For one, terrifying moment, she felt like she was drifting without an anchor. This wasn't her. It wasn't how she was. She was sensible, she was safe. She went to bed by nine every night. She didn't have sex with strange men in opera boxes.

Tears pricked her eyes. She was horrified. She didn't want to cry in front of him, not after coming like that in his arms. It was heaping mortification on top of mortification. Because no matter how she regretted it now, there was no pretending she hadn't wanted it. That she hadn't been an equal partner, if not an instigator.

She had wanted it. That was the part that scared her most. Her body still ached, still hummed with the aftereffects of her recent release. And her frame was shaking with the effort of holding her tears at bay.

"I have to go," she said.

"The show isn't over," Alik said tightly, his eyes burning in the darkness.

"Yes, Alik. It is over," she said, not talking about the opera. "It's over for me."

She turned and swept the back curtain aside, walking out of the box and into the hall. There were people there, people milling around who could have easily walked in on them.

Her heart thundered, her legs shaking, her stomach nauseous as she made her way down the curved staircase and into the lobby, then out the front door. She ran along the line of cars idling at the curb until she found Alik's driver.

She opened the back door and the man jumped, his head rising sharply. "Mrs. Vasin?"

She didn't bother to correct him. "Yes. I need you to take me home."

"Where is Mr. Vasin?"

"He is not ready to leave yet. Take me home."

"But what about Mr....."

"If Alik bloody Vasin is as damned resourceful as he would have me believe, then he can find his own ride home and I won't worry about him for a moment. Now take me back to the town house." She leaned back against the seat, her heart thundering.

The driver put the car into Park and started to pull away from the front of the theater. Jada looked back and saw Alik burst through the front doors, his jacket gone, his tie still loose. Then she looked at the road ahead, at the streetlights and the light reflected in the rain-covered street, and said nothing.

CHAPTER NINE

ALIK CURSED JADA AT LEAST a hundred times on his way back to his town house in his ill-gotten limousine. He'd greased the palm of a waiting driver and snagged another opera attendee's ride. He couldn't be bothered to feel bad about it.

Actually, if Jada hadn't run out on him there would be very little in the world he could be bothered to feel bad about. Not when his body was still burning with the aftereffects of his release.

Not when Jada had gone up like flame in his arms, flames that had consumed him. Damn the woman. He should have gone to a club and gotten drunk instead of following her. But for some reason he needed to be home. Needed to follow her.

Dimly, through the haze of his anger, he wondered if her kiss, her body, *had* transferred her passion to him. It was why he never should have touched her.

But it was too late for that. Much too late. The floodgates were open and they were both going to have to deal with the consequences.

The limo pulled up to his house and he got out, slamming the door behind him and stalking into the house. He could not recall the last time he was so angry. Anger required emotion, loss of control, and both of those things were rare for him.

But now, he was in the thick of both.

He prowled up the stairs, tugging his tie off and throwing it onto the floor, then continued down the hall, his heart pounding, his body aching for more. For another taste of the woman who had brought him to heaven and then looked at him like he was the devil.

He could have caught up to her at the theater, but he'd paused at the middle of the stairs and watched her instead, watched her run out of the theater, deep crimson against the pale marble surroundings. Like a rose in the middle of stone. Triumphant, alive.

Only Jada was also angry. The emotion coming from her in waves, undeniable and somewhat awe inspiring. And then it had been as if some of it had attached itself to him, coated his skin. And then he'd felt it, too. Only he wasn't angry at himself. He was angry at her. How could she experience what they just had, the same damn thing, and then run off?

It wasn't simply that she'd left, it was that she'd looked like she wanted to cry. As if he'd hurt her in some way when they both knew all he'd done was give her pleasure. Mind-blowing pleasure at that.

He wasn't being conceited—it was the truth.

He wrenched open the door to her room without knocking and she shrieked tugging her dress up against her breasts, attempting to cover herself.

"What the hell was the meaning of that?" he asked, aware that he was showing his loss of control and temper, not sure that he cared.

"I might ask you the same question," she fired back, her eyes stormy. "You just…you did that to me in a public place. A public place! We could have been seen. We could have been—"

And his control snapped. "I *did that* to you?" he repeated, his voice low. "I did it. *To* you."

"Yes," she said, lifting her chin.

"Aren't you a pretty little liar. Making up stories that suit your reality. I did nothing to you. You grabbed me. You kissed me. You were the one who wrapped your hand around me and put the condom on, so don't you dare act the part of wounded maiden." He advanced on her and she shrank back. Good. Finally she saw what he was. Finally she was afraid. Just like everyone else. And he would not hold himself back, not for her, not now. Not when it was her fault that his armor was cracked, that all of this was leaking out. "If there is a part for you to play in this little opera you're conducting in your head it would be the whore, and make no mistake."

"And if I'm the whore," she spat, "what does that make you?"

"No less and no more. But I know my part, and I don't pretend to be something I'm not. I don't pretend to be above the lusts of the flesh even while I'm burning up for it."

"Have you no sense of responsibility? Of right? You act like self-control is some sort of sin, but people aren't animals and we don't just have to go around doing everything we like!"

"So proper, Jada, have you ever stepped out of line other than tonight?"

"I've never wanted to."

"You never wanted to? Or other people in your life didn't want you to?"

"What's the difference? We live for other people. At least, normal people do."

"There is a big difference, Jada. Clearly you needed to let loose. Or tonight wouldn't have happened."

"Tonight," she bit out, "never should have happened at all. I must have been crazy to let you touch me."

"Is that right?" he asked. A new kind of heat was flowing through him now, reckless and dark. So often in his life, he felt like an observer, standing above things, watching them, manipulating, but not engaging.

He was engaged now. And the closer he got to Jada, the more tightly he embraced the anger that was pouring through him, the looser his grip on his control became.

He took a step toward her and she didn't back down, didn't shrink. Whatever moment of sanity she'd had before was gone now. Now she was ready to challenge him.

"Yes," she said, her voice thinner now, less confident, betraying the fact that, no matter how straight she stood, she wasn't as fearless as she appeared.

"Is that so, princess? You despise my touch so much?" She looked at him, stared him down, golden eyes burning. "I am so abhorrent to you?" He reached out and skimmed her cheekbone with his thumb, drawing it down to her lower lip, tracing the outer edge of her tender flesh. And he saw her react. Saw her eyes darken, her pulse flutter at the base of her throat. "Yes, clearly you could not stand to have me touch you again," he said, his tone mocking.

She jerked back from him. "I shouldn't be able to stand it," she said. "I don't know you. I don't like you, I sure as hell don't love you."

"What does love have to do with sex?" he asked.

Her mouth dropped open. "What does love have to… Sex is incredibly intimate—that I just shared it with a virtual stranger makes my skin crawl."

"There is nothing intimate about sex."

Jada thought she'd reached her limit on things Alik could say that she would find shocking. She'd been wrong. "Nothing intimate about… How can you think that?"

"Sex is just chasing release, using someone else's body to find it."

That assessment of it, of what they'd just done, was worse than anything she could have imagined. She felt used, but worse than that, she felt like a user. Like she'd pushed her pent-up sexual energy and frustration onto him, used his body to satisfy hers. Like she was no better than he was.

She shook her head, her throat closing up, her heart pounding so hard she felt dizzy. "That's not right, Alik. It is intimate. It's important."

"How?"

"You were inside me!" she shouted, not caring if the au pair, who was installed in a room next to Leena's, could hear. Not caring if people on the street below heard. Not caring about anything but venting her anger, her frustration. Her confusion. The rage that was only directed at herself. "How is that not intimate?"

He looked frozen then, like a block of stone, his features hard, uncompromising. He was silent for a while, and when he spoke, it was like all of the color had drained from his voice. All of the anger, the frustration that had been boiling over a moment before was gone. Leaving in its place an icy calm that chilled her to her bones.

"I am not accustomed to hysterics from a woman I've just treated to so much pleasure. I would have expected a thank-you." He was using that calm, smooth voice that she was sure had seduced countless women, but beneath the words, she could hear the total detachment. Could hear them ring false.

"Why do you have to do that?" she asked.

"What?" He took a step back and leaned against the door frame.

"Why do you have to stop being angry. Stop being...anything. Why can't you just scream at me if you're mad?"

"Why can't you just admit that you want me?"

Her heart rate picked up. Why couldn't she admit it? Because it felt like a betrayal. No, not of Sunil. He was gone. She knew that, she understood it and accepted it. It felt like a betrayal of who she was. Of what she'd always believed in.

Of who she'd always thought she was. And in that, was a betrayal of her memories.

She didn't know the woman who had grabbed onto Alik's jacket, the woman who had devoured his lips like she was starving. The woman who had taken him in her hand and squeezed tight, who had urged him to take her, hard, fast and without regard to the people in the auditorium.

No, she didn't know that woman at all, and she didn't have time, or the inclination to get to know her. She had a child to raise, a dysfunctional man to try and fix so he could be a father to his daughter, and introducing her own issues into it would just mess everything up.

More than it already was.

"Because it doesn't matter," she said. "This doesn't matter. Leena matters."

"When we touch, we burn, princess. This…this isn't normal…you have to know that." His voice was low, husky. Genuine.

"I know it's not normal," she whispered. "This is as far from my normal as possible. Look at what happened tonight. I don't…I don't do this."

"You know all about sex, Jada, I can see that you do. So why does this scare you so much?"

"Because I know about sex in a committed relationship. I know about sex in bed. The wildest I've gotten is leaving the lights on. I…I never even wanted more than that. How can I want this?" The admission was torn from her and it left her feeling raw. Exposed. This whole evening had. As if a veil had been ripped away and shown the world pieces of herself she hadn't even known were there. The deepest, most secret parts of her brought to the surface for everyone to see.

"If there's one thing I know about, it's satisfying desires. If you want it, take it, Jada. There's nothing wrong with chasing a little fulfillment."

He was offering her forbidden fruit. And she wanted to take it. "Alik, it's not fulfillment. That's what you don't understand. And we can't…we can't bring this into our arrangement. I'm not like you…I can't stay detached. I can't see it as just sex, because there is no such thing as just sex to me. It means more to me than that and…I'm not going to get it from you."

He shook his head. "I won't lie to you."

"I know. I appreciate it."

He backed out the door, his hand on the knob. "I will see you tomorrow." He closed the door, leaving her to herself.

She sat on the edge of the bed and let the dress fall to the floor. She just felt numb. No, not entirely numb. She wished she could feel numb. Her body was still on an adrenaline rush from being in Alik's arms, from sparring with him. And her heart hurt from the exchange that had just happened between them.

He'd been angry. So angry. She'd never seen that depth of emotion in him before. It was encouraging in some ways that he could express it, that it existed in him. And she wondered what she'd done to bring it out.

Had she hurt him? It didn't seem possible. But if it was only sex, which was something she knew he could get anytime he wanted, why would he care if she regretted it?

She groaned and lay facedown on the bed. She was an ass. She had told him she'd regretted being with him.

You despise my touch so much?

She'd imagined him above things like that. Above emotion. The fact that he wasn't was a comfort in some ways. In others…well, she felt like a terrible person.

A terrible, unsatisfied person who knew what she wanted, knew she shouldn't have it, and who didn't feel half as guilty about her actions tonight as she knew she ought to.

She rolled onto her back and looked at the unfamiliar ceiling. She'd uprooted her whole life for Leena. She wasn't compromising that now. Wasn't going to create an unstable environment. She had to be the rock here. Had to somehow bridge the gap between father and daughter and, at the same time, be the mother Leena deserved.

There was no time for angst about the situation with Alik. No time to sit around and self-flagellate over what she'd done tonight.

So she would push it all down deep inside of her and put a cap on it. Ignore it. And tomorrow, she would be back to normal.

There was no other option.

CHAPTER TEN

ALIK'S MEETING HADN'T gone well.

He'd gone to meet Michael LaMont with the full intention of taking on the other man's project. But he hadn't done it.

He hadn't done it because he'd uncovered some very unethical practices happening in the other man's corporation. He'd never cared about that kind of thing, not one bit. His loyalty was for sale and always had been.

But there were reports, multiple reports, of sexual harassment by executives in HR files, which he normally would never have looked at. But it had seemed important.

And as he'd been sitting there looking over the files, reading a report from an eighteen-year-old temp who had been groped repeatedly by an upper-level exec, then fired when she'd complained, he'd had one thought only: If anything like that happened to Leena when she went into the workforce, the offending hand would be removed from the man who dared touch her.

By the time LaMont had come into the office to ask Alik what he thought, Alik had very nearly shown the man, physically, what sort of mood he was in.

Instead of resorting to violence, he'd turned the job offer down flat, and had walked out. Then he'd urged the HR director to talk to the women in question about pressing charges, and promised that if the man lost his job as a result, Alik would find him work elsewhere.

He was turning into a damned altruist.

He slammed the front door of his town house, just as Jada was walking down the stairs with Leena on her hip. His heart, which seemed to be doing a lot more than pumping blood through his body lately, jumped into his throat.

It was very different than when she'd come down the stairs the night before. Her hair was tied back in a ponytail, a simple T-shirt covering her curves, a pair of gray track pants riding low on her hips, disguising the shape of her legs.

He regretted he hadn't seen her naked. If he had, he probably wouldn't feel the need to stare at her like this. He probably wouldn't still burn for her. And his heart probably wouldn't be in his throat.

He couldn't remember feeling curious about a woman after sex. Couldn't remember feeling drawn to her in a particular way. His sexual relationships were brief and mutually beneficial. One woman wasn't more important than the one that came before, or the one that would come after.

So the fact that he'd had sex with Jada, but hadn't seen her body, must be responsible for the lingering feeling of the unfinished.

That and the fact that she'd been the first woman to end things with him. There hadn't even been things to end. A brief screw against the wall and she'd run like Cinderella at midnight. Then when he'd found her, she'd made it abundantly clear that she never wanted him to touch her again.

Rejection on that scale was unheard of for him, and he found he didn't like it. He didn't even find it tolerable. And the memory of the rejection, combined with his current mood, was starting to feel a bit deadly.

"Good afternoon," she said, her tone a touch too bright. "Lunch is just about to be served on the patio. I didn't know if you would be home, but just in case, I had a setting put out for you." She whisked past him and toward the back of the house.

He followed, unsure of what to think. Now she'd succeeded

in putting him on his back foot twice in less than twenty-four hours. He didn't like that, either.

The little fenced-in patio that sat behind the house was, in fact, prepared for lunch. Ham and mushroom feuillités, macaroons and café au laits were spread out on the bistro table. There was also a plate of fruit and a high chair for Leena.

"You have taken over as mistress of the house, I see," he said, taking a seat and a bite of feuillité.

"I am your wife for all intents and purposes, Alik, and we are attempting to be a family. That means I should be at home in your homes, right?"

"I suppose," he said. He hadn't thought much about it before. Not initially. Because he had thought of them as guests in his home, a home that he wouldn't be in. Now things were becoming complicated. More tangled together.

He found that, for some reason he no longer saw it as sufficient to simply leave Leena in a luxury home to be provided for monetarily. Perhaps that was because of what Jada had said to him about fathers. About her father.

He'd never had one, not that he'd known, so had no idea the function a father could serve. But he did know that he didn't want his daughter growing up to be like him.

"Yes," he said, this time firmer, more sure, "it is right that you should take over that position. And also, I wanted to talk to you about living arrangements."

"What about them?"

"We must live together. I do travel a lot, and when I'm on short-term trips staying in hotels, I imagine Leena would find it more stable to stay at home. But when I am on a long-term business trip, for more than a month, or when I change residence for part of the year I would like you both to come with me."

Jada's eyes widened as she finished buckling Leena in her high chair and took a seat across from him. "Really? And what about your...social life?"

She meant women. He could tell by the frost in her tone. He didn't know why, but he found her jealousy gratifying. "I will find a way to manage it discreetly. It will not be a problem for either of you."

"I see." She looked down into her coffee. "What made you change your mind?"

"What you said the other day about your father. About all the difference he made to you. About how his presence taught you what sort of treatment to expect." He looked at Leena, so small and innocent, her cheeks round. And she looked at him, a smile spreading over her face. He'd never really paused to look at her before. Not once in the past few weeks. Not closely.

Now that he did, he felt like his chest was too full. Like his heart would be crushed with the pressure building there.

"I would not want Leena to choose a man like me," he said. He thought back to the reports he'd seen today. No, he'd never been the sort of man to press unwanted advances on a woman, but he still felt disturbed by it all. By the thought of Leena as a woman who would have to go out in the world and deal with men who wanted to hurt her. Or even men who didn't want to hurt her, but might, as they used her for their own selfish ends.

"I wouldn't want to teach her to expect that the man in her life should be absent, that he should be concerned with his own well-being, rather than hers. I would not want her to believe that she should accept money and physical comfort over love."

"Alik...you can give her more than you think. I know you can."

"I don't know it," he said, the pressure in his chest growing stronger, more unbearable. "I know what she should have. I know what's important. I see it, I understand it, but I don't know how to feel it."

"That's not true, Alik. I think you feel more than you let yourself."

"Such confidence in a man you don't want touching you," he bit out.

She looked down. "How was your meeting?"

"Neatly done, Jada. And my meeting was unsuccessful. I turned him down."

"Why?"

"I can't work for a man like him. I don't know why. Only that I can't."

She looked up at him, golden eyes shimmering. "I know why."

"Enlighten me."

"Because you do feel."

"Is that what you call this?"

"You're already changing, Alik. Two weeks ago you wanted to drop us off in Paris and never see her. Two weeks ago you thought she needed a nanny, not a mother. And now you see the difference. Now you see what she needs."

"I still have no idea what I'm doing."

"I don't, either. Still, caring, even if it's confusing, has to be better than spending two weeks with Leena and not changing the way you feel about her."

"All I know is that I want her to have everything, and I fear I don't have the ability to give it to her."

"All parents feel that way," she said, reaching across the table and putting her hand over his. A comforting touch. Not sexual, which was the only way he was used to being touched by women. Not violent, which was the only way he'd ever been touched by men.

He couldn't recall ever receiving comfort from another person before. Two weeks ago he would have said he didn't need it. In this moment, he felt like he did.

Perhaps he was changing. And he had no idea what that might mean. For the future, for the way he handled his life.

"Then I suppose I'm partway to the point I need to be."

"Worrying?"

He nodded. "I've never worried much," he said. "Because in my experience, worry fixes nothing. When I was starving, worrying about where food would come from wouldn't deliver it to me—it required action. Worry wouldn't serve me on the battlefield—it would distract me. And yet I find with her...I worry."

Emotion was coming easier these days. Odd, after a life spent chasing feeling, it would come so suddenly now. Anger with Jada. Rage at LaMont. Worry for Leena.

"You worry because you care, don't you?" he asked, looking at Leena again, watching her attempting to pick up a slippery piece of melon.

"Yes, Alik," Jada said, her voice choked. He looked at her then, at the moisture glistening in her eyes. "That's why you worry."

Jade closed the door to Leena's room and let out a long breath. Leena hadn't been that nasty about going to bed in a long time. But tonight, she'd been more interested in gripping the crib rails and bouncing on the mattress than she'd been in sleeping.

And the mostly adorable hyperactivity had turned into wailing when Jada had shut off the light and insisted it was time to settle down. All attempts at rocking and singing had been resisted bitterly.

But her wailing had eventually turned to whimpering, which had turned into reluctant sleep. And Jada was now way past ready for bed and on her way to whimpering too.

She started down the hall and stopped when she saw a dark shadow separate from the wall and start moving toward her.

"Alik?"

"She was upset?"

"Just having a princess fit because she didn't want to go to sleep, that's all."

She could see the tension leave his silhouette. He drew

closer, a shaft of moonlight coming in from outside illuminating him. Shirtless, a pair of athletic pants low on his hips.
He was a beautiful man.

Beautiful, rough, broken. And he called to her. Made her
heart beat fast, made her body ache. She'd been intimate with
him—no matter what he might want to call it—and she knew
him now. Her body knew his.

Though, she didn't feel like she'd explored him enough.
Not to the degree she wanted to.

And you won't.

Stern, sensible Jada chimed in, the voice of reason. Which
was a nice thing to have on hand because her body wasn't in
a reasonable place. Her body was just remembering how it
had felt to be near him, to have him kiss her, to have him take
her to the peak and push them both over the edge.

She blinked. "You couldn't sleep?"

"I was concerned."

"Why didn't you come into the room?"

He lifted one shoulder, a casual gesture, but she knew him
well enough by now to know it was anything but casual. Alik
feeling concern for another person wasn't usual, or casual. "I
didn't feel it was my place."

"Of course it's your place, Alik. You're her father."

He nodded slowly then lifted his arm, drew his hand over
his hair and let out a sigh. "I feel like you have something
with her. That you understand things I do not."

"You aren't the only one to feel that way."

"You make me feel almost normal," he said, his tone dry.

"Nobody feels like they know what they're doing with their
own kids, Alik. We just sort of hope for the best."

"Even you?"

"Yes. Even me. Especially me. Deciding to adopt while
I was single was something I struggled with. Because I always believed that a child should have a mother and father."

"Why didn't you and your husband have any children?"

Jada still felt protective of Sunil when it came to that subject. His family had started asking when they would start having children from the moment they'd gotten married and hadn't let up until his death.

She'd never told them, never told anyone why in their six years of marriage they hadn't managed to conceive. It had hit at his pride. That he could provide for her financially, but couldn't give her something she wanted so badly had been the source of so much pain for him.

No matter what she'd said, he could never really believe that she didn't resent it. And eventually, he hadn't wanted to talk about it at all.

"We couldn't," she said. "We couldn't have children. I mean…he couldn't. But we were married and that made it *us* who couldn't."

"And you decided not to pursue artificial means of conception?"

Jada almost laughed. Leave it to Alik to ask the most personal, inappropriate questions and not have a clue he was being personal or inappropriate. "My husband wasn't comfortable with the idea of me carrying another man's baby. And frankly, he wasn't all that interested in the adoption idea, either."

"Even though you wanted children?"

"He did, too. But…but he hadn't worked through the disappointment of the fact that it wouldn't happen for us the way he'd imagined. He took it personally."

"See what emotion gets you? Logically, he should have just made sure you could have the children you wanted regardless of how."

"You say that, Alik, but even you were all about the blood connection."

"I know. But I see…I see now that it's not the blood connection that builds the strongest bond. You…you effortlessly connect with her and I struggle."

"But you do connect. You have."

He nodded slowly. "I turned down working with LaMont because he was covering up the fact that one of his top execs is sexually harassing female employees. And all I could think of was that if some man did that to Leena I would...I fear I would kill them, Jada, and I don't mean that figuratively. I would. I could."

"Alik..."

"Emotion...it is not logical. It is inconvenient. It makes it almost impossible to...live with myself."

He let out a sound somewhere between a groan and a growl and leaned against the wall, his head tilted back. He needed something. Emotional comfort, emotional connection, and she knew he would never allow it. Would never recognize it.

She wanted to give it. Wanted to tell him everything would be okay. She wanted to...

What she wanted to do, what she really wanted, was to touch him. Because he understood the physical. He understood touch and sex. It was how he connected. She wanted to cut through the confusion and give him something familiar. And at the same time, she didn't want to be familiar. Didn't want to be just another body.

She wanted to reach him. To help him.

If she was really honest—really, really honest—she just wanted to touch him.

But she wasn't going to be honest, because honesty might stop her. And she didn't want to stop.

This could be okay. If she kept it separate from emotion, like he did. Kept it separate from marriage, then it might be okay.

She took a step toward him and put her fingertips on his chest, on the start of his tattoo, the one over his heart. The one he'd gotten before he'd risked his life to rescue his friend, the man he thought of as a brother.

His hand shot up and caught her arm, held it away from

his body. "Be careful," he bit out. "Because I swear if you touch me again, I will have you naked and in my bed before you can protest."

"I'm not going to protest so you won't be able to test the theory." She said it with a lot more boldness than she felt, but she realized that she'd made the decision the moment she'd taken a step toward him.

She wanted him again. If they left it at the night at the opera, it would never truly be over. It had been too fast. Too intense. A memory that was scorched around the edges, covering it all in the hazy smoke of fantasy. There was no way it had been as good as she remembered. No way it had been so all-consuming, so soul-destroying.

She lifted her other hand and cupped his cheek, sliding her thumb over the rough shadow of stubble that covered his jaw. "I want you," she said.

"Really?" he bit out. "Because I seem to recall you running from me as though I had forced you the last time you begged me to touch you. I wasn't a fan of that."

"I'm not going to run this time," she said, her voice trembling. Even as she said it, she wasn't sure she could keep her promise.

Because the closer she got to Alik, the less hazy her memory became. The longer she left her palm on his face, against the heat of his skin, the more he burned into her. And she was shaking, terrified that being with him again would reduce her entirely to ash. She was shaking, afraid of what she felt. Of what she intended to do.

But she couldn't turn back, either.

"Promise," he said, leaning in, his lips skimming her cheek. He nipped her ear, lightly, leaving behind a light sting that he soothed with the tip of his tongue. "Promise me," he repeated.

"I promise," she said.

"Tell me you want me."

"I want you, Alik."

It was enough for him. It must have been. He pulled her up against his chest, kissing her hard, deep. She wrapped her arms around his neck and held him to her, kissing him back, matching his desperation, his hunger.

The beast he woke up inside of her was something she'd never known about before. The desire, the need, from a part of her she hadn't been aware existed.

She knew about desire, she knew about pleasure, but this... this was new. This need that verged on pain, this hunger that bordered on insanity. She felt like he was air, like having him was essential, something she couldn't live without.

It made it impossible for her to think. And that thoughtlessness was bliss.

"Bedroom," she panted as he kissed down her throat, his teeth scraping her collarbone.

"Mine or yours."

"Whichever is closer."

"Yours," he said, picking her up and carrying her down the hall. She wrapped her arms around his neck, awed by his strength, which, she was sure, was the reason he'd done it. That and to make her feel tiny and feminine. Both had worked.

He pushed the bedroom door open and set her down, then slammed it shut behind them. He flicked the light on, a wicked grin on his face.

"What?" she asked. "Why did you turn the lights on?"

"Didn't you say that you've had sex with the lights on?"

"Yes, but..." Just not quite so purposefully.

"I want to see you," he said, pushing his pants down his narrow hips. "It's a priority this time around."

Her jaw slackened a little bit when he was naked in front of her. Completely. She'd seen most of him, but not all of him at one time. He was utter masculine perfection, hard-cut lines of muscle, deep scars that were marring his skin, a map of his life, marks that had been inflicted on him by those who had meant him harm.

And the ink on his skin, marks he'd chosen for himself.

"They say men are visual," she said, "but I'm feeling pretty visual myself right now."

"As am I," he said, skipping over the compliment. "Show yourself to me."

Her breath shortened, became labored. It was such a strange way to put it. Evidence of the fact that English wasn't his first language. But it meant more this way, too. She was showing herself to him.

A part of herself she had never seen or known about. A part no one had ever seen or known about. Deeper. More sensual. The only question was if she was brave enough. Not simply to uncover it for him, but to reveal it to herself.

Maybe if she'd had a choice, she wouldn't have done it. But there was no choice. This thing, this desire, it was bigger than she was. And tonight, it won over everything else. Over reserve, over fear.

She slowly peeled her top over her head, leaving her breasts bare for him. She shivered, nerves and the chill in the air raising goose bumps on her skin, arousal making her nipples pucker.

She pushed her pants down her legs, and her panties with them. "Just for you," she said. And she meant it. This part of her, this woman who would make love in a box at the opera, she was just for Alik. Somehow, he made her different.

Later, she would worry about it. She might even regret it. But not now.

"I am a lucky man." He crossed to her, cupping her cheek, the gesture tender, at odds with the heat and intent burning in his eyes.

She wrapped her arms around his neck and pulled his body against hers, pulled him in for a kiss. Skin to skin. She needed it. Needed him, his touch. Needed him to push her past the point of reason, past the point of thought.

He'd done it before, with such ease, and she needed it again.

He gripped her thighs and lifted her so that her legs were wrapped around his waist and he was supporting all of her weight. It brought the heart of her against the hard ridge of his erection, sending a spark of pleasure through her, deep and all-consuming.

And she was there. Beyond thought. Beyond anything other than feeling.

He kissed her neck, whispered things in her ear. Husky, dark words. Some she understood, some she didn't, but the intent didn't need translation.

"Take me," she whispered, broken, needy. Alik would fix her. He would answer the ache inside of her body. The one that went deeper than the physical.

He lay down on the bed, bringing her down on top of him. She started to adjust her position, to take him inside of her body. His hands tightened at her hips. "Stop."

"What?" she panted.

"Condom."

"Where?" she asked.

"Drawer."

"Oh." She hadn't looked in her nightstand drawer since arriving in Paris. And there they were. She might feel weird about it later, might feel bad that Alik had protection everywhere, because clearly he was the sort of man who did what he wished when the mood hit. But for now, she was just grateful.

She handed the protection to him and he applied it, then she moved back where she'd been and lowered herself onto him. Slowly, as slowly as she could manage, enjoying the tease. Enjoying the pained look on his face.

She liked that she had the power to torture him. To make him sweat and shake. It made her feel strong. It made her feel beautiful. Like a woman. A woman who was enough for the man she was with. A man who felt no inhibition, no issues with himself or who he was, or his ability to satisfy her.

Being with Alik was like waking up. Like bursting through the surface of the water after being under for too long. She hadn't even realized she was suffocating.

He gripped her hips tightly, thrust up inside of her. Her head fell back and she put her hands on his shoulders, rode him, found the rhythm that worked for both of them.

She looked down at Alik's face, the intensity, the focus. She bent down and kissed his mouth, sliding her tongue against his and he stiffened beneath her, shuddering out his orgasm. He swore and turned her over, reversing their positions and then pressing a kiss to her breasts, sucking on a nipple deep inside his mouth, continuing down her body.

He gripped her legs and hooked them over his shoulders, gripping her buttocks tight in his palms and pulling her up to his mouth, burying his face between her thighs before she had a chance to catch her breath.

"Alik…" She shuddered, his tongue tracing a streak of fire over her damp flesh.

He pushed two fingers inside of her, working them in time with his lips and tongue, pushing her higher, farther than she imagined possible.

Nothing had ever felt this good. Ever. Alik knew her body, knew just what she needed. Knew when she needed more, knew when to bring her down just so he could push her back to the edge again.

He kept it going until she was sure she would die from the pleasure. She opened her mouth to beg him to stop, to beg him to end it and let her come, but the words died on her lips, incoherent moans taking their place.

Still holding her lower body tightly with one hand, he took his other hand and reached up, pinched her nipple lightly between his thumb and forefinger while continuing his sensual torture with his mouth and she broke completely, shattering into a thousand, glimmering pieces. She wasn't sure she would ever be whole again, and she wasn't sure she cared.

She was lost in the pleasure, in the release that kept coming, wave after wave, so big, so intense she didn't know if she could withstand it. He kept tasting her, kept sliding his tongue over her damp skin until she shook, until her body was racked by tiny tremors, aftershocks of the release that had undone her completely.

And when it was over, Alik was there. And she wanted to run. But she'd promised she wouldn't. So she lay there instead, shaking.

Alik rose up and kissed her lips, his skin damp with sweat and her own arousal. He sat on the edge of the bed, his expression flat. "I don't know what happened," he said.

"You don't…"

"Usually I am more considerate than that. I lost my control for a moment. It won't happen again. Good night, Jada." He sat straight for a moment, indecision flashing across his face, then he leaned in and kissed her again. "I'll see you in the morning."

He got up and walked out of the room.

Jada hadn't run. But Alik had.

CHAPTER ELEVEN

ALIK DID HIS BEST TO WASH the impression of Jada from his skin with a cold shower. When that didn't work, he went for a run, hoping the rain and a bit of physical punishment would take care of things for him.

It didn't. By the time he collapsed in his bed, the sky was turning gray, the sun rising up behind the clouds.

He growled and got back out of bed, stalking down to the kitchen. His cook had just gotten in. He gave terse orders in French for her to prepare breakfast to be served out on the patio again. He wanted to eat out there like they'd done yesterday morning. Like they'd done before Jada had stripped his skin from his bones, left him feeling raw and exposed.

It was because he'd come before she had. That had to be it. He hadn't been that quick on the draw since he'd been a teenager. But damned if he could have stopped himself. And that was just far too telling.

He had never considered himself a man who held control in high esteem. He did what he wanted, when he wanted to do it. Some had called him debauched, and they weren't that far off. There were years of his life that he could barely remember, and it wasn't for any good or honorable reason.

Now he wondered how much of himself he'd truly kept bound up. How much of that sense of emotionless came from control. How much he had inflicted on himself. Because what had happened with Jada disturbed him, and it was beyond a simple matter of male pride.

"I thought I heard you growling down here." He turned and saw Jada behind him, in the clothes she'd been wearing the night before. Clothes she'd stripped off for his pleasure.

"I am not growling."

"You most certainly were. I could hear a rumbling coming from down here and no distinct words."

"I didn't sleep well last night."

"Join the club."

She was angry, he could tell. Not shooting sparks at him with her eyes, but definitely angry.

"Where is Leena?"

"Sleeping. Like a sane person. It's barely five o'clock."

"And why are you up?"

"The same reason you are, I imagine."

"We aren't going to have a heart-to-heart, Jada. Something like that requires both parties have a heart."

She stalked forward and fisted his T-shirt in her hands, tugging hard. And he followed the direction of the pull. She pressed her mouth to his, took his lower lip between her teeth and nipped him lightly. Then she released him.

"You can't run from that, Alik. I tried it already, remember?"

"Yes, Jada, I remember. And I don't run. I've withstood artillery fire...I'm hardly backing down from a woman who barely comes up to the center of my chest."

"Yeah, yeah. I keep hearing about all that. Big Bad Alik Vasin. But you ran last night."

"I don't spend the night with women I..." The look on her face forced him to swallow the last crude word he'd been about to say. "I'm not the kind of guy who cuddles after."

"Fine," she said, so clearly not fine it was almost comical. "But it would be nice if you stayed for more than five seconds. I know I'm not your wife. Well, I am, but you know what I mean. We aren't in love. The vows we took…we didn't mean them. I know that. I know someday you're going to get tired of me and go back to doing what it is you do with women." She took a deep breath. "I'm not your real wife. I'm also not some bimbo you picked up at a club."

"I know that."

"I don't think you do," she said. "Because you treated me like one last night. You left so fast it made my head spin. I'm not experienced at this. I've only been with one other man and not until after I married him."

"You are married to me," he said, "whether or not you love me."

She sighed. "I suppose. But the point is, this whole sexual thing…I'm not sure what to do with it. I'm not sure how I feel and the last thing I need is for you to confirm what I'm afraid is true."

"And that is?"

"Am I…is something wrong with me that I want this? That I don't care if I love you, or if I even like you?"

"Sex doesn't have to be connected to feelings, princess. In my experience it never has been. Sex is your body."

"My body wants things that are bad for me. All the time. Take chocolate cake for example," she said. "I love chocolate cake. With lots of frosting. And I would eat it all the time. I crave it. If I listened to my body I would be eating chocolate cake for breakfast today, but just because I want it doesn't mean I should have it."

"But that's half of what makes it so good," he said, for his own benefit more than hers.

Maybe that was all it was. Maybe that was part of the excitement of being with her. She was the last woman he should want. She was his wife, but he didn't intend to make her his actual wife. Being with her like this was complicated and messy and bad.

Perhaps that was why his body responded so enthusiastically to it.

"It's human nature," he said. "To want the one thing you shouldn't have. Forbidden fruit is sweeter."

"Is that what this is?"

"Would you dislike it so much if it was?"

"I'm confused by it. I've always done what I should. I've always liked doing the right thing. But…what did it get me, Alik? What did it get me but hurt in the end? If I would have kept playing by the rules I would have lost Leena, too."

"So play dangerous for a while, Jada. Play with me." This he could do…this was easy. It certainly wasn't anything new or different. A little bit of harmless sex. He'd overreacted. He could see that now.

"What about when it ends? It might be difficult."

"Would it be any easier to stop now?" he asked.

She shook her head. "No. I don't want to stop now."

"You like living a little dangerously, don't you?"

The color in her cheeks deepened. "Yes."

"I thought you would."

He advanced on her, intent on tasting her lips again. Leena's sharp cry, carrying all the way down the stairs, made him stop.

"Sorry," she said. "I have to get her."

He wanted to go, too, he realized. But she didn't need him. And he didn't want to interrupt her. So he shoved it aside. It wasn't important.

"I will see that breakfast gets laid out for everyone. A banana, for Leena, am I right?"

"Her favorite."

He nodded. "Then I will make sure she has it."

Jada lay back on the bed, utterly spent. She could hardly catch her breath. Alik was a ruthless lover. He made her beg. He made her scream. And she had no complaints.

She wanted to ask him to stay, but she really didn't want to sound needy. Even though she felt needy. She didn't want him to know.

He kissed her and she clung to him, still hungry for him. Maybe she could tempt him to stay with the promise of more sex. He certainly wasn't going to stay and cuddle. He'd made that very clear and he'd kept that promise for six nights running.

Things were certainly hot between them. They were officially having a physical-only affair. She cared for him, yes. As the father of her daughter. But it was nothing truly personal to her.

You are such a liar.

But, very true to what he'd said at the beginning of their marriage—when had she started to think of it that way?—he seemed to keep sex and what happened during the day completely separate. And that did bother her a little. She was all for separate but he took it to a ridiculous degree.

Except for those moments when their eyes would lock. Over the table at breakfast, when they were passing in the hall, and the fire between them would burn so hot, so bright that it was a miracle they didn't just sweep everything aside and tear each other's clothes off.

They saved that passion for the nights. Half the night, anyway. And then Alik left. Went back to his room. To his own space.

"Alik?" She settled beneath the covers, searching for a topic to delay him. "Tell me more about how…how you're here."

"You know where babies come from, I assume. You just proved you know it proficiently well, actually." He arched one brow. "And that you're also well versed in bedroom activities that don't make babies."

"That's not what I meant," she said, determined not to be offended by his ridiculousness. He *wanted* her offended. She knew him well enough to realize that. A week ago, she probably *would* have been offended. For some reason, she just wasn't now. "You were an orphan in Moscow."

"Yes," he said. "In one of the very overcrowded children's homes. You've never seen anything like that, Jada. Cribs in rows with narrow walkways for the workers to get through. Maybe three people trying to manage all those children. Someone is always crying. And when it gets terribly overcrowded, the older children have to go."

Jada closed her eyes. "Oh no…"

"I was twelve, older than some. Lucky, really. Because while the orphanages are overcrowded and understaffed, they try. They aren't cruel. It's not love or affection, but food and shelter go a long way in helping make a child's life bearable. After that there was nothing. I was lucky, I avoided having to sell my body. I found I had a talent for theft and manipulation. Which, as I told you, caught the attention of the local organized crime family."

He sat back down on the edge of the bed, still naked. "And for them, I did errands. Small things, delivering packages with unknown contents. And then I would also strategize heists. Big heists. And I thought it was brilliant. Here I was fourteen, fifteen years old and I was the criminal mastermind behind some of Europe's most notorious burglaries. Not a bad achievement for a kid with nothing. But ultimately, at some point, I had to face the reality that I was doing work for the Mob and to be honest, morally bankrupt bastard that I am, not even I cared much for that."

"And then what did you do?"

"Disappeared. Which you have to do for a while in my position. I went into Asia. Lived in Singapore, then Japan. Tended bar, ran petty scams, did a lot of things the United States Surgeon General would advise against."

"And you were in Japan when that man approached you to help a militia strategize a government takeover."

He nodded slowly. "You listen well."

"You're interesting."

"Is that what you call it? Interesting. Perhaps I am. But I find very little to be proud of in my past. There's nothing hard about following the money. You don't have to decide what you think is right or wrong. You sell yourself to the highest bidder. Whoever has the money is right. So simple. So perfect. So very easy."

"I'm sure you weren't so bad, Alik."

"I put missions in motion that cost men their lives and to this day, I don't know what every cause I stood with was. I only knew they paid me. And I knew that the thrill of danger made me feel alive. It was only when I met Sayid that I got caught up in the rights and freedom of a nation. Attar was under attack by neighboring factions and Sayid hired me to help wipe them out. They were terrible people, Jada, and I saw the kinds of things they were doing. And then I saw Sayid risk himself, his men, everything, to save the life of a woman. And I realized I would not have done the same. Sayid got himself captured, and I was free. I didn't deserve freedom, not when men of Sayid's caliber rotted in jail. So I made it my mission to free them. There was no money involved in that. It was the first decision I had ever made in my life that was for someone else, and not for me."

"You're a good man, Alik."

He shook his head. "It took a good man to show me just how far gone I was. But I have changed. Now I'm just a corporate killer." He shook his head and stood. "And that's my story, Jada."

"It's not over yet. And you did something different here. You turned down working for a corporation that violated your ethics. To appease a conscience I know you have."

"Whatever I have, whatever I feel…it's because of Leena."

"That's how it should be. It's the same for me. She…she saved my life." *And so did you.* The words hovered on the tip of her tongue, but she held them back. She only looked at him. Because she wasn't sure if they were true. Alik had torn her from her comfort zone. Taken her from friends, from the life she knew, from everyone who had an expectation of her and left her feeling like she was drifting out at sea. Free. Terrifying.

"Do you want to know what this says?" he asked, lifting his arm and exposing the words written in ink beneath.

"What?"

"Little thieves are hanged. Great thieves escape." He lowered his arm. "I was a great thief. And I escaped. I was young and cocky, so I had this tattooed on my body to let the world know that it was my greatness that would keep me from getting caught. But you know what? You can't escape your past. I escaped arrest. I was never killed by an enemy. But my past remains, and I am trapped in it. A creation of it. So you see, no thief escapes, princess. Not even me."

She touched his bicep, her fingers drifting over the muscle. "Will you punish yourself forever?" *Will you?*

Again, she ignored her own thoughts.

"I don't have to. I don't seek to punish myself, but you asked what made me, and the simple fact is, it was nothing good that had a hand in my creation. What I am simply is. It's not me punishing myself, or the world punishing me. But my existence is a consequence for everything that has come before. There's no changing it."

She had seen Alik angry. She'd seen him totally out of his depth. She'd seen tenderness, deeply hidden but evident, when he looked at Leena. But she'd never heard him sound hopeless. Tonight, he sounded hopeless. He sounded like he wanted more than what he was.

And it broke her. Because he didn't see what she did. He didn't see what he could be. But he did want more. He was changing. And he was capable of change, no matter what he thought.

He turned to go and her heart slammed hard against her breastbone. She craved him. By her side, in her bed, her arms. No matter what he'd done, no matter where he'd been.

This dangerous, difficult, damaged man.

She wanted to reach out, to offer comfort. To take comfort. But she was too raw. She needed distance, too. Needed escape.

So she let him go. Because the alternative was calling him back and further cementing a bond that she couldn't handle.

CHAPTER TWELVE

"WE NEED TO TAKE LEENA OUT," Alik said, the next morning at breakfast. "She hasn't been anywhere except the back patio the whole time we've been in Paris."

"*I've* barely been anywhere but the back patio," Jada said, lifting her mug to her lips and leaning back in her chair, soaking in the early-morning window of sunshine that filtered through the trees, casting spots of light and shadow onto the brick floor.

"Liar, you walk to the Eiffel Tower every morning."

"And I bring Leena with me."

"Still, I think… It seems she hasn't been out enough."

For a moment, the strangeness of it all hit her full force. She was in Paris, had been for a few weeks, sleeping with a man she'd only just met. Married to the man. And the things she did with him…the things she wanted from him.

Just thinking of it made her hands shake.

She looked down at her hands, trying to orient her thoughts. And she realized she hadn't put Sunil's ring on her right hand that morning. She'd put on the rings Alik had given her, but nothing else.

She looked back up at him. "You want us all to go out together," she said, realizing slowly that that's what was happening. That he didn't know how to articulate it, or didn't want to. She wondered if he was having the same, surreal moment she was.

"That seems...normal."

"It is."

He nodded once, sharply, as though he'd known, the whole time, that his request was perfectly normal. The thing was, she imagined he didn't. He had no reference for what families did. Nothing beyond what was in movies or TV. And Alik didn't seem like the kind of man who curled up on his couch at night for prime-time sitcoms.

Even if he had, they were hardly scripted television. Nothing about their situation followed a logical path.

"Then, let's go out. What would you like to do?" she asked.

He shrugged. "I don't know."

"You must know, Alik." It came out shorter than she'd intended, but she was feeling edgy. And her right hand felt bare. More exposed skin. Less to hide behind.

"I don't."

"You don't have any ideas?" She didn't believe him. But it was also obvious that he wasn't willing to share his thoughts with her.

"We could just walk," he said, "and see where we end up."

She accepted his evasiveness. Mainly because she was too caught up in her own thoughts. In her own fears of exposure. "That sounds good to me."

"She's getting tired of the stroller," Jada said, looking down at Leena, who was wiggling and pushing against her restraints.

They stopped and Alik looked down at her, frowning. "I suppose I could hold her. But she didn't like it the last time I did that."

"More than three weeks ago, Alik."

That made his frown deepen. "Oh." He bent then, swift and decisive, and freed Leena from her seat, pulling her up into his arms.

Leena's fist curled around his shirt collar, her other hand

going to the hair on the back of his neck. He grimaced when she tugged, but he didn't reprimand her.

"All right, let's keep walking," he said.

She didn't say anything as they kept walking down the busy streets, she just kept watching Alik when she was sure he wasn't looking at her. His hold on Leena was strong, but gentle. His eyes were on their surroundings, not on his daughter.

They went through a narrow alley with cobblestones and bistro tables. People were sitting and chatting, drinking coffee and eating pastries, both of which looked like a good idea to Jada, but Alik definitely had another agenda. One he still wasn't sharing. Which left Jada alone with her thoughts. At the moment that wasn't necessarily a good thing because her thoughts were edgy and confused.

They passed through the alley and back out onto a busy main street, walking in the opposite direction they had been now.

"Are we going back already?" she asked.

"Back to the tower."

"Oh."

They crossed back through the web of streets, in the direction of the town house, cutting through an open-air market filled with flowers, racks of books and fruit. Alik didn't spare the sights a second glance. So very typical of him. He could be so focused on whatever his internal mission was, on getting from point A to point B, that he didn't look at the beauty that surrounded him.

And you've been so different the past few years? You've had blinders on.

Alik stopped then at a carousel, one she passed every morning, stationed out in front of the tower, enticing tourists to spend money with bright colors, glittering gems and music that sounded like it was coming from a jewelry box.

"This is where you wanted to go the whole time, isn't it?" she asked.

He shrugged. "I had thought she might like it."

"She's a little small to go by herself," she said. "But I—" she looked at Alik, at Leena, grinning in his arms "—you could take her."

"I could?"

"Yes. You could. She'll be fine. Look, she's happy with you."

He looked down at Leena and swallowed. "All right."

He approached the man who was running the carousel and spoke to him in French, explaining the situation, Jada assumed. That was one thing about Alik, he might seem out of his element with a baby in his arms, but as a traveler, he was the man you wanted with you. He knew customs, and languages, knew where to go and what to order at restaurants. He knew opera.

There was no end to the general knowledge the man possessed. Not only that, but he'd been shot, had crossed enemy lines, had broken into a horrible prison to rescue his friend.

But put a baby in his arms and he looked like a man scared for his very life.

A curious man, her Alik.

She blinked. When had she started thinking of him that way? When had he become hers? She looked away from him, looked at tourists, the families walking on the green in front of the tower, laughing, holding each other.

No Alik wasn't hers. He couldn't be. Not ever. She repeated it over and over in her mind and tried not to give in to the ache that was climbing her throat. She wrapped her arms around herself, trying to hold the pieces of herself in, so she wouldn't go and surrender any more of herself to Alik.

Alik held Leena tightly against him and climbed up onto one of the white carousel horses, fastening them both in tightly.

He could still remember the first carousel he'd seen, in the square in Moscow. A game for children, and he'd never been a child. Not truly. So he'd never gone on it.

Leena clapped her hands and looked back up at him, her eyes, the same shade as his own, sparkled. With excitement. With trust.

Then she lifted her hand and put it on his cheek. "Da!"

And the carousel started to turn. He held tight to his daughter, held her steady on the horse. The world was turning around him, too fast to make out Jada or any other distinct shapes. Leena was all he could see.

She laughed, deep and happy as the ride turned, slapping the horses head, slapping his leg. Happiness, so pure, so unspoiled pouring out of her with ease. And the trust. That trust that Jada had spoken of.

It's yours to lose.

He didn't want to lose it. More than anything he didn't want to lose it.

Right now, at least, he had it. So he held on tight to Leena and kept his focus on her. Not on the world around them, not on the future. And he tried to grapple with the feeling of exposure, the feeling of tenderness, that was taking him over.

He didn't know himself right now. He very much doubted if he knew anything at all.

"Leena's asleep. I think we wore her out." Jada sat down next to Alik on the couch, a cup of coffee warming her palm. Alik had some sort of alcohol in his glass, and a very stoic expression on his face.

"She has a lot of energy," he said, looking down.

"She does. She liked the carousel."

"I am glad."

So, Alik wasn't going to give anything tonight. At least, nothing in terms of conversation.

"It was a good idea you had," she pushed, "taking her on it."

"Thank you."

Infuriating Russian. The man had a tendency to go Siberia cold on her whenever it suited him. "You didn't think of it last minute, though. It's what you were thinking from the beginning but you didn't want to tell me. Why?"

He looked at her, one dark brow raised. "I wasn't certain it was a good idea. I didn't know if she would like it." He said it so casually, but she had a feeling there was nothing casual in the admission. But when Alik put on his armor, that I-don't-give-a-crap facade of his, it was almost impossible to see through.

"You could have asked me."

"I didn't know if you would like it," he said.

And then she understood. That there was something personal. Something that had made him feel exposed. And he hadn't wanted her to reject it. To reject *him*.

It struck her then, that Alik felt as out of place and different in this situation as she did.

"Even if I didn't like it, I don't make all the decisions concerning Leena. You're her father—you make them too."

"I know. I understand that, but I don't know anything about children or what they're supposed to like at what age I only..."

"What?"

"Nothing."

She set her coffee mug down on the table by the sofa and put her hands in her lap, angling her body toward Alik. "You only what, Alik? Don't play stupid games with me."

"I am not playing a game," he said, standing. "I only knew that when I was a child, there was a carousel I used to walk by. After I left the orphanage. It cost money, and I would never have spent money on such a thing. I had to use what I had to buy food, or shelter if I ended up with enough. But never for something like that. Well, now I have money. Leena, by extension, has money and she can go on a carousel if she likes," he finished, his voice rough, fierce.

"Of course she can." She wasn't used to seeing Alik overcome by emotion. More and more though, it was starting to come through. More and more, he was connecting with Leena, but it was challenging him. She could see it.

And the more it came through for him, the more she felt drawn to him. And it scared her to death. Challenged her just as much as it challenged him. She didn't like the feeling she had when she was with him, and yet she craved it. So strong and compelling, so utterly frightening.

She didn't know what to call it, but she knew that Alik Vasin had a hold on her. One she couldn't shake free of. One she wanted to break away from and cling to all at the same time.

"There were no parents to care for me. To make sure I had what I needed, much less anything I wanted. I was a burden to my mother. So much so she had to give me up."

"I'm sure she wanted to keep you, Alik."

"It doesn't change anything. How she felt about it doesn't change what happened to me after. It doesn't replace what I lost." He looked down, dark eyes unfocused. "Leena deserves to have everything," he said, his voice lower now. "How will I know what to give her? I don't know what to give her."

"Just keep giving her you, Alik. She's so happy with that. Did you see her today? When you held her? She loves just being with you. She loves you."

"But what about when she realizes just what a pitiful excuse for a father I am?" he asked, his words sounding torn, broken. "When she realizes I don't know what I'm doing?"

"I don't know what I'm doing, either, Alik, I just hope that I can love her enough to cover all the mistakes I make."

"What if I can't do that, either?"

She swallowed hard, tried to speak with confidence she just didn't have. "You will."

"What if I don't?" He set his glass down hard on the mantel.

"What would you have wanted from your parents?"

"There's no point wishing for what you don't have."

"You never thought about them? Never wondered about your mother."

He shook his head once. "No."

She bit her lip, trying to keep from crying. From shouting. "But what would you have wanted? Would you have needed them to be perfect? Or would you have just needed them to be there? Just be here, Alik. Be here for her."

He paused, turning the tumbler in his hand. "I will," he said. "That I promise. I swear it."

"Then she has nothing to worry about."

Alik looked back at his glass, then back at her. His expression was raw, open, revealing the depth of his pain, his insecurity, his need. And it was so vast she was afraid that it could never, ever be filled.

Alik wasn't emotionless. Alik was hiding everything, because there was simply too much to deal with. She saw it plainly in that moment. Saw the wounds inflicted on him, over and over, during his life, and the high cost of them.

And then it was gone, replaced by the stone wall he had spent his life perfecting. "Let's go to bed," he said.

"You don't want to talk?"

"I'm done talking," he said. "I want you. Now."

"Alik…"

He stalked to the couch and bent down, bracing his hand on the back of it, his lips crashing down on hers. His kiss was rough and desperate. She was almost used to the edge of utter abandon that came with their attraction. Almost. But this was different. This wasn't about his need for her.

She didn't doubt he wanted her, after their time together she couldn't doubt that, but the need to escape that flavored his kiss wasn't about her. It was about him.

He wrapped his arm around her waist and drew her up against him, made her stand. And she clung to him, answer-

ing his need, because there was never anything else she could
do with Alik.

She should resist. She shouldn't let him use her. And yet,
she couldn't. She *needed* him. The moment he touched her
she was lost. She had been from the moment she'd met him.
She didn't know what that said about her, didn't know what
it might mean. And in that moment, she honestly didn't care.

He made her want, a deep, aching want that she had yet to
find satisfaction for, no matter how many times they made
love. Could it even be called making love? She didn't know.
She knew Alik would never call it that.

Sex isn't intimate.

Not to him.

"Alik." She said his name, pulled away and looked at his
eyes.

He didn't allow it. He leaned in and kissed her neck. "Get
behind the couch," he said. Hard. Demanding.

"Alik..."

"Now."

The command excited her. But everything Alik did excited her. She was experienced—she'd been married for six
years—but she'd never played games like this. Though, looking at the hard glint in Alik's eye made it hard to think of it
as a game. And she found that excited her even more.

She obeyed him, rounding to the back of the couch. He
stood on the other side of it, watching her, his expression
strangely flat. Detached.

"Hold on."

She obeyed that command too, bending at her waist and
curling her fingers around the wooden frame.

"Good."

He started working his belt buckle as he rounded to the
back of the couch and her heart stopped beating, climbed into
her throat and made it impossible to breathe. She heard his

belt slide through the loops, heard the zipper on his pants, and she tried to look back.

"Eyes ahead, princess."

And she obeyed again, because she didn't want him to stop.

He slid his hand down her back, cupped her butt, bunched the material of her dress into one hand and tugged it up. "Perfect."

He dragged her panties down her legs, and she closed her eyes, letting him touch her, tease her, heighten her arousal. And then she heard him opening a condom packet, and still she followed his orders. Still she looked ahead.

He pushed a finger deep inside of her and a sharp gasp escaped her lips.

"Ready?" he asked.

She could only nod, but it was taken as permission.

He pushed into her slowly and she dug her nails into the couch as he filled her. He went deeper at this angle and she found that she liked it. The only thing that she didn't like, was that she couldn't see him.

As he starting thrusting hard into her, she wondered if that was by design. But the thought was only a twinge of pain, swallowed quickly by the pleasure roaring through her.

Alik reached between her thighs and slid his fingers over her clitoris, bringing her release, sharp and fast, while he continued to chase his own. But even after she found hers, he didn't let up.

Tension, heat, coiled in her tightly again while he continued to work his magic on her. He slowed his rhythm, going slow so she could feel every inch of him. She bit her lip, trying to hold back the desperate whimpers that were building inside her. Trying to hold back the crash of another orgasm. She wasn't ready yet. Not yet.

One more flick of his clever fingers and he pushed her over. Her thighs were shaking, sweat beading on her brow. He kept on, pushing her higher, further.

"Alik…I can't."

"You will," he said, his voice rough, his breath hot on her neck. "With me this time."

He thrust harder, faster, his fingers moving in time with the rest of him. Impossible, she felt another wave building, bigger, frightening. It was slow, rolling, and, she feared, more than she could possibly withstand.

Alik froze, one hand gripping her hip hard, his fingers biting into her flesh. He pulsed deep inside of her, sending her over. There was no sight, no sound, nothing but the all-consuming pleasure. She was drowning in it, in Alik.

She was still catching her breath, still trying to keep her legs from collapsing beneath her weight, when Alik moved away from her. She could hear him righting his clothes. She imagined she was allowed to look at him now. But she was afraid.

Afraid of what she might see. More afraid of what she might feel. Afraid that if she looked, there would be no more secrets at all. That he would see straight into her soul, see things no one else ever had.

He was tugging away a mask she hadn't realized she'd had. A mask kept so easily in place by her desire to please, first her parents and then her husband. She'd been happy with it. Her life had been quiet, and easy.

This wasn't quiet. It wasn't easy.

"That is more what you should expect from me," he said, his voice smug. But it was off somehow. It wasn't genuine. He was back to playing a part.

His words made her angry. Angry enough that she wasn't afraid to face him anymore. He was looking at her, his expression dispassionate, his eyes flat, his clothes righted.

"You know what, Alik, if you want to use me as your therapist, then maybe you should lie down on the couch instead of bending me over it."

"What does that mean?"

"I'm not interested in letting you use my body so you can work your issues out."

"You flatter yourself if you think sex with you is somehow connected to working out my issues."

"Do I?" she asked, her throat tightening. She wasn't going to cry. Not now. Not when he was being so spectacularly un-emotional and horrible.

"I already told you, sex is sex. It's not connected to any-thing outside of it. It is what it is. Thank you for the orgasm."

"Stop it, Alik," she said.

"It's reality, the reality of being with me, Jada, so get used to it, or find another man."

She didn't want another man. Not any other man, not even the one she'd loved. A shocking, jolting realization.

But she didn't particularly want this one, either. Not this version of him.

"I'm going to bed," she said, turning away from him.

"No thank-you for me? I made you come three times."

She whirled around, anger coursing through her. "And? I can get my own orgasms, Alik, without having to deal with this kind of treatment after! The thing you don't understand, is that what makes sex better than your own hand is the con-nection you get from it. But you don't offer that and you don't accept it. So there's no point, is there?"

It wasn't true. Sex with Alik was beyond anything in her experience. But it had also forged a bond with him she didn't want. One that was tearing her apart from the inside out, strip-ping away every defense. The way he was acting hurt, but it wasn't why she was pulling away from him. It was because of what he made her feel.

Because of who he made her.

"I suppose not, for you. Good night."

He made no move to go. He picked his glass up from the mantel and walked over to the bar, pouring himself another drink. As if nothing had happened. Nothing that mattered. And he was dismissing her now.

"Right," she said. "Good night."

She stalked from the room, only realizing later that she'd left her underwear. If Alik didn't get them, the housekeeper would. She decided it was less of a humiliation than going back for them in Alik's presence.

So she just went up the stairs and flung her bedroom door open, and resisted the urge to slam it closed. She didn't want to give him the satisfaction of knowing how hurt she was. But then, would it even mean anything to him?

"Ah, what does this mean when you slam doors, Jada? I do not understand complex human emotion." she said to herself, imitating Alik and his accent, poorly. "It means I'm mad at you, you jackass, because you are the most insensitive and horrible human being on the planet!"

She flopped down on the bed and stared at the ceiling with gritty eyes. This was the time when she had to figure out if Alik was worth it, or if she should just abandon ship.

What do you want from him? Surely not love and marriage? Real marriage? You had that. This is not that. It never could be.

No. It never could be. Partly because Alik wasn't her first husband. And partly because she didn't think she could ever be that woman again. She was changing. But this wasn't the same kind of change she'd made in her first marriage. She wasn't changing to make Alik's life easier, to make their marriage more harmonious.

She wasn't changing to fit a mold. The change seemed endless, with no boundaries closing in. It was the kind of freedom she hadn't wanted, the kind she didn't truly understand.

She had always tried to please the people in her life, but Alik seemed to ask her to please only herself. And this woman that she was…this woman wouldn't have been happy with her life three years ago. She would have wanted more from her marriage. More passion. More honesty. Less hiding.

She was afraid of what he made her want. But she didn't want to walk away, either.

She didn't like that Alik wasn't simply in her present, that he hadn't just changed her future, but that he was changing her view of the past, as well.

CHAPTER THIRTEEN

IT HADN'T WORKED. Alik didn't like failure. He rarely failed. In fact, his only failure to date was the condom failure he'd suffered more than a year and a half ago during Leena's conception. If he'd failed otherwise, with the sorts of endeavors he'd engaged in, he would be dead.

But he had failed in putting things back into place inside himself. He had failed in his attempt to feel normal again after the carousel ride with Leena.

He had failed in holding Jada at a reasonable distance. He had failed in putting her back there. He had tried.

He'd thought if he couldn't see her face. If he just took it back to sex at its most basic, then he would stop aching inside. That it would give him the high, the euphoria that sex had always given him.

But sex with Jada had a cost. And each time it seemed higher.

If only the price could be paid in money. He had that. This was asking for pieces of him, demanding he lower his guard to pay, and he really didn't like that. He had emotions. He knew it now. But he'd built up a wall around them so thick, so high, that not even he had been able to pull it down at his own whim.

He'd given all the credit to Leena before. But Jada was the one with the wrecking ball. She was taking down his defenses, and everything was spilling out now. Years of need, of unmet emotional longing, bleeding endlessly from him.

He found he couldn't even scowl about it, because he was, at that moment, sitting on the floor in Leena's room, watching his daughter toddle around in a circle. She was wearing a short, pink dress that showed off chubby legs, the skirt flaring out in the back, thanks to her diaper.

"Fashion forward," he said to her, as she wobbled and her legs folded, dropping her straight on her bottom. "And practical for you, I imagine it cushioned you some."

She gurgled and let out a long string of jabber that she seemed to think were words, because when she was done, she looked at him expectantly.

"I don't know what you said."

She responded with more jabber and flapping hands. In spite of his foul mood, he felt a smile curve his lips. Jada was right about one thing, babies were very cute. Although, he didn't think babies in general were all that cute. But Leena was. Leena was the most beautiful thing he had ever seen. So perfect and tiny.

He shifted and lay down on his stomach, propping himself up on his elbow and taking her hand in his. He counted her fingers. Five of them. Then he took her other hand and counted the fingers there too before moving on to her toes.

"Ten and ten," he said. "Had to check."

"That was the first thing I did when I held her at the hospital."

He looked over his shoulder and straightened into a sitting position. "Is it?"

"Yes." Jada walked into the room and he wondered how long she'd been standing there. He didn't like her being witness to all this stuff. Mainly because he didn't want anyone to witness it. These feelings for Leena, the feelings he kept having in general, were like new skin growing over wounds. Tender. Raw.

"I wanted to make sure."

"Well, yeah. You have to do it."

"I didn't get to hold her at the hospital," he said, suddenly choked by regret. "I wish I would have known about her. And I hope if I had I would have cared."

"Are you honestly afraid you wouldn't have?"

"Seeing Sayid with his family…that started changing my thoughts on babies. But…a year ago? I'm not certain what I would have done."

"You would have done the right thing, Alik. Because it's what you do."

"No, Jada, it's not." He pushed up into standing and Leena shrieked, holding her arms up and looking at him plaintively. He couldn't deny her. He bent and picked her up and she giggled, triumphant. "I've spent my life doing what was best for me and to hell with everyone else."

"What changed?"

"I don't know. Maybe me. We can only hope."

Except last night he'd done it with Jada. Done what pleased himself. Had looked out only for his own well-being. Although, it hadn't gone as planned. There had been none of the detachment he'd bragged about to her in the beginning.

"Do you want to change, Alik?"

"If it's possible."

"You hurt me last night," she said.

Her words hit him like a slap to the face. "Where? What did I do?"

"Not physically," she said, her cheeks coloring. "Physically it all felt good. But the way you treated me after… Alik, I understand that you don't want love and all of that—that's fine. But I don't want you to try and prove the point that you feel nothing every time you're with me."

"Do you want love, Jada?"

She shook her head slowly. "Not from you."

He didn't know why, but the admission stabbed at him. "Then what is it you want from me?"

"Respect. Being treated like more than a whore."

"I don't treat you like that."

"You do. You did last night. Like a woman who was there just to satisfy you."

"I gave you pleasure," he said, "more than I did the night that..."

"You know what? I preferred the night you came first," she said, the color in her cheeks deepening.

"How?"

"Last night was balm for your ego, Alik. You can't pretend otherwise. So you proved you were a stud and you..." Her eyes drifted to Leena. "I know she doesn't know what we're talking about but I can't help thinking that this could be a scarring early life experience for her."

Alik set his daughter down in her crib and put a shape sorter in front of her, and even though she shot him an indignant look, she didn't scream. "Outside."

He and Jada walked out of the nursery and he closed the door behind them. "You may finish telling me why I left you sexually unsatisfied now," he said dryly.

"You were proving something about yourself," she said. "You weren't giving to me. That other time? You just lost control. And I think I liked that better. It was honest, at least. I'm tired of...I'm tired of not having honesty."

"When have I not given you honesty?"

"You did at first, but now...now you're protecting yourself and I've had that relationship, Alik. Where everyone is hiding what they want so they don't hurt anyone, so they don't hurt themselves."

"I thought you didn't want love."

"I don't."

"Then why bother to make comparisons?"

"You're right. I shouldn't. But I would rather have fast, than pleasure brought from your calculated control."

"That makes no sense, Jada. Sex is about pleasure."

"That's not all it's about. Didn't you hear what I said to you last night?"

Yes. He'd heard it. That she would have been better off alone than with him when it came to getting pleasure. He hadn't liked it at all. The rejection had cut through his compromised defenses with stunning accuracy.

"Hard to miss."

"Sex is about intimacy with someone. About connection. It's not about an adrenaline rush, or feeling good for a few minutes. Until you realize that you're missing out on a huge piece of what sex is. You're missing out on making love."

"And you're an expert?"

"Alik, I've had the best sex with you. No question. In terms of pleasure, in terms of excitement…I didn't have any clue it could be so good. But I'm lonely after. And I'm cold. And I've had quite enough of that."

He didn't like hearing that. That he hurt her. That he was spreading the chill inside of his soul to her. She was so warm, so beautiful and full of light. Thinking he might be damaging that…the pain of it stabbed right through the walls he kept around his heart.

"I am sorry for that," he said. "It wasn't my intention to hurt you."

He'd been too busy trying to protect himself to worry about what pushing Jada away might do to her, because until he'd listened to her talk just now, he hadn't truly understood how sex could be connected to emotion. To the way you felt about yourself.

That wasn't entirely true. He'd been on a journey to understanding it since the first time he'd touched her. Because when they were done, the feel of her lingered. Her smell haunted him, feminine and exotic, jasmine and spice and pure enticement.

He had never been able simply to have her and put her out of his mind. He'd never been able to look at her and then put her out of his mind. Like her spice lingered on his skin, Jada always lingered in his thoughts.

"I know, Alik. You never intend to hurt anyone. You just don't always understand how other people...feel."

He didn't. Because he didn't feel in the same way other people did. And he hated that in himself now. Hated it because it had caused Jada pain. Because it might cause Leena pain later.

"I always thought if I smiled enough," he said, "then I would start to feel happy. If I did enough things that made me feel good, it might turn into something more. It doesn't work that way. It never made me feel a damn thing. But Leena does. You do."

"Me?" she asked, her cheeks paled.

"Yes. I am sorry I hurt you. Knowing that I did...it hurts me."

"Empathy."

He nodded slowly. "New for me. I am pleased to have found it. I owe you, for the way I treated you last night."

She shook her head, her dark ponytail swinging in time with the movement. "No, you don't, Alik. That's not how it works. It's not a trade system. Just don't do it again."

"I want to take you out," he said. He did. He wanted to make her smile. Wanted to be in public with her at his side, wanted to show everyone that she was his. It was a strange desire, new. So many new feelings and needs in the past few weeks. He was starting to feel like a different man. Finally. After so many years of trying.

"What about Leena?"

"Marie is here."

"I know, but I don't like giving her all the responsibility."

Jada had a hard time giving up control to the au pair, but Alik, selfishly, liked that it ensured she had more free time in the evenings with him.

"One night out is hardly giving her all the responsibility. Please, come with me."

"All right, but I have to change. I'm not going out in my sweats."

"Wear something red."

"I haven't been to a club in…maybe ever," Jada said, eyeing the crowded room. People were seated at bistro tables that circled the dance floor, all of it packed in tight. The concept of personal space a total loss.

It wasn't like a flashing lights techno club or anything, for which she was grateful. It was dark and smoky, live jazz music provided by a band on stage.

"You've never been to a club?"

"I got married very young and got busy with being a homemaker. We went out, but not dancing. And certainly not anywhere like this."

"Didn't you ever want to?"

"We just…we didn't."

He frowned. "And now, are you here because of me only? Because it is something we do? Or do you want to be here?"

"I want to be here, but it's not…it's not like he was holding me back. At least, I didn't think so. I liked what we had. Yes, the baby thing caused some problems but I know we would have worked it out."

"But tonight you want to dance?"

"Yes. Tonight I want to dance."

Alik tightened his hold on her and turned her to face him, his eyes skimming over her body. She had followed his order and put on a short, red dress that hugged her figure a bit more lovingly than she normally cared for. Or maybe that wasn't true anymore.

This was a dress she'd bought last week, and it had seemed perfect. And she'd had Alik in mind when she'd bought it. He was even changing her taste in clothes.

"The last time I danced was at my first wedding," she said.

"Too long, Jada."

He released his hold on her, then laced his fingers through hers, leading her into the center of the packed dance floor. The crush of bodies around them wrapped them in an intimate cocoon and when Alik pulled her against his arms, she melted into him.

They danced slowly, her head tucked against his chest. It was so simple, so romantic.

"This doesn't seem like the kind of club a billionaire would frequent," she said, trying to dispel some of the misty haze that had descended around them.

"Maybe it isn't, but it's exactly the kind of place I used to go to when I came to Paris for the first time. I thought it would be nice to...show you. To share with you."

That made her heart tighten. "Thank you."

The music stopped for a moment, then the bassist started plucking strings, fast and hard, setting up a rhythm that didn't support the gentle sway she and Alik had been moving in. A smile curved Alik's lips and he dropped his hands from around her waist, took her hands in his.

She wasn't experienced at dancing, but Alik was easy to follow. He twirled her and drew her into his body before releasing her again. She laughed, a light, fizzing sensation filling her chest, her head.

The music kept going and she kicked her shoes off at some point, throwing them under one of the bistro tables. She and Alik danced until her brow was damp with sweat, until her voice was hoarse from singing and laughing.

"Last song," Alik said, in response to the announcement from the lead singer. "Want to dance to it?"

"I'm going to fall over, Alik. You've exhausted me," she

said, wandering back to the table and bracing her hand on the surface, tugging her shoes out from beneath it and putting them back on. "That was…fun." The most fun she could remember having in years. "Thank you. I didn't know I would like dancing so much." It was on the tip of her tongue to say they should go again. That she wanted to make it a regular thing. But there was no point to that. None at all.

"I didn't, either," he said. He took her hand and led her out of the club, back into the crisp night air. It felt cool and dry on her skin after the moist heat of the dance floor. "I didn't know a lot of things about life until you, Jada," he said, pulling her close, kissing her lips. It was tender, sweet. Frightening.

"I want you to teach me," he said, his voice rough.

"Teach you what?" she asked.

People were leaving clubs all along the street, weaving around where she and Alik were standing. But she didn't want to move, didn't want to break the spell of the moment.

"Teach me what it means to make love."

No. Her heart screamed in denial. The request, so simple, was scarier than anything else she'd faced with him. And now she wondered if she should have simply been content with their encounter on the couch. If she should never have told him she needed more. Because this was too much. Too close to her deepest fear.

She'd been with him so many times, and yet, this was the time she feared might break her. Because he wasn't asking for her body. He was asking for her soul. Asking her to go deeper than she felt she could.

The further she went with Alik, the more distant her past became. The less her image of the past appealed, because the woman she was turning into wouldn't fit into it.

She was terrified of losing it, of dishonoring it. Of what it would mean if she took another step away from it, another step toward becoming this person who seemed almost entirely different than the one she'd been with her husband.

All she had were her memories, and the way she saw those was changing, too.

She was trembling inside, but as she looked up into Alik's eyes, she knew she could deny him nothing. "Yes. I'll teach you, Alik."

He had the strongest desire to get drunk. To ask Jada for a reprieve when they got back to his town house so that he could stop by the bar and down a few shots.

But when he stopped and looked at Jada in the bright light of the entryway, in her short red dress that revealed her tanned, toned legs, he was grateful for his sobriety.

Still, when she approached him, he shook like an adolescent. He couldn't recall ever feeling nervous before sex. Not even his first time. He'd been too filled with the kind of bravado a teenage boy who'd spent his life on the streets needed in order to survive.

But he felt on the verge of coming undone now. Yet if he did anything to dull the experience, he knew he would miss something. Because with Jada, he always wanted to feel it all. Hot, rough, perfect. And every time she left him hungrier for more.

She was already beneath his skin in a way no other woman had ever been. Was there any point in fighting? Not tonight. Not now. Now he was going to embrace it, because this was the kind of feeling he'd been chasing all of his life.

There was no drug, no alcohol, no beautiful woman, who had ever brought him this close to the edge of ecstasy. Just looking at Jada put him there. And it wasn't just the promise of physical pleasure. It was all-encompassing heat. Like standing in front of a fire, warming every piece of him, burning inside and out.

He had tried to create something like this for most of his life. Had tried to heat the frozen spaces, tried to bring to life parts of him that were dead.

Here he was now, and he was afraid. Afraid he couldn't handle it. Afraid she would be displeased with him. When all of his protection burned away, and left only Alik, would she still want him?

He didn't have time to dwell on that. He couldn't. Because she was walking toward him now, and her eyes were focused on his. As though she saw into him. As though she saw everything. It was impossible, of course. Because if she could truly see into him, if she could see all he had been, if she could truly understand the pain, the damage that was beneath the stone walls around his heart, she would turn away.

But she didn't. She kept walking to him.

"As exciting as I found the couch, I thought we might make use of the bed tonight."

"You're in charge tonight," he said. "This is all you."

"No, Alik, this is us." She held her hand out and he took it, her soft, delicate fingers curling around his, her thumb skimming a rough patch of skin on his wrist. Her fingers were unsteady and he saw that her eyes were glistening. He couldn't figure out why. And he cursed his inability to simply understand her emotion. "This whole night is about us. That's the first difference between sex and making love. It's not my pleasure. It's not your pleasure. It's ours."

He nodded slowly, his heart thundering, low and steady. She led him from the room and up the stairs and he felt a tremor go up his spine. He laughed.

"What?" she asked, turning to him, the light from the top of the stairs backlighting her, hiding her expression.

"I have faced down enemy gunfire and not felt any fear. There is little fear in death to me. And this, connecting with another person? That's frightening."

"I trust you're brave enough to withstand a night of making love with me." She leaned in and kissed him, her lips soft, perfection.

And he wasn't so sure. It took everything in him not to

pick her up and carry her in the room for a bit of hard and fast. That was easy. That was all physical release. This, this slow walk was forcing him to let the pressure build.

He wanted to hide behind what he knew. Wanted to take charge. But he was too fascinated, and he was far too self-destructive to turn away from something that had this much power to wound.

A sobering and very true realization about himself. Hadn't he spent all of his life acting like whether he lived or died didn't matter? Hadn't he spent his life daring whoever was in charge of the universe to simply finish the job? Rather than having him exist, a physical, intact body that was empty inside?

This might be the thing that set him free, that took all the walls down, once and for all. Or it would be the thing that secured his place in hell.

He only hoped he didn't bring Jada down with him.

They went into his room this time. They'd never been together in his room. Because it put Jada in control of what happened afterward. Whether she left. Whether she stayed.

"Take your clothes off," she said.

He obeyed, and she did the same. Then when they were both naked, they lay down on the bed. She wrapped her arms around him and held him against her, burying her face in his neck, inhaling deeply.

She sighed. It was a sweet sound. One of contentment, of happiness. It made emotion swell in his chest, emotion he wanted to push down. If he just rolled her onto her back, he could take her, bring her to the height of pleasure and make her forget about this.

But he wanted to keep the torture going. Wanted to wallow in this newfound form of punishment. A vision of what could be. If only. If only he wasn't broken beyond repair.

She leaned in and kissed him. Slow and deep, erotic torment for his body and soul. She was attuned to him, to every tensing of his muscles, to every sound of pleasure. Her kiss was for him. Just for him. And he wanted to give her pleasure like it in return. Not just pleasure derived from his knowledge about sex and his experience with it, but knowledge from his experiences with Jada.

And so he did. He tore his mouth from hers, then dropped a teasing kiss back on her mouth, took her lower lip between his teeth and bit her gently, because he knew she liked it.

He was rewarded with a low hum and a sweet smile, and it only made his chest feel fuller. Made his whole body feel like it was trying to hold something far too big for one man to carry.

But too wonderful to pass off to anyone else. Jada was his. This was his.

He lowered his head, pressed a kiss to the valley between her breasts. "You are the most beautifully formed woman I have ever seen," he said.

He cupped her, traced the outline of her nipple with the tip of his tongue before sucking it deep into his mouth. She arched into him, her fingers laced in his hair. And he smiled against her skin. She always did that. Always held on to him as though he was anchoring her to earth.

He loved it.

Her skin was soft beneath his hands, and he traced her curves with his fingertips, memorizing every inch of her. There had never been another woman like her. At the moment, he couldn't even remember another woman. They were inconsequential. Everything was.

The violence, the pain, it all fell away beneath Jada's hands. Her touch burned away the memory of everything else. Her voice, soft, sweet, whispering things in his ear, promises of pleasure, words of encouragement, drowned out the visions of violence, the hard, angry, ugly words he'd been exposed to from the time he was a boy.

And when he slid inside of her, it was like the world fell

away. And there was nothing but the two of them. And they didn't even seem like two people anymore.

She wrapped her legs around his waist, moving in time with him, until he could no longer tell who was in control, could no longer tell where he ended and she began.

He felt her tense beneath him, felt her internal muscles tighten around him, and he let go. Let his release wash over him in a wave, drowning out sound and light, pouring through him, into every part of him.

He thought his heart would burst through his chest, thought the walls would cave in around him. But when he came back to himself, everything was the same.

And nothing was. He felt changed. Totally and completely.

Jada wrapped her arms around him, and he adjusted himself, pulling her against him. She rested her head on his chest, her hand over his heart.

And for the first time in his life, Alik wasn't in a hurry to leave the woman by his side. He wasn't on to the next time or place in his mind. On to the next lover. Jada filled his senses, and he was happy to leave it that way. Replete. Satisfied.

"The anchor doesn't mean nothing," he said, not sure why he felt compelled to share. Except it seemed right. After experiencing intimacy with Jada it seemed right to try and deepen it.

"The anchor?" she said, her voice sleepy.

He lifted his arm and showed her the tattoo. "They told me my father was in the navy. At the orphanage. At least, I think that's what my mother told them. I have no idea if it's true. But I thought...I thought it might make me feel closer to him. Sailors have tattoos like this and I thought we might share a trait. I was seventeen, on the run, making my way through Asia and I thought it might make me feel connected with someone. With something. It was stupid. It didn't work, either. I like the tattoo, though."

"I like your tattoos," she said, tracing the line on the anchor with her fingertip. "They keep the past close to you. Permanent reminders of a place you used to be."

Jada looked up at him, the sadness in her eyes stealing his breath. And he wondered who had put it there. If it was past memories, or if it was his fault somehow.

"Memories are good," he said. "But there is no time in my past I would choose to return to."

He watched her face closely, watched pain flash across her face. He reached out to cup her cheek and she turned away from him. Then she sat up, clutching the blanket to her chest. "I should go back to bed. I need to be by Leena's room."

"You should be able to hear if…"

"But I might not be able to," she said. She got out of bed and picked her clothes up off the floor, dressing quickly.

Was this how she felt every night when he left her? Bare? Exposed? Rejected? Because he felt every bit of that and more.

"Don't go."

"It's just…better. I'll see you in the morning."

She turned around and left, shutting the door behind her. Tonight, Alik had had his first taste of true intimacy. And his first taste of what it was to have intimacy rejected.

The latter made him feel that the former was unbelievably overrated.

There was no way he was sleeping tonight. He got up and put on his sweats and running shoes. He had to think. And in order to do that, he needed to run. And he wouldn't stop until he came up with an answer to the burning hunger in his chest.

CHAPTER FOURTEEN

"Good morning, Alik."

"Good morning," he said, sitting down at the breakfast table. Leena was in her usual position and Jada was in hers.

Funny how they all had usual positions now. Jada wanted to scream and run from it. Why hadn't she realized just how much making love with Alik would cost her? She'd thought she could do it. She'd thought she was strong enough. And now she was coming apart inside. Over crepes and coffee. Which was about the stupidest thing ever.

"Breakfast is really, really good this morning," she said, her words shaky as she spooned a bite of banana, wrapped in crepe and cream, into Leena's mouth.

"It looks like it." Alik sat down across from her, his expression sober, and his eyes far too perceptive. "Finish eating because I want to talk to you."

"I'm taking Leena out for a walk so maybe after…"

"I have called Marie and she will be by to walk Leena. You're going to talk to me."

She nodded slowly. "I'll just finish up my coffee."

"Or bring it into the sitting room with me."

Just then, the lovely, dark-haired woman who took care of Leena walked onto the patio. *"Bonjour."*

"Marie, can you finish giving Leena her breakfast?"

"Of course!" she answered far too brightly. So brightly it gave Jada a headache. And stole her excuse for avoiding Alik.

Jada stood grudgingly and Alik did, too, but not before he dropped a kiss on Leena's head. The sight made Jada's heart crack further. He loved Leena. She saw it whenever he looked at her, and now...he could even show it.

It was all she'd needed. For Leena and for him. And it made what she had to do now, what she had to do for her, easier.

Not easier, nothing would make it easier, but it made it less risky. She'd taught Alik to love and he didn't need her anymore. Not as a lover.

And she couldn't afford to play with fire anymore.

"Why are you running from me, Jada?" he asked when they were alone.

"I'm not. But now that you mention it, there is something going on. Something I've been thinking about since last night."

"What?"

"We always said this...this thing between us would end, and I think it needs to end now."

Alik looked like she'd slapped him. "What?"

"It's going to end, Alik, and I want to do it now. While we like each other. While we respect each other and...you're such a good father. You're doing amazing with Leena and..."

"Bull."

"What?"

"You're lying. You don't want to end things while we like each other. I don't believe you." He was right. She was lying. But she had to do it. Everything she'd been, everything that had mattered, was starting to get fuzzy in her mind as Alik grew clearer, sharper. She didn't understand her feelings. She didn't understand herself.

"We talked about this. It was always going to end, and I think we need to do it while everything is healthy between us."

"What is healthy about two people who can't keep their hands off each other, Jada? Tell me. What is healthy about that? I am not an expert on healthy human behavior so I can't comment."

"It's passing," she said.

"Is it?" he bit out.

"It is for me," she said, the lie stabbing at her deep.

"Don't end things."

"Why?"

Alik looked down, then at her, his gray eyes blazing with intensity. "I have fallen in love with you."

It was the admission she'd longed for most. The one she'd feared the most. The one she absolutely couldn't answer. "No, Alik, you haven't."

"Are you going to tell me now what I feel, Jada? Because you are an expert on emotion and I know nothing?"

She almost laughed. She'd never felt less expert in her life. She felt so confused, so crippled by pain and uncertainty. But she had to do this. "That's not it, it's just…this has been a very different and challenging time for you and I think you might be…"

"No. Jada, if you don't want this then say it, but don't you dare question what I feel. I damn well love you and I will not have you force me to deny it."

"I don't want you to love me."

"I don't care," he said, advancing on her, grabbing her hands and tugging her against his chest. "I don't care what you want. I love you. I have never loved anything in all my life until I saw that child in the courthouse. It burned me, Jada. It burned my heart to see her. My flesh and blood, the only flesh and blood I have. And then there was you. So bright and fiery, challenging me, tempting me." He dipped his head, his lips a whisper from hers. "You let me inside you…doesn't that count for anything?"

She felt light-headed, pain slicing through her like a knife's blade. But it was nothing compared to the fear. Nothing compared to the terror she felt at the idea of losing him. The thought of caring enough, of giving enough of herself to him that if he were ever gone from her she would never be able to put herself back together.

She pulled away from him, swaying on her feet. "You don't understand, Alik. I've had love," she said. "And this isn't it. This isn't...this isn't what it feels like. This isn't me."

"Of course it's not the same—I'm not the same man he was. You're not the same woman you were. You've walked through hell. Did you honestly think you would come out the other side needing the same things you needed before you went in?"

"Of course I'm not the same! There's no way I could be. But what you're asking? It's impossible. You want me to just forget him, to..."

"I never said I wanted you to forget him."

"What other option is there? I'm getting further and further away from him and I can't even...I can't even capture the way that I used to feel anymore. I have been...drowning in this grief and pain for so long, and before that I had a life. I had a life and dreams enough for the future, and if I just keep...moving away from it, then what did it mean? It's like I'm making it so it doesn't even matter."

"Why can't it matter, too? Why can't you just let it go and..."

"How would you even know what I can and can't let go of, Alik? What any person could? You've clung to your pain, shielded it, all your life. You've spent all these years running from your feelings, from your pain, so don't you dare tell me what I should let go of!"

He advanced on her, his lip curled into a snarl. "You're right—I've spent enough time running, Jada, so I know what that looks like. But you aren't even running. You're just standing in the same spot, glued to it because you're afraid to move on. I know your path changed, I know it's rough and scary and I know it hurts, but you still have to walk on it, dammit.

You were the one that told me life moves on. But you aren't moving, Jada. You're standing still."

"So I should just go on like he didn't matter? Like everything is fine?"

"You didn't die three years ago. He did," Alik said, his voice hard. Angry.

"Stop. Just stop."

"No. You listen. You are alive, Jada Patel, but you choose to bury yourself. To try to live unchanging and unmoving. There is life here. There could be life with me. But you won't take it."

Her eyes glistened, with tears. With anger. "Just because I don't want you doesn't mean I don't want to live," she said. "I did change. I got Leena, didn't I?"

"You didn't change—you simply didn't have anyone standing in the way of what you always wanted. Because he did stand in your way, Jada, whether you want to admit it or not. He stood in the way of Leena. Of who you are."

"He didn't, Alik. He was a good man, he—"

"Better than me?"

"Yes." He jerked back, as though he'd been slapped. But still she kept going. "I want a simple, normal life that doesn't hurt all the time. I want to raise my daughter, with you because you're her father and it's right, but I don't want to be your wife."

"You are in luck, then," he said slowly, taking an envelope off the desk. "The adoption is finalized. You don't have to be my wife."

She blinked slowly. "I don't?"

"No."

"Oh."

"You listen to me," he said. "I will divorce you. I will give you what you ask for. I will put you in a house of your choosing. Here, in Attar, in New York, back in Oregon. I don't care. But before I do that, I am going to say it one more time and when you reject it, you be sure that you don't want it because I will never say it again…do you understand me? Reject me again and I withdraw it."

She closed her eyes, a tear sliding down her cheek. And she nodded, biting her lip, trying to hold the pain at bay.

"I love you."

She shook her head, a sob escaping her lips, more tears falling. "No." It was all she could say.

"Then that is the last time I will torture you with the words. Now get out."

"Alik…"

"Out."

Alik watched Jada walk out of the room, and he felt his chest tear in two. It was like everything in him had come to life, new and raw and bleeding. He felt it all now. The loss, so intense, crippling, and with it, the love that beat behind it. Too strong to be wiped out, no matter how cruel the rejection.

This was why he had left himself numb for so long.

Because his life would have been nothing but an endless hell of pain if he hadn't learned to numb it. But if he had spent his life feeling, then perhaps this moment wouldn't be quite so devastating. Perhaps he could have built up a security system against it. As it was, there was nothing to prepare him for it. For how it felt to tell a woman he loved her. To have her throw it back at him.

He wanted to hurt her, as he was hurting. He wanted to take Leena from her. Just for one, small, ugly moment, he wanted it. And then he imagined the pain it would put her through and his own doubled.

Love was hell. To want to make her feel his pain, to know that if he did it would hurt him even more.

No wonder he had guarded himself against this. He had been smart.

He wished he could close himself up again. Wished he

could go back to life before Jada. Wished he could unlearn intimacy. Wished he had never made love with her.

But if he wished it all away, if he turned back to the man he was, then he would lose his love for Leena, too. And Leena was worth the pain. She was worth any pain.

So strange. He had lived his life for so long, and he had had nothing to live for. So he had flirted with death. With danger. Now he had something that was truly worth dying for. He would lay down his life for Leena without hesitation, but for her sake, for the love of her, he wanted to live now more than he ever had.

He also wanted to cut his heart out of his chest.

It was too damned early in the day to drink. And he had no way to numb his pain. So instead he walked out of the sitting room and back to the patio. Marie was still there talking to Leena.

"Let me take her," he said.

He picked her up and smelled her hair, and a strange feeling of calm cut through the pain. He had Leena. No matter what, he had Leena.

He didn't need Jada. He only needed his daughter. And he wouldn't hurt his daughter by taking her from his wife. The woman who would be his ex-wife soon enough.

After giving Leena back to Marie, he walked outside into the chilly Parisian morning and did his best to ignore the word. Ex-wife. It kept repeating itself in his mind. Over and over again, in time with his footsteps.

He gritted his teeth. It didn't matter. She didn't matter. He had made a vow. He would not tell her he loved her again. He would not even think it. Jada had missed her chance with him. She could have her freedom. She could have her safety.

She could cling to the memory of a husband who could no longer hold her.

He would not look back. He would not offer his love again.

* * *

He'd sent Jada and Leena back to Attar, while he'd taken a different plane, had gone back to Brussels to check on his earlier deal. The one that had been interrupted by the discovery of his child. And the acquisition of his new wife.

Now he was walking downtown, the streets cold and wet, the clubs inviting. In there was every tool he needed to forget. Women. Alcohol. Especially women.

He jerked open the door to one of the clubs. The music, cigarette smoke and thick smell of sweat and booze hit him hard. It was all so familiar. So much more familiar than this feeling of raw vulnerability in his chest.

Here, there was no pain. No need to be honest. Here, there was oblivion. Shallow and perfect. The strobe lights were blinding, the bass deafening. A hostile takeover of the senses. Everything he could have asked for.

He went to the bar and ordered a drink, then surveyed his surroundings. Until he spotted her. Blonde, tall and bombshell curvy. All the things Jada wasn't.

She was leaning against the other end of the bar, a drink in her hand. She lifted a toothpick from it and put it in her mouth, sucking the cherry from the end. Subtle she was not. Good. He didn't want subtle.

He wanted easy.

He put his glass to his lips and made eye contact with her. And on cue, she worked her way down the bar toward him, her hips swaying. He felt no desire for her. But this wasn't about her.

"Buy me another drink?" she shouted over the music.

He nodded and signaled to the bartender.

He knew the steps to this dance. Everything about it was familiar. Except for the sick feeling in his stomach. Except for the total absence of adrenaline. Of the thrill.

The woman approached him, put her hand over his, tilted

her head to the side. She talked. She played with her hair. She licked her lips.

His vision blurred. Until he saw Jada. In a white dress, walking down the aisle toward him like she was going to the gallows.

And then he heard their vows. Over and over again.

Promises of togetherness until death. Of faithfulness.

And Sayid's words, echoing in his head.

You think what happened here today, the words you spoke, you think those won't matter?

It mattered. Regardless of what he wanted to believe. It mattered.

She mattered. And the simple act of her not returning his love didn't erase it.

"I have to go." He put his drink down on the bar and turned away from the woman, walked back toward the door.

Someone ran into him, laughed, a strange-sounding laugh. Drunken. Not genuine.

No wonder he had never found anything lasting here. No wonder this had never brought him satisfaction. There was nothing real in this. Nothing of substance.

Jada and Leena were the real thing.

They were all that mattered. And if he had to put himself through the pain of her rejection a thousand times, he would do it.

Because before Jada, he had been a prisoner in himself. And now, pain and all, he was free.

Alik had been gone for days, leaving Leena and Jada alone in Attar.

Jada couldn't complain. She badly needed the space. Needed to get her head on straight. Find herself again, whoever that was.

Although the idea that space would somehow ease her

pain was terribly flawed. She knew that. Space, separation, caused so much pain.

Leena had fallen asleep already, which was nice in some ways. Not in others. Because without her daughter to entertain, all Jada had were her thoughts. And her thoughts were a sad, bitter place at the moment.

Bitter at herself, mostly. And at Alik for demanding so much of her.

Jada sighed and rested her arms on the railing, looking out over the ocean. She missed Alik. She missed his touch. His kiss. His laugh. She missed how she felt happy around him.

You're not the same woman you were.

She couldn't get his words out of her mind. That was what scared her. That she'd changed so much. That all her memories were fading into a vague, colorless past. Happy, but no longer so poignant. No longer something she felt desperate to recapture. No longer something she idolized as utter perfection, but something she now saw as flawed. Real.

She was standing on the edge of a cliff, and she wasn't sure whether or not she should jump. She was afraid that by embracing her new self with Alik, she would lose who she'd been with Sunil.

But Sunil was gone. And there was no way to know how things would have played out if he was still here. No way to know how she would have changed, or not changed.

The simple truth was, the woman who was here and now, wanted Alik, and no other man. The woman she was now wouldn't go back, because this life, her life, was everything she hadn't known she'd wanted. And she wanted Alik, so much. So incredibly much. His touch, his laugh, him.

She waited for the guilt that admission should bring, but there was none. Just a sort of sweet ache in her heart.

She closed her eyes and lifted her face to the sky, the ocean breeze skimming over her skin like a caress. That made her think of Alik, too. When she thought of the word *husband,* it was his face she saw. When she thought of love…

She couldn't go forward while she had one foot in the past. She realized that now. She also realized that she'd been doing it by design. That she'd been doing it to keep herself safe.

But Alik, stupid Alik, sexy, wonderful Alik, wouldn't let her stay safe.

He had pulled her open, exposed her, made her care and laugh and love. Made her hunger for life, for the next chapter instead of the ones at the beginning of the book.

She had been terrified of shedding her old self. That her new skin seemed to fit so much better. Because she hadn't been sure how to reconcile it all. She had been happy with Sunil. But…but with Alik there was the promise of something true. Something complete. And it had all been too much for her to handle.

And now she'd ruined everything. Alik would never offer his love to her again. His face when he'd said that…it had been so cold. So horribly cold.

"How dare you?"

She turned and saw Alik, walking toward her. He was wearing the remnants of a suit, no tie, his shirt rumpled and the sleeves pushed up to his elbows.

"How dare I what?"

"How dare you…storm into my life."

"You were the one who stormed into mine," she said.

"Then why am I the one left devastated?"

She flinched, the haunted look in his eyes almost too painful for her to witness.

He took her arm and pulled her to him, his expression fierce. "You stripped me of all of my protection. Of everything that was holding me together. And then you took yourself from me too."

"How dare I?" she asked. "How dare you! I feel like…I don't even know who I am anymore. No, that's not it. I feel like I found myself for the first time and I have nothing to hide behind. I have no excuse now, not to be this person, not to…not to grab what I want and I'm afraid of what I want, Alik. Of how badly I want it."

"And what is it you want?"

"You," she breathed. "No matter what…I…all I want is you. I've made some bad choices lately."

"You have?" he asked, his expression frozen.

She nodded. "Alik, I was so stupid. I was so focused on protecting things that have already passed that I missed something I could have had now. I was too…I was too afraid of the person I was becoming and it made me want to cling to the past even more."

"Emotion," he said slowly, "is a very strange thing. As I am learning. I tried to feel for most of my life, and I failed. I tried to create deep feelings from shallow things but that doesn't work. You can't protect yourself and embrace love."

"Sometimes you can't stop it, either, even though you want to. I wanted to stop it, Alik, but I couldn't."

He laughed. "You wanted to stop what, princess?" The tenderness in his voice made her want to cry. Then she realized she was already crying.

She wiped a tear from her cheek. "Alik, I tried so hard to fix you because it was easier than looking at myself and seeing what a mess I still was. I was so afraid that wanting different things now, becoming a different person now, would make my marriage obsolete. That it would dishonor my husband's memory. More than that even…that I just wouldn't be able to hide anything of myself. You distracted me, made me start to forget."

"My sex appeal, I think."

"You *would* think that, and I won't lie, it was that in the beginning."

"And now?"

"I am the most self-righteous, ridiculous, un-self-aware person on the planet."

"Are you?"

"I must be. I had myself convinced that my past was perfection."

"And I know that I'm not perfection."

Her heart seized. "Alik...no...let me finish. I thought moving on from my past would somehow be disloyal or that it would...that it would erase it. That wanting something different now might mean that what I had then was somehow less. Alik, you made me want again. You made me dream. You took me dancing. You made me happy. You showed me that I wanted things I hadn't even known I wanted. And with all of that...I don't need my memories anymore. And those memories meant so much. They're warm and sweet, calm. They're what my idea of love was."

"We are not sweet and calm, are we?"

"No. We aren't. You challenge me. You arouse me like no other man ever has. I've spent my life doing things exactly how I should, and no one has ever made me want to deviate from that path. But you...you had me up against a wall in an opera house! You make me lose my control. You make me dizzy. And this isn't anything I've ever felt before, anything I ever wanted before. And I didn't understand how this could be me. I didn't understand how this thing between you and me could be love."

He put his hand on her cheek, his eyes filled with sadness so deep it made her heart squeeze. "For you, maybe it isn't."

She shook her head. "No. You were right. It's different because you're different. Because I'm different. Because I need to be different. I realized it then, Alik. And that was when I ran. When you said you loved me, I had to face the fact that I loved you, too, and..."

"You love me?"

She nodded, the words sticking in her throat.

"Then why did you…why did you walk away from me?"

"I was running. You should know all about that."

He slid his thumbs over her cheeks, wiping her tears away. "Will you stop running from me? Will you stop running from us? I have. I tried to go back, Jada. I'm not proud of it. I tried to go to a club, to pick up a woman. I found I didn't even want to. I couldn't. I am too changed by what has passed between us."

She nodded. "I am, too. I don't want to go back, either, and that's what scared me, Alik. That I've moved on. Finally. Really."

He took her hands in his, pinned them to his chest. "I have broken down every wall inside of myself so that there could be nothing between us, and I swore I wouldn't offer it again, but, Jada, my pride can burn in hell because if I don't have you… there is no meaning. Pride won't keep me warm. Pride won't show me beauty. You are what I have been chasing all my life. This is the feeling. I thought I was dead inside, thought I could never, ever have this…and then there was you."

Jada looked at Alik, at the man who had changed her. At the man who was offering her healing. "I'm so sorry, Alik."

"What?" he asked, his voice choked.

"This is what I did to you, isn't it? I dragged you out of your safety, out of your comfort zone and I made you face everything that scared you the most."

"You did. But it needed to be done. Protecting myself… protecting myself from the pain of losing my mother would have kept me from truly connecting with my child. It would have kept me from connecting with you. From loving you."

"I was so arrogant to think I wasn't hiding, too. I was. I was hiding behind grief and excuses. I…I don't want to hide anymore. Alik, please, please forgive me. Please love me. Please tell me it's not too late."

He pulled her in, crushing his lips to hers, stealing her breath. When they parted, she was dizzy. "Of course it's not too late. In fact, I was planning on mounting a full-scale attack on your defenses."

She laughed. "As if you hadn't already!"

"I'm a strategist, remember? That's what they pay me for. And I had a plan to win you back."

"What was it?"

"I don't remember. I discarded it somewhere between the plane from Brussels to Attar, then I spent days in a hotel room, sulking and then I went and got this." He held his left hand up. There was a dark band tattooed around his ring finger.

"What is that?"

"My wedding ring. It doesn't come off, which, I thought might make for a nice line about why you actually have to stay married to me."

"Alik…"

She took his hand in hers and ran her finger over the band. "What does it say?" She looked up at him. "It's in Russian."

"Jada. And Leena. My family. I am committed to you, always."

"What if I would have told you I didn't want to be married to you?"

"Are you going to tell me that?"

"No."

"Then it's moot. But that was when I figured I would redraft a strategy and start working on ways to exploit your vulnerabilities."

"My vulnerabilities?"

"Yes. For one, I thought I could take you to the opera and get you alone in a private royal box."

"You are shameless."

"Always. But now…only for you. I have tasted every empty, meaningless pleasure life has to offer and I've come to the conclusion that those things are only there to distract us from the real meaning in life. A man can get lost in the fleeting things and forget to look for anything real. I am so thankful you brought something real into my life."

"Alik, I want you to marry me again," she said, thinking back to their wedding day. To the dress that she didn't like. To the lack of music. To her sadness. "And this time, I want to take your name. So we all have the same name. So I have your name."

"But what about…"

"The past is the past. I have good memories there. But now I'm not afraid to simply let memories be memories. Not anymore. I have too much ahead of me to keep looking back. You are my future. My heart. My love."

"And you have brought me love. For the first time, Jada. It's like seeing the sun, seeing color, when before there was only darkness. Only gray."

"Like waking up," she said, and she realized that it was true for her, too.

"Yes. Like that."

"I'm glad I woke up," she said. "Because this is so much better than dreaming."

"So much."

"So, will you marry me again?" she asked.

Alik looked at Jada, at his wife, at his heart. He had spent his life not feeling, not caring. And now that he did, he loved with all of himself. "No one ever loved me," he said. "And now, I have an embarrassment of riches. You and Leena? I am the luckiest man on earth. There are so many broken things in our lives and now…we get a chance to make something new. Something perfect."

She arched one brow and gave him an impish smile. "So, will you marry me, then?"

"Nothing could stop me."

"Don't go challenging fate, Alik."

"When I look at how things have played out, how I found Leena, how I found you, I think fate is on our side, don't you?"

"I think you're right."

EPILOGUE

JADA ADJUSTED HER RED VEIL and held her arms out in front of her, examining the intricate designs that had been painted onto her skin during the henna ceremony the night before. Sayid's wife, Chloe, had helped with that and Jada was pleased that she'd found a friend in the other woman. Sayid was the closest thing Alik had to a brother. And now they were all family.

She could hear the music coming from the courtyard and her heart swelled, the smile that had been on her face since she'd woken up that morning spreading wider. She grabbed her bouquet from the dressing table and lifted her heavy skirt, adorned with gold fabric that caught fire when the midday Attari sun caught a hold of it. Bright, vibrant. Happy.

She ran down the stairs, her fingers skimming the stone balustrade. Two attendants opened the double doors for her, and she saw Alik, waiting for her at the head of the aisle, Leena in a red dress that matched Jada's, resting in his arms.

She nearly laughed, her heart taking flight. She looked up into the bleached sky and smiled. The heaviness that had been inside her for so long was gone, burned away by the sun, by the heat of Alik's love. She felt light again. She felt new.

Then she started to walk down the aisle. Toward her family, her husband. Her future.

Alik took her hand and she looked down at where they were joined, her hand small and dark in his. "I searched for this moment all my life," he said, his voice low. "What a gift to have finally reached it."

"I didn't realize I was searching for this moment," she said. "But I was. Out of grief came the most beautiful path. And it was taking me toward you, Alik."

"I'm so glad you followed it."

"So am I, Alik. So am I."

* * * * *

TEMPT ME

CAITLIN CREWS

CHAPTER ONE

RORY MORTON KNEW perfectly well she wasn't supposed to be in this room of the extraordinarily posh
Parisian private home she was meant to be cleaning.
The many bedrooms, studies, and other public areas
were to be dusted and carefully made even more
beautiful than they already were. The kitchen was
to sparkle, the bathrooms were to be left immaculate, and all the glass, chrome, and marble was to
shine. The office—visible behind glass and neat as
a pin—was not to be disturbed. The garage was not
to be entered. The grounds on this parcel of land in
the Golden Triangle, located in Paris's upscale 8th
Arrondissement, were tended to by a different service and should be left alone—unless, of course,
Rory noted some cause for concern.

And the locked door on the second floor was to
be read as a KEEP OUT sign and obeyed.

It had all been clearly laid out in the pages upon
pages of instructions she'd received from the fussy

assistant of whoever owned this surprisingly large property set down in the middle of the city that she'd been hired to clean.

Rory had come to Paris because it was *Paris*, which should have been reason enough. She liked to say it just like that and stare at whoever asked as if there could be no other possible answer.

But another layer to that truth was that she'd become deeply bored with her life, all of which had been lived in and around Nashville. She'd grown up in Nashville. She'd gone to college in Nashville. She loved Nashville—but Rory wanted to see more of the world than Tennessee.

When her two best friends moved to opposite coasts, Natalie to Los Angeles and Blair to New York, it was possible Rory had felt the need to throw down a power move in the shape of Paris. And yes, she now spent most of her life taking clever pictures to plaster all over her social media accounts to indicate, whenever possible, how much more amazing her life was *on the Continent*. #expatlife.

Once in Paris, she'd started a cleaning service because it was the most un-chic thing she could think of to do in the chicest city on earth, and therefore made her seem more authentic. It was a bonus that it also deeply horrified her parents—especially her mother, who liked to point out that she had come all the way to the States from the Philippines so her children could exceed expectations. Not clean up after other people.

Her long-suffering father preferred to drink his horror in the form of Tennessee whiskey, which he liked to say his people had been making in one form or another since they'd found their way to the Tennessee hills from Scotland or Ireland or both in the 1800s. But when he wasn't drowning his sorrows, he was still Marty Morton, and his contacts through his decades of producing music provided Rory with a roster of wealthy clients who were only too happy to hire her to clean their Parisian second, or third, or fourth homes.

Rory liked to pretend that she was doing this because it was art. *Everything is art if it's done by an artist,* she'd captioned one of her last posts, of her in profile near a priceless painting in a client's flat, on her hands and knees with a sponge to scrub the floor.

She liked to be provocative. She could admit that. And so far it had gotten her hundreds of thousands of followers, so she figured she was doing something right.

And if Rory found she enjoyed the actual act of cleaning more than she'd expected—that it became almost meditative and reminded her in some ways of dancing—she wisely kept that to herself. It was one thing to do important work as a kind of digital performance artist. It would have been something else entirely to *actually be* nothing but a house cleaner.

Not that Rory was concerned about her art at the moment. *Darlin, you can't tell me cleaning a toilet is anything but cleaning a got-damn toilet,* her father had said the one time she'd loftily used that word to describe her work in his hearing. And she didn't bother rolling her eyes at her father from across the ocean because what she *was* concerned with was the very private room in this place that had been locked up tighter than a drum for three months now.

Frankly, she thought she deserved a medal for her restraint and respect of her client's privacy. And for not trying to jimmy the lock. Not even once.

Of course, the reality was that every other time she'd come here the door to the room had been sealed up so tight it didn't budge. Meaning that Rory didn't so much practice any kind of restraint as she'd repeatedly tried the dramatic, medieval door handle— every time she cleaned here—and always, always found it locked.

Maybe no medals, then.

But today, at last, the secret room was open.

Rory had finished up her normal rounds, leaving everything sparkling and bright and *lifted*, because that was what actually made her happy. Then she'd taken a few artsy photos and posted them, because that was her *brand*. With all identifying details concealed, naturally, because her clients certainly didn't want the masses showing up at their homes. Then, on her way out, she'd gone ahead and tried the extraordinarily over-the-top door, fitted as it was in a stone arch, complete with iron studs and scrollwork bands across the sturdy oak planks.

When everything else in this home was sleek and modern, as if to play off the old church's gothic architecture.

She expected it to be as immovable as it always was, but instead, when she tugged on the iron handle, it opened.

A thrill shot through her, a wild tingling thing that was hot and cold at once—

"It's just a door," she muttered at herself, trying to tamp down all that absurd sensation.

It didn't work.

She pulled her mobile out of her back pocket and hooked her spray bottle—filled with the noninvasive, nonchemical, nonharmful green cleaner she preferred, because she wasn't a Boomer, hell-bent on destroying the world on her way out, thank you very much—on the waistband of her jeans. Then she took a few snaps of herself trying the handle of the secret door she'd posted about before, making faces upon finding it open and then pushing the door in as she went inside.

The first thing she noticed were the stained glass windows. She assumed this must have been the nave of the church, where the altar would have been, and the glass seemed warm and remote at once as the summer afternoon light streamed in. She ran her fingers over the wall beside the door, trying to blink her eyes into focus, and found what seemed like a particularly involved panel of light switches. Dimmers and another line of switches and who even knew what.

She flicked on the light switches, blinked, and then paused. Because she'd expected…a wine cellar, or something. A recording studio, like her father's back home that he liked to treat like it was the Pentagon.

But not…*this*.

It was a large room with warm hardwood floors. There were area rugs that looked soft and inviting. The ceilings were high and airy, with whitewashed walls wherever the stained glass windows weren't, and loads of exposed beams and brick.

It was nicer than her current flat in the Latin Quarter, if she was honest.

But it was also outfitted with a great many things she'd never seen in person before. There was a bed with four very high and sturdy-looking posters, all fitted with bolts and things that clearly indicated it was used for bondage. There was a chair nearby that looked like a throne but…wasn't. There was a huge X-shaped cross against one brick wall. On either side of where she stood, stretching down the walls, were…tools. Of all shapes, sizes, and descriptions. Whips and actual chains. Obvious sex toys she could identify and a great many she'd never seen before in her life.

Her heart thudded at her. Her pulse felt too hot and weighted, somehow, in her veins.

The rest of the room featured a giant mirror on the wall across from the X that she imagined could also take in the bed. There were a variety of different benches, many with interesting-looking additions, or better still, subtractions, that made her head spin. There was what looked like a padded massage table, if she ignored that the space beneath it was an actual cage. There was a hammock sort of thing slung from one of the beams, what looked like a hanging pull-up bar, and incongruously, high above, one of the biggest and most beautiful chandeliers she'd ever seen.

And for some reason, the sight of all these things made her breath go shallow.

If Rory wasn't mistaken—and how could she be in the face of all this clear evidence?—this was a *literal* den of iniquity. A red room of pain, as such places were sometimes known. Though this room was not red.

On the contrary, it didn't scream out *sexual deviant* at all. If she squinted and pretended she couldn't recognize the fetish equipment all over the place— all of which she and her high school friends had tittered over when they'd stolen their mother's Fifty Shades books—it could have been an upscale, hipster coffeehouse.

And she told herself it was surprise and astonishment that was making her heart beat double time in her chest. While an unfamiliar sensation seemed to sink down into her belly, then deep between her legs. It was…warm.

Very, very warm.

Rory didn't know what that was, since she'd concluded at some point in college that she was incapable of feeling such things. So intensely, anyway. In that area.

She rubbed a bit absently at her chest, where her heart was going mad. And sure, this place was a converted church, when she had always been a secular person—except here, now, she could have sworn she could hear a choir singing hosannas in the distance.

Maybe it had something to do with the way the light came into the stained glass, sending beams of color this way and that, like an invitation.

Rory drifted farther into the room, skirting the fascinating furniture as she went. All of which, she was happy to note on a purely professional level, looked even cleaner than the house. She stopped at the foot of the huge bed, swallowed hard at all the metalwork she could see in the four posters—not to mention the bolts in the floor—and decided to take a few pictures of the windows. The stained glass glory of it all.

It took her a few moments to figure out how to take a reasonable breath, and to start thinking of something clever she could post as a caption to hint at what this room was without actually giving anything away. She told herself it was because she didn't want to risk getting in trouble with the mysterious owner, but deep down, there was a part of her that wanted to keep this private anyway.

And not because she was afraid of getting in trouble, but because there was something about that *warmth* and the way she felt like she might be glowing like the stained glass up above. Or that the choir she almost heard was singing inside her.

Breathing too hard still, she turned, wanting to see the rest of the room—

And Rory forgot about the room.

Because there was a man standing in the doorway.

"What, exactly, do you think you're doing?" he asked in crisp French.

His voice was precise and something like polite, though it was also so chilly it made her flinch. Especially when she noticed that chill was matched by the frigid navy blue gaze leveled on her.

She could feel the thrust of it, everywhere.

She knew, even though she'd never met him before, that this was the mysterious owner of this place. The man who was too busy to ever interact with his cleaning service, which was fair enough. But he was also so unknowable that even after three months of cleaning his bedroom and bathroom, she knew absolutely nothing about him. Not even his name.

Not even what side of the bed he slept on.

She wanted to launch into a passionate defense

of herself and how she happened to be here in this room, clearly breaking all the rules. Rory considered herself pretty fluent in excuses, after the past few years of what her father liked to call *unfortunate aimlessness*.

But when she opened her mouth, nothing came out.

It was him.

He was…forbidding.

He was tall and built like none of the men Rory tended to date. He was not willowy and slim, with tousled hair. He did not look as if he could wear a smaller size of trousers than she could. He looked like he was intimately acquainted with his own body and decidedly physical. There were lean muscles everywhere, and it was obvious that if he were to strip naked, he would look like the sort of glorious male sculpture that belonged in one of the museums here.

He looked as strict as he did beautiful. It was those eyes of his, so decidedly dark blue and cold, like the Atlantic in winter. And his mouth, set in a hard, firm line. His dark blond hair was close-cropped and only made him seem that much more masculine. That much *more*. There was obvious power and authority in him that he wore as easily as he did the dark trousers he had on and that leather jacket that whispered of near incalculable amounts of money, particularly because it did marvelous things for his wide shoulders.

Or maybe that was just his shoulders.

If asked, Rory could have given a dissertation on the kind of man she liked. A boyish-faced, agreeable poet sort. Wispy, nonthreatening men who wanted to sing her songs and tell her about their dreams.

That was not this man. At all.

He looked as if he might have been fashioned out of a hatchet or sword, all planes and angles, all solid. Not only deeply, inarguably male, but very much as if he might at a moment's notice turn himself into a weapon.

Or already was one.

Rory had no idea why looking at him made her knees feel weak.

"Do I need to call the police?" he asked in the same cut-steel voice.

Rory told herself that his voice was getting to her because he was speaking French. That was all. It was flawless French, though she could hear the hint of an accent, and she always had to play catchup when people were speaking French. Even though she'd imagined herself fluent after all her years of studying the language in high school and college.

"I understand French," she told him. Maybe a little hopefully. "But I'm much better in English."

"Forgive me," the man said with exaggerated patience. He still stood there, taking up the entirety of the arched stone doorway and all of the oxygen in the room, and he didn't look as if he was all that interested in forgiveness. "I cannot think of a single reason why an American should be in my home at all. Much less in this room."

He said all of that in English. So that she could be certain to hear the derision in his voice when he said *American*, Rory assumed. But that made this interaction feel something like normal, so she beamed at him.

"I'm happy to clear that up," she said brightly. "I'm your cleaning service."

"You do not look like a service. You look like a single person. And one who is not where she ought to be."

Everything about his voice and that cool, assessing way he looked at her made her heart kick around inside her chest. It made that warm thing expand, hot and unwieldy and barbed, almost.

As if he was electric. And inside her, somehow.

"I've been cleaning this property for months," she told him, as if that should make him feel better about her invasion of his privacy.

"Have you indeed."

It didn't sound like a question, but she took it as one anyway. "I have. I hope you've noticed the care I've taken with your things. That's part of what we promise at CleanWorks."

"And were my instructions unclear in all this time?"

There was something about the way he continued to stand there that should have scared her, she thought. He was so still. So focused.

So…intent.

But instead, the warmth in her turned into a blast of heat. And it made her pussy ache.

"There were six pages of instructions for this property," she said, trying not to stammer as unfamiliar sensations flowed through her. Her breasts felt heavy. She could feel her nipples harden. She thought she might even be *sweating*. "Single-spaced. To be honest, I skimmed them."

An expression moved over his face that she thought might have been laughter, if he'd been someone else. On him it looked like a storm.

"You skimmed. And you feel comfortable telling me this as you stand here in the middle of the room I expressly forbade you to enter."

"The door was open." She shrugged casually, as if she felt in any way relaxed or at her ease while her lungs stopped working and her whole body was… freaking out. "I thought maybe that meant you wanted it cleaned this time."

"No," he said. With quiet conviction. "You did not think that."

His words seemed to fill the room. Or maybe it was the way he looked at her, those dark blue eyes so intent that she nearly collapsed to the floor and started blurting out confessions. Anything to make him stop looking at her like that.

But he didn't stop. And to her astonishment, she felt herself flush. She felt her cheeks get hot, and somewhere in her belly, she felt a little curl of shame.

Which was even more unusual than the heat everywhere else.

She opened her mouth to protest, but he stopped her. He did something with his head, barely shaking it at all. He just looked as if he *might* shake his head, and whatever she'd been about to say died unsaid.

"I will ask you not lie to me," he said.

In that same quiet voice that was all steel. Steel that didn't have to flash or carry on—it was just steel.

And it was bizarre, then, how she suddenly wanted to impress him with the force of her honesty.

"Maybe…" Again, that almost shake of his head, and she pulled in a shaky breath. And dropped the *maybe*. "I wanted to see what was in this room."

"Why?"

"I guess…"

"Don't guess. Tell me."

It occurred to Rory to wonder why she was still standing there, trying to impress a man who looked as if nothing could ever impress him. Or worse, as if she was desperate to keep talking to him when she didn't even know his name.

When he obviously—*and rightly*, something in her piped up, straight from that flush of shame inside her—thought the worst of her.

"I guess I'm the curious type."

"You guess? Or you are?"

She had no idea why she felt chastened. Or why she, who could talk to anyone about anything and usually did, stood there. Silenced.

"Not only curious," he continued. "You thought you should document your findings. What do you plan to do with those pictures you took?"

Rory had completely forgotten that her mobile was in her hand. She stared down at it, as if it was a scarlet A branded on her palm. "I… I don't know."

"Don't you?"

Her cheeks felt even hotter than before. "I take a lot of pictures. And okay, I post some of them online. All of my friends are back in the States, and I like to make it clear that I made good choices in coming to Paris. Plus, you know, I have followers."

"Followers," he repeated, as if the word felt foreign and unpleasant on his tongue. "Are you a student?"

"Um, no. I graduated from college almost four years ago."

"A tourist, then. Cleaning houses for fun as you travel? Or perhaps to raise money for the next leg?"

"It's actually my company," she said, and she felt as if she was back on even ground again. Or more even ground, anyway. "CleanWorks is more than just a housecleaning service. I like to call it an artisan experience that *results* in housecleaning."

"Does this experience normally include an invasion of your clients' privacy, or is that a bonus?"

He didn't move when he said that, and still, she felt it like a shock to her system. A literal electric shock. As if he'd leaped across the space and *done something* with his hands—

Though she almost staggered back a step when she realized that no small part of her wished he had. What was *happening* to her?

"I really did think the door was left open because you wanted this room as part of your clean this time," she said loftily, because it was better to double down on something that he couldn't *prove* was untrue. "My bad. I'll just pack up—"

"No," he said in the same mildly reproving way, all steel and disappointment, shaming her all over again, "you did not think that. And I believe I've already told you that I dislike lies."

She took a breath and realized she couldn't remember if she'd done that in a while. And once she did, she could again feel the wild racket her heart was making.

Meanwhile, that ache in her pussy was bordering on astonishing. She felt...slippery.

And something like needy.

"Do you know what I use this room for?" he asked.

"Unless it's an art installation, I imagine you use it for sex," Rory replied, matter-of-factly.

She had always taken particular pleasure in being provocative. In talking about sex as if she'd done it all a thousand times over, for example, to people who expected her to stammer or blush. She liked to give them a direct stare, a faintly superior sort of smile, and a frankness they never saw coming.

But none of that worked here. With him.

He only gazed back at her, one dark brow raised higher than the other, and she felt herself...quiver.

"Yes," he said in that voice of his, with that accent she couldn't quite place. "Sex. But not just any kind of sex, obviously. I like tools. And props. And all kinds of games. It's a very particular kind of sex that I don't care if you understand or not. But I prefer, all the same, to do the deciding about who I share that with."

"I get it," Rory said, nodding maybe a little too vigorously. As if that would make all the dark, wicked images his words had stirred up dissipate. It didn't work, but she kept going. "I grew up on Fifty Shades, so..."

The man did not sigh. He did not roll his eyes. Yet somehow he gave the impression of doing both.

Without moving an inch or lifting that navy blue, winter sea gaze of his from her.

"There are normally consequences for lying to me in this room," he told her. Very calmly. "Consequences I have no doubt you would not wish to pay, for all your posturing."

"I'm not *posturing*—"

"What you are is fired." This time his voice was all steel, and though he didn't change his volume, it wasn't quiet. "But before you leave here, never to return, I would like you to give me your mobile."

Rory blinked. She would do nothing of the kind.

But before she knew she meant to move—or even breathe—she found herself crossing back to the door, her hand outstretched toward him, so caught up in that stare of his she thought she might have leaped off a cliff—

She only caught herself at the last moment, rocking to a halt and frowning at him in a flush of confusion.

"Wait."

But he reached over and tugged her phone from her grip, managing to do it without touching her at all.

Something that shouldn't have made her feel so... raw.

"You really can't go around taking people's phones," she protested. "Right out of their hands."

He tapped a few buttons, deleting the photos she'd taken, and then raised that cool gaze to hers again. "It is such an invasion of privacy, isn't it? I understand."

And she felt that rawness inside her turn into something else, too quickly, as if he'd flayed her open with such a mild reproach.

The shame inside her seemed to swallow her

whole. It was hot and awful, and she couldn't seem to feel anything but the press of it.

And the way he looked at her, as if he knew.

"I'm sorry," she heard herself say, as if from a very great distance.

In a voice that didn't sound like hers at all.

The man handed her phone back to her in a peremptory way that nearly had her *thanking* him. And then he studied her, something about that slow, intense perusal making her fight to keep from shivering.

She wanted to back away from him, but she didn't.

"I think that's the most honest thing you've said to me so far," he said. And she had the strangest notion that he approved.

A kind of glow lit her up, washing through all the places she'd felt shame, like a changing of the tide.

She didn't know what the hell *that* was.

"Look, Mr.—" but she stopped. Because she realized she had no idea what his name was.

His eyebrows rose even higher, and for a dizzying sort of moment she was sure he looked as amused as he did astonished. "Vanderburg. Conrad Vanderburg."

And it wouldn't occur to her until much later that he paused after he said that, clearly anticipating that she would recognize his name. She didn't.

She plowed on. "Okay, Conrad. I think this is a terrible misunderstanding. I should never have come in here and I've apologized for that. I probably shouldn't have taken pictures, either, but really, I was just…doing what I do. I didn't think about it."

"Do you make a habit of thoughtlessness?" Conrad asked in that same low, steel-infused way. It shouldn't have bothered her. It shouldn't have registered with her at all.

But there was something about the way he asked those calm little questions that made her think her entire body might shake itself apart.

Right here and now, with her spray bottle hanging off her jeans, her hair in the work braids she preferred, and all this *shame* she couldn't seem to jettison.

And shame wasn't what was coursing through her, making everything *ache.*

"I don't think you should fire me," she threw at him, desperately. Or maybe she imagined she needed to challenge him? *You want to challenge him,* something in her whispered. *You want to see what he'll do.* "I feel like that's a pretty over-the-top response, all things considered."

He studied her. It wasn't as simple as holding her gaze. He saw too much, too deep.

And for the first time since Rory had looked up and seen him standing there, it dawned on her—really dawned on her—that she hadn't thought any of this through. For one thing, she didn't know anything about this man. Except that he was nothing like any man she knew. That was obvious at a glance. He was too…intense.

Too controlled, in a way that sent alarms ringing through her whole body, straight down into her toes.

Dangerous, that same something in her whispered.

Even though, in the very next moment, she felt the strangest certainty that, dangerous though he clearly was, she was perfectly safe.

It felt like whiplash.

And then Conrad made it worse.

He laughed.

CHAPTER TWO

CONRAD VANDERBURG COULDN'T remember the last time he'd laughed spontaneously.

About anything. He wasn't the laughing sort. He preferred his humor dry, his wit sharp, and if he was forced to suffer a fool, he preferred it to be in a business setting where he could at least make a profit on his exasperation.

This woman was something else.

Women normally did not look at him and mouth off, whatever their proclivities. Women did not have to actually practice sexual submission themselves to get a little silly in his presence. They usually blushed, fluttered, and were still.

Not this one.

He'd walked into his house, aware within two steps that someone else was on the premises. He had only just recalled that his secretary had found him a new cleaning service for this property when he'd seen that the door to what he liked to call his chapel was open.

And he almost never left it open.

He'd lived in this building since he'd renovated it a decade back and he'd left that door unlocked precisely twice.

Three times, apparently, he'd thought darkly as he'd approached the door, prepared to forcibly eject whoever had dared invade his sanctuary.

But he hadn't.

Because the first thing that had crossed his mind when he'd seen her standing in the middle of the room, looking around with a speculative look on her face that made his cock hard—instantly—was that it was a pity he didn't recognize her. Because that meant she couldn't be one of his, come back for more.

Something he normally discouraged.

But she was breathtaking. She had liquid brown eyes, glossy dark hair in a braided coronet, and light brown skin. She looked supple, but not delicate, even though she wore a collection of garments that he could only assume she had chosen because they made her look frumpy.

A fashion choice he felt was an offense not only to his own gaze, but to the whole of France.

"You must think very highly of yourself," he said, mildly, when he stopped laughing—still amazed he'd started. "If you truly imagine that after flagrantly disobeying my clear instructions, you can argue me into retaining your questionable services. Especially by attempting to convince me that it's my reaction to your behavior that's the problem."

And much as his cock might have liked to imagine otherwise, it was clear that this woman—his cleaner, apparently, if the spray bottle hanging from her overly relaxed jeans and the mop and bucket he'd seen outside in the hall was any indication—had never spent any time inside a proper dungeon before. Even if she hadn't mentioned that book, a clear indication that someone was a dilettante, if that, Conrad would have known she was vanilla at a glance.

It was too bad, really.

He decided that, as he had just come back from a grueling business trip that had involved absolutely no opportunities to indulge his typically voracious sexual appetites, it was probably best that he not continue to stand here imagining her tipped over his spanking bench, restrained, and with that sweet ass of hers fully displayed for his pleasure.

Too fucking bad, indeed.

He turned away from her and headed for his kitchen, shrugging out of his jacket as he went. He hung it on one of the hooks in the hall, rolled up his shirtsleeves as he moved, and went to get himself a glass of water.

It wasn't until he had the glass of water in his hand that he realized what he was doing. Drinking *water,* as if he was in a scene. As if he needed to be careful not to let alcohol cloud his judgment.

You wish, he told himself darkly.

He wasn't particularly surprised to see the girl there when he looked up again, standing in the high arch where the granite and steel kitchen melted into the cavernous, loft-like first floor of his church. The one he had personally renovated to his tastes, but had planned to sell when he married appropriately. He'd assumed the appropriate wife would come with the appropriate address. Some whitewashed, stuccoed bore in Belgravia, perhaps? Or worse, a grand old stately affair plunked down in England's greenest hills, where it would likely have stood for centuries, grim and staid against the march of progress?

But he should have known better. He was Conrad Vanderburg. He had been born bent and had only twisted further as time went on. He had tried his best to go vanilla, but that gambit had failed spectacularly when he'd found his carefully chosen fiancée with another man. Another man she'd gone ahead and married, in fact, leaving him to his own devices.

He had therefore resigned himself to being the high priest of his own dark desires, come what may, and had kept his dirty church. And Paris.

And every last kink and twist within him.

"You can go," he told the girl as she stood there, exuding vanilla like a pastry in a shop.

Pity he knew better than to steal a bite. A pastry could never fill him up.

"Here's the thing," she said, as if he'd invited

her to negotiate. Most vanilla girls would have run
screaming from the house by now, so it was hard not
to be impressed—though he couldn't tell if she was
brave or oblivious. "You're by far my best account.
I really wish that there was a way that we could re-
wind and pretend this never happened."

"What's your name?" Conrad took a sip of his
water, amused at himself.

Because he was acting as if he was in a club.
Leading the submissive where he wanted her to go,
one seemingly innocuous question after the next...

His cock hardened even more, reminding him how
long it had been since he'd visited his favorite club.

"I'm Rory Morton," she said helpfully. Even
cheerfully. "Owner and sole proprietor of Clean-
Works, an artisan—"

"Yes, yes. An experience. I heard you."

She frowned. "People treat cleaning like a chore
when it's an art."

"In my case it is neither, as I hire it out to people
who take direction better than you do."

"There are works of art all over this house. Surely
if you have the taste to appreciate them, you can also
appreciate the artistry that goes into creating and
keeping the space around them gleaming and bright."

Distantly, Conrad found himself wishing this interaction was happening at his club after all, because
he would have paid money to watch his friends' reactions to the lofty, vaguely condescending way this

girl felt she should speak to him. His best friend, Dorian Alexander, would have laughed the loudest and longest back when they visited such places together.

Something they no longer did, as Dorian had gone and gotten himself married.

To Conrad's formerly selfish and irresponsible younger sister, of all people.

Though Conrad was forced to admit the two of them not only seemed astonishingly happy—but Dorian had been a good influence on Erika, too. She was currently back at university, finishing up the degree she'd swanned off from years back.

May wonders never cease, he thought now, and not for the first time.

And concentrated on the morsel before him, vanilla-scented pastry though she was.

"What kind of name is Rory?" he asked. "Are you a little boy?"

"It's my name." She wrinkled her nose at him. "And no. Obviously."

"That's it? In its totality? Rory isn't short for something?"

She looked a little less confident, then. Or a little less self-righteous, as the case might be. "My mother named me Aurora, but no one's ever called me that."

"Why not?" he asked. And he almost called her *little one.* The way he would if this was a scene.

He put down his glass of water. And then, internally, shrugged. Because why not enjoy himself? He couldn't be the only man who'd long had the fantasy of coming home from a business trip to find a pretty girl in his house. He could play a little.

Without actually playing, of course.

Clearly his cock was already all in.

"I don't like *Aurora*," she said. "It sounds like an old woman."

"It's a beautiful name." He laughed at himself, but he did it anyway. "Little one."

"Did you...?" Rory blinked. "It's actually really demeaning to be called *little one*, you know. It basically reeks of toxic masculinity."

Conrad smiled faintly. "Then leave."

He was still only toying with her, but she didn't turn around and head for the door. She stayed where she was, those astonishingly beautiful brown eyes of hers looking faintly dazed.

Conrad noted she didn't move.

And he felt all the dark in him catch fire, then blaze.

"Paris is just outside," he said. "If you wish to take on the patriarchy, I suggest you use the front door, let yourself out, and get on with it."

"Well, I just..." She didn't finish that sentence. She seemed to lose track of it halfway through.

Conrad braced his hands on the marble counter in front of him and regarded her.

"I don't need a cleaner," he said with a certain

quiet intent. "I've just returned from a two-week business trip and I'm tired. I need a shower and then I need to fuck."

Rory blinked. "Are you hitting on me?" She sounded scandalized.

"I do not hit on people, as a rule."

His gaze was steady on her, so he could see the beat of her pulse in her throat. He could see the way she kept shifting her weight, moving from one foot to the other, and he was as sure as he could be that it wasn't that her feet hurt in those clearly overly comfortable shoes she wore. He had no doubt that if he reached between her legs, he would find her hot and wet.

For him.

Like the good girl it was possible she was after all, deep inside.

"So you just like talking about fucking in a general sense, then?" she demanded, as if she had the upper hand. Or as if she thought she was discouraging clumsy attempts to flirt with her in some dreadful bar.

Conrad took his time rounding his counter. He found it amusing when she stood her ground in the great arch, her chin tilting a little farther into the air with every inch he closed between them.

Like she thought she could fight him.

Or that he would fight her in the first place, when

he didn't need to. Not when she was so busy fighting herself.

"If you don't want to fuck me, then don't."

He stopped when he was a little too close, because he'd never met a boundary he didn't like to push a little, just to see what happened. In this case, the effect on her was delightful. She stiffened. Her nostrils flared. She looked flushed.

"Are you…asking me to fuck you?"

"I don't ask women to fuck me," he said, trying his best not to laugh. "They beg me for the honor."

He expected her to react to that, and he wasn't disappointed. Rory pulled in a breath, ragged and obvious, and blinked rapidly, as if she didn't quite know what to do with her face.

"Of course they do," she said, and then she rolled her eyes.

Conrad almost laughed again.

"That's not a line," he said mildly. "I'm not trying to impress you. It's a statement of fact. If you weren't here when I arrived home, there is a long list of people I could have called who have already begged me for the privilege of being on that list in the first place."

Her chin jutted higher. "Do you expect me to applaud?"

Conrad did laugh again, then, not sure why he was finding this entertaining. When he was, deliberately, strict and humorless when it came to these things. He liked discipline. Obedience. He expected his submissives to do as he asked, when he asked, or he found a different submissive. He had limited time and even less interest in "training" when that meant, as it so often did these days, hanging about at the service of a selfish woman who thought only of her own pleasure no matter how much time she spent on her knees.

Conrad, famously, had no interest whatsoever in the *bratty sub* phenomenon.

Yet here he was, hard and intrigued despite himself.

And it had been so long since he'd been drawn to anything that he went with it.

"You wouldn't like the way I prefer to receive my applause," he told her, not stepping back. Not giving her space. "It involves your mouth. You on your knees with your hands behind your back. And generally speaking, a healthy amount of tears on your part. That tends to be par for the course in the kind of sex I prefer. Perhaps the equipment you saw in the other room already clued you in."

"You make people cry when they give you blow jobs?"

"They cry because my cock is large and I like to fuck their faces," Conrad said, the way he might discuss mild weather with the Queen of England. "And because crying at their own helplessness while I take my pleasure as I please makes them even hotter."

She was breathing fast. "That sounds revolting."

But her eyes were glassy with heat. He could see it roll over her, making her whole body quiver. And that pulse in her neck beat out the truth.

"Liar," he said, and made a faintly disapproving noise. "What am I going to do with you? If you can't even tell the truth to yourself, how will you possibly achieve the honesty that I require?" He let his gaze sharpen. "Because let's be very clear. Honesty isn't a suggestion. It's a commandment you break at your peril."

"Wait a minute. I haven't agreed to anything."

"Rory. Little one. You haven't left."

It seemed to occur to her that they were standing too close, then. That she was breathing too hard, her skin was too hot, and her nipples were poking hard against her oversize T-shirt—and worse, that he could see all of those things. She scrambled back a few feet and caught herself against the exposed brick wall behind her.

He made no move to follow her, and he could see that confused her.

"I'm not opposed to a sexual interaction," she said after a moment, though every bit of her body language suggested that she wasn't nearly as blasé as she sounded. "Necessarily."

"I'm delighted to hear that." Conrad watched the way the hand she'd shot out against the brick wall trembled. "But I generally require consent to be far more unambiguous. And enthusiastic. And occasionally documented."

She shook her head at that, but sharpened her gaze on him as if that could keep her confusion at bay. He rather liked that she came to it naturally.

"But there are some things that you should know about me," she told him, in the same lofty voice she'd used to lecture him on artisanal housecleaning, of all ridiculous things.

"Don't worry too much about that," he said. In what he liked to call his soothing voice. Not to be confused with his commanding voice. Though both usually had the same effect. "If I get my hands on you, I'll know everything about you. Sooner or later."

Her lips parted at that and it seemed to take her a long moment to shake it off. "First of all, I'm going to need you to respect my identity."

"Which identity is this? An artist whose medium is bleach in a bathtub? An American who distinguishes herself by wandering around Paris dressed appallingly?"

She frowned, swaying on her feet like she couldn't decide where to swing first.

"I'm pansexual," she announced, and nodded, as if cosigning her own declaration.

"Again, you have my felicitations."

"I'm pansexual for sure and *probably* demisexual, and—"

"Explain to me what these words mean to you," Conrad said, interrupting her.

Her frown deepened. "What do you mean, what they mean *to me*? They have specific definitions."

"Most things do. But what are those definitions? As you understand them."

"I can be attracted to anyone, and am," she threw at him. "I like all kinds of actors and actresses. But I only really enjoy sex with people I have feelings for."

"You cannot possibly have feelings for me. You met me moments ago, while trespassing in my private area. What do we do if these definitions fail us?"

"I guess you could consider me het-curious." She inclined her head like royalty, which made him want to do all manner of filthy, glorious things to her. She was that lovely. "That means I'm curious about the behavior of heterosexuals. Though I should assume that's what you are?"

"Among other things," he agreed, perilously close to laughing again.

"Well. Okay then."

Conrad thrust his hands in his pockets and kept his gaze on her. "Everyone has a sexual identity, Rory. I like power differentials, personally."

"Both ways?"

He smiled. "No. I like power games, I insist on obedience, and when I fuck, I'm always in charge."

She…fluttered. There was no other word for it.

"And before you tell me how little that interests

you, you should know that I can see how aroused you are," he said quietly. "Arousal is not action, I grant you, but let's try to be honest about it."

"You can't see that. You can't *see* any of that."

"I can. For example, the look on your face right now tells me that for all the many attractions you claim you've had to all and sundry—all on screens, I assume, given you mentioned their job descriptions—you haven't had a lot in the way of decent lovers. Is that wrong?"

Rory blew out a breath. "What do you mean by a decent lover?"

"One that made you come," he said dryly. "A lot."

"I'm really more focused on intimacy."

"So the answer is no, then." Conrad shook his head. "How can you decide what your sexual identity is if you've never had good sex?"

"I've had great sex," she retorted.

"Great sex without coming?" He lifted a shoulder, then dropped it. "What is that?"

"Just because you're psychotically goal oriented doesn't mean everyone is."

"Rory. Sex is about orgasms, or you could simply have an intimate cup of coffee with a friend. When a man has sex, he can expect that he will always have an orgasm. Why as a woman should you expect any less?"

"I—" But she stopped. She stared at him, and he could see the way she had to catch herself, as if her knees weren't quite working. Once again, he was struck by how beautiful she was, this absurd argument and all. "It's the closeness that really matters."

Conrad sighed. "Do you know who says things like that? People who don't know any better. Or men who don't care to do their jobs."

"I have a million orgasms," she assured him. "All the time."

"Rory. I can make you come in minutes. Right here. That's the very least you should expect from a person you take into your body. It pains me to imagine that you have careened through life allowing your lovers to treat you so shabbily."

"My lovers, of which there are many," she said, in a tone of voice that suddenly made him wonder if she'd had any lovers at all, "know, as I do, that there's a lot more to sex than just coming."

"Of course there is." He found himself smiling again. "Or everyone would simply masturbate and call it a day. I hope you do, by the way. Since you don't achieve satisfaction anywhere else."

"I'm a sexually liberated, infinitely satisfied woman. I am fully in charge of my own orgasm—"

"That's a yes, you do. I think. I'm pleased to hear it."

"I demand, and receive, exactly what I want in bed."

"Then it's sad that what you demand and receive is so paltry. And unsatisfying."

"I think you're full of it," she threw at him, her

eyes overly bright. "The truth of the matter is, everyone has different bodies. You can't make sweeping statements like—"

"Like, I can make you come?" Another laugh came out of him, astonishing him. But then, this whole scenario was astonishing, and here he was. Still participating in it. "But I can. In minutes, as I said."

She moved forward in a display of aggression that he would never have tolerated in any of the women he normally played with.

But there was something about Rory that entertained him. He couldn't have said why. She was different. All wrong, in fact.

Yet that wasn't really what he was concentrating on as she put her hands on her hips, stuck her face in his, and scowled at him.

Actually scowled.

At him.

"Okay, big guy," she threw at him, which was obviously unacceptable on every level, and yet only made him hard. "Then prove it."

CHAPTER THREE

RORY HAD MADE a mistake.

A huge mistake, she thought while everything inside her shuddered and those dark, navy blue eyes of his seemed to…turn to steel.

It was as if he'd put on a mask, suddenly.

Or worse, a voice in her suggested, *taken one off.*

It wasn't that his face changed, really. He was still as beautiful. As striking, no matter he wasn't her type. It was as if he was suddenly…*more* than all that. And she could feel her response prickle all over her, inside and out, until she felt almost feverish.

Hot. Cold.

Back and forth.

While she was wholly unable to jerk her gaze away from his.

Rory had the insane notion that he'd picked her up and was holding her in the palm of his hand, though he was only staring down at her in that darkly unreadable way of his. And wasn't touching her at all.

Another man might have reacted. She'd banked on a reaction, but Conrad only *burned*. And studied her as if he was a sheathed weapon she had no business getting near.

She could suddenly see nothing else when she looked at him but that danger.

Rory couldn't say she'd ever paid that much attention to her nipples before in all her life, but now they were so sensitive that the weight of her T-shirt against them was almost unbearable.

But if she let herself think too much about why, she thought she might pass out on the spot.

And the way her heart kept battering at her ribs, that was a very real worry.

"See?" She made herself demand, aware that her voice was a little too much on the uneven side. That wasn't good. But she was still standing there, hands on hips and her face in his, and she was sure that if she didn't double down, she might die. *Or worse,* something in her whispered. "All talk and no—"

"That's enough."

There was something about that voice of his. It wasn't harsh. It wasn't sharp or loud, even. If she'd had to describe it, Rory would have said it was *patient*, and surely there was no reason that word should have rattled around inside her like that. Particularly when it wasn't the sort of patience she would normally think of when she used that word. He was no saintly, self-sacrificing grandmother type.

His patience was charged, somehow. Weaponized.

But the truly astonishing thing was that she simply...obeyed. Her mouth shut with an audible snap. Her hands slid off her hips. She didn't exactly shrink or cringe, but she stood normally.

It was the strangest thing.

"I will tell you what I want you to do," Conrad said. It was almost as if his voice became another unbearable fabric against her skin, but inside her, too. It was so...rumbly. The kind of deep that seemed to move through her, fusing to parts of her she hadn't even known were there.

She felt her clit pulse and nearly doubled over, because the only time she could remember feeling it quite like that was when she'd gotten her piercing down there. On a whim one night in Nashville because maybe she'd thought she needed to prove that just because she was still there didn't mean she wasn't *doing things*. And what she did best was something sexual in one way or another, because that was easy enough to perform. Especially online, where it was much easier to cut and filter and create a scene. She'd made a little video of the proceedings and gained thousands of followers. All for a little U-shaped barbell through the hood over her clit so that any pressure at all made it sing.

Except there was no pressure. There was only Conrad's voice.

She fought it.

Because she was much more used to the way things looked. The way things might make her look. What certain images or opinions said about her.

Feeling something was new. And searingly, breathtakingly different.

"I thought the point was that *you* were going to do something," she said, trying to focus on him instead of the ruckus in her body. The downside of that being that her mouth took over. "I thought that was what all the posturing was about. You were going to do something in thirty seconds and rock my world forever, blah blah blah, like every other guy I've ever met. Guess what? Your penis isn't world peace. It's not even that interesting. It's just a penis—lots of people have one just like it."

The intensity in his gaze didn't drain away, but it changed. And he let out what she would have categorized as a reluctant laugh.

"Are you going to issue stage directions?" He still hadn't touched her, and she felt wrecked. But she didn't break his gaze. Or run. "Or do you think, perhaps, that your personal history might suggest you're not the expert in these things?"

"You're the one who seems to think it's a problem."

"If you don't think it's a problem, Rory, I once again invite you to leave," he said, in that quietly masterful way that made her want to slink off. And also cry. But mostly, it made her want to do anything he asked, if he would just *ask it*. What was *that*? "I assure you, my altruism only stretches so far. I can certainly find better things to do with my time than perform public services for ungrateful young women who I already know to be astonishingly disobedient."

He kept telling her that she could leave. She kept not leaving. And Rory honestly couldn't tell why it was that her feet seemed fused to the floor beneath her.

This wasn't how she liked to play. She was never normally so…out of control. And, like it or not, convinced that this man might know something she didn't.

Though she would bite off her own tongue before she told him that.

But there was that look he got, like now, all navy blue and certain, that made her think he already knew.

She felt that pulse in her clit again and really did have to bite her tongue, then, to keep it to herself.

"Move back against the wall," Conrad said. Very calmly.

Rory took a breath as if to argue, but thought better of it. The wall behind her was brick and she kind of liked how solid it was, there at her back, when she felt so off-balance.

"Breathe," he told her. Looking amused again.

The men she dated never found her amusing, at

least not like this. It should have made her furious that he did. It was patronizing, at the very least. But instead of demanding he stop *laughing at her*, she felt her cheeks heat up. And somehow, feeling that flush move all over her skin, and deep inside her, made her more comfortable. Instantly.

Because whatever Conrad Vanderburg was—with his sex room and all those things he'd said that she wanted to dismiss as bragging, but sensed wasn't him being boastful at all—he wasn't scary. Or, she thought, revising that a little, he wasn't scary in any kind of predatory or gross way.

He scared her all right, but because he was so quiet and still. So obviously confident. And so wholly uninterested in attempting to impress her.

She expected him to jump on her, or something. To throw himself against the wall on top of her, and do whatever it was he was going to do.

But instead, he stayed where he was. He crossed his arms, lifted one hand to his mouth to toy with his lips in a quietly sensual way that made her *ache*, and then…studied her.

Intently.

She felt herself actually flinch. Her knees buckled and his gaze darkened.

"No," he said, still very calmly, but his orders were perfectly clear. "Stay still, please."

And she did.

Rory kept the bricks at her back, and she pressed

her palms against the stones until she could feel the faint, rough abrasion against her skin.

He regarded her as if he was looking at a work of art in a gallery, like the many scattered all over Paris. She had the impression that those midnight blue eyes of his saw every single part of her. That they touched every bit of skin that she'd left exposed, from her neck to her wrists to the tips of her ears. More than that, she was sure he could see her body behind the baggy careless clothes she wore to clean.

She wanted to shout at him. She wanted to make sure he knew that she was no *commodity*, to be analyzed so closely and picked apart and judged, as if there was something wrong with her—

Rory felt her breath pick up. And in the next second, she realized that all the sensation she could feel charging around inside of her—lighting everything up and making her feel as if she was melting, from the top of her head to deep between her legs, wasn't her feeling like there was something *wrong* with her at all.

She'd never felt *less* wrong.

"Take off your shirt," Conrad told her.

And a part of her wanted to stop and discuss that *voice*.

She still couldn't figure out the particular flavor of his accent. It wasn't British. She didn't think it was Australian. And anyway, it was the *tone* that seemed to careen around inside her, setting her on fire wherever it touched.

Because the calmer he sounded, the more she wanted to please him.

A thought that should have horrified her, but didn't.

And at the same time, Rory had no doubt that no matter how calm and mild he might have sounded, that had been an order. An order he expected her to follow, clearly, or he'd throw her out of his house.

Rory wished she could understand why she absolutely, positively couldn't have that.

She told herself she was entirely too feminist to take orders from some strange man with an en suite pleasure palace who thought he was Christian Grey.

But then she reached down, pulled her shirt off, and stood there in nothing but her bra.

Because apparently she took orders after all.

Something she would have to interrogate herself about later.

"Take that off, too," he told her, his gaze inviting her to look only at him, think only of him, and let her head go quiet. She shuddered at the thought. "And then you may drop your clothes to one side."

Something about that made a kind of kick reverberate inside her, as if she was a tuning fork and he'd set her to humming. It started in her spine and then bloomed outward. Because it hadn't occurred to her that he intended to control even what she did with the clothes she removed at his command. It seemed so over-the-top to her—so fussy—and yet, something in her found it thrilling.

That he noticed details, maybe, when in her experience the moment she showed a little skin it was basically a race to the finish.

His finish, something in her commented. *Never yours.*

She dropped the T-shirt to one side. Then she found herself too hot, awkward and sweaty—yet still too bright, straight through, with all that molten longing—as she wrestled her bra off. She finally managed it, tossing it to the floor beside her as well.

Rory braced herself for him to jump on her, then. To reach over and grab her breasts, the way men did, and fumble around until all the cool control disappeared and he forgot himself. Because that was what men did, wasn't it? All kinds of promises, but then they did as they pleased.

But not Conrad.

He hardly seemed to notice that she was now naked to the waist. He stayed where he was, observing her from a foot or so away, as if he could do nothing but that forever.

Rory had no idea why she wanted to weep. Again. Why her eyes felt hot with too much emotion when she should have felt nothing at all. Because nothing was happening. Her breasts were hanging out between them and *nothing was happening*.

She couldn't bear it. "I really can't believe—"

"No, thank you," he said, so casually. So very, very casually. "No talking, I think. I've heard enough about my penis from you tonight."

Rory couldn't tell if the flames in her were temper, desire, shame—or all of the above. "That's fine, but I think it's already been ten minutes. Your big promises are all bullshit. Just pointing that out."

"It has been ninety seconds," he replied, matter-of-factly. "If you keep talking, it will be longer. It's up to you."

She closed her mouth. And though he didn't actually smile, there was something about the gleam in his gaze that made her think he considered it.

It made her skin prickle, and that jangly, greedy thing inside her seemed to hum again. Louder than before.

"I like where your hands are," Conrad continued, pleasantly, as if she hadn't said anything. "Keep them there."

He paused, as if he expected her to say something else. Acknowledge him, maybe? But it was only for a scant second and then he seemed to collect himself.

And then, finally, he moved toward her.

Still looking the way he had when he'd appeared in that doorway. Like he belonged on the cover of *GQ*. The only thing he'd done was remove his jacket, but otherwise, he looked rich and corporate, astonishingly *capable*, and deliciously…stern.

All things that should have repulsed her.

But instead, she was standing in a converted church, pressing her hands back against a brick wall with her shirt off because he'd told her to strip, holding her breath as she waited to see what he would do next.

Something inside her, panicky and desperate, seemed to swell—

But then he touched her, and she settled.

She *settled*.

All he did was smooth his palm over her cheek.

Rory blew out the breath she'd been holding, long and shuddery.

He was so close that she could smell him. And she didn't understand how a man so big, so *intensely* male, who had been wearing a *jacket*, could smell good in the middle of a Parisian summer. But he did. There was a hint of something too fresh to be cologne, more complicated than soap, and the rest was simply him.

Heat, maybe. Sheer confidence, if that was possible.

And God, his *hand*.

His palm was hard, and large. And he moved down, slowly, over her cheek to her neck. He paused for the scantest moment, long enough for her to gulp and possibly to feel her traitorous pulse, and then he kept going.

He stood there before her, his attention on what

he was doing, not her. So intense, so *sure*, that it didn't even occur to her to hurry him along. Or say something to break the spell. Or attack him, more likely, because she felt so off-balance and uncertain.

And then he filled his palms with her breasts.

His eyes gleamed when she made a broken little noise. Rory waited for him to bend his head. To take a nipple in his mouth, or start treating them roughly with his thumbs, but he didn't do any of that.

Instead he only tested their weight, noted the color on her cheeks, then moved lower.

She thought maybe he was going to do some slow, languorous thing with her navel, just to drive her truly crazy, but he ignored it. He moved instead to the waistband of her jeans. She heard a clunking sound, but only dimly recognized that as him removing her spray bottle and tossing it aside. Rory couldn't really seem to do anything but press, and press harder, against those bricks.

Until his gaze lifted and pinned her even more firmly against that wall.

He didn't speak. Her world narrowed to that demanding navy blue gaze while below, he snapped open her jeans.

Then slid one hand down the slope of her abdomen and directly into her panties.

She expected him to tease her. To play.

He didn't.

Conrad's fingers were bold and as rock hard as the rest of him. He cupped her pussy, then squeezed, and she knew the exact moment he felt her piercing.

There was another pause, and his gaze caught fire.

But all he did was stroke into her. And whatever else she might have told herself, whatever she kept telling herself about what she *should* feel, there was no argument here.

She was slick and wet and molten hot. Already swollen with need, the ache of it almost too much, and he didn't wait. As if he knew.

He didn't pause again.

Conrad lifted one hand and covered her breast again, and she couldn't seem to help but arch into his palm, making that sharp ache in her nipple better and worse at once.

The hand in her panties moved at the same time. He twisted his wrist so that the heel of his hand pressed down hard against her piercing and therefore her clit, pinched her nipple between his thumb and forefinger, and then he speared two fingers deep inside her.

All at once.

It was all a shock. An intrusion. A bright burst of too much sensation to bear—

He retreated. He lessened the pressure on her nipple.

Then he thrust in deep below. Pinched above.

And again, ground that heel hard against her clit.

And everything inside of her seemed to spin, in a dizzying, breathless, pulsing loop—then collide.

It was as if there was a train bearing down on her, something huge and awful and wonderful and terrifying—

Rory was arching off the wall, or she was shaking apart, or she was convulsing, maybe. Her hands were supposed to be on the wall, but she could feel his shoulders beneath her fingers, and she was lifting, trying to outrun it, trying to stop the growing swell of it—

"Don't fight it." His voice was a dark invitation. A command. "Come, Rory. Now."

One more deep, lush thrust of his fingers. Stretching her, invading her, claiming her, while his palm ground down on her clit, and that lancing bite where he pinched her nipple—

It walloped her, then.

And she was lost.

Her eyes went blind, and maybe she was sobbing.

She'd had orgasms before, but this—

But Rory couldn't analyze it. She was too busy falling apart, somewhere between that hard hand still thrusting in her pussy and the other one on her breast. And if she could have, she would have given thanks for the wall behind her, too.

Because she was limp and she was a livewire. She was *lost*.

She shook and she shook. And the world disappeared. And everything was the howling roar inside her that went on and on and on.

Years could have passed.

She could hardly handle it, not sure where one endless, glorious convulsion began or ended.

Until vaguely, somehow, the shaking lessened. And she became aware that her face was tipped forward and she was surrounded by his scent again.

It took her a lifetime or two to realize that Conrad was holding her and her face was buried in his chest. She was breathing, so loud and so heavily she was surprised her lungs didn't pop.

She thought he moved, though she couldn't be sure until she felt his hands, surprisingly gentle as they shifted her back and propped her up against that wall again. She had to grip onto the bricks again, her head lolling forward as if she couldn't hold it up of her own volition.

And for a long while, she tried to breathe. She tried to make sense of all the eddies and swirls of sensation that still moved around inside her. Her clit felt swollen, and she was so wet she was tempted to imagine there was something wrong with her—

But there couldn't be. Not when she felt like this.

As if everything had changed.

As if nothing would be the same.

As if this whole time she'd been staggering around

talking boldly and confidently about color in black-and-white spaces, only to discover that she'd never known color at all. She'd never even glimpsed it.

She felt another wallop, but this time, it was emotional.

Rory lifted her head, feeling panicked and exposed, and somehow wasn't surprised that Conrad was still standing there before her, still studying her, with the same expression on his face.

Infinitely patient, with that dark edge.

She felt all that rawness inside her ease a little. A lot.

Wordlessly, he handed her the T-shirt and bra she'd discarded. Rory clutched them to her, covering herself, but not trying to wrestle her clothes back on. Not quite yet. Not when her arms felt like noodles and she was desperately afraid that her knees might give out, or her pants might fall down, or any combination thereof.

She didn't know what she was supposed to do now. Praise him? Thank him?

Cry?

Rory tried to pull herself together, which was hard to do under all that dark navy regard.

She'd never felt so naked in her life, and she understood the piercing irony of that, given how often she posted seemingly accidental scantily clad photos of herself on the internet because she knew her followers loved it when she did.

And she didn't know if what she felt then was shame—or where that curl of heat was directed, maybe. At all the skin she had shown, with no inkling of how she could feel? Or the fact that it had taken a stranger to show her—despite all her protestations about her feminism and her sexuality and what she owned and what she didn't, and all the long, involved conversations she'd had about this or that identity—that she didn't know her own body at all.

That she never had.

As if it was more his than hers.

But something in that triggered her temper, and she was glad.

Fiercely, wildly, almost giddily glad.

"Let me guess," she said, with all the carelessness she could muster for what she really wanted. "This is where you tell me that it's my turn, and you make me suck your cock."

But this was Conrad. He was confounding.

So perhaps she should have known that all he would do was laugh.

At her.

Again.

"I don't know what makes you imagine that you could possibly have earned that kind of privilege," he said, all that rich amusement in his voice. "You certainly haven't."

She scoffed, temper getting the better of her.

"What do you mean? Who thinks it's a *privilege* to blow you?"

He only smiled, darkly, and she flushed. And even though it seemed impossible to her, Rory had absolutely no doubt that when he talked to her of lists and begging, he meant every word.

She believed it against her will.

Inside this body that still felt like his.

"Well, I'm willing to do whatever," she said, still gripping her shirt to her chest, not sure if she was trying to clear a debt. If she thought she was supposed to. Or stranger yet, actually wanted nothing more than to take him deep in her mouth. "In return for...this."

"A tempting invitation, I'm sure," he said dryly, sounding insultingly uninterested. "Regretfully, I must pass. Put on your clothes, Rory. Pick up your things. And then go. And the next time you have sex with one of your little puppies, remember. You're supposed to come. That's the whole point. Accept no substitutes."

And to her astonishment, he actually walked away.

"Wait..." she began.

He didn't even turn around. He only made what she assumed was a kind of backward *shooing* gesture with one hand, and walked off toward the living area of his sprawling house.

"If you're still here in five minutes," he said, in

that same maddeningly calm way of his, "I will either bodily remove you or call the police. Neither will be fun for you. If I were you, Rory, I'd go now."

CHAPTER FOUR

TWO WEEKS LATER, Rory faced her latest date outside a café on the Left Bank, where they'd had a long dinner and drink during which she'd felt...nothing.

Absolutely nothing.

Trouble was, she could no longer remember if she'd ever felt anything on these dates of hers. Was this a new thing, now that she knew what she *could* feel? Or had it always been like this and she just hadn't known any better?

"Are you sure you don't want to come back to mine?" he asked in the charmingly accented English she'd been enjoying all evening, flashing his dimples at her from beneath his floppy hair. "I've a bottle of wine I'd love to share with you, Rory."

The dimples were why she'd gone on a date with him in the first place. And the way he said her name, rolling the first *R* so it almost sounded like *Lori*, had seemed almost unbearably cute when she'd offered it to him like a ripe peach outside the

Musée D'Orsay. He was from northern Italy, was in graduate school of some kind or another in Paris—he had told her all about it at great length, but she'd been surreptitiously checking her phone—and a couple of weeks ago, Rory would have loved nothing more than to let him take her home to whatever flat he lived in.

Wine or no wine.

She would have rolled around with him all night long and taken great pleasure in the provocative things she could say to him while they did that. Bold, careless, contradictory. He would tell her how amazing the sex was, she would smile mysteriously and talk about *the sensual* and *the erotic* while never coming close to any climax herself, and he would follow her around for months thereafter. Begging for another go, which she would deny him.

Rory had always liked to think of herself as madcap and mercurial, and that was why she liked to play with boys but rarely get serious. But now she wondered if all along, her body had been hoping she'd wise up and stop wasting her time with *puppies*.

She had been on three other such dates since Conrad.

All of them cute, just like this one. Boyish. Eager to please and impress.

She hadn't bothered to have sex with a single one of them.

Because every time she drank a little more wine

and told herself she might as well, because she was young and free and in Paris, she had Conrad in her head.

That navy blue gaze, pinning her to his wall. And her clit would light on fire all over again, and she would have to clench down hard to keep herself from coming just from *thinking* about him—

And every time that happened, the prospect of getting fully naked with some boy who would do nothing for her at all…paled.

"I won't change my mind," she said, smiling to take the sting off it. *"Au revoir."*

And then she walked away quickly, throwing herself into the late night crowd milling about on the cobbled stones of Rue Bonaparte, so there could be no further wrangling.

Conrad had wrecked everything. He'd wrecked *her*. She should never have let him touch her.

She glared at the old abbey across from the café, rising into the Paris night, because it made her think of him. But then, so did everything else. Even walking up a famous street toward the Seine, which had nothing to do with him. Ever since she'd staggered out of Conrad's converted church with her cleaning supplies and her shirt on backward, she'd been… flustered. Days later. Two weeks later she still wasn't right.

Rory hadn't felt like posting, for once. She hadn't felt like much of anything, for that matter. She spent more time than she wanted to admit feeling listless and a whole lot less interested in the brand she'd been building. Because what even was *a brand* when she was nothing but one person trying to pretend social media likes were the same as…well, as anything? When all she could think about was one person and whether or not he, personally, liked her.

Or ever could.

Even if he had threatened to call the police on her.

She went out on dates, because they'd already been scheduled, but it was always the same. They were nothing but a waste of her time.

Puppies, she could hear Conrad say, as if he lived in her head and had complete control of her clit.

She felt that same jolt that she should have been used to by now, out there on the historic street in the thick, warm, summer dark.

All she thought about was sex. And that locked room of his. And the amusement in those navy blue eyes of his. The magic in his fingers. And she thought he might actually have wrecked her. For good.

Because she didn't understand how she was supposed to survive now that she *knew*.

Now that she was entirely too aware that there was a world filled with pointless men who didn't have the slightest idea what to do with her body. And that she happened to possess the name and address of the one man who knew all too well.

And had proved it.

Tonight, the weather was mild. There were people strolling down the boulevards, talking happily, probably all on their way to have mind-numbing, life-altering orgasms with each other. Meanwhile Rory could do nothing but brood her way along the Seine, everything inside her clamoring for one more taste of Conrad Vanderburg.

Who, by now, she also knew a whole lot more about.

She walked along the Left Bank of the river, lost in thought, turning over the information she had about him now in her head. The accent she couldn't place likely came from a childhood he'd spent between his native South Africa and swanky European boarding schools. Not to mention his time at Oxford, la di dah. He had taken over the management of the family fortune after his father had died, and was therefore very, very wealthy. He was the kind of wealthy that impressed her father, who liked to call himself "comfortable" when he was clearly rich.

Rory had never heard of him, but she had heard of his sister, Erika, who she was pretty sure she'd been following on social media for years and years. Especially during Erika's scandalous phase. When she thought about Erika Vanderburg, she pictured images in the white dust of Burning Man. She'd thought that was wildly romantic and devil-may-care, and the outfits were always so delicious, but Rory did not camp. In a desert. With or without costumes.

She'd read a lot a distressingly boring corporate online magazines that talked about Conrad in glowing terms. He was apparently not only good at what he did—growing the family fortune from astounding to stratospheric—but he was considered something of a prophet, too, if one gushing blog was to be believed. *The way Vanderburg sees markets is nothing short of extraordinary,* said one otherwise deeply staid British article.

At the same time, he was also renowned for his discipline. His quiet ruthlessness and implacability. Better to be on his team than against him, numerous financial papers had declared.

Even when his high profile engagement to Lady Something or Other had ended some two years back, he had seemed…unmoved. Icy straight through. Fierce and immovable, which had made the paparazzi less interested in following him around. *Might as well try to snap a glacier,* one had complained.

You should really consider those warning signs, Rory told herself. Not for the first time.

But her pussy had a different take on the whole thing.

And the next breath she took was a shuddery one, as ever, because she was hot and damp and needy. All the time now.

Rory crossed the river and made her way into the Golden Triangle, a collection of lovely old buildings packed full of famous stores not far from the Champs-Élysées. She had found herself here almost every night since she'd met Conrad, no matter how she vowed that she would stop. Sooner or later, no matter where she was in the city, she found herself walking down these same grand old avenues until she found the little side street, hardly more than an alley, that sneaked around to what had once been a churchyard and was now his domain in the center of Paris.

Sooner or later she was simply drawn there, a moth to the flame, whether she liked it or not.

She told herself it was enough to simply walk to the place where the street snaked away in between two upscale shops that catered to the wealthy, then leave. She told herself that tonight would be the night that she broke the spell. That she absolutely would not make her way to the front gates surrounding his converted church, where there were trees to lurk behind, cobblestones to slip over, and looming buildings all around.

But she didn't keep walking when she reached his turn.

She didn't double back when she reached the end of the building that opened into the small plaza where the church stood.

And she didn't pretend she was anything but sad when she found herself at her favorite tree. The only surprising thing, she'd thought repeatedly throughout these two weeks, was that there weren't besotted idiots like her behind *every* tree.

Because once again, the hold he still had on her—even though she was pretty sure he'd already forgotten she existed—won the day. She stood there outside that old, Gothic church, her head spinning.

Paris was electric and alive on the other side of the stately buildings that surrounded the church, but down on the old plaza stones, it was quiet. Dark. That meant there was nothing to distract her as image after image of the things he'd done and could do to her plagued her. With sensations to match, storming around inside her body, making her feel deliciously weak.

Her clit felt swollen. Again.

Always.

Rory had barely slept these two weeks. When she did fall asleep, her head was filled with all the images of the deliciously dark sex acts she'd spent entirely too much time researching online. Because she wanted to know what all that furniture in Conrad's locked room was used for.

And now she did.

If anything, that made the chaos and greed inside her burn all the brighter.

She was opposed to all of it, of course. Actively appalled, and so on. As a feminist.

Rory told herself variations of that all day long, while she cleaned for her various clients with a fervor she had never before applied to her work.

She would get home to her flat in the evenings, filled with righteous indignation. *Certainly not* thinking about the kind of things *that man* got up to. Not that she begrudged consenting adults their fun, but *she* was certainly not going to do those things.

"I'm an influencer," she would remind herself out loud. "Not a pony. Or a *little one.*"

And then the next thing she knew she would be hunched over her laptop, one hand between her legs, looking at things that shouldn't have turned her on at all.

But they did.

The things that most horrified her by day made her wettest, and hottest, when she stopped pretending she was *horrified* at all.

Suddenly, there in the hushed darkness behind her tree of choice, she remembered when she—with all of her self-righteous zeal—had decided that Christmas dinner, the year after she graduated from college, was an excellent time to demand that her father accept her as pansexual.

Because she had decided, after much careful consideration and deep conversations with her friends, that she was. Therefore, she thought everyone should know.

Especially her parents.

Her mother had sighed and reached for her wine, then headed back to the kitchen to direct the staff.

Her cousins had either laughed, sat forward to watch the show, or both. Her aunt Melinda had invoked the Good Book, and none of her uncles had ever met her gaze directly again.

But Marty Morton had stared at her over the turkey he was carving with a studiously blank look on his face and his signature Santa hat slightly askew.

Darlin', he'd said, in his usual booming way, *do you want me to stand here with my hands in the Christmas turkey and talk to you about what I do with my drawers down?*

Ew, Dad. She'd been horrified. *No.*

Then why don't you concentrate on the gotdamn baby Jesus in Bethlehem and not whatever the hell you just said about Wonder Woman. Everybody thinks that woman is attractive, darlin'. That's her gotdamn job.

She'd posted a selfie from the bathroom five minutes later to detail how her father had silenced her truth.

But here, now, it occurred to her for the first time that finding people attractive wasn't the same thing as wanting to have sex with them. It had always appealed to her, deeply, that she be seen as carefree, sexually. That anyone who followed her online might think that they had a chance with her. She'd always loved the notion that sex could be anything, and if it was anything, than anyone was an appropriate partner.

Just as she'd always imagined that, if given the opportunity, she would love nothing more than to dance down mountainsides in the moon.

But loving the image of a flower child on a mountain beneath the stars didn't mean she wanted to take up hiking. And loving pretty images of pretty people didn't mean she wanted to have sex with all of them. In both cases, it just meant she liked pretty things.

Because actually having sex with people—in her case, only and ever men, no matter who she claimed she was attracted to—was a remarkably low impact, mechanical sort of thing. For her. So much so that she'd come to the conclusion that she maybe wasn't the sort of person who felt a lot of things deeply. Sexually, anyway. And she'd been starting to think if there were words she should use to describe that part of herself, too. Because all of those things—attractions, erotic moments, sex—operated on that same low frequency in her. Like soft notes she could play or not play, when what she thought she really liked about the whole thing was the attention.

She liked a curated picture of a thing, she realized now. Not the thing itself.

Because curation was comforting. It kept her safe. It let her stay in control, always.

Except then she'd met Conrad.

And literally none of the words she'd ever use to describe herself seem to be remotely true anymore. None of them fit.

She barely fit in her own skin.

Rory still couldn't decide if she wanted to cry about that, punch something, or just find him and beg him to show her more of the intensity she hadn't known was out there. Or in her. To show her parts of herself that either thrilled her or scared her—she couldn't decide.

But whichever it was, she wanted more.

She blew out a breath and told herself to walk away again. The church was dark, the way it always was. What was the point of creeping about like a stalker if she couldn't actually *see* him? She would go back to her little flat, look at more things that should have disgusted her, and pretend her own fingers in her panties were his.

But before she could do any of that, she saw headlights dance across the facade of the church. And then a sleek, low-slung sports car coming down the little alley. It had a low, authoritative rumble that made her think of his voice, and she knew it was him even before it turned in to the church and remotely opened the gate.

All the other nights she'd stood here, hating herself, she'd never seen him. Not even a whisper of him. She'd imagined Conrad off in some sex club— and if it hadn't been Paris, literally brimming with such places, she might have gone and tried to find him in one of them.

She was gripping herself, hugging her arms across

her abdomen in a way that only hurt, but she didn't stop. The gate closed behind the car that then slid into the garage that waited. The garage door closed, too. And for moment, Rory was simply alone on a cobbled Parisian street, spying on a man who had already threatened to call the police on her once.

When she was usually the one who had to roll her eyes and shoo away boys who didn't get the picture and leave when she told them to.

She watched the lights go on inside. And the church stood, bright and beautiful and compelling, claiming its own little plaza the way it must have done for centuries.

But all she could think about was the man who lived there.

Rory made herself a promise, there and then. If she actually did what she wanted to do—cross the street, knock on his door, and beg him for…anything, really—

If she actually *begged*—

No matter what happened, if she did these things, it would be the last time. She made a vow to herself as she stood there, the summer night close around her. If he said no, as she expected he would, and then demanded she leave and never come back, that was what she would do.

Even if she had to leave Paris just to keep herself from ending up in his street no matter her intentions, she would.

But first, tonight, she would try.

Rory was already crossing the stone plaza before the thought was fully formed inside her head.

She skirted the gated part of the church's grounds and went instead to the big, ornate doors. They rose high and proud, but she headed for the smaller door tucked inside them, and didn't bother attempting to use the code she'd had when she'd worked here. She felt certain that he had changed it, but even if he hadn't, she wasn't foolish enough to think he would find her letting herself in the least bit entertaining.

The truth was, she doubted he would find any of this entertaining. But here she was all the same.

She rang the bell, not surprised to hear that it sounded like church bells. A cascading sound that filled the plaza and soared up toward the night sky.

This is a terrible idea, she told herself. *Run while you can.*

But she didn't move.

A light flicked on above her, flooding her face and making her blink. But Rory stayed where she was, her arms folded, and—she hoped—no particular expression on her face, because she knew he could see her on his security video.

An eternity later, she heard the heavy iron of the dead bolt slide free, and then the door swung open.

She held her breath.

Conrad stood in the opening, light from inside and the light above bathing him and making him look like…a god. And tonight he wasn't dressed like a page out of *GQ*. Tonight he was dressed in dark jeans and a dark black T-shirt that made her brain short out. Because she could see his biceps and every ridge in his abdomen, and she was suddenly afraid that she might actually explode.

Right where she stood.

His mouth was hard. A stern, flat line.

His navy blue eyes blazed.

"What an unexpected surprise," Conrad said, and that *voice*… It was worse—better—than she remembered. It seemed to crash over her like a wave, even as it was already inside her, filling her up. It made her breasts ache and her pussy pulse and even her hair down her back felt provocative. When all she was doing was looking at him. Listening to him.

"I don't how to do this," she told him, feeling jittery. Practically like she was on drugs. "I'm sure it's all wrong. I've never… I mean I don't know…"

"So far, all you have done is ring a doorbell and stammer," Conrad replied, quiet and sure but not, she was almost positive, *furious*. He didn't even look annoyed. She was going to cling to that. "It would appear you know exactly how to do that. Is that why you came here?"

She remembered her hands on the brick wall and some dark thing inside her pulsed hot, so she did it again. She held out her hands like that, like a supplicant.

And scarier by far, she held his gaze.

"Please," she heard herself say, in a voice that sounded like need. Not like her. "I... I want more."

CHAPTER FIVE

FAR BE IT from Conrad to refuse such a pretty little act of surrender.

"You'd better come in, then," he said, a sense of inevitability kicking through him in a way he would not have liked if he'd allowed himself to focus on it.

He focused on her, instead. She looked different tonight, his little cleaner, who he'd had every intention of forgetting as soon as he walked away from her that night. Before he walked away, even. He'd been sure that it would take very little doing on his part. He would go out, he would indulge all of his appetites in all of his favorite ways, and that would be that.

But it hadn't worked out that way.

He'd discovered that the appetite he had was very specific, no matter how he wanted it to be otherwise. No one but a disrespectful American would do, a state of affairs that so appalled him that he'd upped his usual ninety-minute daily workouts to twice that to see if he could sweat it out.

Alas, he could not.

And of course, Conrad had her contact details. They had been part of the email his secretary had sent him when Rory's cleaning service had been hired three months ago, but he hadn't bothered to look at it until now. It had been lowering indeed to find himself digging out that email, clearly indicating he could not conquer this desire he didn't want. And he'd spent entirely too much time over the past two weeks arguing with himself about whether or not he would do something with them. Something like call her, God help him, when he had always been known as a master so exacting, so precise, that only the most graceful, obedient, and service-oriented submissives ever dared imagine they might have a chance with him.

He hadn't bothered with graceless, ignorant, mouthy beginners in a long, long time.

He hadn't planned to change that. Ever. If anything, the debacle of his attempt to marry had made him an even sterner master, not less.

And yet it had taken him far more self-control than it should have to keep from calling the little cleaner.

Wasn't it convenient that now he didn't have to?

He studied her as she walked inside his house, looking jittery and hectic, even though she tried to hide it.

Her hair was down, and he liked that. It was inky

black, glossy, and fell below her shoulders in lovely waves. She wore a hint of cosmetics on her face, and unlike some who made it look as if they'd used just a hint by using a great deal, he had the impression her use was actually sparing.

Conrad had no opinion on cosmetics one way or the other, but he filed that away anyway, because it told him things about her. That she was confident. That she liked how she looked enough to both enhance it and not hide it.

Rory was dressed in clothing far more becoming tonight. A figure-skimming tank top over a loose, flowing sort of skirt that showed him acres of her sweetly formed legs straight down to her bright red painted toenails inside a pair of sandals. Around her neck she wore a frothy sort of summer scarf. And down one arm, a collection of bracelets that chimed and sang when she moved.

She looked bright and almost too pretty to bear. He remembered discovering her clit ring, and stopped pretending everything about her didn't fill him with an impossible heat.

Conrad beckoned her, with exaggerated chivalry, to precede him into the part of the grand space on the first floor that he liked best. For a variety of reasons. It was a living room, first and foremost. It was set with various chairs and couches, tables and art, all arrayed around the fireplace he enjoyed in winter. But this part of the house was off the plaza, and on nights like this, he opened up the French doors and let his garden in.

Conrad loved cities—any city. He craved that kind of pulsing energy, because there was nothing better than setting out on a long walk at any hour and feeling the heartbeat of the city as he moved through it. He loved Paris particularly, because it was his. No ghosts of his father here. No interference from his overbearing mother. Here he had built himself a company, a fortress, and a life, and all of it made sense only here in the center of the city.

But a man needed green to grow, his father had told him long ago. Conrad had taken that to heart.

Assuming he had a heart, that was.

A topic that was often up for debate. With his mother, the impossible Chriszette, and occasionally one of her unfortunate lovers. Who seemed always to feel the need to chime in on Vanderburg family matters—but rarely more than once. And with his sister, of course—though Erika had changed since she'd started up with Dorian. All for the better, Conrad had to admit, after years of assuming Erika was a lost cause. It was why he'd cut her off.

Something he'd remedied once Erika and Dorian had actually started living together. Little as he wished to think about the things that must be true about his sister if she'd ended up with his best friend.

Given that Conrad and Dorian had discovered

they'd shared a great many of the same interests when they'd been teenagers, shunted off to the same boarding school and prone to the sort of confessions that could only be made at age fourteen.

He shoved that away, as he always did, because surely he could wish them the best without allowing himself to imagine *his sister* as the submissive she must be if she was the right woman for Dorian. Or if Dorian was the right man for her, which it was clear he was.

Conrad's oft-disputed heart could only take so much.

But happily, unsolicited comments on his heart or lack thereof were not something he had to contend with when it came to lovely women begging him to perform his favorite acts all over their bodies. For his own pleasure and amusement.

Especially not when they turned up at his front door to commence said begging, a practice he would normally strongly discourage. And certainly not reward like this.

But her bloody contact details had been taunting him for two weeks, and his body did not understand why he kept going to the gym instead of the dungeon.

There was a faint breeze through the windows as he led Rory to the chair he wished her to take. The sound of the Champs-Élysées from afar. The luxury flats and penthouses in the tall buildings surrounding his private plaza seemed like their own galaxy of sorts, lights beaming down through the canopy of trees in his garden.

He expected Rory to balk, or start ranting at him again. That she sat down quietly and obediently was one more indication the past two weeks had impacted on her.

Conrad was egotistical enough to enjoy that. Even if he was also experienced enough to understand that it might not be him she'd come back for as much as another taste of dominance.

If a person had a taste for it, it was difficult—after sampling it for the first time—to think about much of anything else.

He knew that all too well. He remembered.

Conrad took the chair opposite her, sitting down with his legs thrust out so that he claimed the greater part of the space between them. And so that he was giving the impression of caging her between them without actually resorting to chains or bars. Though the night was young.

And then he...did nothing. He propped his head on one hand, kept his gaze on her, and was silent.

Silent and watchful, while his quiet house stood hushed all around, like another observer.

Faint sounds of traffic floated in the French doors. Music from somewhere up high. The hint of laughter on the breeze, but gone the next moment.

He could have turned on music, but didn't. He waited.

And watched, entertained, as Rory lost her nerve and began to fray, right there before him.

First she began to fidget. She arranged and rearranged the hem of her skirt as it flirted with the middle of her pretty thighs. She pressed her lips together, then straightened them. She fiddled with her bracelets. She moved her hair forward over one shoulder, then back. Then she did it all again.

And again.

And all the while, her breathing got faster and shallower. He watched her pupils dilate. Faint beads of nervous heat appeared at her temples. Conrad wondered how long it would take before the panic completely overwhelmed her.

"Aren't you going to say something?" she asked, finally. The words sounded torn straight from her, and she looked like they must have hurt, coming out.

"I am not the one who appeared at your door, in what I can only assume is desperation," Conrad said, coolly. As if he hadn't stared at her bloody mobile number for far too long, though she didn't need to know that. Not when her anxiety made her nipples this hard. "What is it you have to say?"

She blew out her breath in a telling huff and wriggled in her chair, likely unaware that she was broadcasting her need to him. "I…"

But that was all she could manage.

Conrad didn't let himself smile. "Let's start here. What is it you want?"

His voice was kind, but implacable all the same. He watched as she blinked, clearly considering how she might answer that.

"I hope you remember what I told you at our last meeting," he continued, while he could practically see her thoughts scrolling across her forehead. "Don't lie to me. If you don't know something, say you don't know. If you don't want to answer a question, say that. If it turns out that you thought you wanted one thing only to discover that really, you wanted another, that's fine, too. But everything that happens after this moment must be based on trust and honesty."

Her gaze brightened. "You mean, like, safewords?"

"I see you've been doing your homework."

"It seems straightforward enough. As a concept."

He smiled, then, unable to help himself. "I certainly hope not. What would be the fun in that?"

She frowned at him. He took that as evidence that she was remembering herself. Recovering her equilibrium, getting her feet beneath her. Rediscovering that mouth of hers.

Good. He wanted her desperate for release—and desperate to please him—not actually desperate.

"You're acting like I'm some big pathological liar, which I'm not," she said, rudely. But that was her equilibrium coming back, so Conrad didn't react to it. "But I don't know how I'm supposed to be setting new records in honesty when you're... doing stuff."

Conrad sighed, let her hear it, and watched as her frown turned more worried than defiant. Excellent progress. "We're not concerning ourselves with 'doing stuff' right now. That comes later. Maybe. Depending on how this conversation goes."

She switched back to frowning at him. "Well, I didn't come here for conversation. I came here for—"

"I understand exactly what you came here for." He let his voice shift, then. All dominant, as an experiment, just to see what she would do.

But he already knew.

And she didn't disappoint him. Rory's eyes widened, and then she went quiet.

"This isn't a blind date," he said quietly, with all that authority still there in his voice. And the way he gazed at her, patient enough—but hard and stern. "You already know what's behind the locked door in my house. I felt your pussy tighten around my fingers while you came."

She was breathing heavily again. He doubted she realized he could hear it. "I remember."

"I'm sure that you do, or you wouldn't be here now. But this isn't a seduction, Rory. This is an interview. One you might very well not pass."

She looked flushed and cranky, then, which was truly one of his favorite expressions any woman could wear. Particularly this woman.

"Okay. I don't really know what that means, but whatever you want."

He reminded himself that for her, that was the equivalent of rising to her feet, putting her hands behind her head, and presenting herself for his sensual inspection.

"That's an excellent start." He settled back in his chair. "I asked you a question." When she only stared at him, he relented, though he kept his expression stern. "What do you want?"

She didn't toss an answer right back at him. Maybe she might actually have listened to what he'd told her, would wonders never cease.

But his cock stirred at the notion that this girl could truly be taught.

"More," Rory said after sitting with it a while. "I guess I want more."

"More of what?"

She shifted in her chair again, and Conrad knew that if he asked her to bare herself, her pussy would be swollen already. Wet. Needy.

Just the way he liked it.

"The whole thing," she answered him, sounding almost solemn. "I can't stop thinking about it."

"What makes it different from any other situation you've had?" He lifted a brow. "I seem to recall you boasting at some length about your vast sexual prowess."

She flushed at that. He approved. "I've had sex,

sure. But I've never... I mean, you know..." Rory clearly fought to settle herself. "I've never come before. With someone, I mean."

"What I'm trying to figure out," Conrad said, all quiet intent, "is if you came back here because you liked the way I made you come or if you just like that I made you come at all."

She looked down at her hands. "Both."

Conrad nodded. "Do you to like to be controlled?"

Rory jerked in her chair, and he could almost see the denial on her lips. She stopped herself. "I wouldn't have thought so. But when I think about..." Her gaze slid from her hands, over toward that brick wall where he'd taught her that first lesson. "If I think about it, that's the part that makes me..."

"Good," he said, and smiled when her eyes shot back to his. "If it didn't excite you, there would be no point in you coming here. You already know I like control."

"Have you experimented?" She cleared her throat. "With, you know. Doing it both ways? Just to see?"

"That sounds like you've been on the internet." He made a tsking sound. "No, I'm not now, nor have I ever been, a switch."

"But I thought it made sense that the way to learn how to do something was to feel it, first."

"I know how to drive," Conrad said dryly. "Without the faintest idea how it feels to be an engine. Don't you?"

Rory's gaze moved over him, and he would not ordinarily have allowed that, but she was different. This wasn't a club. She'd never done this before.

And she was just different. Full stop.

"How did you know you were…?"

"A sexual dominant?" Conrad shrugged. "It was always clear. All sex can be good, but the kind that works best for a person has something else, doesn't it? I've heard people say that it's brighter. That it has more edge to it. Greater highs and lows, certainly. Whatever you call it, it was always clear which I pre-ferred. I gravitated toward that more and more the older I got. And now?" He didn't quite smile. He let his gaze do that for him. "I don't really see the point in pretending to be something I'm not."

"Have you ever? Pretended, I mean? Not neces-sarily to be on the other side, but to be…" She waved a hand at him. "Not *you*."

"As a matter of fact, yes."

And maybe he shouldn't have been surprised that this conversation was straying into ground he never, ever shared with the submissives he played with. Because none of this was standard. The submissive women he met in the clubs would never dare show up at his front door. Or do any of the other things Rory had already done.

Maybe, too, he was feeling a little more at his ease

than he should have, because he'd been completely unable to get her out of his head and she was here anyway. Without him having to break.

That was the only justification he could come up with for why he kept talking. "Not long ago I decided that it was better for everyone concerned if I committed myself to conventionality."

More to the point, his mother had carried on about *what he owed the family name*, and Conrad had already lost Erika, at that point. He'd been certain his version of tough love was what she needed after she'd abandoned her education, but that hadn't made it any easier. Especially when she'd been so gleeful in her hatred of him. He'd been more susceptible to Chriszette than usual.

And perhaps, deep down, he'd viewed it all as an act of redemption. A way to prove that everything he did was in the family's best interests, from cutting off Erika to finding himself the sort of fiancée his mother would approve of, social climber that she was at heart. Surely that would show everyone that his heart was in the right place whether they could see it or not.

"Conventionality?" Rory blinked, and this time, when her gaze strayed from his it went toward his chapel. "You?"

He felt his mouth curve in one corner. "Me."

"But what would that even look like? Whips only twice a week and chains on alternate Thursdays?"

She amused him. That was the part he couldn't seem to get past.

"I was prepared to commit myself to a vanilla life," he told her, because now this was becoming another way she could entertain him, and he had no intention of analyzing that, thank you. "*Vanilla* means—"

"I know what *vanilla* means," she said, rolling her eyes at him. Cute, but unacceptable. He filed that way "I'm pansexual, hello."

"How foolish of me to forget." Her eyes narrowed a bit at his dry tone, but he ignored it. "I picked the perfect vanilla bride, prepared to march happily down a vanilla aisle, and had I done so, I would have carried on dutifully, vanilla to the end."

The truth was a bit more complicated than that. Lady Jenny Markham, his perfect vanilla bride, was perhaps a bit more delightfully twisted than he'd anticipated. Or known, since he'd never touched her during their whirlwind courtship.

When he'd had the distinct displeasure of walking in on her and the man she'd ended up marrying, he'd recognized their dynamic instantly. It certainly hadn't been anything he'd sensed in her on their few dates, though he did wonder, now and again when he thought of that strange period in his life, if that was why he'd chosen her. When he could have chosen anyone.

But then, he'd always had an eye for submissives

hiding in plain sight. Like his house cleaner, for God's sake.

Not that any of it mattered now. He and Jenny would have married for convenience's sake, but she'd chosen someone else. Someone far less convenient who clearly made her far happier than he ever would have. And he couldn't help but think that despite the considerable embarrassment of being so publicly jilted, he'd had a lucky escape.

Because here, now, he couldn't imagine how he'd ever imagined that he could be vanilla for an evening, much less a lifetime.

"No one should have to spend their life pretending to be someone they're not," Rory told him, very seriously. And he let her, because she didn't realize that she ought to have been intimidated by him, and for some reason he found that charming. "The world is filled with people who are withering away and dying because they think they need to wear masks all the time. I think it's a good thing that you're living your truth."

Conrad endeavored not to wince at that. "Yes, thank you. 'Living my truth,' indeed. How… American."

Rory shrugged, and gifted him with another eye roll. "I know, I know. Americans, so embarrassingly in touch with their feelings. How gauche. Whatever is the world coming to, with all this maudlin sentiment?"

That she had a point was one more thing Conrad chose not to examine. He concentrated on her, instead.

"You keep pushing us away from the conversation we ought to be having," he pointed out mildly. "If you're having second thoughts, you know where the door is. I will continue to enjoy my evening, uninterrupted. You can go back to doing whatever it is you were doing."

"I was on a date." He'd spent years perfecting his facial expressions—or rather, his lack thereof. And yet despite that he must have done *something*, because she grinned. "I've had a lot of dates since I last saw you. I've always liked dating. It's like a social media post, but in person."

"I'm happy to say I have no idea what that means."

"Everyone knows that social media is all about curating, yes?" She waited for him to shrug and clearly took that as assent. "Picking the best parts, leaving out anything that's sad or weird. Which I think is a good thing, by the way. Some things you *should* save for your friends. And dating is the same. You have to take all the best parts of you and kind of act them out for an evening. They do the same. Then, if all the performances match well enough, you get to have sex. It's fun."

"That sounds delightfully progressive-minded," Conrad murmured. "I applaud you. But I can't help thinking about the fact that all that curation led to you against my wall, begging me to make you come for the first time. So was the curating worth it?"

She sighed a little. "I've been having some trouble coming to terms with that myself."

"Did you experiment with your dates?" And he was amused at the little scrape of something inside him that almost felt like possessiveness. *Possessiveness.* He'd been sure he'd left that far in his past. The closest he'd come in recent memory was walking in on Jenny and her lover in that club in Sydney. And not because it had hurt him, because it hadn't. At all. But because she had agreed to marry him, and when Conrad claimed something, he preferred it remain his.

He'd only collared one woman, long ago. If he ever collared another, it would be for good.

And because he was in no rush for that unlikely event, he kept his scenes intense but his relationships with the women he played with otherwise casual.

There was absolutely no reason he should care if she'd gone out and slept with half of Europe since he'd last seen her. He'd intended to do much the same himself.

"I really wanted to experiment," Rory told him, again with that solemn expression. "But I couldn't do it. I kept meaning to. I was certain all through each dinner that I would, but then it was just so… Boring. So I kept going home. Alone."

Conrad assured himself that he felt nothing upon

hearing that. That this was about gathering information, nothing more. "And then? What did you do when you got home?"

"I spent a lot of time online." Her eyes got wider, her voice rougher. "Looking at a lot of pictures. And some videos."

"And?"

"And...thinking about you. About what happened here."

"Did you, now. I like that. But tell me, where were your hands while you entertained these thoughts?"

She was red-faced and sweating with it. She was lovely.

Especially when she didn't look away from him.

"Where yours were," she whispered, and then flushed again, and brighter.

"I can see that was difficult for you, Rory. You didn't want to tell me that."

"No," she agreed, suddenly sounding winded.

"Do you know why honesty is so important?"

Her eyes widened, almost comically. "Because of all those things in that room of yours. I don't think anyone would enjoy pretending that they were into it only to find that they really, *really* weren't."

"It doesn't quite work that way," he said, once again finding that what he wanted to do was laugh. When he was not exactly known for his hilarity in a scene. "Honesty is vulnerability. Only vulnerability allows for intimacy. And for all the closeness you claim you had while tragic, untutored boys heaved about on top of you, it brought you no real pleasure at all. I can promise you that this will be different. If what you truly want is that kind of closeness—that vulnerability and intimacy—then this is where you will find it, within the confines of the games we might decide to play. Do you understand?"

"I think so," she said. "Or I want to, I guess."

"Wonderful," he said. He smiled. "Then get down on your knees."

Conrad saw the shock go through her, electric and encompassing. "What?"

"You heard me."

"H…here?"

He nodded toward the floor between them and opted not to point out how benevolent he was because there was a very soft rug there. Her knees would be pampered—a gift she could not possibly appreciate while this was shiny and new.

But her knees weren't the point. Her head was.

Conrad watched her panic. He saw her eyes move this way, then that, as if trying to figure out how she could get out of this—while still getting what she'd come here for.

He waited, enjoying the show. There was more wringing of her hands. Her bracelets danced and jangled. He saw her toes curl in her sandals.

"Okay," Rory said, very softly, her voice thready. "But how isn't this demeaning?"

He didn't *quite* laugh at that. "For whom?"

"For women!" When he only gazed back at her mildly, she shook her head. "For me, then. It's one thing to wander around making people come at the drop of a hat. But kneeling? Isn't that…?"

"Isn't that what?" he prompted her when she fell silent. "If you don't finish the question, you can't expect an answer."

"I have to wonder what you get out of it, that's all."

Conrad settled back in his chair. "I'm so glad you asked. I like it. That's what I get out of it."

He nodded, again, at the place between them where he wanted her to kneel before him. And he could actually see, to his delight, the goose bumps that marched their way over every inch of her bare skin. Far more bare skin on display tonight, and all of it reacting to him.

She only got more and more delightful.

"I mean, saying that you're in charge, or controlling, or bossy, or whatever…" Her chest moved dramatically as she fought to breathe. "That's not the same thing as telling people to get down on their knees. This is basically everything that's toxic about cishet sex."

"I'm sorry," Conrad said, allowing himself to sound bored. "I'm not following this conversation. Are we having an academic debate about the great many social and cultural issues that inform the world outside this building? Because I thought we were talking about what it is *I* like. What pleases *me*, in my bed and out of it. And there are a great many things that I like, as a matter of fact, but I asked you to do just one of them. And you would rather bludgeon me with buzzwords."

"You don't think it's problematic to ask women to kneel before you?"

"Not for me." He bit back a smile at her appalled expression. "Or, Rory, for the women who choose to kneel before me not only for my pleasure, but theirs."

He let her sit with that, because she clearly had to breathe through it. And unless he was mistaken, she wasn't doing a great job of it.

"*Their* pleasure?" she asked, her voice practically strangled.

"You seem to be under a common misconception," he told her, almost kindly. "I told you that I'm dominant sexually. I told you that the kind of sex I'm talking about begins in a conversation like this. And that vulnerability and honesty is how intimacy is built."

"Yeah, that part sounds great. It's the kneeling down I'm having trouble wrapping my head around. Weird. It's almost like it's a gross power trip."

"Yes, Rory, because the only thing you're thinking about is you."

And that time, his voice was a whip. Sharp and fast, and devastatingly accurate.

She went still, then. Very still.

And silent.

Conrad continued. "You're concerned about your orgasm. You want another one. Maybe a night filled with so many you'll lose count. You want me to act as a kind of instrument to make that happen. A fully grown, autonomous vibrator. That's not to say I couldn't do that, of course. You already know I can, which is why you've come back here. But what's in it for me?"

Her jaw actually dropped open a little. "I don't... I thought *that* was what was in it for you."

"Don't get me wrong. I enjoy making a pretty woman come apart in my hands. Who wouldn't? But I'm not after your orgasm, Rory. I could make any woman come, and have. I've already proved that."

"What do you want, then?" she asked.

The very question he'd asked her, though her question was far more...fragile.

Conrad could feel the intensity in him. His gaze, his face. He did nothing to curb it. "I want your submission. Your surrender."

"What..."

She looked as if she was reeling, there where she sat. As if the breeze from out in the garden might topple her over.

He loved this part. These sweet, hot moments of struggle.

Before she gave in to what she really wanted.

"Do you know why I let you in my door?" He

didn't wait for her to respond. He wasn't sure she could, just then, all goose bumps and slick, shocked eyes. "It was your surrender, Rory. It was written all over you. And that's what this is about. That's what I want, not that you asked until prompted. I want the exchange."

"How...how is it an *exchange* if I'm the one surrendering?"

"I'm not going to force you to surrender," he said. "Or to do anything else. You should do the things I ask you to do because you want to please me. And I'm not foolish enough to imagine a temporary scene isn't highly motivated by the prospects of orgasms, especially in the case of someone like you, who is so new to the things her body wants."

He could see she wanted to argue with that. But didn't.

"You're here," he pointed out. "I didn't force you to come here. I won't force you to stay. If I had to force you, how would that be any fun?"

"But..." She looked at the rug between them. "But you want..."

"I want you to kneel because you want to kneel," he told her with a quiet intensity. "Because, even if it scares you or repels you or worries you, you want to please me more than you want to stay where you are. Stuck in that chair. Stuck in your life. Stuck pretending you're happy with puppy love and pointless sex."

"I'm not..."

"It's up to you, Rory," Conrad told her, intent and sure. "Do you want to change? If you don't, you're welcome to go at any time. But if you do…" He lifted a shoulder, then dropped it, and nodded once more at the floor. "You know what to do."

CHAPTER SIX

RORY THOUGHT SHE must surely be ill, because she was considering it.

More than considering it. Her body was a mess. It hardly felt like hers. She was all…electrical surges, shivering that reminded her of the flu, and a great, heavy sort of rawness that just *sat* there. Deep inside her.

Thick and rough and greedy.

Conrad looked beautiful and remote. And above all, demanding. There was something about the contrast between his stern mouth and the blazing heat in his navy blue eyes that made her breath hitch.

While down below, her pussy was soft and wild and making its own demands.

Louder and hotter by the second.

Rory had watched so many videos. She'd looked at so many pictures. The images were shocking— *disturbing*, she would even have said, had anyone been there to ask. Except it was the ones she'd found most personally disturbing that she'd looked at the longest. It was those same images that played over and over in her head as she thought about doing them with him.

And she thought about doing all of those things with him, no matter what words she flung at those fantasies in the light of day. When the sun was out, she was faintly embarrassed to discover, she was more of a pearl clutcher than the fearless warrior for alternative sexual experiences she'd always imagined she was.

But despite all her fantasies, each more feverish than the last, nothing had prepared her for this.

For sitting here in a converted church in a soft leather chair that she could feel like a caress on the bare skin of her thighs. For Conrad himself, sitting there so casually and yet clearly and indisputably in control.

Of himself.

And, unless she was very much mistaken, of her.

Worse—or better—when she stopped telling herself how offensive that ought to have been, she could tell that her body thrilled to the notion.

She thought of all those *things* of his, implements and devices and tools, carefully locked away beneath the stained glass. She thought of collars and hard hands against her ass, all those things she'd imagined when she was alone, and none of that imagining had been even half as intense as sitting here.

Just sitting here.

Fighting with herself.

First something like self-pity washed through her. Why didn't he simply take control the way he had before? Why didn't he handle things—particularly her—so that she didn't have to do all this…choosing?

Her heart beat a little faster at that, but she had a terrible inkling that she already knew what the truth was.

And it was a galling thing indeed to realize that despite all the time she spent shouting about what consent was and what it should look like, and all the many ways in which she personally liked to indicate her enthusiasm to her dates, it was clear that all of that was easy. Because it required so little of her.

This, however, required a whole lot more than a speech on her part.

And this is what she knew already. Whatever she did, or didn't do, she was never going to get Conrad Vanderburg out of her head. She'd tried already and failed. Miserably.

More than that, she was fairly sure he had changed her body, and her, forever.

She didn't think she could go back to thinking that a good night with a lover meant her lying there, sphinxlike, acting lofty and mysterious when once again he came and she didn't. Talking about *closeness*, and *choosing to have control* of her own orgasm, and then not having one.

How could she go back to any of that when he'd

taken a wrecking ball to everything she thought was true—about her body, about what she was capable of, about the things that she could want and feel and need?

Rory understood that this would all remain true even if she got up from her seat right now and let herself back out of this gloriously Gothic church of his.

And the rawness inside her grew bigger and bigger, more unwieldy, more insistent.

She tried to imagine what it would be like if she left. She couldn't help thinking that no matter what it might demand of her to stay, leaving would be the kind of regret she might never get over.

And she had no illusions. If she left, there was no way that Conrad would let her come back.

It's just sex, she told herself stoutly. *Kinky sex, that's all. Why are you being so dramatic about it?*

And that helped. That put her back on familiar ground. She was a goddamned sex positive, progressive, proudly kink-friendly woman. Even if, until now, the kinkiest thing she'd ever done had involved playing with candle wax with a boyfriend in college. The same boyfriend who had introduced her to girl-on-girl porn, which had played a huge part in her deciding that she must be pansexual.

She realized she was waiting for Conrad to say something else, but a glance his way—at all that brooding, weaponized patience—made it clear that he wasn't going to do that.

So Rory would have to do what was necessary.

It really was necessary, she told herself. Because even if she hated every single thing that happened with this man—which would certainly be a change from what had already happened with him—it would be experience.

She was supposed to be the kind of person who collected experiences. That was part of her brand.

And she almost laughed out loud—granted, a little bit hysterically—at the thought of what Conrad would say if she mentioned her *brand* just now.

Rory braced herself. She took hold of the skinny little string of the bag she liked to wear out to dates and things, because it was so little and easy, and slipped it off her shoulder. She placed the bag on the table closest to her, and maybe she made a little production out of that. Eating up minutes.

Dawdling, her father would have said, *only makes dread into a decision*.

For God's sake, this was not the time to think about her father.

Yet in that moment, Rory suddenly realized exactly why her father had been so appalled that she'd wanted to talk about her sex life with him. She'd never understood before. All the sex she'd ever had was about as meaningful as a sneeze. Why not debate and discuss over food with family? Why not talk it up all over the place, because what did it matter if everyone knew her thoughts on every last detail? They were only *thoughts*.

But she understood, at last, that when other people talked about sex they weren't talking about their thoughts and philosophies and *what ifs*. They were talking about *action*. About actual *acts*. And all the acts *Rory* had ever taken part in had been about as intimate and vulnerable as a high five.

But that wasn't true for everyone.

Because everything with Conrad already felt more intimate, more raw, more meaningful or powerful—in the sense of consequences, in this body that no longer felt like her own—than literally all the sex she had ever had.

That made a different sort of sensation go through her like a long, sad ripple.

And then Rory banished her father from her head and at the same time, put her hands on her knees and tried to imagine how she was going to make herself do this. It should have been simple. Sliding out of the chair, getting down on the rug—no big thing.

But it felt...huge. Like flinging herself off a cliff.

Like changing her life, as he'd said.

She looked at Conrad for help, but he remained as implacable as stone. As if he could sit there, watching and waiting, until the end of time.

Maybe that was comforting. She blew out a

breath. Then heaved in another one, because oxygen no longer seem to be doing the trick.

She shifted a little and realized that her pussy was ridiculously wet. That there was that low, throbbing ache that made her wonder whether, if she just squeezed her thighs together, she could make herself come just like this.

Just at the idea.

And then oddly, she felt her eyes well up, even as her nipples prickled to life again, poking hard against her tank top.

Something shifted inside her, the way it had when she'd been standing outside this church earlier. It was the sense that she was already ruined, so what was a little more? Rory wanted to call that defeatist, but she had the sneaking suspicion that it was nothing more and nothing less than that wholescale surrender that he'd been talking about.

The very word made her want to sob. It made her want to put her hands between her legs and make herself come, over and over.

It made her want him.

It made her feel as if she was caught in a terrible undertow, tossed and rolled by the waves and then dragged out to a sea she hardly knew—

And then finally, in the end, it was such a simple thing.

She slipped off the chair. She took herself down to the rug.

Rory knelt there in front of him, her chest heaving and her pulse a drum inside her, as if she'd performed an Olympic feat.

For a moment, the noise inside her head was so loud, and her body shook so much, that she thought she might crumple down into a puddle—

But Conrad smiled.

A genuine smile, and it changed everything.

Everything inside her seem to…lift. Then spin a bit, like hope.

He sat forward, and that was when it occurred to her that she wasn't simply kneeling, which was bad enough. She was kneeling between his legs, in front of his chair.

But she didn't have time to worry herself to death over that little detail, because he was sitting forward and putting that palm of his to her cheek.

His hand was big and hard, and she knew from last time that he burned hot to the touch. But his palm felt cool against her cheek, which only made her flush harder, because she understood in a flash that he could tell. That he could see all these reactions she was having, no matter what she might say.

Conrad brushed his thumb over her cheek, and she felt everything inside her settle. All that noise, all that jangling and worry, smoothed out into a kind of humming.

Like once again, he'd used a tuning fork on her,

and all she could think to do was offer him what little music she had in return.

"I'm proud of you," he said.

And for a terrifying second, Rory thought she might actually burst into tears. Great, racking sobs. The sort of thing that would leave her messy and red-faced and swollen eyed for days—

But somehow, she managed to hold that all back.

Somehow, she managed to keep herself in one piece. Nothing more than eyes too blurry to see and a sob that had nowhere to go, because she held her breath.

Like her life depended on it.

"It's all right," he told her, his hand still on her face and his voice so calm and *sure* she wanted to melt. "Tears are a good thing. You can let them out. I promise you, little one, that there is nothing that you could show me, or do, that I can't handle." His thumb moved against her skin, her hot cheek, as if he was rubbing peace into her with every stroke. "There is no *too much* here."

It felt like a far worse surrender when tears flooded her eyes and then tracked down her cheeks, no matter the horror in her. And no matter what he said.

But true to his word, he simply let her cry—and that made her cry harder. One big sob, then another, and his hand stayed where it was. She even sagged against him, there against the hard certainty of his thigh. And his other hand came up to hold her there too, smoothing its way over her hair.

Then, after the storm took her and shook her, it let her go.

And Rory felt...washed clean.

"I must look..." she began, as his hands helped her kneel upright again.

"You look beautiful," he told her, matter-of-factly.

"I know that's not true," she started, wiping at her face.

But he caught her hands and drew them away. And then held them, so there was nothing for her to do but look up at him. Rory found it hard to breathe, yet again, because the way he was looking at her was so intense she was sure she must have caught fire.

"Stop thinking about how you look." Conrad's gaze was deep. Dark. Another demand. "Think instead about how I see you. You look beautiful, Rory. You look vulnerable. Open and honest. You could not please me more if you tried."

And again, it was as if she suddenly grew wings and could fly. As if she was already soaring somewhere high above Paris. When instead, she was kneeling down in front of a man because he'd asked her to.

He was still toying with her hair. He'd dropped his hand from her face, but he held a long strand of her hair between the fingers of his other hand, and he was...simply playing with it.

And for a long while, he concentrated on that, with so much focus and intensity that she found herself shivering hot and cold once again.

"Here's what I want you to do with your hands," he said after a while. As if it had only just occurred to him. "If you're kneeling the way you are now, sitting back on your heels, you can rest your hands on your thighs, palms up. If you're kneeling up, I'd like your hands in the small of your back. Do you understand?"

"Do you really… I mean does it really matter…" He shifted that look of his from her hair to her. Steady. Implacable. Her pulse skipped. "I mean… I'm just…there are so many details. Aren't you afraid it will get lost somehow in all the *rules*?"

"The details are what make it fun," Conrad replied, and that gleam in his eyes made her think he was laughing at her. Again.

"I thought it was the sex that was fun."

"Sex is always supposed to be fun, Rory." He didn't shake his head, but she had the impression he could have. "If I were to indulge in a little spot of vanilla sex, I would expect that to be fun, because it's sex. Everything else is like spices. Some people don't like spicy food at all, which is perfectly fine. Other people like a mildly spicy food, and enjoy it at that temperature to their heart's content. Do you see where I'm going with this?"

"Sure. Ball gags and cilantro. Totally the same thing."

Rory was so close to him now, kneeling there before him. She could see when that gleam in his eyes turned to something else. Something that made her think instead of how stern he could be. And all the uses he might have for that hard hand of his.

She repressed a little shudder.

"Just like any other kind of sex, the kind I prefer is highly individual," Conrad said, that patient tone laced through with something more like steel. It made her sit a little straighter on her knees. "You can go into any club and expect to see certain trappings, but every practitioner is different. We all want different things. We have different enthusiasms. Different things get us off."

As he spoke, he wrapped that glossy black rope of her hair round and around his finger.

"For example, some people like a little hint of pain with their pleasure." He tugged on the hair he held, and she gasped at the little pinch at her scalp. While at the same time, she felt her nipples pinch, and her clit throb. "You, for example, respond beautifully to pain."

"I don't..." But she didn't finish that sentence.

Conrad eased back on that tugging pressure. "Some people like quite a lot of pain, and only through it do they find their pleasure," he said. "It's all in the details, Rory. Like anything else in life, it's an infinitely customizable menu."

"What do you want?" she asked.

And when his mouth curved, she remembered the pointed comment he'd made about how she hadn't asked him that first.

"If I were to get philosophical about it, I would tell you that what turns me on the most is radical trust," he said, and the quieter his voice got, the more intensely his dark blue eyes gleamed. "You put yourself in my hands, literally, and take whatever I choose to give you, trusting that what I will do with it will not only make us both come, but, truly, make us better people."

There wasn't anything particularly sexy about what he said. And still everything inside her reacted as if it was. She wanted to pick her hands from where they rested on top of her thighs, just as he told her, and *do something* with all that greedy energy. All that throbbing, greedy heat.

"And if you weren't being philosophical?"

"There are many dominants," Conrad said, a different gleam in his gaze. "But I tend to skew more toward high protocol. With a healthy amount of discipline."

Rory felt as winded as if she'd run up six flights of stairs. "What does that mean?"

"It means I expect, and demand, that you speak to me in a certain way. Using certain words. And that you assume the appropriate positions that match those things."

"That...doesn't really tell me anything."

"If we were in a club, I would expect any submissive who approached me to do so on their knees," he told her coolly, his gaze never shifting from her face. "I would expect them to sit before me as you are now, in either of the two kneeling positions I described to you, but keep their eyes lowered unless I asked them to look at me."

She thought maybe her mouth dropped open at that.

Conrad's eyes crinkled in the corners. "I insist on being addressed respectfully. And I take a dim view of being spoken to unless I've issued an invitation to do so. That's a basic overview of high protocol." His gaze moved over her, and she knew he could see how fast she was breathing. There was no hiding it. "As for discipline? It can take any number of forms, but I'm a big believer in maintenance spankings."

Every conversation with him made her feel as if she was being buffeted by high winds while standing on some unprotected mountaintop. This was no different. Every word he said seemed to spark a new fire inside her, even as her mind reeled about and tried to keep up.

"Okay. Wait. What about all that...bowing and scraping and whatever else is hot to you?"

"All of it." And again, his laughter was in his gaze, if not out loud.

"Doesn't that make you…"

But there were some things even she didn't dare say.

Conrad knew. How did he always know? "Rory. Are you asking me if there are some who are drawn to this particular lifestyle because it accords them an architecture they can build around their innate bullying behavior? Of course there are." He shrugged. "But that's true of anything—of any people in any kind of relationship. Whatever our gender, whatever our sexual identity, there are no spaces—anywhere—that are one hundred percent safe from people who might manipulate those spaces to their own ends. But I will tell you that the people in the spaces I inhabit, while certainly not perfect, tend to be significantly more self-aware than the average puppy dog of a boy you might find in a bar."

"They're self-aware about the way they like women to kneel in front of them and call them… what? My liege?"

"Sir, generally. Or Master, depending." He tilted his head slightly to one side, his dark eyes glittering. "But what on earth makes you think that it's only women who kneel?"

Rory blinked at that, a bit shocked with herself. Because, of course, the internet had been filled with images of all sorts of people in all sorts of submissive poses. Why was it she couldn't seem to remember that all of this could apply to all kinds of people who weren't her?

Maybe she was as selfish as he'd suggested she was.

She didn't know what to do with that possibility. "You're right. I knew that. I…"

"Do you really want a seminar on BDSM throughout the ages?" Conrad asked, with a hint of that amusement again. "I prefer more practical applications of philosophy, but you can waste all the time you want, Rory. I already know how this works."

But that other thing he'd said was still rattling around inside of her. "Well, but… I also want to know what you mean by *maintenance spanking*."

The way he almost smiled then struck her as deeply unholy. It was like a completely different note rang through her then, wicked and wild.

"Maintenance spankings are when the spanking is simply part of the calendar. Once a week, every night, whatever works for the relationship. Meaning," he said when she frowned at him, "I would not wait for you to do something wrong, then spank you. I would spank you not only whenever I pleased in the general course of things, but also on a schedule."

"A *schedule*?"

"I find that expectations and anticipation lead to the most delicious places," Conrad told her.

"Is that how you...keep them obedient?" she asked, feeling as if she was flailing around, trying to get the vocabulary right.

Or maybe it's not the vocabulary you're worried about, but how much you long for all these problematic things he's talking about so casually—but she didn't want to listen to that voice inside her.

"I expect obedience, yes," Conrad said, and she could hear *layers* of steel and stone in his voice, then. She could feel it like his hand against her pussy once again. "There are some BDSM relationships that appear to be predicated on the submissive acting like a brat and the dominant punishing that brattiness as it occurs—or not, to the dominant's taste. But I don't do brattiness. I don't much like it in a single scene and I would not tolerate it at all in a more permanent arrangement."

"Because all of your orders are so perfect?" she demanded. A little hotly, she realized after she threw the words out.

But Conrad only regarded her in the same patient way he always did. "Some people will tell you that BDSM is all a great bit of theater around the fact that despite everything you might see to the contrary, the submissive has control. And on some level, that's true. Because it is her consent to any act that gives it its heat. Its power. But if you go deeper than that, there is a power exchange. And the power exchange is not about who's dominant and who's submissive, who gives consent or who capitalizes on it. It's exactly what it sounds like. An exchange."

Her throat was dry. Her eyes felt wet again. What was happening to her?

Conrad's dark eyes were a blazing thing, hard and beautiful. "As much as you trust me to work within your boundaries, and perhaps push them a little, I trust you to allow me those things. It's a balance. One can't work without the other. I could tell you a thousand different theories about why that is, and what it is, but what it comes down to is that BDSM is a highly stylized practice of intimacy."

This time she didn't try to make a joke about cilantro or ball gags.

And she thought he nearly smiled again. "Because the difficulty with intimacy, Rory, is not in you. But what you, through the other person, see in yourself. Most people do not enjoy that mirror."

"Have you had that?" she dared to ask.

"Yes."

And he offered nothing more. But her ribs seemed to hurt, because all of this was significantly more direct than any conversation she'd ever had with a man before.

But of course, that was his point.

It occurred to her that she didn't actually know what kind of man he was. Did he play around—

either with or without a partner's knowledge? "Do you have it…now?"

"No," he told her. "I haven't had that kind of relationship in a long time."

"What happened to your last one?" she asked, and was confused when he laughed.

"You sound so scandalized. What are you imagining? That I beat her black-and-blue and she escaped me with nothing but a collar around her neck?" As he had once before, he gave the impression of rolling his eyes without actually doing it. "That is a story of abuse. What I had was a relationship. A mutually exclusive relationship of consenting adults involved in a power exchange. And when it had run its course, we separated. Is there something about that that is inherently more dramatic than your average divorce? Or even a run-of-the-mill breakup?"

"How did she break up with you if she had to ask you permission to speak?" Rory asked.

Conrad's mouth was still curved. "What makes you think she was the one who broke up with me?"

"Okay, but if you're the one who broke up with her, why? If this power exchange thing is the be-all and end-all—"

Conrad sighed. "I don't think you're really all that interested in my ancient history, Rory. I think it makes you feel braver to question me. I take the responsibility for the kind of sex I enjoy very seriously. That's part of what I like about it. You have your casual dates. Your curation. But I have scenes in which I sit down with a woman and discuss, frankly and honestly, what is going to occur. And then I arrange an experience to both of our mutual satisfaction."

"But—"

"And what I think you're really interested in is spanking."

She shook a little at that. Maybe a lot. "I wouldn't say *interested*, necessarily."

"Maintenance spankings, in particular. I find them fascinating myself. But don't worry, that's more of a relationship thing."

And Rory, who had never been spanked in her life, felt suddenly outraged that he was excluding her from the option of whatever *relationship spankings* were.

When his eyes lit up again, she knew he could tell.

"Do you have any other meandering questions or vague accusations?" he asked. "You look so lovely on your knees, I could answer them all night."

She realized, with a start, that she'd forgotten that she was kneeling.

Something about that struck her hard. Like a gong. The very fact that something that had been so difficult for her to even contemplate seemed almost quaint now... Surely that should have upset her. Surely that should have been something that took a long time to get her head around.

But the reality was, it was him.

The way he looked at her. That *voice*. His marvelous hands.

He hadn't even touched her in any particularly sexual way tonight, and he was still the most exciting man she'd ever met—and by far the best sex she'd ever had.

She hardly knew where to put that.

"Well," she said, considering all of those factors and her own feelings. And everything he'd said. Or better yet, implied, all midnight blue and that relentless gaze. "I appreciate you telling me all of these things. But I have to say… I kind of thought that kinky sex would have a lot more fucking. If I'm honest."

His expression didn't change, though somehow, it got significantly more…*wolfish*.

He smoothed his hand over her hair, and the way he looked down at her made everything inside her tighten.

"Rory," he said, so softly. Almost gently, if it weren't for the steel beneath. "How wet are you?"

She was so wet it should probably have been embarrassing. Hot and aching besides. She was so wet *it hurt*. "What?"

He looked almost tender, if an expression so intimidating, all steel and intent, could be any such thing.

"This is BDSM, little one," he said, rumbling and

dark, and too delicious to bear. He made her heart slam against her own ribs like a mallet. "I like to start it off with a long, slow, lazy mind fuck. Or what would be the point?"

CHAPTER SEVEN

CONRAD COULDN'T REMEMBER the last time he'd had this much fun.

He'd had a lot of sex, certainly. And the push and pull of BDSM always made that sex excellent.

But this was on a different level altogether.

He couldn't remember the last time he'd been with a brand-new submissive, because he preferred to avoid them. He didn't want to waste his time training a woman to his standards, when he only intended to enjoy her for a night. Or a short scene. His experiences with Marie Jeanette, the only submissive he'd claimed—and when he'd been much younger—had left him uninterested in collaring anyone since.

The aversion had faded as the years passed, but these days he hardly had time to play, much less maintain a woman in the way she required.

Because, much as he and Marie Jeanette had suited at the start, things had changed. Things always changed—he understood that—but the way they'd changed had ruined them. Conrad had come into himself as he grew. The more responsibility he took on in the outside world, the more intensely he'd wanted sexual power.

But Marie Jeanette had turned out to want less sexual dominance, and more of a conventional life. The more intense he became sexually, the less in to it she was. And the more she cried and wanted more fancy holidays abroad than scenes, the less he wanted to do any of it. It became unworkable.

These days, Marie Jeanette was far happier with a gentler, kinder dominant partner, who was happy to keep her as she preferred. They had married some time ago, and Conrad had attended their wedding. Happily.

But he couldn't say that he had been particularly inspired to repeat the collaring experience since then. Or even training a submissive to please him, because he rarely played with the same woman twice.

Until now.

And little as he wanted to accept that Rory was different, he was not in the habit of hiding from truths. However unpleasant. Even if it meant that apparently, he was in the market to train this unexpected—and if he was honest, unacceptable—American.

"Am I supposed be doing something?" she asked, her eyes wide. "Or is this part of the mind fuck?"

"It's all part of the mind fuck," he replied. And

felt a surge of something it took him a moment to identify.

Affection.

He had to pause a moment to process that. This woman was everything he would have sworn to anyone who would listen, in any club he frequented, he detested. And yet here he was, so hard he was beginning to worry it might actually threaten the limits of his control.

Imagine that.

"The last time you were here, you indicated that you are no stranger to sucking cock." He let his fingers move over the delicate curve of her ear, enjoying the way she shuddered. "But as I told you, that is a privilege. A little bit of kneeling, however pretty, would never be enough to earn it."

He watched as the pulse in her neck went wild. And he wasn't sure she knew, yet, the way her body betrayed her. The way her eyes dilated. The way she swallowed, hard, then moistened her lips.

His cock was becoming a problem.

"Then, of course, there's spanking," he said sedately, as if he wasn't considering throwing her over the back of the chair and finding some relief. "Which obviously fascinates you."

"I wouldn't… I wouldn't say that I'm *fascinated*—"

But that breathy voice told him otherwise.

"Were you ever spanked as a child?"

She actually wriggled, there between his outstretched legs. "Of course not."

"Well, Rory, that explains a great deal about you. And I can certainly see that there would be instant benefits to reddening that ass of yours." He made a show of considering it. "How do you feel about breath play?"

"Is that…?"

He slid his hand to her throat and cupped her neck, gently. Very, very gently. And then, holding her gaze with his, he tightened his grip. Infinitesimally.

She let out a soft little sound, and he could see the shudder that worked its way over her, then. Her nipples punched out, tight and hard, into the fabric of the tank top she wore. Even her goose bumps seemed to have goose bumps. And better still, he could actually smell her arousal.

God, she was perfect.

"I can see that you like it very much." He moved his hand away from her neck, biting back a smile as she made another sound, this one a kind of grief.

"There are so many ways to fuck," he mused. "And so many practical things to consider. Those pesky details again."

"You love those," she said, and he imagined she meant to sound her usual confronting self. But she couldn't manage to get her voice above a whisper.

"You should know, of course, that if I choose to fuck you, I'll want to fuck that ass of yours just as much as I'll want to fuck your mouth," he said. Conversationally. "Maybe I'll fuck you in both of those places instead of in your pussy, and before you ask, the answer is because I might feel like it."

She shook at that, a flush working its way down her neck, while her gaze stayed glued to his.

"And because it will make you want it more," he told her. "And because I'm going to like seeing you desperate. Because sometimes, not giving you what you want will give you exactly what you want, in the end." His mouth curved. "Or exactly what I want. If we're doing this right, that should be the same thing."

"Are you going to do *all* those things?" she asked, breathlessly. "Tonight?"

"Let's concentrate on protocol." Conrad made his expression cooler. Harder. "I have been allowing you to question me while you got comfortable, but you look perfectly comfortable to me. Now I don't want you to use your voice unless I ask you to. Do you understand?"

Rory balked a bit at that, as he'd expected she would. He could see that this was another shift, like that beautiful struggle she'd had to come to him in the first place, down on her knees.

"I understand what you're saying, if that's what you mean. The actual words, but..."

"The only time you can violate that rule—speaking only when I ask you to—is if you feel that something is happening that requires a safeword. You mentioned safewords earlier. Do you know what they are?"

Her breath sounded like a pant. "Am I allowed to answer that?"

"No need," Conrad said calmly. "I may ask you to tell me your safeword, and if I do, you can respond in one of three ways. Red, yellow, or green. Just like a stoplight. Green means everything is fine. Yellow means you'd like to pause, because perhaps you're overwhelmed, or confused, or think you need to catch your breath. Red, obviously, is stop. Yellow and red are the only two words you're welcome to use at any time, whether I ask you to speak or not. Do you understand all of that?"

"I mean... I guess I understand the stoplight but why I have to—"

He brushed his fingers over her mouth, quieting her. And finding her lips as soft and lush as he'd thought he would, which didn't exactly help the wild greed in him.

"No editorializing," he said, making his voice a little more stern and watching her stiffen in instant response. She really was a natural. "You will answer yes or no, unless I ask you specifically for your thoughts or feelings. It won't be confusing. I'll tell you exactly what I want. Do you understand?"

Her eyes were taking on that glassy, glorious sheen. "Y....yes."

"Good girl," Conrad murmured, and he knew

that she was slipping into the right frame of mind when all she did was moan a little at that. No arguments. No commentary about derogatory language or whether or not she felt demeaned.

He could see that she did not.

And it pleased him that whether she could have put it into words or not, some part of her understood that here, at his feet, was the time to experience power differentials. Not debate them.

"First," he said, "I want you naked. I don't want you to stand up. I want you to take off your clothes right where you are. Stay on your knees, please."

Rory looked like she might topple over, but she didn't. And she was breathing like she was running a race, but she didn't argue with him. Her shoulders dropped, and then she shrugged off the summer scarf that had long since fallen to each side. She pulled off her tank top, and the strappy bra beneath it, and set them to the side. She rocked forward on her knees to push her skirt and her panties down, then back again to wrestle them over her knees, and forward one more time to get them off.

When she was finished, she was flushed and looked cross.

But he could see all of her, at last.

And she was a confection. She was a petite little thing, all silky limbs, full breasts, and a pouting pussy.

Mine, something in him growled, dark and deep.

He concentrated on the task at hand. "You spent a lot of time in the past two weeks looking at filthy things on the internet." And when she started to speak, to answer him, then stopped herself—he smiled. "You must have made yourself come, Rory. Again and again, I would think. Show me."

He heard the huff of the breath she let out. He could almost see the word she wanted to say trembling there on her lips, but once again, she caught herself.

Even though her chest heaved.

"Keep your eyes on me," he told her, with silken command. "Put your hands between your legs. Spread your thighs. And show me what you do when you're alone in your flat, watching dark and terrible things that excite you and make you think of me."

He heard the low, almost pained sound she made, but she rushed to do exactly as he'd requested. She slid her hands to the inside of her thighs, and adjusted the way she knelt there, widening her thighs to give him a better view, and then moving her hands to cup her pussy.

"I don't know if I can—"

Conrad simply reached out and pinched her nipple. Hard. She made a squeaking, outraged sort of sound, but he didn't let go.

"That's called a consequence." His voice was perfectly calm. "And it was such a mild one, wasn't it?" Even as he spoke, he was rolling the proud little peak between his finger and thumb, soothing the sharp pain he knew he'd given her. "What did I say about editorializing?"

She swallowed, hard, and he thought she got a little mixed up the way she was breathing, because she made a ragged sound. "You said not to."

"Indeed." He flicked his thumb over the crest of her nipple, and she shivered. Her body bucked a little, and he could see that the shock of arousal and pain had mixed together for her. Just the way he liked it. "And when you speak to me, Rory, you call me Sir."

Her eyes looked damper. Shinier. But they were still fixed to his face.

He lifted his hand to smooth it over her cheek. "You may thank me, Rory, for training you like this."

He watched her struggle with that, or maybe fight her way out from under the weight of it. Either way, she looked jittery again, as if she didn't know what her own body was doing.

"Th… Thank you, Sir," she managed, her voice sounding thready. Insubstantial.

Perfect.

"I don't like to be kept waiting," he warned.

He could see a kind of anguish over her face, then. And he knew what she might have wanted to tell him, if he'd let her speak. That she didn't know if she could make herself come on command. That she hadn't done it before, like this. That this was all too much for her, naked and kneeling, her hands between her legs, about to give herself pleasure—by giving him the pleasure he'd requested.

He shifted his legs slightly so they hemmed her in a bit more, truly caging her there, and waited.

And slowly, beautifully, she began to move her hands between her legs, finding her slick flesh and moving her fingers through her folds to find her clit and the piercing that marked it.

Conrad reached out and fit his hand to her cheek again. Caressing her as she caressed yourself, yes. But also holding her there where he wanted her, with her face exposed to him.

He knew the precise moment she realized that. That he was keeping her face tipped up like that so he could see every glimmer of emotion, thought, anything at all, as it moved across her face.

And he could hear how slick she was, how wet, as her hands moved. It was quiet in this room and the sounds she made were greedy, rude, insistent. She rocked her palm into her pussy, very much the way he had the other day, her gaze fastened to him.

He liked the fine tremor he could feel build in her, and the way she moved quicker, with more confidence, as she went. He thought about that hot little clit ring and how it must be helping her get there as she worked.

And what he could do with it, in time.

Again, everything was quiet save the sound of her breath and her pussy. Her face got brighter, redder.

And he waited, watching her for the signs. The way her lips parted. The way she began to strain a bit, and then stiffened.

"You have my permission to come," he told her, his voice low and commanding.

Right as she was on the edge.

He heard the stutter in her breath, the little cry, and then she threw herself over.

And he held her there between his legs, naked and kneeling at his feet, as she came for him. She shook and she bucked, and through all her shaking apart she tried her best to keep her eyes glued to him.

As if she dared not look away.

"Beautiful," he said, his voice rougher than it should have been.

Because she was getting to him. She'd already gotten to him, but her willingness to submit was making his cock pulse and, far more worrying, his chest feel tight.

But he would deal with that later.

He stood, pulling her with him, and he loved how pliable she was. Supple and close to stumbling, really, though she didn't. Quite. He turned her, so he could guide her with his hand wrapped around the back of her neck, and propelled her to an archway that led into a little alcove. Inside the alcove there were some bookshelves, a window overlooking the garden, a sturdy bench, and directly in front of the archway, a giant antique mirror tilted back against the wall.

Conrad saw her eyeing the bench, still fighting to catch her breath. He stood her there in the archway, waiting for her eyes to lift from that bench to the mirror. He met her gaze.

"You come beautifully," he told her. "Thank me for allowing you the privilege, please."

"Thank you," she said, and he could hear the confusion in her voice, the pleasure and the wonder, the worry in the dark need.

"Thank you, who?"

Her eyes widened almost comically. "Sir," she said in a hurry. "Thank you, Sir."

"Good girl."

He left her standing there and watched her in the mirror as he went into the alcove, opening up the bench to pull out the toys he wanted. He watched her fight to stay balanced and upright. She looked around the room, but only for a moment before directing her gaze back to him. And then keeping it there.

Something in him shifted at that. Because he'd forgotten what it was like to be looked at with so much…awe. Better still, they weren't in a club, so there was no question that this was any kind of performance for the evening. Rory really was focused entirely on him.

His cock ached.

He had what he needed, so he walked around her

to make her more nervous, then set about putting it all together. Briskly, as if the naked girl in the middle of it all hardly signified.

Conrad loved the way she watched him, as if she couldn't decide if she was terrified or delighted.

Particularly when he attached his chains to the subtle eye hooks at the top of the arch. He let them drop, so he could watch her reaction at the clattering sound they made against the floor.

She had just come, but he could see her flush with a new arousal. Her nipples, soft after her climax, hardened again. And she was naked for him, so he could enjoy everything from the way her hair moved against her back to the ubiquitous tattoos she had, one behind her left shoulder and another on her leg.

If she was his, he would ink her soft, light brown skin with designs of his choosing. He could almost see the tattoo he would insist upon, stretching up one side and wrapping beneath one breast.

Then Conrad shook his head, because she wasn't his. He wouldn't be tattooing her. He didn't know where such a thought had come from.

"I'm going to restrain you in a few different ways," he told her, severely. "And sometimes the idea of bondage is quite different from the reality. That makes it a good time to think about your safewords. Tell me what they are."

She looked as if she might come out of her skin.

"Um. Green if everything is good. Yellow if I

need a pause. Red to stop." Her eyes widened when his brow rose. "Sir."

"Very good."

He went to her neck first, buckling a play collar around it, a sturdy, stiff leather to help give her the sensation of his hand there. Sure enough, she responded immediately. He felt her go distinctly pliant, and her eyes took on that glassy sheen he wanted.

"Okay?" he asked, moving his hand as he studied her face, down the sweet length of her spine to the intriguing curve of her ass.

"Yes, Sir," she whispered.

And while she was concentrating on having a binding around her neck, he picked up a pair of cuffs and moved behind her, letting his hands travel down the length of her arms before securing her wrists in the small of her back.

"Stand straight, please," he told her, with just enough edge to make her jolt before she obeyed.

He pulled her elbows toward each other until she arched her back. "This is how I want you to stand. I like the curve here." He smoothed his palm along it. "I like that it raises your breasts and puts all of your beautiful body on display for my pleasure."

Conrad gathered her hair in one hand, and began to twist it into a smooth, glossy rope. Then he pulled back when it was good and tight so she tipped backward, her head resting against his shoulder. Then he held her there before him.

"Look in the mirror," he ordered her.

He liked the image himself. Rory was bound with a thick black collar around her neck. She wore nothing else but the flush on her skin and lovely goose bumps to mark the way. He watched her, pleased at the contrast they made in the mirror. He was all in black, his sternest look on his face, and she was melting, trembling, lost in that exquisite distress that he adored.

She was such a little thing, particularly in her bare feet, slender and curvy at once. He liked how lush her hips were and the way they flared. And when he trailed a hand down her side, where he could see that tattoo if he squinted, he cupped her breast and the little sigh she let out arrowed straight through him. Heating him up almost to the boiling point.

Soon, he promised himself.

"Now I'm going to make it interesting," he said. "Because I think you like a little pain with your pleasure. But then, whether you do or don't, I do. You want to please me, don't you, Rory?"

He watched her in the mirror. And the way her eyes were on him, only him, even as her body trembled.

"Yes, Sir."

"Good." He pulled out the clamps he'd put in his pocket, and held them so she could see them. "These are vicious. And effective. You'll see what I mean."

Conrad let her hair fall, then moved around in front

of her. Then he enjoyed himself. He played with her breasts, watching the expression on her face change as she felt the way the cuffs and the collar restrained her. He grabbed a handful of her ass, gripping her hard so she went up on her toes. And he slid a demanding finger through her folds, to confirm that she was molten hot and ready, to play with that clit and his favorite piercing, and to watch her eyes go dark.

But then he returned to her breasts, holding up each one in turn, and playing with her nipples. Stimulating them, roughly, to see what she would do.

What she did was dance a bit into his touch, and then let out a shaky sort of moan when he bent his head and pulled one nipple deep into his mouth. And sucked.

He felt her react. He felt a kind of lightning shoot through her, and while she was still making a little noise, he fixed the clamp to her nipple.

Rory didn't disappoint him. She howled and bucked, but she was cuffed and he had a hold of her. While she was protesting, he bent his head, sucked her other nipple deep and then clamped it the same.

He waited for her to safeword out, but she didn't.

Conrad was unduly proud.

Then he stood back and watched her deal with it. Her pulse beat in her throat. Her breath was harsh, wild, and she looked shocked. He suspected her head was swimming, every breath a jagged reminder of her submission.

"Breathe," he advised her, with certainty. "The more you hold your breath, the worse it is."

"I thought you'd never experienced it," she snapped at him, furiously.

All he did was stare at her, his gaze dark, one brow raised.

And she...quailed. "I didn't... I'm sorry... I just..."

"With every syllable you utter, you're making it worse," he said with a soft menace that he could *see* go through her like a cattle prod. "Safeword or be silent. Those are your choices."

She wisely chose to be silent. Conrad eyed the placement of the clamps critically, then moved around behind her so he could grip her cuffed wrists, making sure his grip jostled her breasts so the clamps would remind her they were there.

Rory hissed at the sensation.

"Actions have consequences," he told her, his face and voice severe. "If I ask you to do something and you disobey me, that would normally simply...be life. People will do and say whatever they like, after all. But this is a scene. You and I have decided that I have the authority over your surrender."

Her lips were parted, her eyes gloriously bright, as she gazed back at him with beautiful apprehension.

"And you may not understand this now, Rory, but I'm going to tell you the real truth about how to choose dominants to match your submission. It's not how they make you come, because the truth is, anyone can do that. You just did it yourself."

He leaned in close and put his mouth at her ear. "The true measure of a man, in particular a dominant, is how he enforces the agreed upon boundaries. If I allow you to break my rules, how would you respect me enough to truly surrender yourself to me?"

Conrad ran his teeth over the tattoo on her shoulder, pleased when goose bumps followed and her whole body heated up. "If I permit your disobedience, that gives you the power and if you wanted the power, you wouldn't be submitting in the first place. If you didn't crave discipline, your body wouldn't react the way it does under the circumstances." He reached down and stroked his way between her legs, tugging gently on her piercing until she made a rich little sound of need. "And your body is already an addict, Rory."

He propelled her forward, then turned, sitting down on the bench and tipping her over his lap. He knew how out of control this must have felt for her, and yet he was distinctly controlling her at the same time. Because her hands were caught behind her back, and her breasts would feel extra full and aching with the clamps on. He hung her over his knee so that gravity tugged on her breasts and intensified that sensation and she had no choice but to stay where he put her.

Completely in his hands.

Conrad smoothed a hand over her round pert ass. "You told me you've never been spanked, and I'm afraid that you will find this quite painful. I want you to remember, that's the point."

She stiffened and kicked a little. He moved a leg over both of hers, to trap her into place, and he could feel her fight that.

"Yellow," she cried out.

"Are you telling me to pause because you're actually overwhelmed, Rory?" he asked her, his hand on her ass no longer moving. He went still, but he kept her where she was. "Or because you're apprehensive?"

"I don't... I don't want to be spanked."

His hand trailed over her ass again, while his other one held her hands against the small of her back to remind her that he was the one keeping her there. Right where he wanted her.

"I'll give you points for honesty." And somehow, he kept from laughing at her predicament. "But is this about what you want or about what I want?"

"I don't know." She sounded fierce and furious. "Something about boundaries and discipline and whether or not I'll respect you. I feel like I respect you enough already."

"You're attracted to me," he agreed. "Drawn to me, even. But respect? I don't think so."

"But—"

"Enough talking." He traced his way down the dark furrow of her ass and beneath, the hungry wet clench of her pussy. "You feel wet and needy to me, Rory. Are you still yellow?"

He felt her fight, and then submit. He felt the shudder go through her and then she relaxed against him, and he thought he had never wanted another woman more.

"I'm green, Sir," she whispered.

Conrad rewarded her by tracing his finger through her wetness, circling around her desperate clit. Then he returned to the task at hand.

"I'm going to spank you five times." He kept his voice appropriately stern and authoritative. "Because you're brand-new, I'm going easy on you with this low, paltry number. You may thank me."

"Thank you," she gritted out, not sounding remotely thankful.

He bit back a grin. If there was anything on this earth better than a grumpy submissive trying to prepare herself for a punishment she both wanted and hated, he didn't know what it was.

He gripped her ass, hard. "Pardon? Thank you, who?"

"Sir," she wheezed.

He began to rub her, then, roughly, covering both ass cheeks as he got her blood moving.

"I want you to count, Rory. If you lose count, I'll start over. After each blow, you will say 'one, thank you, Sir. Two, thank you, Sir.' And so on. Do you understand?"

She was wriggling, slightly. He could see her shiver, then flush. And her ass was already reddening beneath the rough treatment he was giving it, which made him imagine how lovely it would look with a few handprints.

He could feel his own elevated pulse in his cock, but that was part of the fun.

"Yes, Sir," Rory whispered.

"You can make all the noise you want," he assured her. "That, too, is a gift. No matter how much it hurts, or how much you scream, you will still count. Is that understood?"

"Y…yes, S—"

And before she could really finish that sentence, he spanked her.

Hard.

CHAPTER EIGHT

HE ACTUALLY HIT HER.

Spanked her.

And it hurt like hell.

Rory jerked in his hold, though it was pointless. He was holding her bound hands against her back, pressing her down into his knee. And his leg was over her feet, so she couldn't kick.

Pain exploded through her like a bright, sharp wave.

And when she jerked, those horrible clamps bit hard into her nipples, so she was strung out somewhere between the pain in her breasts and the sharper, hotter pain in her butt.

For a narrow, impossible length of time that could easily have been forever, everything was pain. Everything was that endless, encompassing wave, washing through her, over her—

This was *awful*. What was she *doing*? Why the hell had she not only gone out of her way to make this happen, but had enthusiastically participated—

"Was that a free one?" came his cool, maddening voice from above. "Just practice? Or are you counting?"

Rory wanted to kill him. Her eyes were blurry with pain and fury, and she opened her mouth to tell him exactly what she thought of him. But his hand was on her ass. Right where he'd spanked her, and it hurt, but then again, there was something else threaded in there beneath the pressure of his palm.

She took a breath instead of swearing at him, and when she did, she could feel all the same things she already did. That bright, painful place where he'd spanked her. The teeth of those clamps making her nipples feel hot and glaring, but also...him.

That big hand, hot against her ass. His strong thighs beneath her, and the leg holding her in place. The fact of his clothing against her nakedness, adding to it all, making her skin feel even more sensitive.

And that was different, somehow, to think about him. To *feel* him, and that impossibly gorgeous body of his, so hard and toned. It didn't change the pain, or make it better, but it made it bearable.

"One, thank you, Sir," she managed to get out, though her voice was choked.

"Next time louder, please," he said, as if he was a professor somewhere, asking for a different font size on a boring paper.

That struck her as ridiculous. Though really, no more ridiculous than the fact she was naked and trussed up like a turkey, and not because she'd been kidnapped or taken against her will—no. This was worse.

She had *chosen* to be here. And just now, she'd reinforced that choice.

For some reason, that made something in her seem to yawn open, then. Wide and dizzying.

And almost unutterably raw.

Smack.

He hit the other cheek, and it was the same. Worse, almost.

That bright bloom of sharpness, the awful burn of it. Rory knew better than to jerk the way she had before, but she did it anyway. And it had the same result, so she yelped in reaction, not sure what to do in all that confusion of pains. Should she try to move away from that slap or away from the persistent ache in her nipples?

It was like she was trapped in the tumble of it, the pull, and then there was his hand again, rubbing the ass cheek he just slapped.

Making it better. Making it worse. Somehow taking all that confusion and smoothing it, not away, but down through her body to make her clit seem to glow.

With a hunger she was surprised didn't make her implode, there and then.

"If I have to tell you to count again, Rory," came his implacable, ruthless voice, "I will double the amount to ten."

"Two, thank you, Sir," she forced herself to say, though there was something in her throat. She felt thick and agonized. Somehow both hideously connected to everything that was happening to her and as if she was across the room, watching him spank her.

All the while her clit pulsed, sending a different sensation rolling through her, until it all mixed together and was *too much*—

The next time he spanked her, it was exactly the same spot as the first. He did it again on the other side. She did her best to count.

Each wallop was worse. While inside her, everything was chaos and that rawness, too big, too tight, *too much*.

She didn't realize that she was sobbing until she felt the tears on her cheeks. And that only made her cry harder.

"Stop tensing," Conrad said, his voice descending as if from on high somewhere. Dispassionate, disengaged.

And even that seemed to work in her like heat, going directly to her pussy and sharper into the pain.

Rory tried to make her body obey her. She strained against the cuffs, too aware as she sobbed of that stiff collar around her neck.

She thought, then, *there is no part of my body he's not in control of right now. There is no part of me that doesn't feel* every single thing *he's doing, and he knew it. He knew what this would do—*

But that last slap was cruel.

He hit her low on her ass so that the reverberation lit her up, everywhere. From that collar to the clamps to the cuffs, and her poor, red ass, because she could feel it. Sharp and bright and painful.

"Five," she somehow made herself get out, though she was sobbing so hard she was surprised she could form words at all. "Thank you."

And she wasn't sure she could get the last bit out. She wasn't sure... But there was something about the pain. About that rawness inside her. If she focused, on him, it wasn't like it went away, but it felt less overwhelming. "Sir. Thank you, Sir."

She thought she heard him murmur something, probably *good girl*, or some other such thing that should have outraged her.

But it didn't. She felt scraped clean, a jangle of sensation she couldn't quite sort through. Especially when everything was tipping all over itself, again.

Rory hardly recognized that she was on her feet again, because Conrad was the one doing all the work. Holding her and moving her around as if she was some kind of doll.

A notion that should have appalled her, deep into her core.

But instead, it had the opposite effect. Because his hands were big and he knew how to hold her. And she went with him willingly enough—or more to the point, it didn't occur to her to resist—as he took her back to that archway. She was trying to figure out how to breathe in a way that she didn't set off that same chain of sensation—collar, cuffs, clamps, and ass.

And her greedy, impossible clit.

Though there was so much noise inside her that, after a moment, she couldn't separate one sensation from another. It was too complicated to pull one strand from the next.

There was nothing but that noise, everywhere.

Except him.

Conrad was the center of everything, still and strong. Stern. Unmovable.

Rory focused on him. She looked at him in that huge mirror. His dark blond head to the black clothes he wore that made him look dark and dangerous, but not nearly as much as he really was. The way the floor seemed to rise to meet him where other men simply stood. The more she centered herself on him, the more she felt less like one great cacophony.

The more she felt, instead, like she was in a kind of mountain pass with noise on all sides, but Conrad there as the horizon.

And the more she concentrated on him like the sky, the more she felt all the noise…combine. Into the greedy pulse in her clit, as if all the other things— the pain and the noise, the fear and the delight—was fuel for it.

It was only when he pulled those chains closer, the ones she'd been doing her best to forget, that Rory realized she hadn't bothered to look at herself yet. She'd only been studying Conrad in that reflection.

She looked...like an extraordinary mess. Her face was red and blotchy. Her eyes were swollen. But that collar around her neck kept her chin up, and there was something about that, about the way it pressed against her throat, that streaked straight through her, to pool in her pussy. Her breasts looked obscene, her brown nipples clamped tight, and the more she concentrated on them the more the jagged edges of the clamps seem to dig in.

But then it all got worse, because Conrad was attaching the delicate little chain between the clamps to those chains. And then pulling on the slack until she yelped.

And when his gaze returned to hers, she felt it like another smack against her ass. Except this time, it seemed to hit her everywhere.

"Perfect," he said, looking as if he was enjoying himself thoroughly.

He left her standing there, and she watched in the mirror as he went behind her and picked up a chair with a high back. She began to breathe, sharp and heavy, as he set that chair up in front of her. He eyed the chains again and made some adjustments.

"You're doing very well, little one," he told her as he worked. "Now you get your reward. There'll be pain, of course, but I think you'll find that as it mixes with pleasure, it creates its own cocktail. I suspect you will find it addictive."

She was afraid she already did and, for the first time, was glad that she wasn't allowed to talk and tell him so. Conrad finished with the chains and moved to her face. He studied her expression, then wiped the water from beneath her eyes.

It amazed her how much she craved his touch. How the tenderness seemed to mix itself up with a dull ache in her nipples. How it turned into something molten as it sank into her pussy and made her clit seem to swell.

"You don't have to do anything," he said, so stern, so commanding. "If I want you to do something, I'll tell you. Unless I do, assume that everything is precisely as I want it to be. I don't want you to help. I don't want you to do anything at all but surrender yourself into my hands. Can you do that?"

Rory didn't know the answer to that. She didn't know what he was talking about—which she assumed, at this point, was part of why he'd said it. She didn't know anything, but she knew that there was really only one response.

Because the idea of surrender didn't make her want to cry any longer.

"Yes, Sir," she said, and whatever uncertainty there was inside her, it seemed to flip over into something like joy when his mouth crooked in one corner.

"Good girl," he said.

And then his navy blue gaze was all fire.

He moved her back a few steps, bringing the chair with him. She stood there, aware of the chains connecting her to the ceiling, but not sure why. Conrad straddled the chair, facing her.

Then, his gaze hard on hers, he unzipped his trousers.

And Rory thought she had never been so excited for a glimpse of a man's cock in all her life.

But his took her breath away.

Because he was huge.

He held her gaze while he stroked himself, grabbing his own thick length in his fist. The way he moved that fist made her think that he was doing nothing so much as preparing yet another tool to torture and tempt her.

Rory's mouth watered.

Conrad reached into his back pocket and pulled out a condom packet, and then she watched him roll a condom into place with the same brutal efficiency.

She couldn't quite understand why watching this was charging around inside her, more thrilling than it should have been. When it was just a cock. A condom.

But then again, it wasn't *just* anything. It was Conrad.

He sat down in the chair, then pulled her over him. So that, if her arms had been free, she could have gripped the back of the chair as he settled her down on his lap.

But as he pulled her down to him, she felt the resistance from the chains attached to her nipple clamps. The bite. She sucked in a breath.

Conrad's eyes blazed. His hard, wicked hands held her hips and positioned her where he wanted her, so that she could feel the whisper of his cock-head against the outer lips of her pussy.

"Stop helping," he ordered her, and even with his cock out, clearly about to enter her, he sounded… exactly the same. Cool. Remote.

She shuddered.

"You're a fuck toy, Rory," he said, the way other men might read love poetry. "You're a tight, hot pussy I'm going to use to get myself off. You don't have to do anything at all but take it."

Those words tumbled through her, leaving marks she couldn't identify. They could have been wounds, badges of honor, or new tattoos she would wear proudly—but all of them felt like fire. Conrad gripped her, his fingers digging into her ass, and then he slammed her down onto his cock. Sheathing himself fully in one hard thrust.

Rory came in a delicious, almost terrifying rush.

But that didn't stop him. He lifted her and then he slammed her down again.

Over and over.

That first orgasm was vicious, thorough. It about

knocked her out, but there was too much happening for her to let that happen, to fully fall off that edge.

Every time he slammed her down hard, he buried his cock completely inside of her, and each time he was almost too big. So big, she thought it might have hurt if she hadn't been quite as wet as she was. The fact that he had neither checked, nor made certain, made something thorny and bright unfurl inside of her.

And some part of her wished it had hurt a little, so she could revel in that.

He was absolutely true to his word. Conrad held her tightly and levered her up and down, over and over, creating the rhythm he wanted.

The truth was that Rory couldn't have helped if she'd wanted to. Her toes touched the floor, but they had no purchase because he kept lifting her up and slamming her down as he pleased.

And those chains were demonic.

Because every time he was thrust fully inside her, the chains from the ceiling tugged on her nipples. Just enough to make those clamps bite at her, as if they were new.

Her wrists were still bound behind her back, so she was nothing but an offering to him. A fuck toy, as he'd said, and the more those words careened around inside her, the more she felt them like his mouth on her clit.

Her breasts were thrust forward in this position

and the way he was holding her, arching her back, she could do absolutely nothing but feel the twin wallop of his cock so deep inside her and that bright tension in her nipples.

The second time she came, she screamed.

But Conrad kept going, fucking her deep and hard, giving no quarter.

His eyes were so dark and that stern expression had given way to pure intensity.

His fingers dug deep into her ass cheeks, pulling them apart as he lifted and dropped her, and that added to it. A wicked little stretch where she least expected it, and somewhere in there, between all those points of pain and the relentless onslaught of wild orgasms, the pressure at her throat and her bound arms, the way her toes kissed the floor but never held, Rory felt herself...bloom.

It was almost as if she lost track of herself, even though she had never been more aware of every square inch of her body than she was now.

She was more aware of Conrad. His cock like a weapon, like a blessing, hard and huge and something like magic as he worked it in and out of her, never in any kind of rhythm that she could anticipate. Never anything she could get used to.

And there was a point at which she could no longer tell if she was coming or about to come. It was all coming, it seemed to her, and something far better and brighter than a mere orgasm.

The more she simply let it happen, the more it happened. The more she seemed to feel herself spin out and fall back into all the ways he held her—collar and cuffs, clamps and his cock, the more she felt like herself.

But when she thought of herself, she thought of him. As if he amplified her. Enhanced her. As if in that place where his cock was too deeply buried in her and she was too wide-open to bear, they were the same.

Rory came again at that thought, in a bright, delirious wave of forever, and then he held her there. He kept her down hard on his cock, then held her there while she jerked and moaned. Something flashed, dark and wicked, over his austere, beautiful face.

And then she felt him tug at those clamps. But this time, he removed them. She opened her mouth to thank him, but that was when a new, different kind of searing pain shot through her, burning up from her nipples, connecting to all the other sensations inside her, and hurtling her into a deeper, harder abyss.

"That's the blood coming back," Conrad told her, his voice still completely unaffected by what he was doing, which only made the way she was falling apart worse.

Or better.

And then he wrapped his arms around her, holding her cuffed hands to the small of her back. He held her and he fucked her, hard, so that everything was that pain, and everything was pleasure, and she was nothing but a lush streak of sensation, existing only for every deep, life-altering stroke of his cock.

Rory thought that part lasted forever.

She wanted it to.

And when Conrad finally came, she joined him once more. Then she felt herself disappear completely, with the oddest, strangest notion that she had never been more desired. Or more beautiful. Or more appreciated.

Or more inexplicably safe than she was in his arms.

CHAPTER NINE

CONRAD FELT SOMETHING LIKE...shaken.

Rory was slumped in his lap, her head against his shoulder. He was still deep inside her, and there was a part of him that wanted nothing more than to simply stay right there.

Forever, something in him whispered.

But that was foolish. He almost laughed, because that was the response of the newbie that she was, not the seasoned master he'd been for years.

It was endorphins, he lectured himself. Not emotions.

He should know the difference.

Conrad pushed away the clamps and the chains that still dangled down around them, though they were no longer connected to her flesh. Then he angled Rory back, so he could check the state of things. Of her.

Her eyes were closed and her lips parted, but her color was good. When he reached down to test her nipples, she murmured something, but he couldn't tell if it was pleasure or protest—both, perhaps, at this point. She should have been good and sensitive.

He lifted her off him, then switched places with her to deposit her in the chair. He dealt with the condom, then tucked himself away. And when he turned back, he took a moment, because his chest tightened almost unbearably at the sight of her.

Conrad had thought she was remarkably pretty when he'd first seen her, standing in his chapel, surrounded by his equipment—even though she shouldn't have been in that room. But now she was so much more than that. She was naked, save for the cuffs that she held to one side, that still pushed her breasts forward as she lolled there in the chair. And that play collar around her neck like his hand.

Like a brand.

Like a wish, something in him offered.

He ignored that. Or tried.

He squatted down next to the chair, and had the uncharacteristic urge to push her hair back from her face when it didn't need any rearranging, but he didn't. Because somehow that felt tender in a way he never was in these moments, and he didn't think it would be wise to follow that urge to its conclusion. He released her hands instead, pulling her wrists in front of her so he could rub them and make sure that her circulation was as it should be. Because his duty to her was not about his feelings here. Her physical well-being came first.

"Any numbness?" he asked her, his voice quieter than before.

She murmured something vaguely negative, her head still lolling back against the chair and her eyes still shut.

And his cock stirred all over again at the sight of her in nothing but a collar he'd put on her.

Stop, he told himself.

He made himself remove the collar, and then he stroked her neck as well. He felt for her pulse, making certain that while she was likely depleted after the intensity of the scene, that was all she was. When he was satisfied, he stood and scooped her up into his arms.

And the tight feeling in his chest intensified as she nestled into him, one hand coming up to rest just over his heart.

He was sure she could feel it kicking. Hard.

Conrad carried her through the living room, grabbing a throw from the back of an armchair as he went, then continuing straight on through the French doors and out into his garden.

The night was cooler than before, so he draped the throw over her as he carried her down the stairs, taking her beneath the thick canopy of trees that protected them both from prying eyes and the buildings looming overhead. He took her over to his gazebo, where a hot tub waited and comfortable, cozy chairs and chaises ringed it. He settled her on a chaise, tucking the throw around her.

Her eyes stayed shut, so Conrad tended to the practicalities. He made sure the water was bubbling hot. He checked her vitals once again, then left her for a moment. He returned with a glass of water and a small plate with a selection of sweet and salty snacks, placed them down on the table beside her, and picked her up again. Then he settled them both down on that chaise, with her resting against his chest, between his legs, and cuddled up warm and safe.

For a long time, she dozed in and out of whatever space she was in. Conrad relaxed against the chaise, stroking her hair with one hand and opting not to pay too close attention to the perfect weight of her there against his chest. The way her face fit there in the crook of his neck. Or the way she held her hands up in front of her, clasping them together, right there against his heart.

He had always had the courage of his convictions—maybe to a fault—but that didn't matter here. It couldn't. She was brand-new to the scene, and there was no way to tell how she would feel on the other side of her first BDSM experience. Some new submissives retreated into shame and self-recrimination, afraid of their own desires and the pleasure they'd received from things they were afraid to name in the light. Others went in the other direction, so desperate for more of that same sweet drug of submission that they took any risk to get another hit.

Whatever route Rory took, the last thing Conrad needed to do was start acting like he had aspirations to be her master when all she needed was a dominant for the night. An introduction, not a claiming.

He couldn't believe that word was in his head.

Conrad shook his head in the dark, wishing once again that his friends could see this. He could hear Dorian laughing from a thousand kilometers away in Berlin.

Eventually, Rory stirred. He saw her eyes flutter. She screwed up her face and stretched a little and then she lifted her head, looking around as if she hadn't the faintest clue where she was.

"We are out in my garden," he told her, before she became alarmed. "Drink some water. Eat something."

Rory pushed herself into a more upright position, slowly. Very, very slowly, as if she wasn't entirely certain her body still worked in the same way in had before. Conrad watched her closely, seeing the instant she started remembering what had happened tonight—because her cheeks began to look flushed again.

But she obeyed him, no doubt still stumbling her way back out of subspace and into her own head again. She picked up the glass of water and gulped at it, greedily. Then she ate a little, looking almost guilty.

And only when she'd demolished the plate he'd brought for her and drank the rest of the water, did she pull even farther away from him to wrap that throw even more tightly around her.

"Where are my clothes?" she asked, her voice rough and sleepy.

Conrad stayed where he was, lounging there with one knee up and one leg straight. He reached over and helped himself to that hair of hers, so glossy and so silky to the touch.

"Inside where you left them, I would imagine."

She nodded, vigorously. "Well. I guess I'd better—"

"Rory."

She stilled at the sound of her name in his mouth, and he liked that far too much. He reminded himself that this wasn't about him. He had a duty here. And it wasn't to satisfy himself as much as it was to make certain that *she* was satisfied, in every possible way, so that she would have a healthy introduction to the lifestyle. Safe, sane, and consensual, the way it was meant to be.

He was more than happy to lecture others on how they ought to treat newcomers to the scene, but he had never felt this invested before. In her, not the scene.

In her, full stop.

"There are two parts to a scene," he told her, getting his lecture on again, because that felt like solid ground. "Both equally important. One part gets all the attention because it usually has equipment, and vanilla people are afraid of it. All those scary whips and chains. But this part is called aftercare, and it's necessary."

"Aftercare," she echoed him, and he knew that particular note in her voice now. She sounded lost.

He tugged her into his arms again and held her there against his chest, making a soothing sort of sound.

"Aftercare," he confirmed. "Sometimes it involves attending to bruises or marks, depending on how rough and exciting things got. And that's important, but the most important component is an emotional resetting."

"You don't have to worry about me getting emotional," she told him, very seriously. "I don't do that."

"Everyone does that." Conrad found himself resting his chin on her head because it fit there so nicely, as if… But no. He wasn't going to analyze it. "Remember what I told you. The point of this is intimacy. You can't have intimacy without emotion, or sustained intensity without vulnerability. Aftercare allows you to process intimacy, emotion, and vulnerability, while we slowly regain our equilibrium."

She smelled like him now, and he wasn't going to pretend he didn't enjoy that. He did. But he also felt her harsh intake of breath. "We?"

"Of course, *we*," he said, and he didn't sound the way he should. Aloof. Unmarked. "I took you apart—I need to make sure that I put you back together. That's my job. And it's also my job to protect you. To make sure that you're in the right state of mind to go rejoin the world after what happened between us."

"Oh," she said, an odd note in her voice. "This is just a mandatory thing, then."

"It should be mandatory, yes," Conrad said darkly. "Of course, it varies, because people have different needs and philosophies. The main purpose of aftercare is to make sure that everyone is okay on every level."

She shifted and looked up at him, her gaze vulnerable and direct. "Are you okay?"

It took him back, though maybe it shouldn't have. But he couldn't remember the last time anyone had asked him that. Normally, in club situations, the submissive might share some feelings—usually threaded through with thanks and some angling for a repeat—and then they would both go their separate ways.

But there was something about Rory, damn her. And the solemn way she regarded him, as if she knew more about the state of his heart than he did.

"I am," Conrad replied. He wanted to say, *more okay than I've been in some time*, but he didn't.

He wouldn't.

It was only when his heart started beating a little

too hard that he realized that one of her hands was stretched out over his chest as if she was holding it in her hand.

"Come," he said, feeling grumpy with all the things he felt, but shouldn't. "Let's get you in that hot tub."

She frowned as he shifted her off him. But when he stood up and walked over to the large tub, she followed him. The tub was done in wood so that it seemed almost to blend into the garden all around. The water bubbled quietly, the soft light inside the tub illuminating the benches that lined its walls and sending a sweet little light dancing around the gazebo.

A man liked to see who he brought out here in the dark. Especially when she was as perfect as Rory.

He tested the water with his fingers, then nodded for her to climb in.

She continued to frown at him. "Are you...giving me a bath like a toddler? Sir?" Her frown deepened. "Do I still have to call you *Sir*?" When he only eyed her, she let out a small sound of frustration. "Do you want me to call you *Sir*?"

Rory continued to frown at him, so Conrad set about removing his own clothes. And watched, torn somewhere between amusement and sheer lust as she...gaped at him.

"I'm glad you appreciate me, little one," he rumbled at her when he finally stripped off. Her eyes had

dropped to his cock, which was already ready for another round. "But I do need you to get into that tub."

She gulped and then obeyed him, climbing into
the hot tub and making a sound of appreciation as
she slid into the water.

Conrad followed, sinking into the heat and sitting
on one of the built-in benches. Rory stood before
him, her breasts above the waterline as she tied her
hair into a knot on top of her head. And then she sub-
merged herself to her chin, letting out a deep, long
sigh that seemed to come from the very center of her.

"Tell me about that clit ring," he said, idly, as he
lounged on the bench across from her. "You don't
have any other piercings. Okay, your ears. But nothing else quite so interesting."

She moved her arms in the water, as if feeling the
weight of it against her fingers. "I guess I wanted it
because it seemed cool. You know, a conversation
piece, anyway. It's always a surprise. And usually
a good one."

"That's not the real reason."

Her gaze flew to his, then back to the water.
"No, that's not the real reason, but I didn't think it
worked."

"Because the real reason is…?"

"I wanted to feel," she said, her voice cracking a
little on that last word, her gaze trained on the surface of the water. "I wanted to be…more. I thought
it would help."

"But it didn't."

"It was a conversation starter." Her smile was rueful. "It let me think that I was kinky and mysterious, I guess. But until tonight, it was really just jewelry."

He didn't think there was a single part of her that was *just* anything, but he didn't say that. It would be too much, surely. Too dangerous tonight.

"I like it," he told her instead.

She smiled, though the smile seemed fragile. "Whatever else it is or was supposed to do, I like it because it's wearable art." Her gaze moved over his face, searching for something. "Do you want to know why I really moved to Paris?"

It surprised him not only that he did, indeed, want to know—but that the wanting was an intense thing that seemed to grow inside him as she gazed at him. He restricted himself to a nod.

"I love art," she said. Shyly, he thought, as her smile began to look self-deprecating. "When I went to the Musée Rodin, I cried. I always thought that I could stare at a Manet for a day or two, and at the Musée d'Orsay, I have. And then I go back to my flat and take pictures for social media and pretend they're the same, when I know they're not. I can't draw or paint or even take a good photograph of anything, unless I'm in it. But I love art all the same."

She kept her gaze on the bubbling, frothing water. "If you can't make art, you can make your life art, I guess."

"Rory." Her name had sounded so silly to him when he'd met her. Such a strange diminutive of the far more beautiful—and apt—Aurora. But now it tasted sweet on his tongue and to his ears it might as well have been a song. "You are the art. You don't have to make it. You are it."

She lifted her head, her lovely eyes dark. A different sort of sheen in them.

And when she smiled, it was like dawn breaking, bright and hopeful.

"Do you think it's possible that your whole world can change when you least expect it?" she asked.

"That's the only way the world changes," Conrad replied. Maybe a little too gruffly.

And he shouldn't let himself do this. He was good at the usual banter. The usual game. Easy conversation, nothing too demanding, keeping everything light and easy so it was no hardship at all to cross back over to the real world.

"Come here," he said, his voice stern as if it was an order. Though he feared it was something far closer to a request.

And she did, skimming her hands over the water as she crossed the tub. When she reached him, she stood there before him, achingly beautiful, her gaze open and her mouth soft.

Conrad reached over and pulled her close, so he could curve his hands around her neck and rest his thumbs on either side of her throat. He could feel her pulse kick into high gear—and his did the same, to match.

And then he did his job.

"You seem to spend a large quantity of your life doing things so that others see you in a certain way. But you can't curate the best parts of life, Rory. You have to live them."

"You live in a converted a Gothic church," she whispered, because of course she was going to argue. "Talk about a curated life."

"Answer me this," he said, because this was what he did. He opened them up and they told him how they were broken, and then he fixed them. Even if he couldn't seem to recall the face of another woman, just then. There was only Rory. "What would you do if you had nothing to prove?"

She jerked in his grip as if he'd spanked her again. The look in her dark eyes was something like betrayal. "What would you do?"

He held her gaze. "I'm doing it. I don't have anything to prove."

"Really?" she asked, too solemnly for his peace of mind. She shook her head. "You keep a dungeon in a church, Conrad."

"I'm perfectly comfortable with my life, Rory," he gritted out, and he knew as he said it that it wasn't as true as it should have been.

Worse, he thought she knew it, too.

"What is…" She pulled in a breath, and he could

hear that it was ragged. He could see emotion in her eyes. And more, he could see the reflection of himself, not quite as composed as he should've been. "What is this, Conrad?"

"You tell me," he said, in a voice so low he hardly heard it.

But she did. Because something shifted, there on her pretty face. She smiled, which was bad enough.

And she leaned forward, as if pushing herself farther into his grip.

Or deeper into your heart, something in him contradicted.

And then she ruined everything, and kissed him.

CHAPTER TEN

SHE HADN'T MEANT to do that.

Or maybe she had, Rory thought, in the last seconds that she was even capable of thought, because kissing Conrad was like magic.

That stern mouth of his was so hard. So impossibly ruthless and beautiful. And even though she felt him stiffen, he kissed her back.

And of all the things that had happened since she'd met him, all of it so confronting, life-altering, and impossible to get her head around—this was almost...sweet.

Or it would have been, if she couldn't feel the tremor in the air between them. The hush of anticipation. That little spark that reminded her that what was between them was fire, not sugar.

She capitalized on the little moment before the flames kicked in. She kissed him because she could. Because she'd wanted to since almost the first moment she'd laid eyes on him. Because he was letting her.

Because he tasted like everything she'd ever wanted.

And then he made a low noise, grasped her head firmly between his hands, and took over.

And all that sweetness skyrocketed into something else.

Something spectacular.

Conrad claimed her mouth, boldly. Unapologetically.

He wrapped his arms around her, and Rory clung to him, kissing him back as he rose from the water and let it cascade all over them.

"Hold on," he growled against her mouth.

An order. An invitation. She didn't care which—she just wrapped her legs around his torso and clung on for dear life as he carried her out of the tub and over to the chaise they'd been lying on before.

He bore her down, coming down on top of her. Hard.

She could feel everything. His chest, crushing her into the chaise with that delirious weight of his. The wetness of their skin, cool against the summer night. The faint sprinkling of hair on his chest that seemed specifically put there to tease her poor, sensitive nipples.

He was so hard, so heavy, and best of all, she could feel his cock between them. It pressed hard against her belly, and Rory felt herself begin to shudder.

As if he didn't have to be inside her to make her pussy so wet and hot, or the rest of her start to shake. As if this was enough.

Still he kissed her. Again and again, as if he couldn't get enough.

The way she couldn't get enough.

Rory kissed him, filled with thanks and emotion and art. All the parts of her she'd trotted out into the light and let him see. All that vulnerability and hope.

She kissed him as if her life depended on it.

As if she'd been living all this time completely unaware what her life was supposed to be, but his mouth on hers had revived her. Renewed her.

She'd started this night in the shadows outside his house and now she was here in his garden with him on top of her, and neither one of them was quite who she'd imagined they were when she'd come here.

And Rory knew that she would never be the same again.

"Reach up and grab the chair," Conrad ordered her, that stern voice of his as authoritative as ever, if lanced through with the same fire she felt burn in her. "And hold on for dear life."

Rory thought her heart might actually claw its way out of her own chest. She kept pulling in breaths as best she could, but they sounded like sobs.

But, of course, she obeyed him. She didn't think twice about it—a far cry from how she'd started this evening with him. She reached up and grabbed hold of the slats, exulting in the way that made her back arch, so she could present her breasts to him. Because she knew he liked that.

Rory thought a person could spend a lifetime trying to please a man like this.

And loving every moment of it.

Because the way Conrad expressed his pleasure made her entire body quake, a new kind of hard-edged excitement that was already pulsing through her again.

While she'd been following his last order, he'd found another condom and was already rolling it on.

Conrad knelt above her on the chaise, then, and the look on his face was…savage. A kind of storm crashed through his eyes, but there was still that intense, glorious focus on his face.

Something in her melted at that. At the evidence that even when she pushed him, she was safe.

He moved between her legs and reached over to one of the tables beside the chaise. He pulled something out, a small tube, and squirted something into his hand. As he warmed it between his palms, the look he narrowed on her was…pitiless.

Ruthless straight through, and this time, Rory understood that the fear that made her shiver was as much anticipation as it was joy.

Sheer, unadulterated joy, in the middle of something that she'd expected would only ever be a game of charades to her. In theory.

Rory had expected Conrad would make her feel what she had that first evening, up against his wall. She'd expected he would give her more of that pleasure. She hadn't anticipated that he would take so much in return.

Or that she would want so very, very badly to give it.

She felt as if something shook inside of her along a deep fault line she hadn't known was there, sending out earthquake after earthquake, but she didn't have time to worry about that. Not when all she had to focus on was him.

"How flexible are you?" Conrad asked, almost casually.

"Very," she replied. "I do yoga at least three times a week. When I remember."

The gleam in his eyes made her shiver.

"Put your ankles on my neck," he ordered her.

"Yes, Sir," she breathed.

And she didn't have to ask what name to use here. Not now.

She arched up from the chaise, using her grip on the slats behind her to help lift her hips. Then she slid her legs onto his shoulders, locking her ankles around his neck, as ordered. And then, for a moment, they were looking at each other down the length of her body.

Rory felt as if she was nothing but a display for his pleasure. A piece of art in a museum, pinned to a wall and helpless to do anything but accept that edgy stare of his. Maybe that was the only time paintings—she—came alive.

That idea made her clit begin to pulse, dangerously close to throwing her over the edge already.

Before he'd done a thing.

"Lovely," he murmured, as if he knew.

The way she imagined he would always know.

With one hand, Conrad reached down and slid his hand over the curve of her ass. She could feel the slickness on his palm and understood with one shaky breath that he'd used whatever was in that tube to make them that way. And in the next breath, she could feel his slick, blunt fingers probing the tight entry to her ass.

"I told you earlier," he said, his voice not sounding precisely calm, but a distinct order all the same. "I want all of you."

She tried to breathe out, not wriggle away, but there was nowhere to go no matter what she did. She was trapped by her own position, locked into place, and she watched his face as he waited for her to accept that. For that rush of panic to ease a little, and a hot, red flush to take its place.

When it did, Conrad calmly worked one finger, then another, deep inside her ass.

It hurt at first. A sting and then a duller sensation that wasn't quite an ache. She moaned, not sure where the sound had come from—only that she needed to get it out. And it still stung.

But then, she suspected it was meant to.

Conrad looked even more savage and focused than before. He used the hand wrapped around her to lift her higher, so he could fit the broad head of his cock to her pussy.

His eyes found hers, as sensation pounded through her in time with his probing, demanding fingers.

"You can move your legs from my neck," he told her. "But I want them on my shoulders. Do you understand?"

"Yes," she panted. "Yes, Sir."

He bared his teeth in some semblance of a grin, wild and thrilling, and he slammed himself home.

And deep inside her at last, he pressed her down to the chaise, but more importantly, deeper against the fingers in her ass.

Sensation went through her like a bomb, too intense to catalog. Everything was him. Everything was Conrad and the way he took her in two places, making her entirely his.

Rory could do nothing at all but surrender.

Her legs were draped over his shoulders as he settled in, propping himself up with one hand, and began to teach her a deep, pounding, profoundly electrifying lesson about rhythm. Possession. And that the limits of her desire were his to push.

And hers to take.

Because every slick slide of his cock and his fingers made her…blossom.

Conrad thrust deep with his cock while retreating with his fingers, then reversed it. Over and over. Again and again, until she felt as if she was suspended between the two, penetrated and conquered and never in her life so beautifully taken.

Seen and sampled and claimed.

She felt as if with every thrust, pussy and ass, he made her new.

His free hand was next to her head, and then his mouth was on hers again, his tongue a new torment, as irresistible as the rest.

And she was coming again before she knew she meant to, or could.

Because Conrad filled her, and kept filling her. Her ass, her pussy, her mouth. He took all of her, demanding everything and taking more.

Rory lost any sense of herself. She was only sensation. She was only need.

He'd called her a fuck toy, and now she understood how glorious that was. How freeing and beautiful.

To be a receptacle instead of a sphinx. To give so much that it became her own kind of taking, there in the magic of this. He was in control, but she took back control and made it…this.

Joy.

Again and again, over and over, too much sensation that spilled over into a hint of *too much*, and then became joy.

All that perfect friction and rhythm, and the marvelous things her body could do with both.

With him.

Once again, she lost track of the difference between coming and coming down, between ramping up and falling over.

And when he came again, lifetimes later, she thought they both exploded—bursting apart into the night, like stars.

This time, Rory was wrecked in a different way.

There was the same slow surfacing, returning to her own body instead of the one they made together.

She drank another glass of water. She ate a bit more of the food he gave her from his own hand, and this time, he didn't lounge there like the Lord of the Manor. He didn't ask her questions or talk to her about rules and expectations.

Maybe there was nothing to say after something so profound.

That great, beautiful darkness that was in them both now. Part of them forever.

Rory kind of thought she'd grown new bones here tonight, and his name was etched on them all.

Neither one of them spoke, there on that chaise in the last of a night that had already lasted forever. In the hot tub again, he held her close and they soaked together like that until she started to get sleepy.

And when Conrad picked her up and took her out of the tub, then toweled her dry, Rory knew she had no choice.

She had to leave, and now.

The old version of her, the one who'd showed up here tonight, would have stayed. But then, she wouldn't have been as altered. The version of her who knew she could never go back to who she'd been knew that she had to take stock of…everything.

And she couldn't possibly do that when Conrad was in front of her, stealing all the light from the sky.

Even in the middle of the night.

"Thank you," she said, holding his gaze as he brought her into the house again. "You didn't have to let me in tonight. I'll never be able to thank you enough that you did."

Conrad only stared down at her, as imposing naked as he was fully clothed.

And she couldn't say anything else, because if she did, she feared that he would see far too much. When she knew that no matter what, she had to see herself first.

Maybe for the first time.

"I'm going to go now," Rory told him when he'd set her back down on her feet. Next to the chairs where they'd sat together what seemed like a lifetime ago. The floor where she'd knelt despite how much it had scared her. The little pile of the clothes that she hardly recognized, because she'd become a stranger.

His hand moved as if of its own accord and smoothed over her hair. "I'm not sure that's a good idea."

"Are you worried about me?" It hurt to sound dry. Arch and amused. But she had to start building back her walls, or how would she walk down a street? The sensory input would kill her within a few steps. "You don't need to be. I'm good. Really, Conrad."

She wasn't sure he believed her, not with the way he looked at her, all narrow and dark. But he only nodded, with his usual authority.

Maybe she wasn't the only one who needed to find her footing.

He insisted on calling her a car. And when it arrived, he led her outside, wearing nothing but a pair of lounging trousers, low on his hips. He stopped her when she went to climb in, once again with his hand in her hair.

Then he held it—and her. Possessively, she thought.

Like her hair was a kind of leash, and her body responded by melting all over again, as if it could never get enough of him.

Rory doubted that could change. How could it change? Even her bones felt new, and they melted, too.

She thought he was going to kiss her, but he didn't. He looked down at her, his mouth a stern, almost grim line. His gaze was harsher than she'd ever seen it and still, somehow, connected to all the parts of her he touched.

All the parts of her he'd changed.

"Be well," he told her, making it a command.

Then he let her go.

And Rory did the only thing she could.

She fled into what remained of the night, hoping that when dawn came, she would find herself whole.

CHAPTER ELEVEN

A WEEK AFTER that night, Conrad stood outside of one of Paris's most decadent, exclusive clubs. A place he was well-known, having spent so much time there over the years. He knew exactly how the night would unfold if he went inside. He could have his cock sucked within the first ten minutes, as an appetizer, as he worked out how he should further indulge himself.

But he couldn't seem to summon up the slightest bit of interest in going inside.

He'd thrown himself into work in the wake of that night with Rory and told himself that he hadn't had time to indulge his usual appetites. Now he did.

But he'd been staring at the secret door, conveniently placed down at the end of a dark alley, and couldn't quite bring himself to go in. His appetite wasn't for a buffet.

He told himself it was an aberration.

Because he had done everything he should have

done. He'd found her phone number and called two days later, to make sure she was still all right. It had been a strange, stilted conversation that had left him unsettled. Wound up with a bizarre energy he'd tried to work off in the gym.

I'm well, she'd said. *You told me to be well and I am.*

Miles and miles he'd run to try to dislodge those words from where they were stuck inside him, with no luck.

He'd thought a night out at his favorite club might do the trick.

But he didn't bother to go in. A week later, it was the same.

Two weeks after that, Conrad was forced to accept that he simply didn't want anyone else.

He came to this conclusion in the bright light of a late summer day, sitting in the office building that he walked to every morning from his own personal church. It was located in one of those lovely buildings that lined the Golden Triangle, where he could look out over Paris and be glad. La Tour Eiffel. The American Cathedral. The plush green trees that lined Avenue George V. And in the distance, Tour Montparnasse.

Usually having Paris at his feet was soothing.

But today he raked his hands through his hair, wondered what the hell had become of him, and called his best friend.

"I don't understand the issue," Dorian said after Conrad had laid out the scenario for him. Grudgingly, because still Rory felt like his. Only his. "So she's brand-new. So what. If you don't handle her, someone else will. How do you imagine you'll feel about that?"

"I'm not in the market for feelings," Conrad said darkly.

Dorian laughed. "You can control anything, brother. But not that."

Conrad sighed, glaring out at Paris and seeing only Rory. And the things he wanted, even when he knew better.

"The trouble is," he said, "even if I thought it was appropriate, I don't know if I have it in me."

There was a pause, then. Conrad could hear Berlin street traffic. The muffled sound of conversations in animated German.

"Listen," Dorian said after a moment. "Marie Jeanette wasn't a referendum on your life. I know that your narrative is that she changed, but she didn't, Conrad. She lied."

Of all the things he thought Dorian might have said, it wasn't that.

And Dorian wasn't finished. "She never wanted the things you did. She wanted a meal ticket. When's last time you saw her and Claude in any kind of scene? That's not part of their life."

"Many people take their play private," Conrad said. "Including, as an example, you."

He regretted it the moment he said it, given said private play involved *his sister* these days.

"But it's still a huge part of my life," Dorian said, then laughed at the expression on Conrad's face he must have sensed was there. "Though I will spare you the details."

"I have no idea what you're talking about," Conrad said dryly. "My understanding is that you and Erika both took holy orders."

Dorian only laughed again. "Marie Jeanette didn't want to play, ever. Now she doesn't have to. She used you, you rightly scraped her off, and I don't think you should allow the memory of that situation to inform what you do now. You're allowed to care, Conrad. That's not a detriment to who you are as a dominant or as a man. It's what makes you both of those things."

Because, though his friend wouldn't say it, Dorian had never been among those who thought Conrad was heartless.

And it was with his best friend's words ringing in his ears, whether he wanted them to or not, that Conrad told his secretary to hold all his calls and cancel his appointments, because he was going out.

He assumed that Rory might be anywhere, really. The whole city was available to her, after all, since she went about cleaning people's houses. He assumed

she would be off intruding on the privacy of others—
and why did he now find that amusing?—but when
he went to her flat, the chatty man in the boulangerie
below was only too happy to inform him that Made-
moiselle Morton did not work on Tuesdays.

Conrad hadn't quite believed where the man had
said she was instead.

The truth of the matter was, he had never heard
of a *cat café*.

But when he stalked his way down the street and
to the very edge of her neighborhood, the evidence
was impossible to ignore. Sure enough, there was
a cat café.

A café. With cats.

And not merely a motif of cats, as he had convinced himself on the walk over.

But a café in which there were actual cats. Roam-
ing about.

Conrad wrenched open the door, looked inside,
and was not the least bit surprised to find Rory sitting at a café table, a coffee at her elbow, a white cat
with a smushed-in face in front of her and a giant
ginger one on her lap.

There were cats everywhere. They were covering
all the surfaces, climbing up and down trees made
of furniture, presumably put there for that purpose.

If you do this, a voice in him that might have been
himself all those years ago, flush with certainty after
ending things with Marie Jeanette, *you can never tell*

yourself later that you didn't know what you were walking into.

Because, when he stopped to think about it, of course Rory wouldn't be in a typical café, like every other tourist and Parisian. Of course, though she was in Paris, she was here.

Rory shifted in her chair, the enormously fat orange cat on her lap, and glanced over. And she didn't startle. She didn't look at all surprised. She kept her gaze on Conrad as if she'd been waiting for him to come.

That, too, felt very nearly inevitable.

He made his way to her table, distantly amazed that the place was doing a brisk business. All these people, gathered here to…pet the cats, apparently?

When he arrived at her side, he claimed the only empty chair—as the others were occupied, by cats— and sat down. And for a moment, he and Rory stared at each other. The cat in her lap stared too, and Conrad could not have said in that moment which heavy gaze on him was more disconcerting.

And this was all so deeply absurd, so comical and yet somehow perfectly Rory, that Conrad might have sat there forever.

But Rory shifted in her chair again, hugged the lummox of a cat in her lap closer still, and surprised Conrad completely by smiling.

It was like sunshine breaking through the clouds, when he knew it was a perfectly pleasant day outside.

He felt his chest tighten and resisted the urge to rub at the place where his heart seemed to beat triple time.

She was even more beautiful than he remembered, even here. Even though he found himself surrounded by animals, literally, mewling and butting up against his leg. He gazed down at the two below him, and they both flattened their ears—but stopped.

When he looked at Rory again, her smile had faded from her mouth, but was still there in her lovely eyes. It made them gleam.

"Conrad Vanderburg in a cat café," she said, and shook her head. "This must be a dream."

"It is certainly not *my* dream," he replied darkly.

And he couldn't help himself. He reached over and took her hand. Maybe because, once he did it, he wanted to see if it was still there.

That spark. That kick.

That impossible connection that had haunted him since the last time he'd seen her.

Nothing changed when he touched her. Neither one of them stood up, started yelling, or tipped over the table. There were still improbable cats, winding this way and that. But at the same time…everything changed.

He felt that *click* inside him. That bright edge. That space between them was only theirs, filled with desire and surrender, power and pleasure.

It was tempting to imagine that with a single touch, he could feel the truth of her. And of him.

That whether it was a simple touch of hands, or the darker games they'd played that night, it was all the same. And would always be the same.

God, how she tempted him.

"You came to find me," she said after a moment, her voice soft. And threaded through with something like wonder. "I have to tell you, I really didn't think you were going to do that."

"What happened between us was unusually intense," he said, gruffly. "I should have checked in on you sooner. In person."

She sighed a little and looked down at their hands. "To discharge your duties, of course."

Conrad felt that like a slap upside the head.

He had walked out of his office when he never, ever interrupted his workday. He'd been uninterested in carrying on with his usual club activities, because he simply didn't feel the need any longer. There was only this. There was only her.

And pretending otherwise was perilously close to the kind of lies he'd always detested.

But he needed to do his duty no matter what he wanted. For her, not him.

No one had ever said that duty was easy. Or that it gave anyone what they wanted. Hadn't he spent his life learning that lesson?

Why should this be any different?

"I have duties where you're concerned, whether you like it or not," he told her, keeping his gaze and voice stern.

He watched her melt at once. He watched her wriggle in her seat, then put the cat down to one side as if she needed to concentrate fully and totally on him.

Something he obviously approved of, he thought, as he felt his pulse drop down into his cock, then begin to drum.

"I introduced you into a lifestyle that means a great deal to me," he continued. "One of the things I feel strongest about is that brand-new submissives not be taken advantage of. By me or anyone else."

"Has someone taken advantage of me without my knowledge?" She laughed. "I understand that you must think I'm foolish in many ways, Conrad. But I'm a little more sturdy than you think. Or I wouldn't have taken myself off to live in a foreign country, all alone. And then stayed here, for a good year, taking care of myself."

"I don't think you're foolish," he said, still concentrating on the touch of her skin against his as their fingers twined. "Or if I do, I find myself charmed by it. But that's not the point."

She smiled again, more faintly this time. "I don't see why it couldn't be the point. Would it kill us if it was the point? For a minute or two?"

And he felt the weight of the past month, bearing

down on him, but still. She made him want to laugh. She always made him want to laugh. He compromised with a smile. "You know you're charming."

"*I* think I'm an endless delight," she said, and her nose wrinkled up a bit as she looked at him, her dark hair falling to one side. "It's what you think that remains a mystery."

"That's why I came to find you," Conrad said, very seriously. "Because above all else, it's important for you to explore who you are. To discover where submission can take you."

Her eyes were still gleaming. "Is it a bus ticket?"

Conrad ignored that because her hand was in his, and he wanted nothing more than to pick her up. Wrap her in his arms, put a collar around her neck, and call her his. But he had responsibilities. Hadn't he always? And whether he thought that was fair or unfair, it was reality.

And he would acquit his responsibilities appropriately, come hell or high water.

Even if that meant restraining himself around this woman who had somehow wrecked him in a single night.

That wasn't something she needed to know, he thought. Yet.

"I assume you've already experimented," he said, amazed how much it cost him to keep his voice even. Easy. "How were those experiences?"

Rory regarded him for a long moment, a frown gathering between her eyes. "Which experiences?"

He made his gaze direct. "Many submissives find their first experience overwhelmingly addictive. As you did not show up at my door again, I'm assuming you went off to find the power dynamics you now know you enjoy wherever you could. And this is Paris. There are clubs everywhere."

Conrad felt as if he was having an out-of-body experience. Because he'd had this conversation many times before. Usually when a submissive had found it impossible to let go of him and had required him to gently, if firmly, guide her in the right direction. To tell her that everything she was feeling was normal, but not as personal as she believed.

And never once in all the many times he'd had versions of this conversation had he ever found that the thought of that woman with another...

Infuriated him.

Even back in the early days with Marie Jeanette, when he'd been so certain that they were well suited to each other forever, he never felt like this. As if she truly belonged to him, in every possible way. Her soul, her sex, inarguably his.

He ordered himself to calm down.

Rory pulled her hand from his, and he didn't like that, either, but he let her go. This wasn't a scene.

Since when had he had trouble telling the difference?

"I think Paris sex clubs are your department, not mine," she said, suddenly unreadable. Her dark brown eyes were opaque. Even that lush mouth of hers was in a neutral line.

"Then I will be happy to be your guide," he told her, proud of how calm and generous he sounded.

She stared at him for so long that time, almost as if she was frozen into place, that he could no longer continue to block out the chirpy Japanese pop in the background.

But then Rory cleared her throat, and he forgot everything, save her. "My guide," she repeated.

"I can tell you which dominants would be good fits for you, and which would be best avoided," he said, still fighting to keep his voice as cool as possible.

He watched her swallow, as if her throat was tight. And he flashed back to that night. To the depths of her submission, her glorious surrender...and how the hell was he supposed to move on from that?

Because for all his talk about exchanges, he had never felt anything like that before—as if the two of them were entwined at all those different points of pain and power, pleasure and release, but one.

And then she'd kissed him. He'd lost control, and he wasn't sure he had ever felt so good, so right, in all his life.

But this was about her, not him.

And he tried to look...benevolent. Or whatever

she needed to see so that she knew she was safe. That she could experiment as she wished—as she should—and he would…wait, he supposed.

He would have to.

"I want to be very sure that I'm understanding you," Rory said, sounding a bit stiff. Her gaze was still unreadable. "You tracked me down. I know you have my phone number so you probably know where I live. But how could you possibly have found me here?"

"That was a rhetorical question," she said when he made as if to answer. And Conrad saw the flash of what he very much believed was temper in her eyes. "You had to want to find me. You had to go out of your way to do it. And now I'm finding it hard to get my head around the possibility that the reason you did that was so that you could…counsel me on how to fuck other men?"

Something shifted in him. Blood, maybe, heating up in a way that was not precisely wise. Or safe, for either of them.

"Perhaps you don't need my counsel," he managed to say without succumbing to the fire in him. "I'm sure you have puppies aplenty."

"I'm done with puppies." And her eyes flashed, telling him that it absolutely was temper. And quite a lot of it, if he wasn't mistaken. "That's why I like to come hang out with cats these days. And just to be perfectly clear, I haven't been trolling around in sex clubs, either. Because it turns out, Conrad, I don't really want to just…be tied up."

The only surprising part about this woman, he reminded himself, was that she never ceased to be surprising herself. He never had any idea what she would say. And he had never imagined that she would say something like that. He thought of how she'd melted. How she'd delivered herself into his hands, and come so beautifully—and so often—that memories of it still woke him in the night.

"I was under the impression that you loved being tied up," he said, trying to sound neutral.

She scowled at him, and even leaned forward. Were she his, she would have to account for that kind of aggression. Likely while getting spanked.

But he needed his cock to calm down, or he never would.

"I like it when you do it, you dumbass," she threw at him.

And he was so astonished he actually laughed, but that only made her madder. She started brandishing her finger at him, and he was…astounded, certainly. But captivated all the same.

"I don't need to experiment with submission," she said furiously, "or whatever the hell you just said."

"But you should." He tried to sound patient. "You should view this as the beginning of your journey—"

"I'm not on a journey, Conrad," she said, throwing her words at him, though that gaze of hers never wavered. "I'm not interested in submitting. I've never had the slightest urge to do any of those things, ever. I've always liked to be the one in control. The only difference now is you."

His heart was kicking at him. That sounded a little too close to the things he wanted, but did not dare allow himself.

"I understand that BDSM can bring up very intense emotions," he began.

And she snorted. Inelegant, graceless, and still he wanted nothing more than to get his hands on her.

"Are you going to pretend that that's not the point?" she asked him. "Because you told me it was. You can't claim that it's all about intimacy and vulnerability and then pretend you're surprised when that's what happens."

"Are you lecturing me on BDSM?"

"I'll leave the lecturing to you, Professor," she said, somehow both dry and hot at the same time. "But you can stop trying to foist me off on random other dudes in leather who happen to be prancing around Paris, doling out spankings and paddling on every street corner."

"So you have dated," he said coolly.

"I only want you," she said, matter-of-factly, throwing that down in the middle the café table. A squirrelly looking tortoiseshell cat jumped on the table between them, looked back and forth between them, and hissed. But Conrad hardly noticed.

"That's not a decision you can make after only one night." He kept his eyes fixed on her, though his ears rang. "You need to separate actions and the person you're acting them out with, because the truth is, they may not be the same."

"Why?" she demanded. "As someone once said to me, I know how to drive a car without knowing how the engine feels. Or does that only apply to you?"

"I'm the one with the experience. You may think that I don't know what I'm talking about, but I do."

"Then why did you come here?"

There was a note of something else in her voice, then. Exasperation, maybe. And something else that clawed at him. Some kind of futility that he hated to hear in her voice.

"I know it was one night," Rory said, her voice as turbulent as the look on her face. "Two nights, if you want to be technical. And I told myself everything you said to me here, and more. I know exactly how to go back to your house, but I didn't. Because I didn't want to be that girl, clinging to your trouser leg and begging for more."

She blew out a breath. "I had already told myself that when I came to your house that night that no matter what happened, that would be it. And I stuck to it. But my feelings didn't change, Conrad. I don't think they're going to."

He needed to say something, but all he could seem

to do was stay where he was, trapped in her gaze. Her honesty. All her vulnerability, there before him.

"And I was perfectly happy to sit with my feelings and figure out a way forward," she said fiercely. I didn't ask you for anything. But you came here and I want to know why."

"I've told you—"

"That's your excuse. Why don't you tell me the real reason? Or does honesty only work one way?"

She could not have said anything that devastated him more.

He was surprised she didn't feel the earthquake that rocked through him, razing Paris to dust outside, while he could do nothing but stay where he was.

Caught in that gaze of hers—and called out.

"I want to see how it plays out between us," he said, as if from some great distance, where he was still in control of himself. "I want to explore our dynamic. But I know it's too soon for you to commit yourself to anyone, particularly in the ways that people in the lifestyle commit themselves. I was hoping that I could be one of the dominants that you play with. I was thinking of you, Rory, though this level of insolence makes me wonder why I bothered."

"You love this level of insolence," she shot back, lighting up with temper again. "For two reasons. First, because I'm betting that nobody talks to you like this. They all bow and scrape, scurry around, and I'm not even talking about sex when I say that.

And second, because you like to sit over there and imagine what consequences you can visit upon me whenever I'm something less then scrupulously polite. Don't bother denying it. I know you do."

"Do you now." Something in him stirred, dark and greedy. "You'll have to forgive me. I can't quite sift through all of that invective and rudeness to find the part where you either said yes, you would like to explore our dynamic, or no, you would rather not."

She leaned forward so abruptly that the cat there hissed, then jumped off the table.

"Everything you told me BDSM could be, it was," she said, intensely. "I have never felt so vulnerable, or exposed. It took me a good two weeks to feel like myself again—that was how profoundly changed that night left me. And that's not all. I haven't posted a single thing online in a month. I stopped cleaning houses, because that's not art, and I don't know why I ever pretended it was. I stopped going on dates. My friends think there's something wrong with me, but there's not. I've never felt better. I know exactly who I am, and exactly what I want, and neither of those things would've been possible without you, Conrad."

"Rory—"

Her brown eyes looked something like wise, then. Almost sad, he would have said, and that killed him.

"I don't want to 'explore dynamics' with you, Conrad," Rory said, very distinctly. "I want so much more than that. I want to marry you, and I don't even believe in marriage."

He must have made a face, because she laughed. And then she reached over and took his hand, reminding him suddenly of the way she'd kissed him in that pool, changing everything.

This time, Rory smiled when she pulled his hand to her mouth and kissed his palm, the same one he'd used to spank her until she came apart. "I'm in love with you, Conrad. And don't tell me I'm not, or that I don't know my own mind or heart. I do."

CHAPTER TWELVE

RORY HAD IMAGINED this scene a thousand times over the last, long month, but every time she had, she hadn't imagined that she would feel like this.

So *alive*.

Hopeful and a kind of outsize version of happy—or almost happy—at the sight of him. Something like supercharged—plugged in again—because he was here, and everything seemed to crackle with electricity around the edges near him.

She had looked up from what she considered her primary form of self-care these days to see him coming toward her, and if she'd been entertaining any doubts about what had been happening in her heart for the past month, they disappeared.

Just like that.

Because even outside that Gothic church, out of context, and in the last place she had ever expected to find him in all his brooding *maleness*, Conrad was magnificent.

He made her glow with happiness, simply with his presence. He made her squirm in her seat, so instantly was she soft and wet and ready for him. She felt as if she'd been ready for him since she'd last had him.

He made her all kinds of things. Even mad, when he looked at her so calmly and talked about experimenting with others—but not the kind of mad that made her want to storm away, burn bridges, or figure out ways to forget him. This was a kind of mad she'd never felt before. The kind of mad that made Rory want to sit here in this café with cats and coffee, and keep talking to him until they understood each other.

And all of that, she had to believe, was love.

Rory had always thought that love was the sort of thing that would build up over time, like dripping sand through her fingers until it became a castle.

But instead, one night had ripped her wide-open, showed her who she was and what she wanted, and that was it. She was done.

And as Conrad stared at her now, looking as close to dumbfounded as she supposed a man so stern and austere ever could, she only felt more certain.

It wasn't going to go away. It wasn't going to change. She had known that beyond the shadow of a doubt when she'd been certain she might never lay eyes on him again. She knew it now, while he was here.

All she had to do was touch him, and it was like that collar he'd put around her neck. It affected her breathing. It was impossible to ignore. Something held them both in a tight, unbreakable grip.

"I collared and claimed a woman once," he told her, and for once, his dark eyes looked like a storm. "That means—"

"I know what it means, Conrad."

Rory didn't tell him that she'd spent an inordinate amount of time this last month studying the BDSM lifestyle. Not just looking at sexy pictures, though she'd done that, too. She'd read books, a thousand articles, and had even gone to a few lectures.

But that was something she could tell him later.

Because she had to believe, now he'd tracked her down in what he didn't need to tell her was a very unlike-him move, there would be a later. Hopefully a lot of laters.

"I would have told you that we simply changed," Conrad told her, sounding something like bleak. "People do. But it's been pointed out to me that I misjudged her from the start. And I can't be sure that I won't make a similar mistake again."

Rory understood that was supposed to set her back, but she only shrugged. "Everybody has problematic exes. That's why they're exes. My college boyfriend could only get it up if I wore white cotton panties, lay on my back in corpse position without moving, and let him drip candle wax on my nipples.

Totally not a serial killer, I'm sure." She grinned at him. "We all make mistakes."

Not for the first time, his eyes did that thing where she thought he was about to tip over into a temper, but instead, he laughed.

"I have no place to put any of that." He ran a hand over his face. "What I'm telling you is that I—"

"Will never trust again, blah blah blah," she interrupted him.

Rory felt his hand tense, but she didn't want to let it go. And she reveled in it when their eyes clashed, because she could feel the dominant in him roar. She had the immediate, overwhelming urge to slip off her chair and find her knees on the floor, and only remembered that they were in public at the very last second.

She managed to breathe, but there didn't seem to be anything she could do about the ache in her pussy.

"If I were you, Rory," he said, stern and dark and authoritative, which made her heart beat faster, "I would be very careful with how dismissive you plan to be during this conversation."

And the desire to please him warred with her longing to save them both the only way she could. By risking his displeasure now in the hope it would lead them where she knew—*she knew*—they needed to go.

"Conrad," she said, very seriously, "haven't I proved that you can trust me? I'm not saying that it isn't hard, because I know that it is. I thought that getting onto my knees in front of you would kill me, but it didn't. It made me stronger. It made me understand myself better. And everything else that happened that night just made everything more and more clear. I want you to do the same."

One of his brows rose, making him seem dark blond and more dangerous than usual. Her breath caught. "I will never kneel."

She found herself smiling. "I would never ask you to kneel. Perish the thought."

Again, that ring around them seemed to tighten. And when he pulled his hand from hers, she felt a shot of desolation, straight through her. But all he did was lift it to her neck and hold it there, where he could rub his thumb over her lips, her cheek. Or simply hold the weight of his hand there, like the grip she felt all around them.

Like eternity.

"You are absolutely nothing that I would ever want," he said, and something about the way he looked at her as he said it made it sound like an endearment, not an insult. And his hand was on her skin, so she found herself melting instead of bristling. "You are too brash. Too mouthy. You say whatever's on your mind, and what's on your mind is always…extraordinary. You make me laugh, Rory, when no one has managed that in years."

"I sound terrible," she whispered.

His eyes crinkled in the corners. "You are."

And again, that should have hurt her feelings, but he was smiling. He was looking at her the way he had when he was inside her, fierce and bright, and she felt spellbound. If that was terrible, she would commit herself to being as terrible as possible forevermore.

"You came out of nowhere," Conrad said, his voice low and dark but all that bright light in his gaze. "My cock is prepared for anything. But my heart..."

"I know you have one," she said quietly. Intently. "I felt it beat."

He looked as if that hurt him. As if she'd swung hard and landed a blow.

"I don't make spontaneous decisions," he told her, severely. "I am a rational, measured, meticulous man, in word and deed."

Rory leaned her cheek into his hand.

"I love you, Conrad," she said, calmly. Because when he was touching her like this, when she was lost in his gaze, no matter what else was happening in her body or her head—she felt still. Calm. Whole. "I don't care if that's not rational and measured and meticulous. It's a fact. No one's expecting you to drop down on your knees or, God forbid, become a switch—" and neither one of them smiled, but the look they shared warmed, all the same "—but I think that just this once, you should trust me. See what happens."

An eternity seemed to tick by. A muscle in his jaw tensed.

"If we jump into this," he said, and her heart flipped over inside her, "I don't think it's going to be halfway. Are you ready for that? No brakes. Just you and me and all the intensity we can handle. And while we're on the topic of intensity, there will be no one else. When I claim something, I keep it to myself."

It took everything she had to keep her expression neutral, when inside she was melting. Jumping up and down. Filled with a hope so encompassing that it almost hurt.

"I've never claimed anything," Rory said, solemnly, though everything in her was a single, solid scream of yes. "But you better believe that I'll be more than happy to claim you."

"I've never jumped off a cliff in my life," Conrad said, a note of something like wonder in his dark voice. And a light she hardly dared believe in there in his navy blue gaze. "Why do you make me feel like that might be a great idea?"

"Because you trust me." Rory was unable to keep the emotion out of her voice, her eyes, *her*. "And I trust you. And everything else will sort itself out."

He shook his head, but his grip only tightened. "I don't think you know what you're signing up for. When I told you about maintenance spanking, I wasn't kidding."

She shivered at that, that delicious, spiked kind of terror going through her once more when she'd thought she would never feel it again. It kicked up everything inside her, turning it into that thick, pulsing desire that only he created in her, and it headed straight for her clit.

"I'm sure I'll hate them," she said, and smiled.

His eyes darkened with promise. "Only if I do them right."

"Just as long as you do it." She burrowed more deeply into his hand. "I promise you, you can trust me to take what you give. All that you give, Conrad. All that you are."

His stern face changed, then, lighting up as he reached to hold her face in both his hands. Caressing her and trapping her at the same time, and it made her heart seem to spin in place. "I'm going to love you something terrible, aren't I?"

She let her grin get wicked and insolent, just for him, the man who hated brats but couldn't stay away from her. "Conrad, you already do. Or you would have thrown me out of your house the second you found me your secret room and never let me back in."

Something flashed in his eyes, as good as vows from another man, and then he was kissing her. A deep, wild claiming, right there in a cat café.

He kissed her like he owned her. And better yet, he kissed her like he was hers, body and soul, the way she'd hardly dared let herself imagine he could ever really be.

But oh, how she'd hoped.

Then he pulled away, smoothed her hair back from her face, and smiled at her.

And Rory felt as if they really had taken a dive over a cliff, but instead of falling, they were flying. Soaring high, with no fear at all of any hard landings.

Not as long as they were together.

And when he pulled away, his eyes had gone stern again, and the spinning in her heart sank through her, making her molten hot and fearful in the most exciting way possible.

"Conrad—" she began, but he put his finger over her lips.

"That's enough now, I think."

Just like that, everything around them shifted. Like a shimmer in the air, and suddenly, they were in that red-hot circle that was only theirs.

And Rory understood in a flash that this is how it would always be. That they would shift between their different worlds, wherever they were, at his whim.

"No talking," he told her, his voice a dark command that she didn't just hear. She felt it. Everywhere. "We're going to get up from the table. You're going to take me back to your flat, and when we're there, you're going to strip down and present yourself to me. I'm going to inspect my property. And then, Rory, there will be a reckoning, which I doubt very much you will enjoy."

She was so happy she thought she might die, or come, or break down into sobs, right there.

Instead, she stood with him, unable to contain her joy. Because it was streaming down her face. It was the way she was breathing, or not breathing. It was making her cheeks hurt from the wideness of her smile.

And inside, she quivered as if he'd set her on fire.

Especially when his hand settled around her neck like her favorite clamp, then propelled her outside when she'd settled her bill.

"We're going to have a long talk, you and I," he told her as they walked, a delicious threat in his voice and Paris around them like a song. "We're going to talk about insolence. The astonishing use of the word 'dumbass.' And when you're finished experiencing the consequences for both of those things, to my satisfaction, we will have a little talk about maintenance. My favorite."

But when he slanted his beautiful dark blue gaze her way, out there in all that sunshine, she knew that his favorite was her.

Then, and always.

And he would prove it to her one spanking at a time.

CHAPTER THIRTEEN

CONRAD HAD ALWAYS assumed that he would get married with great pomp and circumstance, as suited a man of his fortune and position. His attempt at a great vanilla wedding had been just that sort of thing—stately and stuffy, so every business associate he'd ever had could come and gawk.

Even then, when he'd balked at the madness surrounding what had been, to him, little more than a business arrangement, Chriszette had always indicated that her children's weddings were for her, not them. Conrad had really never seen any reason to argue with that. He didn't care enough about weddings to care whether or not he enjoyed his.

But he hadn't been sorry when it had all fallen through.

And now there was Rory, bright and hot and not in any way a lie.

Unsurprisingly, she had all kinds of opinions on weddings. And she lectured him a little too intensely about the evils of *the historical marriage mart*, whatever that was, the wedding industrial complex, and her feelings about proclaiming her role as chattel with a blood diamond *from his homeland* on her hand.

She paid for those lectures, of course, but that only made her rant at him more.

Accordingly, they celebrated their engagement—which involved Conrad ordering her to pack up her things and move into his church with him roughly two or three days after he'd found her in that ridiculous cat café—in private. In his little chapel, with the light streaming down her body as he carefully tied her to his Saint Andrew's Cross.

That night he not only introduced her to his whip, he claimed her as his by switching out her clit piercing for one of his choosing. With a nice big stone with no blood on it. A bigger, more aggressive piercing that made her come screaming at the slightest touch and necessitated she take a solid week to get used to walking with it.

Conrad thought that was an excellent opportunity for her to think about what she was signing up for.

Because he was a man who did everything slow. Who prided himself on doing it right.

Except when it came to her.

Nothing about Rory and him made sense, because it all made too much sense to explain. They fit together and that was the end of it.

"I'm going to say this as clear as I can," her father boomed at him when they visited Rory's family in Nashville. Her mother had claimed to adore Conrad on sight, but big Marty Morton had taken a moment. "That's my baby girl. I don't understand a single thing that comes out of her mouth, but if you break her heart, I'll take your head off with a pocketknife."

Conrad grinned and lifted his drink in Marty's direction. "I will hand you that pocketknife if that happens, and take my beheading like a man."

And when the other man had muttered something gruff to Rory that sounded like *about gotdamn time*, he'd taken that as the best blessing he would receive.

That was how Conrad Vanderburg, head of his family and corporation and lauded throughout the business world, married Rory Morton, internet "influencer," within two months of meeting her.

Their wedding was so private—on a solitary beach in the Philippines, with just the two of them, their officiant, and the breathtaking blue sea—that Rory only uploaded a single photo of it to her social media account.

It was a picture of Conrad looking stern and indulgent at once, while she was a vision in white, the wind making her skirts flow everywhere, and a look of such joy on her face that it made his heart ache.

Rory didn't wear his ring, but she did wear his tattoo. The one he dreamed of that first night, that marked her as his, indelibly. It wasn't visible in that picture, but he knew it was there. He saw it every time he stripped her naked—a great pleasure he indulged in often.

He had that photo framed and placed on the wall in their living room.

So he would never be tempted to forget himself again. To drift off into all that dire gray responsibility that had weighed him down forever. Nothing could be dire when she looked at him like that.

Because with Rory, he found he could let go, a little. That wasn't to say that he shirked his duties, or suddenly discovered the urge to kneel. Hardly.

But she made him laugh. He had always been all intensity, all the time, but they shifted in and out of the different levels of their dynamic as it suited them.

Or rather, as it suited him.

"You?" his sister asked that first Christmas, when Conrad announced that he would be coming with a woman—but had announced upon arrival that, in fact, Rory was his wife. "*Eloped?* Has the world ended?"

Conrad opted not to analyze the look Dorian gave her, because it spoke of too many things he chose not to recognize. Especially when Erika flushed a little.

But Rory laughed, big and bright and entirely her.

"I've corrupted him," she said. "Utterly."

Dorian laughed. "At last."

"I approve," Erika said immediately from beside him, and when she smiled at Conrad, it was as if something else eased, then. Something he hadn't known he'd held so tightly, until now.

He might have been a hard-ass. His sister might have been a problem. But maybe that had only mattered when neither of them were happy.

But now they both were almost too happy to bear. And the woman he'd almost married, Erika's best friend, who he would have made utterly miserable, was happy, too. As if all those near misses and old resentments had been necessary to bring them all here.

Maybe that was hopelessly mawkish. But what could Conrad do? He was unduly influenced by his very own pet American.

In the new year Conrad bought her an art gallery so she could pursue the things that really mattered to her.

They thought she was a joke at first. They called her snide names and made insulting references to her social media presence, but underestimating Rory was always a bad idea.

She was a force to be reckoned with, as she proved, with hard work and what the snotty art magazines called her *surprisingly incisive eye for new and unexpected talent*.

He loved her to distraction.

"I love you," he told her one rainy, Parisian evening.

She'd come home late from her gallery, bubbling over with excitement at the painting she'd sold that day and buzzing around the kitchen as if she hardly noticed he was in it.

But that declaration stopped her, the way it always did. She smiled at him, that beautiful, melting smile that wrecked him, then made him, and that he never wished to do without.

"But you're late," Conrad pointed out, his voice taking on that edge they both loved. He watched her shift. He watched her body change, moving seamlessly from the high-powered gallery owner she'd become to the woman she would always be—his. "You know what tonight is."

Her breath caught. Her eyes got that sheen.

"I know that it's maintenance night," she began. "But—"

"No excuses, please," he said, quiet and implacable. "You know the rules. You were late. Twenty-three minutes late, by my count."

Her eyes got wide. He saw that beautiful flush work its way over her skin.

"But I—"

Conrad only shook his head. And her words tapered off.

Rory took a ragged breath. Then, without having to be asked, she slowly, gracefully, sank down to her knees before him and held her arms behind her back.

His beautiful wife. This woman who took what he gave her and gave it back to him with her glorious and complete surrender, making them both whole.